Lost Days of the Pinta

by

W.W. Whitten

TELEMACHUS PRESS

Cover designed by Jeremy Savard

Cover art:
Copyright © iStockphoto/2396992

Published by Telemachus Press, LLC
http://www.telemachuspress.com

Visit the author website:
http://www.wwwhitten.com

ISBN: 978-1-939927-15-6 (eBook)
ISBN: 978-1-939927-16-3 (Paperback)

Version 2013.10.21

Printed in the United States of America

10 9 8 7 6 5 4 3 2 1

Lost Days of the Pinta

Prologue: 6, January, 1493

CAPTAIN MARTÍN ALONSO Pinzón's cabin door busted open. It swung into a small table tucked against the wall, toppling a lit candlestick to the wooden decking.

The interloper stood just inside the cabin breathing heavily and staring down at the captain sitting at his table.

Martín glanced at the still burning candle on the deck. "Do you intend on burning my ship into the sea?"

Still the man did not move. His tall frame loomed over Martín.

Martín rose from his table and nonchalantly stepped to the candle and snuffed it out with his boot.

"Captain," a voice called from outside the cabin. It was that of Francisco Pinzón, the Pinta's master and the captain's middle brother. "I could not stop him."

A smile pulled at the corner of the captain's mouth. "It is fine Francisco; I know that our brother is a determined man."

The intruder was Vicente Yañez Pinzón, Martín's youngest brother and the captain of the Niña.

"Where have you been?" Vicente spit out. He tossed a small stack of wax sealed documents onto Martín's table. "You ignore the admiral's orders and then you vanish for 46 days!"

Martín laid a hand on Vicente's shoulder. His younger brother shrugged it off and spun to glare at him.

Francisco stepped into the tiny cabin. There was barely enough room for all three men. Francisco was only inches away from Vicente and staring up into his eyes with disdain.

He said, "You should watch your tongue little brother. You are aboard our ship and you need to show our captain some respect."

Vicente's lips curled. Through clenched teeth he hissed, "This is the admiral's ship, and you are lucky to still be walking about it as free men."

Martín smiled. "Now my brothers, this should be a happy reunion." He placed a hand on Francisco's shoulder and gently turned his brother so that he faced him. "Besides, Vicente is right. We did abandon him, and I am sure that his anger has blossomed from concern for our well-being."

Vicente thrust his hand toward the table. "Those are the letters that I wrote to our sisters," his eyes met Martín's, "and your wife, telling them of their loss." He paused and then corrected, "Of *our* loss."

Martín held his brother's stare. "We *are* sorry Vicente."

Vicente slowly lowered his gaze. The façade crumbled.

Martín smiled. "But know that our absence has garnered great reward."

"So the rumors are true, you found gold?" Vicente asked.

"We found a treasure far greater than gold little brother," Martín replied sotto voce.

Chapter 1: Present day

THE BELLS ABOVE the front door signaled to Garron that he had guests in the gallery. He wiped the paint from his hands on a rag as he stepped out from behind the partition that separated his studio from the gallery. There were two large men in navy blue suits and sunglasses waiting for him near the table he used as a sales counter.

One man, a blonde, removed his sunglasses and asked, "Garron Shepard?"

"Yes, how may I help you?" Garron replied.

"I am Special Agent Whitlock with the Department of Homeland Security. This is Special Agent Jefferson."

Both men held their credentials for Garron to inspect. The second man had black hair and he never removed his sunglasses.

Whitlock spoke, "You're a painter. Are all of these yours?"

"Most are, yes. There are a few that belong to other local artists," Garron answered.

"You have a thing for boats, huh?"

"They're ships actually, but yes."

Garron had been painting tall ships in oil on canvas for nearly five years. He could not explain his interest in ships, only that he had watched as the tall ships entered the Inner Harbor five summers ago when he had moved to Baltimore and was impressed by their majesty and beauty.

"And when did you open your gallery?" The agent asked.

"Two years ago."

"That was about the same time you married Veronica Delgado." Whitlock consulted a notepad that he had pulled from his breast pocket.

It was because of Veronica that Garron opened his gallery in Fells Point. She, in fact, purchased the old storefront and had the building renovated as a wedding gift to Garron.

"Since when is Homeland Security concerned with the marital status and business venture of mediocre artists?" Garron attempted to keep the contempt from his voice.

"You don't give yourself enough credit. Some of these are pretty good." Whitlock applied a practiced smile, too big and insincere. He continued, "We are actually interested in speaking to your brother, Jacob. We were hoping that you might know where we could find him."

"I haven't spoken to my brother in over a year."

"You don't seem surprised that we are looking for him."

"I'm not surprised that he's done something wrong. My brother is no saint. But to get the attention of Homeland Security seems a bit much even for Jacob. But like I said, I haven't spoken to him in over a year."

Jacob had been in a few bar brawls, he had stolen a boat, and he had even beaten a man to within an inch of his life; but to have federal agents chasing Jacob did indeed surprise Garron. With each of his past crimes, Jacob would always argue that he was seeking justice. His girlfriend, who was the bartender of the bar in which he started the fight, claimed to have two unruly and intoxicated patrons molest her when she went into the back for ice. When she told Jacob, he broke the one man's arm and threw the other through a window into the street. They later pressed charges and he served thirty days in the system. When the owner of the boat did not pay Jacob for services rendered, Jacob stole the man's boat and stripped it of parts as compensation for what was owed. Jacob spent six months in jail for that offense. And when Jacob discovered that his buddy, Dustin, was beating his wife, Jacob very nearly killed him. Jacob served three years of a seven year sentence.

Garron asked, "So what has my brother done?"

"We really cannot say, but if you hear from him, please contact us immediately." Agent Whitlock handed Garron a business card.

Looking at the card, Garron said, "Domestic Terrorism Unit. You must have the wrong guy. Jacob is not a terrorist."

"Mr. Shepard, we just have some questions for your brother regarding a business partner of his. It seems that this business partner is laundering money for a terrorist cell through Cuba. Maybe Jacob doesn't know what he is involved in, or maybe he does. Either way he can help us, so in turn we can help him. Tell him to call us."

Whitlock put his sunglasses on and both men headed for the door without Special Agent Jefferson ever saying a word.

Whitlock called from over his shoulder, "You know some of these are really very good."

He pointed to a wall where a painting of a clipper in dark, rough seas hung and asked, "How much is that one, that big one?"

"That one is not for sale."

"Not even for the right price?"

Garron studied his work. "That one is priceless."

The two men walked out of the gallery and were joined by two more blue suits that must have been standing on either side of the door just out of Garron's sight. The four men climbed into a black Lincoln Navigator and drove out of view.

Garron looked up at the clipper battling the stormy seas; he knew that he would never sell this piece. Garron located the figure laying on flotsam in the middle ground of the painting. The figure was difficult to find amidst the churning sea. He knew that most of the gallery's visitors were unaware that the figure was even part of the scene, but Garron knew every square inch of this painting. Written on the bow of the ship, on the name plate in delicate script, was the true subject of the work: Veronica.

***

It was hot and humid. Garron was looking forward to autumn and the relief that it promised after a Baltimore summer. The walk to his car, three blocks from his gallery, was short but the sweat ran down the center of his back nonetheless. Garron started the engine and the hum of the air conditioner vents was comforting, even if the air wasn't yet cool. He pulled away from the curb. As much as he loved this city, he hated to drive in it. No matter the time of day, crisscrossing from Fells Point on the eastside to Locust Point where he lived on the westside of the city was difficult. But he loved his gallery and he loved his home, and would not be willing to give either up. When Veronica was out of town, which was more often than Garron would like, he was able to live comfortably in the upper floors of his gallery. The Fells Point storefront had three stories; the first floor was used as the gallery and studio, and the second and third floors were masterfully remodeled into a two-bedroom apartment with all of the luxuries of a permanent residence. The beauty of the Fells Point studio could only be bested by their mid nineteenth century Locust Point home. Garron had purchased the house just before meeting Veronica. He had planned great things for the home, but he never imagined that it would turn out so wonderfully. And if it wasn't for Veronica, it wouldn't have.

Veronica Delgado was a highly successful business-minded lady with a love for life. She was born to Antonio Delgado and Iliana Tryggvason in New York City. Antonio was the first son of wealthy Spanish immigrants and Iliana was a Norwegian national with sizable wealth of her own. The two met while Iliana was dancing with a ballet troop in New York City, and they fell madly in love and were married within two weeks of their meeting. Veronica was born with her father's swarthy complexion and her mother's brilliantly blue eyes. She was a true beauty, tall and voluptuous with the legs of a model, but she still managed to stay humble. Humble not only of her good looks, but also her intelligence and success. Veronica owned or held positions in many profitable businesses around the world. She founded several charitable organizations and donated eighty percent of her wealth in an effort to feed the world's hungry. Garron never understood why Veronica was interested in a starving artist, but he was happy to be one of her charity cases. If he allowed himself moments of measured self worth, then he knew why Veronica loved him. Garron was generous and kind almost to a fault. He had learned to be devoted and honest in love; something he had learned from a failed marriage. And he did not care that Veronica was wealthy. She was tired of being chased for her money, and Garron loved her before he knew of her wealth. If Garron was pressed to admit it, he knew that they were perfect for each other.

Garron parked across the street from his home and was surprised to see Veronica's car in her parking spot. She wasn't due back from Barcelona until tomorrow, but her schedule was ever-changing. He spotted another black Lincoln Navigator halfway down the block as he let himself in the front door.

"Hello love." Veronica greeted him as she descended the stairs.

"When did you get home?" Garron asked.

"Not long ago." She replied.

She was still wearing a white blouse and tan skirt. Her well-toned legs ending in a pair of red high heels.

He tucked a strand of her espresso colored hair, the same strand that always fell across her face, behind her ear and kissed her deeply.

"What's wrong?" Veronica asked reading his face.

It no longer surprised Garron that Veronica seemed able to read his mind.

"Homeland Security stopped by the gallery this morning. They are looking for Jacob." He answered.

"What did he do? Is he okay?"

"The agents looking for him are part of the Domestic Terrorist Division of the Department of Homeland Security. It has something to do with Jay's friend Murphy, I think."

Garron used his childhood sobriquet for Jacob; Jay was short for Jaybird. Their father would call Jacob shit bird, but of course Garron was forbidden to use that nickname as a child, so he cleaned it up.

"Your brother is not a terrorist."

"The DHS believes that Murphy is involved in laundering money for terrorist cells."

Garron emptied his pockets of his wallet, car keys, and change in the drawer of the entry table. Then they both headed for the couch.

Veronica laid her head in Garron's lap and stretched out on the couch.

She asked, "Do you think that Murphy could be involved with something like that?"

Garron ran his fingers through her hair as he looked into his wife's eyes.

"I don't know, Ronnie. I only met him once. All I know is that Jay loves him, so maybe he could have been manipulated because of his feelings for Murphy."

She looked surprised and said, "You're actually considering it?"

"Maybe. No. I hope not."

Veronica sat up and took Garron's hands in hers.

"I haven't known your brother very long, but I don't think that his morals have been corrupted to allow for such accusations to be true. Even with the trouble in his past, he was always fighting for what was right."

"That was my immediate reaction, but I'm not sure that his moral compass hasn't shifted a bit."

Veronica raised a hand to Garron's face. "You are only saying that because you feel that he betrayed you. And that's a far cry from laundering money for terrorists."

"He did betray me." Garron responded with a huff. "All I'm saying is that I'm not sure how far he might go for Murphy."

"Then maybe it's time you talk to him."

"I don't even know how to get in touch with him."

"You know where he's living, so hop on a plane and fly to Florida."

"If Homeland Security can't find him, then what makes you think that I can?"

"I think that he might want to be found if you're the one who is doing the searching."

Garron stood from the couch and pulled back the curtains to peer down the street. The Navigator was still there. Garron crossed to the fireplace and took a wedding photo from the mantel. Jacob stood next to Garron as his best man. It was uncanny how much he and his brother looked alike. In the black and white photo it was hard to determine age; the two men in the photo could have been twins. Garron looked at his brother's broad smile in the photo.

He said, "I don't want him getting into anymore trouble."

"Then this is what we'll do. I'll have Joe file the flight plan tonight and we can fly out tomorrow."

"No. You have to be in Detroit in two days for the soup kitchen's opening. I'll fly down and take care of this on my own."

"Detroit can open without me." Veronica stood and took the photo from her husband. She smiled at the memory.

"Ronnie, I know how much the opening ceremony means to you. I don't want you to miss it. Besides, if you get involved in this, then it might cause some trouble for your business ventures if the wrong people find out that you are aiding a wanted terrorist."

A true look of pain passed over Garron's face as a thought crossed his mind.

"Shit, just by being Jacob's sister-in-law it could bring a storm of bad press, and you don't deserve to have all of the good you've done questioned. Or have your finances combed through because my brother's a fuck up."

"You know that I don't care about the press, and no one is going to start digging around in my finances without due diligence and just cause. I have too many lawyers at my disposal for a witch hunt. And you forget that we don't know if Jacob's done anything wrong. Besides, I have nothing to hide."

"Oh, I know, I didn't mean anything like that. It's just that I feel that this is something I have to do myself."

Veronica hugged Garron close to her. "I know what you meant. And if you feel that strongly about it, then you should go on your own."

He kissed her again then said, "Thank you. I love you."

"And I you, but you better keep me in the loop."

She gave him a playful slap him on the butt and retrieved her cell phone.

"I'll call Joe and get him started on the flight plan."

Garron watched Veronica's legs and backside as she walked toward her office in the rear of the house. He smiled widely.

***

"Hello Mr. Shepard."

"Hello Joe. Will you please call me Garron; I won't ask again."

The two men shook hands as Garron boarded the plane. Joe Yearly was a handsome man of about sixty years and had been flying for Veronica for ten of those years. Joe was tall with blond hair and blue eyes. His features were sharp and his smile was warm. The two had met many times in the past few years, but Garron had only flown with him once before.

"It's nice to have you aboard again Garron. Is there anything you need before we get started?"

"No thanks, Joe."

Garron still wasn't comfortable with having his own plane; although, he understood Veronica's need for such an extravagance. And he knew that Veronica treated Joe and his family very well.

"Well then, our flight will last about two hours and forty minutes; the flight plan has been filed, and we are wheels up in fifteen. If there is anything that you need, Diana will be available while we are in the air."

Diana smiled as Garron took his seat. This was the first time that he had met this attractive member of the flight crew.

Joe continued, "It's my understanding that you will not be returning with us."

"That's correct. I am not sure how long I'll be in Florida."

"Very well then, we will be off shortly. Make yourself comfortable and enjoy the flight."

Joe left the cabin drawing a curtain behind him and stepping into the cockpit.

Diana smiled down on Garron and asked, "Would you care for a beverage Mr. Shepard?"

"Coffee would be nice. But please call me Garron."

"Cream and sugar, Garron?"

"No thank you, just black."

Diana returned with the mug of coffee and Garron settled back into his leather seat and watched as the plane began to taxi.

It wasn't too long ago that flying in a personal jet seemed impossible to Garron. Growing up on the Eastern Shore of Maryland had taught Garron to work hard and expect little. His father had worked long hours as a plumber and his mother had worked at a cannery when work had been available; Garron's family never had very much. But Garron and Jacob were raised right, they had never gone hungry, and they were happy.

Garron and Jacob were more than brothers, they were friends. They spent every minute of the day together, even sharing a bedroom in their modest two bedroom home. As boys they would leave the house just after breakfast and only return for dinner. They ran over the countryside, biked into town, and fished in the rivers and streams. Jacob was six years younger than Garron, but the age difference didn't stop the brothers from playing well together. Jacob was always trying to keep up with his brother, and Garron was always looking out for Jacob. Even when Garron entered high school, he still spent a great deal of time with his younger brother. That was, until Garron discovered girls.

Garron was a handsome young man; and though his self esteem was shaky at best, he still dated frequently. He always dated one girl at a time, and always treated each girl with the utmost respect. When he would bring a young lady home to meet his parents, the tie between brothers was tested. Jacob would do everything in his power to try and come between his brother's new relationships, interrupting kissing sessions, kicking his brother under the dinner table, standing in front of the television. He had even once set fire to a portion of Garron's baseball card collection, while Garron and his date watched a movie.

Jacob had started the fire in a pot set in the kitchen sink. When Garron saw what Jacob had done, he chased his brother through the house with the smoldering pot in hand threatening to beat Jacob to death once he caught him. Jacob explained, as he ran for his life out the back door, that it was just the duplicates that he burned. Garron caught up to him in the backyard and fed Jacob the ashes while his father laughed from the kitchen window. Jacob learned to make room for his brother's girlfriends after that night, and Garron worked at giving Jacob more attention.

Truth be told, he missed his brother, but forgiveness was not easy for Garron. And Jacob had hurt him deeply. It had been fifteen months since they last spoke, and Garron was worried that Jacob had gotten into something that was well over his head.

Diana interrupted his thoughts, "Garron, we will be landing in twenty minutes, and the captain wanted you to know that we might hit some turbulence on our descent."

"Thank you Diana. Diana, have you been working for my wife very long?" Garron asked.

"No, I haven't. She was kind enough to find a position for me when she learned of my husband's battle with cancer. Veronica wanted me to be able to spend as much time with him as possible." Diana smiled.

"How can you spend more time with your husband if you're flying around the world with Veronica?"

"Oh, I thought that you knew; Joe is my husband. We've been married for thirty nine years this November."

"Joe has cancer? I didn't know. I am sorry."

"Don't be sorry. He is determined to beat it, and so far so good." Diana dropped her voice, "But please don't tell him that you know. He is a private man, and he doesn't want to be pitied. We are both just so happy that your wife made it possible for us to spend more time together. Of course, Veronica first offered to give Joe a leave of absence at full pay, because that's just how wonderful your wife is. But Joe insisted on working, so Veronica offered me a job so that we could be together."

Diana brushed a tear from her eye.

"And don't worry about his health affecting his work; he wouldn't fly unless he was certain that he could deliver your wife safely home. He truly cares for that woman, we both do."

Diana smiled and let her hand rest on Garron's shoulder for a moment before returning to the crew compartment just behind the cockpit. Garron smiled at his wife's generosity and empathy.

Chapter 2

GARRON PULLED THE rental car, a black Nissan Altima, onto US 1 and headed north. He did not expect to find Jacob at his home on Islamorada, but he thought that to be the best place to pick up his trail. It was just as hot and humid as it was in Baltimore, but the view was astounding. The crystal blue green water was peppered with boats and jet skis. Pelicans sailed on air currents eye level with Garron as his car crossed the bridge tying Marathon to Islamorada. Men stood on the bridge fishing the waters below. He understood why the Keys appealed to so many; the island life could be had with the convenience of a bridge system tying you to the mainland no more than three hours to the north. And with the knowledge Jacob had of boats and engines, it did not surprise Garron that his brother chose Islamorada to call home.

Growing up on the waters of the Chesapeake Bay, Jacob used his innate mechanical abilities to repair boat engines at the age of fifteen. He was a strong swimmer, a good sailor, and an excellent fisherman. Jacob was most at home on, near, or in the water. So when Jacob told Garron of a dive boat captain looking for an apprentice, Garron thought it a perfect fit. Jacob had been visiting the Keys after getting out of jail for his assault charge and ran into Ian Murphy at a bar on Marathon. Ian took a liking to Jacob and asked him to join his operation and learn the ropes. Jacob, after working for Murphy for two years, told Garron that he felt a true admiration for the older man and hoped that Garron would have a chance to meet him. Garron met the man later that year, when Murphy accompanied Jacob to Garron and Veronica's wedding as his plus one.

It seemed to Garron that Murphy was filling the hole that was left in Jacob after their father died of mesothelioma. Garron was 22 and out of the house, Jacob was 16 and struggling with growing up. The loss of their father was painful for both boys, but it was felt more deeply by the younger brother. Garron tried to help Jacob through the adversity, but Garron's first marriage was crumbling around him. Garron still harbored regret for not giving his brother what he needed. It was after their father's death that Jacob fell into trouble with the law. Garron felt that Jacob was his responsibility, and that he had let him down. But Jacob always took responsibility for his actions, never attributing them to anyone but himself.

The GPS told Garron to take the next left onto Orange Street. Jacob's was the third house on the left. Garron noticed the Lincoln Navigator parked in the driveway of a neighbor. He wondered if Homeland Security would be so obvious or if the vehicle actually belonged to a neighbor. Garron pulled the Altima into the drive and under the stilted house. The homes on Jacob's street had a similar design and all looked to have been built in the 1970s. The houses were mostly ranch homes with a wrap around deck, each supported on stilts to protect the home from rising water. They were built before hurricane building codes were passed.

He stepped from the car and ascended the stairs to the front door. Garron knocked and then tried the knob. The door and jamb were obviously damaged. He cautiously pushed the door inward and called his brother's name. The house had been ransacked. Furniture was overturned, paper was strewn about; even the window air conditioning unit was lying in the middle of the floor. Garron checked the refrigerator. There was very little inside. What few boxed and canned goods Jacob did have were strewn across the kitchen floor. It didn't seem that Jacob was spending much time at home.

Garron wondered if it was Homeland Security that destroyed the place looking for a clue to Jacob's whereabouts. He decided to ask them, but when he went outside to question the passengers in the Navigator, he found that the SUV was gone. Garron saw an older gentleman trimming a hedge across the street.

"Excuse me sir," Garron said as he approached the man.

"No thank you, I don't need any help," the man said from his ladder. He continued, "I can still manage on a ladder, no matter what my wife says."

"Well, I'd be happy to help, but what I really wanted was to know if you knew Jacob Shepard," Garron clarified.

The man climbed down from his ladder. He pulled his wide brimmed hat from his head and wiped his forehead with a rag he drew from his pocket.

He said, "My God, you look just like him."

"So you do know my brother."

"I didn't know that he had a brother, but there is no questioning that you two are kin." The man offered his hand to Garron. "I'm Gene Lewis. It's a pleasure to meet ya," he said in a southern drawl.

"Well Mr. Lewis, have you seen my brother recently?" Garron asked.

"Nah, I guess it's been 'bout a week since last I saw him."

"Have you seen anyone over at his place?"

"Not that I've seen. Me and Ellen are here most days and I haven't seen nobody."

Garron asked, "Are you sure that you don't need any help with that hedge?"

"No thank you son." Gene shook his head. "Is everything okay with your brother?"

"I'm sure that he's fine. I'll catch up with him eventually. Thanks Mr. Lewis."

Garron turned to walk away and then thought of another question.

He asked, "Mr. Lewis, do you know where Jacob went to drink?"

Gene Lewis said with a smile, "Sure do. We drink at the marina near the Teatable. Shirley's the prettiest bartender in the Keys."

"The Teatable?" Garron asked.

Mr. Lewis nodded, "Teatable Key, south toward Matecumbe, on the left at mile marker 75."

"Thank you again Mr. Lewis. I'll tell Shirley that you said hello."

Garron could hear the old man laughing as he walked back across the street and climbed into the Altima.

***

Garron entered the *Lapsed Teetotaler* and made his way to the stool at the far end of the bar. The *Lapsed Teetotaler* was a mix of seaside wharf, island resort, and English pub. The bar was nearly empty at ten in the morning; two men sat at a table in the center of the room. The bartender came from behind a swinging door that Garron thought must separate the bar from the marina's office.

"Where have you been hiding?" The bartender asked in an English accent.

"You must be Shirley," Garron replied.

Shirley was a woman in her early fifties with bleached hair and brightly painted finger nails. She was busty and her low cut blouse showed skin that was white as snow. Garron wondered how she kept her skin so white in the Florida sun, especially considering the low neckline. A wide belt was pulled tightly just below her bosom. Garron decided that Shirley had once been a very pretty lady and understood Gene's attraction.

Shirley was taken aback and she said, "I'm sorry, I thought you were someone else."

Garron smiled. "Gene Lewis says hello."

"Okay, now I'm really buggered. You know Gene Lewis, and you look like one of our regulars." She said, not hiding her distrust.

"I'm Garron Shepard, and you must know my brother Jacob."

"Damn, you two look a lot alike." Shirley reached across the bar and grabbed Garron's chin. She inspected him and smiled. "You boys sure are handsome. I've been trying to get Jake in my bed for months. How is your brother? I haven't seen him in weeks."

Garron blushed. "I was hoping you had seen him, I can't seem to catch up with him."

"Wes over there might know where our boy is. He's the one in the cowboy hat." Shirley pointed toward the two men at the table. "Can I get you a drink?"

"No thank you, I don't drink."

"Are you sure that you're Jake's brother?" She quipped. "Well, you'll need this just the same." Shirley poured whiskey in a glass. "Give this to Wes."

Garron took the glass, "Thank you Shirley."

Garron could smell the liquor, and his pulse raced. He imagined the warmth of the drink sliding down his throat and his mouth began to water. His hand trembled slightly.

Shirley called out from behind him, "Wes Macomber, that fine looking young man heading your way has a drink for you. Now you be nice or I'll make you pay for it."

As Garron approached the table, one of the men stood and exited the front door. The man left sitting at the table, wearing the cowboy hat, was between the ages of seventy and eighty years old. Time had not been good to him, and the expression he wore was one of distrust. Wes Macomber had the appearance of a tall man, even seated. He was long and lean with a drawn face. His skin was yellowed, but his eyes were keen and engaging.

Garron watched the other man leave through the front door. He said, "Sorry to interrupt."

"Don't worry about him, Jimmy likes his privacy is all. He doesn't like strangers much."

"Mr. Macomber, I'm Garron Shepard." Garron said as he extended his hand.

"Is that for me, or not?" Wes said nodding toward the whiskey. "Cuz by the way you're holding onto that glass it looks like you might be keeping' it for yourself."

Garron set the glass down on the table and slid it toward Wes.

"Yes sir, it is yours. I don't drink."

"Anymore."

"Sorry?"

"You don't drink anymore. I've known my share of rehabilitated men, and when that glass was in your hand you had that look about you," Wes clarified. "How long has it been?" He asked.

"More than four years."

"Miss it?"

"Sometimes," Garron responded.

"Well, I'll wait to drink this one until after you leave, if you want."

"No, please. You don't have to wait on my account." Garron took a seat.

Wes lifted the glass and drank the whiskey smoothly.

"You look like him; or rather he looks like you. You're the older one, right?"

"Yes, I am the oldest. Have you seen Jacob lately?" Garron asked.

"He is usually in here almost every day, but I guess it's been about a week since the last time I saw him. He could be up visiting his sweetheart, sometimes he is gone for a week or two if Murph doesn't have any dives scheduled."

"Does he visit her often?" Garron asked.

"I guess. Unless Murph keeps him busy that is."

Garron turned to see Shirley behind the bar and ordered Wes another whiskey. She brought it to the table and let her hand linger on Garron's shoulder a bit too long.

"Much obliged," Wes said as he tossed the drink back.

"Have you seen Murphy recently?"

"It's been about as long, a week or so." Wes answered.

"Do you know where Murphy lives?"

"He's over on Columbus, just after exit 77, bright blue place with white shutters."

Garron stood. "Thanks Wes. I think I'll try Murphy's next. But if you see my brother, please tell him that I'm looking for him. I'll leave my number at the bar for him."

Wes smiled, "You sure that's wise? You leave that number with Shirley and she'll think that you're interested." He laughed loudly.

"You shut your mouth Wes Macomber, if that fine looking man wants to give me his number then that's just what he'll do. Stop interfering." Shirley called from behind the bar, where she had probably overheard Wes and Garron's entire conversation.

***

The rear door to Ian Murphy's home was standing open. Garron's shirt clung to his body with perspiration. The humidity hung in the air not allowing for the sweat to evaporate. But Garron only needed the view from Murphy's deck to remind him why so many people wanted to live in the

Florida Keys. He had left the Altima on the adjacent street and approached the house from the neighboring yard, taking cover from the main street in case it was being watched by Homeland Security. He wanted to find Jacob before the authorities did. The charges that the DHS were leveling against Murphy were serious; Garron needed to know if Jacob was involved. Jacob needed to turn himself in, but only after they contacted a good lawyer. A lawyer that would ensure Jacob was not secreted away without proper representation under The Patriot Act.

Garron slipped quietly from room to room making sure that he was alone. Murphy's home was ransacked, much like Jacob's. He wasn't sure where to begin or what he was looking for, but he decided to start his search in what was Murphy's office. Books and papers were strewn across the room. Desk drawers were tipped spilling their contents onto the floor. If there had been a computer in the room, then it had been taken. But none of the papers scattered throughout the room pointed to a dive business. There were no invoices or receipts; there was no date book or calendar. It seemed to Garron that Murphy must not have worked from home.

Garron left the office and continued down the hall, away from the living room and where he had entered the house. He next came to a room that held a single bed with one dresser and night stand; a spare bedroom. There was a small bathroom at the end of the hall and the master bedroom to his right.

Murphy had decorated the home in a nautical theme. Not that of a cheesy vacation home, but with the eye of someone who truly appreciated the art of sailing and the beauty of the sea. Throughout the home there were framed maps and blueprint ship drawings, although most had been pulled from the wall and smashed underfoot. Some appeared to be on old paper leading Garron to believe that they may have been original and of some historical value. On Murphy's bedroom wall, in the form of a mural, there was a hand painted map. It seemed to be a recreation of an ancient map from a time when cartographers relied on descriptions by men sailing to points yet unknown. It was well done with a flair that spoke to an artistic talent. Garron wondered if Murphy had painted it himself.

A sound startled Garron. It sounded like glass being crushed under foot from a distant part of the house. Then there came a scuff of a shoe on tile. Someone was in the house. Garron searched the debris for something that he could use as a weapon. He decided on a mirror fragment. He used a pillowcase to protect his hand from the sharp edges and then he hid behind the bedroom door and waited for the intruder. Garron wasn't sure in what he had involved himself, and he began to worry about the consequences of that involvement. He watched through the crack in the door as a man cautiously stepped from the hall. The mirror fragment felt awkward in his hand. He weighed his options; he could hide behind the door and hope to go unnoticed, or he could spring from behind the door in an attempt to take the intruder off guard. But was he truly willing to slash someone with his impromptu knife? What if the man had a gun? Garron decided that the best course of action was to use his only advantage: surprise. He would slam the door closed and lunge at the man. He began to count down; three, two, one …

"Garron?" A voice asked.

"Jay." Garron was relieved to see his brother as he slid from behind the door.

Jacob eyed the wrapped hand and mirror. "What were you going to do with that?"

Garron felt his face flush. "It was the best that I could come up with." He let the fragment fall to the floor and tugged the pillowcase from his hand. "And what were you going to do with that?" Garron motioned to the gun in Jacob's hand.

Jacob stuck the gun into his waistband.

Garron asked, "Did you know that I was here?"

"Jimmy radioed and told me that you were at the Totaler."

Garron remembered the man at the table with Wes who left suddenly.

"I figured that Jimmy was mistaken, but here you are."

"I heard that you might be in some kind of trouble."

"You heard?" Jacob was obviously confused.

"I was visited by the Department of Homeland Security."

"Homeland Security?" Jacob ran a hand across the back of his neck. "That doesn't make any sense. Did they say why?"

Now Garron was confused, "Wait, you didn't know that DHS was looking for you? Then who were you hiding from?"

"From whoever did this." Jacob explained, "I went to work the other day and when Murphy didn't show, I came by here and found the house like this." Jacob waved his hand over the destruction. He continued, "I checked all of Murphy's regular spots, but never found him. When I went back home, I found that someone had trashed my place as well. So I've been laying low at Jimmy's fish camp a few miles off shore the last few days."

"Homeland Security is probably watching this house right now. I think I saw them at your house earlier. We should get out of here," Garron insisted.

"We can't, not yet. There's something that I have to find."

Jacob pulled a chain over his head. Several old keys dangled from the chain.

"We need to find the lock, or locks, that these keys open."

***

The brothers began to search through the wreckage of Murphy's house; Jacob started in the master bedroom and Garron moved from the living room to the kitchen. Garron felt as if he were in a dream. He didn't know what he was looking for or why. The keys looked old and they were each quite heavy. They didn't appear to be a modern day reproduction. Jacob only offered that Murphy had asked him to hold the keys until he returned from an unscheduled trip to St. Augustine ten days ago. Murphy had not explained the significance of the keys, but insisted that it was important for Jacob to keep them safe.

Garron surveyed the kitchen. A small table and chairs were toppled. Every cabinet was opened and emptied. The refrigerator door was standing open and all of the contents were either on the floor or spilling off the shelves. The smell of rotting food was ripe in the Florida heat. Containers of flour, salt, and sugar were poured onto the countertop. The sink was full of tea bags, coffee, silverware, and the remains of a potted plant. Boxes of macaroni, spaghetti, cereal, and cans of soup, vegetables, and beer could be found from one corner of the kitchen to the other. Someone made a thorough search of the kitchen, leaving nothing unturned. Garron left the kitchen feeling hopeless.

Garron found Jacob on his hands and knees on the bedroom floor.

"Can you believe this mess? Any luck back here?"

Jacob sat down on the carpet. "Nothing."

"I think we should assume that someone else found whatever it is that we're looking for. I mean they even searched through flour and sugar containers. The sun is going down, we should get out of here and talk this through," Garron suggested.

"No!" Jacob's frustration turned outward. "You can quit, you can fly back to your studio and paint another boat, but I'm not going to let Murphy down."

"Listen Jay, I know that you're hurting and that you are frustrated, but I didn't have to come down here." Garron could feel years of anger about to boil over. "I am trying to help."

"I didn't ask for your help." Jacob stood and clenched his fists.

Garron turned away from his brother. His muscles tensed, and his heart hammered in his chest. The point of this trip was not to drag out the past. Had Garron been fooling himself to think that he could be that selfless? He could walk away now, or he could confront Jacob and release the cap from his bottled emotions.

"I'm sorry." Jacob spoke. "You *are* trying to help and I am thankful. It's just that I am worried about Murphy and I don't know what to do."

Garron turned to see the pain on Jacob's face and remembered why he was there.

Garron took a deep breath. "Then let's talk about this. Exactly what did Murphy say and do when he gave you the keys?" Garron wiped a hand over his face in frustration.

Jacob considered this for a moment. "He asked me to hold onto the keys, and to keep them safe."

"Had he been acting strangely?" Garron asked.

"Murphy has always been a bit paranoid. Every night after locking up, he would double check all of the locks. He kept a baseball bat by the door and slept with a gun near the bed. But he did seem even more on edge recently."

"On edge, how so?" Garron prompted.

"Well, Murphy had an uncle in St. Augustine who passed away three months ago, I guess unexpectedly because he never mentioned that he was sick, and since then Murphy hasn't been himself."

Jacob continued, "And two weeks ago, Murphy made an unscheduled trip back to St. Augustine. We even had some diving charters planned and he asked me to call the clients to reschedule. Nothing was ever last-minute with Murphy. And when I asked why, he said that he had gotten a call from some of his uncle's business partners and that they needed him in St. Augustine immediately."

"He said business partners? What kind of business?"

"Real estate. Murphy and his Uncle Charles, and I guess a few other guys, owned a fair amount of real estate throughout Florida. He had never mentioned that there were other partners until that last trip. I always believed it to be just the two of them. But I figured the housing crash and Charles's death were making things too uncomfortable for his partners and an emergency meeting was called."

Garron thought about the money laundering and wondered if these partners were involved. "You ever meet any of Murphy's real estate partners, or his Uncle Charles for that matter?"

"No."

"Do you know how to reach them?"

Jacob was clearly frustrated. "I don't even have their names. Murphy never talked about it and I never asked. He was willing to teach me everything he could about diving and running a boat, but he kept his real estate venture to himself."

Money laundering seemed more likely to Garron the more he learned about Murphy. However, if Jacob was being completely honest with him, then Garron was happy that Murphy hadn't involved his brother with these business partners. Jacob would be of less interest to Homeland Security.

Garron sat on the edge of the bed. He said, "So tell me more about Murphy, like where he's from and what else he might be into."

Jacob explained that Ian Murphy's parents were originally from England and that they moved to the States when Murphy was just three years old. Murphy had grown up in North Carolina and then moved in with his Uncle Charles after high school. Charles had immigrated to the States with Murphy's parents, but had settled further south, in Miami. Murphy worked with his uncle on a dive boat out of Miami until he was thirty-three and then expanded his uncle's business by opening an office in the Keys. After his uncle retired to St. Augustine, Murphy closed the Miami office and had been working out of Marathon for the last thirty years. Murphy was well respected in the area as a dive master, boat captain, and a business man. He was also known as the area's foremost authority on seafaring history.

"Murphy has quite a collection of old maps and sea charts," Jacob added.

Garron questioned, "Are any of them valuable? Could that be what, whoever it is, is searching for?"

Jacob pondered, "Some of them are rare. Murphy's shown a few to me recently. To the right collector or museum, they could be worth serious money."

Jacob lifted his chin toward the mural behind Garron. "That painting on the wall ..."

Garron interrupted, "Yeah, I noticed it immediately, nice work. Did Murphy paint it himself?"

"He did. It's a portion of a famous map that was thought to have been lost to history, but turned up not too long ago. There's only one copy known to exist. It is Murphy's favorite. He said that this map is the first time that the New World is referred to as America."

Garron rose from the bed and took a closer look at the mural. Murphy had a talent.

He asked, "Latin. But I don't recognize these islands or this, what, peninsula?"

Jacob stood and approached the wall. He pointed to the center of the painting and said, "This large island marked Isabella, is Cuba. And the island to the right of that is Hispaniola, which is made up of Haiti and the Dominican Republic."

"So the area above that would be Florida and the Gulf of Mexico," Garron offered.

"Yep." Jacob went on to explain, "Murphy said it wasn't just a map, but a work of art. He said the original is beautiful, with illustrations and artistic flourishes."

Garron's eye was drawn to the Florida peninsula. He stepped closer to the wall.

He asked, "Jay, do you see this?"

"What?" Jacob too stepped closer.

"The paint hides it well, but there is a play of light and shadow on these islands drawn in the Gulf." Garron extended his arm and ran his hand across the wall above his head.

"There's something here," Garron said as he traced a small rectangle on the wall that was nearly invisible.

"Yeah, I see it." Jacob picked a lamp off of the floor, removed the shade and switched it on.

The naked bulb caused strange shadows to dance across the room. As Jacob raised the lamp over his head an obvious edge became apparent. The right edge was obscured by a painted line that ran floor to ceiling through Florida's peninsula, Cuba, and Hispaniola, which was meant to resemble a fold or seam in the map. But the lamp highlighted a twelve by sixteen inch pattern on the wall that spread from the faux fold. There was something behind the islands representing the Florida Keys.

Garron pressed on the panel and felt it give slightly. It felt like pressing on a taut drum head or trampoline.

"There's a piece of canvas or fabric here, but it is spackled into the drywall like a patch," Garron said.

"Here, use this." Jacob pulled a pocket knife from his jeans and unfolded it.

Garron took the knife and pierced the canvas panel. He sawed at the heavy fabric, exposing a niche in the wall. Garron folded the knife, handed it back to Jacob and then slid a filing cabinet against the wall, gingerly climbing atop in order to reach into the recess. He withdrew an old leather bound book and handed it to Jacob.

It was a large, heavy book with the worn cover a faded blue. Each corner was decorated with a brass corner protector, and there were two latches securing it closed.

"Ever see this before?" Garron asked his brother.

"No. Do you think Murphy meant these old keys as a hint to the map?"

"It seems likely, unless you think that we should keep looking to see what they might fit," Garron answered.

Jacob hung the keys around his neck once again. "No, I think we found it."

"Yeah, but what is *it*?"

A sound reached the room from outside. Jacob raised his index finger to his lips. Garron stepped into the hall and motioned for Jacob to follow. They walked slowly into Murphy's living room and out of the sliding glass door onto the back deck. They descended the stairs. From the backyard, looking under the main structure of the house between the pylons, they were able to see a patrol car on the street. The brothers moved quickly and quietly through the neighboring yard and into Garron's rental car.

"Where to now?" Garron asked.

"Head north, I have a place where we can crash," Jacob answered.

Garron was afraid that he knew exactly where they were heading.

Chapter 3

FORTY FIVE MINUTES later, the Shepard brothers pulled under yet another stilted home that resembled both Jacob's and Murphy's houses. There had been little conversation on the ride; Garron sensed Jacob's uneasiness in the car. Jacob sat in the passenger seat rubbing his hand over the cover of the book in his lap. They exited the rental car and walked around to the back of the house, where they climbed a set of stairs to the deck encircling the home.

Garron noticed immediately that this house had a different feel. The outside space was set up for entertaining and was thoughtfully designed. There were several distinct sitting areas. Four outdoor wicker loveseats with red cushions enclosed a table with an inset fire ring. There was a large L-shaped bar with eight bar stools. Five chaise lounge chairs faced the backyard and the ocean. Potted palms, ferns, and hibiscus trees colored the deck in green, red, and pink.

Jacob unlocked the door with a key he had in his jeans. He stepped inside and turned on a light. Garron followed and was surprised at the remodel of this mid twentieth-century beach home. The door opened into the middle of a large room that flowed from living space to dining area to kitchen. Furniture, cabinets, light fixtures, and appliances had a sleek modern design. The house was beautiful, even for Garron's more traditional taste in décor. And it obviously belonged to a woman. There were feminine touches throughout. Potted plants, window treatments, throw pillows, and scented candles proved that this was not the home of another one of Jacob's fishing buddies.

"Whose house?" Garron asked, already sure of the answer.

"It's Leah's place. I did all the remodeling myself," Jacob said.

He was not surprised, but having Jacob confirm that they were standing in Garron's ex-wife's home made him uncomfortable.

Jacob could see the unease in Garron's expression and said, "She has an apartment just off campus that she stays in when she has classes. Leah won't be back until tomorrow night."

A few moments passed in an uncomfortable silence with Jacob turning on some lights and collecting Leah's mail from the mail slot at the front door.

Jacob finally spoke, "I'm starving, how about something to eat?"

Garron had not eaten since breakfast. "Definitely."

Jacob pulled the gun from his waistband and set it on the counter near the refrigerator. He set the book on the kitchen's island top. He then opened the refrigerator and browsed the contents. From the freezer he pulled a bag of scallops. From a pantry cabinet he removed a can of crushed tomatoes, tomato paste, a box of linguini, and a bottle of olive oil.

From another cabinet Jacob grabbed onion and garlic powder saying, "Sorry, no fresh vegetables. With only using the house on the weekends, Leah just keeps cans and frozen food around."

Garron said, "I'm not as worried about the ingredients as much as the chef. The only thing I've ever known you to make is a phone call to order take out."

"I've picked up a few things over the last five years," Jacob said as he went back to the refrigerator for a package of bacon.

"Do you get up here often?" Garron asked.

Jacob set a frying pan on the range and lit a burner. "About every two weeks. I work most weekends on the dive boat, so it makes it tough to see one another."

Jacob cut a quarter of the bacon from the package and placed it in the hot pan. Garron's stomach growled when the smell tickled his nose.

Garron suggested, "It must strain your," he hesitated, "relationship, seeing so little of each other."

"It's tough, but we both love what we do. She would like for me to open a shop closer to the mainland, but I would never walk away from Murphy."

Jacob set a pan on another burner and started the ingredients for his sauce. In a larger pot he started water to boil. He moved fluidly and expertly around the kitchen. Jacob *had* learned a few things since moving to Florida. Garron saw something new in Jacob. His brother still showed flashes of his former self, but Garron recognized a depth to Jacob that had not been there previously.

Jacob went to the refrigerator and pulled out two beers. He opened both bottles and set one on the kitchen island before Garron could protest.

Jacob put his bottle to his lips before he realized his mistake. "Shit Gar, I'm sorry. I forgot."

Garron forced a smile. "No problem."

"No, I'm really sorry," Jacob insisted. "How long has it been?"

Garron answered, "Six years, four months, and three days."

Jacob stood awkwardly holding his bottle halfway to his mouth.

Garron asked, "How long until dinner?"

"Oh, maybe fifteen minutes."

"Could I grab a quick shower? It's been a long day."

Jacob smiled. "Sure, towels are in the linen closet just outside the bathroom. Help yourself, and I'll have a plate ready for you when you've finished."

"Thanks. I won't be long," Garron said as he made his way down the hall.

***

"Hey, that smells good," Garron said as he stepped into the kitchen still towel drying his hair. "Did you save me any?"

The smile fell from Garron's face when he saw his ex-wife in Jacob's arms; both were crying. This was the first time that Garron had seen Leah since finalizing the divorce ten years ago. In spite of the sorrow on her face, Leah looked beautiful. The turquoise green eyes were even more striking than he remembered. Her blond hair had been cut short, and it framed those eyes and her fine features nicely. She was wearing a pink and white running outfit that showed off her well-toned physique. Leah had always been a runner, and Garron could tell by her shapely thighs and calves that she was still putting shoe leather to pavement.

Finally, Garron broke the silence. "Sorry to interrupt," he said looking from Jacob to Leah.

Leah handed Garron a newspaper, the article's caption read, "Local Diver Found Dead." Garron looked to Jacob, who took a seat at the kitchen island; the pain was obvious. Jacob's brow was creased and his gaze was somewhere in the middle distance as tears followed the contours of his nose and chin.

Leah said, "They found Murphy early this morning floating near Indian Key. It looks like a diving accident. The article said there was a head injury, the water has been rough the last few days, and that he probably hit the boat as he surfaced."

Garron read the article.

"Most diving injuries take place when a diver is at the surface in rough seas, collisions occur with other divers or, as suggested in the deceased's case, the boat. Cause of death is speculated to be drowning as a result of a head injury. Official cause is pending an autopsy. The medical examiner believed that the deceased had spent minimal time in the water, due to the lack of predation and the condition of the body. The body was found by the Coast Guard just after sunrise this morning. The deceased was positively identified as Ian Murphy of Lower Matecumbe and owner of The Key to Diving, Dive Shop and Tours. The medical examiner does not expect foul play. Authorities are still looking for Mr. Murphy's boat and have asked for local boaters to keep their eyes open."

"If this article is right, then why was Murphy's house tossed?" Garron said after reading the article.

"This wasn't an accident," Jacob answered. "Murphy couldn't have been diving alone. He couldn't even get into his vest."

"I'm missing something." Garron was confused.

"Murphy injured his rotor cuff three weeks ago. He couldn't have shrugged into his equipment without a great deal of pain," Leah explained.

Garron pondered, "I know that it sounds absurd, but could Murphy have actually been laundering money?"

"Money laundering, what are you talking about?" Leah asked.

Jacob guffawed. "It's some bullshit story that the DHS fed to Garron and is trying to pin on Murphy." |

"Maybe it's not bullshit," Garron suggested.

"DHS, as in the Department of Homeland Security?" Leah asked.

Garron explained, "Agents came to my studio. They believe Murphy was laundering money for a terrorist cell."

"It's bullshit!" Jacob stood, anger contorting his face. "Murphy was not involved with terrorists."

Garron extended his arms, and raised his hands, palms out in a defensive posture.

"Okay, not terrorism. But you don't think that Murphy's death was an accident, so then what was he involved in that got him killed?" Garron reasoned.

"It must have something to do with the book," Jacob suggested.

Leah had become frustrated. She asked, "What book? Can someone tell me what the hell is going on here?"

Jacob pointed to the leather bound volume on the small desk, where he had moved it while Garron was in the shower, and walked Leah through the day's events.

Leah ran her fingers over the spine and the brass latches and corner covers. "It looks quite old. Have you looked inside? Did Murphy ever mention this before?"

Jacob shook his head. "No, I didn't want to damage the latches by prying it open. And he's never mentioned it. But it is obviously valuable and of some importance to what is going on here. Do you think that we could have Professor Burke take a look at it? He could help shed some light on what we have here."

Still examining the details of the book, Leah said, "I'm sure that Professor Burke would know exactly what we have here, but I think that you should take this to the authorities and explain yourself so you don't get into anymore trouble."

"No, I can't do that yet," Jacob answered. "Murphy entrusted me with this book, and I intend on keeping it safe. Not knowing what this book is, I'm not going to bring something to the police that could further damage Murphy's reputation."

"That's ridiculous." Leah crossed her arms over her chest and lowered her chin slightly.

It was a stance that Garron knew well. And from the change in Jacob's posture, apparently he was familiar with it, too.

Jacob squared his shoulders and stood straighter. He said, "This is not open for discussion, and no matter how long you lecture me I am not going to turn myself in until I know the significance of this book." Jacob slapped the book's cover heavily.

Leah continued to stare at Jacob, arms crossed. "Garron, tell your brother that he should turn himself in."

"I don't know if that *is* the best thing at this point, Leah." Garron added, "And I am not siding with Jacob merely to piss you off."

In spite of what he had just said, if Garron was threatened with penalty of death, he would have to admit that it did feel good to stand in opposition to his ex-wife.

He continued, "If you could have seen the steps Murphy had taken to hide that book, then you might have a better understanding of how valuable it must be."

Garron saw a slight smile crease Jacob's face.

Garron said, "But I do wonder if it is wise to involve anyone else in this mess. Can we trust this professor that you mentioned?"

"Absolutely, Professor Burke is one of my dearest friends. He has studied history, geography, language and ancient documents his entire adult life. Before coming to Barry University to teach environmental ethics, he taught history at the University of Richmond. He is world renowned in both courses of study," Leah answered.

Garron manipulated Leah more easily than he thought possible. With her defense of Professor Burke, she was strengthening Jacob's case.

Garron smiled. "Well, Professor Burke sounds like our man. Can we see him tomorrow?"

Leah hesitated. "I guess I could call him."

Garron smiled as Leah collected her cell phone from her purse and stepped down the hall toward the bedrooms. Jacob smiled, too.

In a whisper Jacob said, "Nice job. She didn't even see it coming."

"Yeah, if I would've had those kinds of negotiation skills years ago, then we may have never been divorced."

The smile left Jacob's face slowly.

"Listen Gar, I am sorry. I didn't mean for things to turn out this way between the three of us."

"It hurt me, Jay. It still hurts."

"I know, but that was not my intention. I didn't fall in love with her to hurt you. It just sort of happened."

"It just sort of happened?" Garron spit out the question, his voice rose. "It never should have been a possibility!"

"You can't pick who you fall in love with," Jacob pleaded.

"Bullshit! That cliché was probably born out of another twisted relationship. I've got another cliché for you, how about blood being thicker than water?"

Jacob did not reply.

Garron grabbed the opened bottle of beer from the counter, where Jacob had left it earlier, and walked out of the house and into the humid August night.

***

Garron's hand shook as he put the bottle to his mouth. He nearly emptied the bottle with two long pulls. The night was dark; the waning moon obscured by cloud cover. The moisture in the air was palpable. Garron shivered, in spite of the heat, as the humid air cooled on his skin. With another swallow he finished the beer and set the empty bottle on a table. He fell into a cushioned Adirondack chair and listened to the waves lapping the shore. Garron stared at the empty beer bottle and anger was replaced by guilt. More than six years sober thrown away after spending less than an hour with Leah.

Seeing Leah for the first time since their divorce ten years ago caused Garron to feel uneasy. A rush of emotions and memories assaulted defenses long ago erected. Saying goodbye to Leah after the divorce proceedings was awkward and painful for Garron; he remembered the joy in her eyes as she realized a different future lay ahead of her. Garron had felt something else, and at the time he didn't understand how Leah could be so callous. He felt empty, guilty and inadequate. He knew that the divorce was best for both of them, but it was painful. Garron thought that he had come to terms with his divorce. But if he was honest with himself, he often wondered where they had gone wrong.

Garron returned to his parent's home after a failed attempt at obtaining a college education. He had left Cambridge, on the eastern shore of Maryland, to attend Towson University to pursue a degree in secondary education. He had wanted, or thought he wanted, to teach art history to high school students. He had never believed himself talented enough to make a living with his art, so teaching seemed the next logical choice. After all, those who can't do, teach. But after getting a taste of the classroom during the first semester of his junior year, he realized that he did not have the patience or a true desire to teach. Garron returned to Cambridge a bit lost, but still hopeful. He took a position as a sales clerk at Kowalski's Art Supply store, the same job he held in high school. That is when he met Leah.

Leah's family had moved to Cambridge from Washington D.C. Her father, Senator Douglas Preston, had been in the political arena for too long and had decided to move his family away from the grind of the District. Leah found herself in a small rural town where everything moved slowly. Her light burned intensely in the quiet shore town. Leah's ferocity for life immediately won Garron over. With Leah by his side, Garron believed that he was capable of anything.

Leah's experience in the public eye and her exposure to living in the nation's capitol made Leah appear older to Garron then her 17 years. Garron mistook Leah's experience for maturity. When Leah turned 18, Garron proposed. They were married within the year. Living in a small apartment in downtown Cambridge did not sit well with Leah; she had grown accustomed to the finer things in life. So when she learned that Garron's employer wanted to retire, Leah proposed that they buy the business from the aging Janusz Kowalski. And although Mr. Kowalski was willing to part with his business for far less than what it was worth, the newlyweds still did not have the resources available for the purchase. But Leah knew where to find the needed funds.

Senator Douglas Preston had doted over his only child since birth. The Preston's were old money, and the senator would use that money to lavish his daughter with gifts. A beautiful French Anglo-Arabian show jumping horse for her tenth birthday; a Mercedes for her sixteenth; and a $225,000 wedding gown were among the gifts he poured over Leah. And even though he did not approve of his daughter's choice for a husband, Senator Preston was happy to give his daughter "a chance at happiness," which is what he called the money he gave the couple to purchase Kowalski's Art Supplies.

Only three months after taking ownership of the business, Garron's father passed away. The strain of running a business and the loss of his father caused turmoil within Garron and Leah's marriage. Neither knew how to handle the loss of a loved one, and neither knew how to operate a business successfully. The strain proved too much, and the couple separated one year later. Garron moved back into his mother's home, and Leah took her father's proposal and began her education at the University of Miami.

Garron made an attempt at keeping the business going, but soon realized that he did not have what it took to be a successful business owner. He sold the business and stayed on as store manager for the new owner. Garron was paralyzed by a feeling of failure and disappointment. And when Jacob was sent to jail, Garron began to drink in order to cope. He was no longer present in his mother's life and after the one year wait imposed by the State of Maryland for his divorce to be finalized, Garron had sunken deeper than even Leah could have imagined. When the couple saw each other at the divorce proceedings, Leah could see the damage that drink and heartache had done to Garron. During that long year though, some good did come. Garron honed his talent with a paintbrush, and had even sold several of his pieces to local collectors. It was then that he moved to

Baltimore, leaving Jacob, his mother, and painful memories behind in an attempt to redefine his life.

Garron swatted another mosquito. He looked at the empty beer bottle and hung his head in disappointment.

***

Leah stepped out of the house and onto the deck. "You're going to get eaten alive out here."

"They've been biting," Garron answered.

Leah stood beside Garron's chair. She placed a hand gently on his shoulder. Garron stiffened at her touch.

She said, referring to the empty beer bottle, "Do you think that's a good idea?"

Garron stood from the chair. "It's a horrible idea."

"Jacob just stepped into the shower. Why don't you come back inside, and I'll heat up that pasta that Jacob made?"

Garron turned and looked at his ex-wife. "Should I have stayed in Maryland?"

"He's glad that you are here."

"What about you?" He asked.

"I'm surprised to see you, but I guess that I shouldn't have been. You heard that your little brother was in trouble, so of course *you* flew to his rescue. You have always put others before yourself."

Garron didn't believe that. He turned back to the lights on the water. "I surprised myself. It's really hard to be here."

Leah walked to the door and placed her hand on the knob. "Come back inside. You must be hungry."

Garron hesitated, and then followed her into the kitchen.

He took a seat at the island once again and watched as Leah spooned some of the pasta onto a dish and placed it in the microwave. Her round features and button nose gave her a youthful, innocent look, but her eyes could make any monk rethink his vows of chastity. Leah looked more beautiful than Garron remembered. There were a few new wrinkles near her eyes, probably from the hours running in the Florida sun, but they suited her.

"This is one of my favorite meals," Leah said. "Jacob is pretty good in the kitchen. I hope reheating does it justice."

"I'm sure that it'll be great," Garron responded.

"I'm sorry to have showed up unannounced. I'm sure you weren't too happy to learn that I was in your shower."

The microwave beeped and Leah placed the hot dish in front of Garron.

"No, I should apologize to you. I didn't give you a very warm welcome. What'll you have to drink?"

Garron thought wine, but said, "Water."

Garron took a bite of Jacob's pasta dish. It was good. Actually it was great.

"I'm glad that you are here for Jacob. If he's involved in something dangerous, then I am glad that you are here to offer advice. Let's face it, his temper can get him into trouble."

Garron thought of the standoff with his brother in Murphy's bedroom.

Between bites, Garron said, "He seems a bit mellower."

Leah laughed. "Yeah, I guess that he has mellowed a bit. But he still has a tendency to act before he has thought through the consequences."

Leah pulled her own plate from the microwave and sat beside Garron.

"So you think that your professor friend can help with understanding the book?"

Leah took a bite and said with her mouth full, "I looked more closely at the book while you were feeding the mosquitoes. Without opening it I can't be sure, but from what I can see of the pages' edges it looks like some kind of map. Plus, I could see some of the writing. It's in Latin. So, yes, Patrick is the man to go to. He's mastered many languages and cartography is one of his many hobbies."

"It's a map?" Garron asked.

"Not sure, but I think so. The pages are made from folded sheets that are attached to the leather binding, but some of the words and images are visible, and I think that it is a map. Or possibly multiple maps in a single volume. I can see some of the illustrations that appear to border the map, and they are extremely detailed."

Garron finished his dinner and emptied his water glass.

"A map makes sense. Jacob told me that Murphy had a thing for ancient maps, and I saw quite a few maps in our search of his house."

"So after we see Patrick, then what?" Leah asked.

"I don't know. I guess it depends on what your friend tells us."

Leah pushed her plate away and turned on her stool to look at Garron directly.

"No, I don't think that it depends on anything. I think that we should go to the police. The longer we wait the more trouble Jacob could find himself in."

"Jacob wants to better understand what he and Murphy were involved in before he turns himself in to the authorities."

"I think that's a mistake." She was unable to hide her disappointment. "And frankly I can't believe that you would allow Jacob to make that mistake."

Garron attempted to keep his cool. "It is his friend, Leah, his best friend. Jacob feels obligated to protect Murphy's reputation. It is ultimately his decision."

Leah stood and took both plates to the sink. They rattled a little too loudly as she dropped them into the basin. She turned and crossed her arms across her chest.

"His decision yes, but he looks up to you Garron and you could influence that decision."

"Hey, now hold on!" Garron rose from his stool. "Why does it always fall back on me being a role model? Jacob is a grown man and can make his own decisions."

"You know the answer to that question, because you *are* the older brother Garron. Everything that you do or have done influences Jacob, whether you want it to or not. He listens to you."

Garron was angry, and he could not hold his tongue. "He doesn't always listen to me! He's making the same mistake that I once made, no matter how many times I tried to warn him."

"What are we talking about here, Garron? You warned him about what? Me?"

"You know damn well what I'm talking about, Leah."

"It's different now Garron. It's different between me and Jacob."

"Maybe for now, but what happens when Jay can't live up to your lofty expectations? You can't trade him in for the next model Leah, we don't have another brother."

Leah's voice stuck. "That's not fair, Garron. We never meant for this to happen, but it has, and we're both very happy."

Garron could see the tears welling in Leah's eyes. He had wanted to hurt her, he wanted to see her cry, but now that he could see the pain he caused, Garron felt guilty.

He said, "We were happy once, too."

"Yeah, we were. But we both know that neither one of us was ready for marriage."

"Are you ready now? How can you be sure that you won't change your mind in three years?"

"For the same reason that you knew it was time to marry Veronica. But there are no guarantees."

Garron softened. He, too, felt as if he could cry.

Leah said, "Jacob had been acting strangely the last two months, so we sat down to talk about it two weeks ago. After some prying, your brother finally told me what was on his mind. Three months ago Jacob bought an engagement ring, but it raked him with guilt. See, even though Jacob and I love each other very much, neither one of us wants to hurt you. And we knew that if we got married, then that is exactly what would happen. So he and I decided that marriage was out of the question until we patched things up with you."

Garron was physically shaken and sat down heavily. He always thought that Jacob and Leah's relationship would fail. He fought with understanding how the relationship could have begun at all, but he reasoned how a chance meeting could have pulled the two together.

Leah had received her degree in marine biology from the University of Miami and began her teaching career at nearby Barry University. Barry was a small school with a respected School of Natural and Health Sciences. In her Department of Zoology position, Leah excelled as an untenured professor. One of her responsibilities was to set up dive trips into the local waters surrounding the Florida coast and the Florida Keys. By chance she happened to call *The Key to Diving, Dive Shop and Tours*, where Jacob had recently taken a job. After the usual pleasantries, the two decided to meet. Their true motivation was to discover what they could about Garron. Leah wanted to learn how Garron was coping with his alcoholism. And Jacob wanted to know why Leah and Garron had split up; it was something his brother never wanted to discuss. They were two people with a common past, who in trying to understand Garron's pain, developed a deep friendship.

Garron appreciated how it could have happened; he just didn't like it. And learning now that the two were discussing marriage hurt him sharply. Garron was tormented with questions. How could Jacob betray him? If Jacob could make Leah happy, then was Jacob a better man than Garron? Did Garron's failure and Jacob's success speak to Garron's worth as a man?

Leah said tentatively, "I think that you and Jacob need to talk. Garron, you don't have to forgive me, but you and Jacob need each other. Talk this through."

Jacob entered the kitchen. Garron could not look his brother in the eye.

Garron said, "I think … that I should call my wife." He stepped back outside.

***

Veronica answered after the first ring.

"Hello Sweetie. Did you find Jacob?"

"I did."

"Is he okay?"

Garron explained to his wife what had occurred earlier in the day.

"I should call Carroll and have him fly to meet you in Miami."

Carroll Cohen was the lead attorney on Veronica's legal team and a long time friend of her family. He had been serving the Delgado family in one capacity or another for nearly fifty years. Garron liked and trusted Carroll.

"Let's wait one more day before calling Carroll."

Garron told Veronica about the book and their plan to speak to one of Leah's colleagues to have it identified.

He added, "We just want to know what we are dealing with here."

"So Leah is there? How are you coping with that?" Veronica asked.

"To be honest, I'm not coping very well. I thought I had put all of that behind me, but just seeing her today twisted my stomach. And I'm saying things just to be spiteful."

"Don't be too hard on yourself, or Leah for that matter, neither of you had a chance for closure. You were both young and immature, and you never took the time to talk through your decisions." She added, "You both probably harbor some resentment. Just remember that you both deserve respect, so neither of you should do or say anything just to hurt one another."

Garron was silent for a moment.

Veronica asked, "How's your brother dealing with Murphy's death?"

Garron realized that he had been too distracted by his own emotions to help Jacob with the loss that he must be feeling.

He said, "He's obviously in pain, but I've been a bit preoccupied with my own emotions to help."

"Well be sure to give him a hug for me."

Garron marveled at his wife's wisdom. "Do you know how much I love you?"

"You tell me all of the time, but it's nice to hear it again."

The couple said their goodbyes and Garron turned to step back inside to speak to Jacob. As he did he noticed a large SUV parked across and down the street. Two passengers were visible through the windshield by only the glow of their cigarettes.

***

Jacob and Leah were sitting on the couch holding each other closely when Garron entered the house. Garron turned off the lamp in the living room.

He said, "I think we have company." Garron hurried to the window and looked out onto the street from behind the window's frame.

Jacob joined Garron at the opposite side of the window.

Garron said, "About three houses down across the street, in the SUV."

"I see them." Jacob confirmed.

"What do we do?" Leah asked.

"I have some questions to ask," Jacob said as he retrieved the pistol from the counter and stepped toward the door.

Leah grabbed him by the arm. "You are not going out there."

"I need some answers, Leah."

Garron peered through the window. "I think that she's right Jay. It must not be cops or agents out there; otherwise they would have knocked down the door and arrested all of us by now. And if you believe that Murphy was murdered, then these could be dangerous men."

"That's what I'm hoping for."

"So you walk out there and get yourself killed, then what? They just leave? They obviously wanted that book, Jay. So they kill you, then how do you think that Leah and I will fair when they come in here looking for the book?"

Jacob stopped at the door.

He said with obvious sarcasm, "What do you suggest then, big brother?"

"Is there a way for us to slip by these guys? Then we can meet up with Leah's professor friend and stay ahead of whoever is following us."

Leah asked, "How about the boat?"

Jacob nodded. "I think that we can make it to the dock. We can slip out the back and use the neighbor's yards to keep out of sight."

"Good. But we'll need a vehicle at some point." Garron thought about the rental car that he would have to leave behind. He wondered how long before he could recover it and return it to the car rental office.

"We'll take the boat to Wes's and borrow one of his cars," Jacob offered.

"Let's turn these lights off," Leah said as she flipped the switch for the overhead kitchen light.

"Good idea, but turn on a light in the bedroom that faces the street. They might think that you are just heading to bed for the night. It might buy us some time," Garron added and then thought to ask, "Is it safe to travel by boat at night?"

"Of course it is. I know these waters well, and they are well marked. Don't worry," Jacob replied with a grin.

"Okay smart ass, forgive me for my cautiousness."

Jacob secured Murphy's book into a red waterproof backpack and the threesome slipped out the back door and down the stairs to the backyard. They waited a moment in silence, allowing their eyes to adjust to the night sky. Jacob led the way through the neighbor's shrubbery that separated the two yards, with Leah close behind him. Garron waited just a heartbeat longer to see if there was any movement in front of Leah's house. All was quiet and still.

Before long they had reached the dock and climbed aboard a twenty-foot Grady White with a center console. Leah expertly untied the boat from its moors, while Jacob checked for a few items and primed the engines. Starting the engines could draw unwanted attention, but they thought that the distance and cover from the surrounding houses should help to muffle any noise. The engines started easily, but in the silence of the night the noise was intense. Jacob slipped the boat away from the dock and out toward the channel markers heading westward.

Garron looked over his shoulder back toward the dock and saw headlights appear. The front seat was illuminated when the SUV's passenger door was opened. Two men were visible. It was difficult for Garron to make out in the low light, but it appeared that the driver was on a phone while the passenger standing beside the SUV was watching their boat with what must have been thermal imaging binoculars. Garron tapped Jacob on the shoulder and pointed back toward the dock. Jacob took in the two men near the dock; he raised his arm and extended his middle finger toward the onlookers. He smiled and throttled the boat's engine.

***

The trip was quick and without incident. Jacob steered the boat down Tavernier Creek. The creek's banks were highly developed with large homes eagerly eating up all waterfront property. Tavernier Creek connected

Florida Bay with the Atlantic Ocean. A home owner on Tavernier Creek would have the waters of the Atlantic or the Gulf of Mexico available from their personal dock. But there was no boat at Wes Macomber's dock.

Leah once again used her skill on the lines and secured Jacob's boat to the dock. There were a few lights on in neighboring houses, but Wes's house was dark.

Garron stepped closer to Jacob and whispered, "Maybe he's not home."

"What?" Jacob asked.

"There's no boat, and there aren't any lights on, maybe Wes isn't home."

"Wes had to sell his boat a few months ago, his health has been spiraling downward and he couldn't keep up with the maintenance. And Wes is probably in bed, it is getting late."

Garron remembered Wes's jaundiced appearance from the bar earlier that day. Wes did not look well.

Garron was surprised to see that Wes's house was different from what he had seen since arriving in the Keys. The house was three stories high, with the garages occupying the lowest level. It was made of concrete with a stucco finish and the majority of the walls were angled. The windows were two stories high, and Garron thought that it would have been a spectacular sight during the day.

"No stilt house?" Garron asked after admiring the home.

Jacob responded, "This is Wes and Ginny's retirement dream. They sat down with their architect and created a home that is not only stunning, but nearly hurricane proof. Those windows have retractable shutters, the walls are made of concrete, and those angles allow the wind to flow around the house. But Ginny never had the time to enjoy it."

"She died shortly after moving in one year ago, completely unexpected," Leah added.

"That's terrible." Garron sympathized with the man that he saw earlier in the day.

"Wes was devastated. Wes hasn't been the same since. He never believed that he would outlive Ginny, he's been fighting cancer for three years now." Leah sounded as if she could cry.

Garron now understood why Wes had been at the bar. Garron was sure that if he found himself in the same situation, alone and dying, that he, too, would have his own stool at a bar.

Garron asked, "How much do we tell Wes?"

"As little as possible. Let me do the talking and I will come up with a story that he might believe," Jacob answered. "Let's see if we can get the old man to answer his door." Jacob led the way through the yard.

They climbed the stairs to the deck and crossed to the door. Jacob raised his hand to knock, but the door stood ajar. Jacob turned and made eye contact with Garron.

Jacob pushed the door inward and called out, "Wes? Hey Wes, you home?"

As he stepped through the door, Jacob pulled the pistol from the waistband of his jeans. They had entered through the eat-in kitchen, and Garron could see that indeed this was a dream home. The appliances, countertops, and furnishings would make any professional chef jealous. As the moon shone through the windows, it confirmed to Garron that the views would be stunning during the day. Just beyond the kitchen was the two-story great room that was surrounded by a balcony.

Something in the shadows caught Garron's attention. He reached out and grabbed Jacob's shoulder, stopping him at the edge of the room. Leah let out a gasp. There in the shadows, across the room, hanging from the center of the balcony was Wes's body. Jacob dashed across the room and grabbed Wes around the legs, raising him upward and sitting the man on his shoulder. Garron found the stairs to his left and climbed them two at a time.

Garron came to the noose and attempted to untie the braided nylon rope from the balcony. He called down to Jacob. "Is he alive? Is he breathing?"

"He's not moving," Jacob answered. "Wes? Can you hear me?"

Leah stepped toward Wes and took his wrist. She could feel no pulse. She looked up at Wes's face. The man's neck was stretched unnaturally. His tongue was visible at the corner of his mouth. Wes was dead.

She whispered, "We're too late."

"What?" Garron demanded.

"We're too late," she repeated. "He's gone."

"Untie him Garron," Jacob said as he hoisted Wes's body higher.

"I can't get the knot ..."

Jacob screamed, "Get him down!"

Leah put her hand in Jacob's jeans and pulled out a pocket knife.

"Good, cut him down. Please," Jacob pleaded.

Leah ran up the stairs and handed Garron the knife. He unfolded the blade and called down to his brother. "Ready?"

"Yes," Jacob answered.

Garron took the blade to the rope and it severed quickly. He looked down from the balcony as Jacob took the weight of Wes's body and carefully laid him on the couch, placing a pillow behind Wes's head. Jacob knelt beside the couch and placed his ear on his friend's chest. Garron and Leah descended the stairs and stood behind the couch and looked down on Jacob.

Jacob looked up at them, with tears in his eyes. "He's gone."

"I'm sorry honey." Leah stretched her arm over the couch and ran a finger down Jacob's jaw line.

"He was a fine man. He didn't deserve this." Jacob stood.

"He didn't deserve ..." Garron hesitated. "You think ... you don't think that this was ... suicide?"

Jacob did not answer.

"People, friends, even family won't accept it, but sometimes we don't understand just how deep that person was hurting," Garron reasoned.

Jacob just looked Garron in the eye.

"With the loss of his wife and his illness, maybe it was just too much ..."

"Just stop!" Jacob interrupted. "Can't you see what is happening here? First it was Murphy and now Wes. Someone is killing my friends."

Garron was not convinced.

"It's just a bit too coincidental, don't you think? Our houses being trashed, us being followed and monitored, the hidden book, it must all be connected." Jacob spit out the last few words.

"Okay Jay, you're right, it is too much of a coincidence." Garron agreed, without conviction. "So what do we do next?"

"I think that we stick with our plan. The further we get away from the Keys, the better for our safety," Jacob answered.

"What about Wes? We can't just leave him," Leah said.

Garron thought about the evidence that they must have left throughout the house. What had he gotten himself into?

"We call 9-1-1 and get the hell out of here." Jacob strode across the kitchen and grabbed the portable phone from the base. He called out to Garron, "Near the front door, on the wall, there are some boat cleats. On those cleats are some keys; grab the ones on the mini snow globe keychain."

Garron pulled the keys from the cleat.

Jacob dialed 9-1-1, and set the phone on the kitchen counter. He grabbed his backpack and pistol from the floor near Wes's body. The threesome hurried down the stairs to the garage. The garage held only two vehicles, an old pick-up truck and an RV. Jacob unlocked the door to the small RV, told Garron to open the garage door, and he pulled the vehicle into the driveway. They all climbed into the RV and drove down Wes's street and turned onto US 1 heading north.

The Winnebago was spacious for being less than 25 feet in length. Garron sat on a bench seat near the side stairs, which faced the center of the cabin just behind the passenger seat. Opposite of Garron's bench was a dinette table that was directly behind the driver's seat. Swiveling the chair, the driver's seat could also function as a dining chair. Behind the dinette was a bathroom with a shower stall. There was also a small kitchen, including a refrigerator, sink, and a small range. And at the back of the vehicle there was a bedroom, with what Garron guessed was a queen-sized bed.

Garron asked, "Aren't the police going to notice that Wes's RV is missing?"

"Actually, this is not Wes's. It belongs to a snowbird neighbor who only lives in the Keys during the winter months. Wes keeps it in his garage and maintains it for him the rest of the year. Unless Wes's house was under surveillance, we should be in the wind," Jacob answered.

Garron looked at his watch; it read 12:42. "Listen, I know that it is late, but I want to call Veronica."

"Are you sure that's wise? Someone might be tapping your phones or tracking your calls," Jacob said.

"That's exactly why I want to call her. I want her to get out of town in case she's being watched. Maybe she can visit one of her offices abroad and stay out of this mess."

Leah agreed. "I think that's a great idea."

Garron rose from his bench. "Are you okay to drive?" He caught Jacob's eye in the rearview.

"I couldn't sleep if I wanted to," Jacob replied.

Garron made his way, a bit unsteadily, toward the bedroom at the rear of the RV. He pulled the curtain closed behind him. He looked down at his cell phone, the battery was nearly dead and he had left the charger in his suitcase, the suitcase that he left behind at Leah's house. He dialed his home number.

***

After five rings, Veronica answered the call in a sleep-heavy voice.

"Sorry to wake you," Garron apologized.

"It's fine. Are you alright?" Veronica asked.

"Yes, we are all okay." Garron suddenly felt tired and weary.

"It's worse than you thought, isn't it?" Veronica knew her husband well.

"I'm not sure what we are in the middle of." Then Garron told his wife about Wes.

After hearing the tale, with her uncanny ability, Veronica asked, "You're not sure if the death was self-inflicted or not, are you?"

"How do you do that? How do you know exactly what I'm thinking?"

She replied, "You're not that hard to read, my love."

"I'm worried about you."

"I'm fine. But I'm glad to hear your voice." She adjusted her position a little higher in the bed.

"If Jay is right, and people are being killed, then I'm worried that this thing may come home."

"You think that I'm in danger?"

"I just want you to take some precautions. Do you have any business travel plans after Detroit Saturday?"

"I'm to be in …"

Garron interrupted. "Don't tell me where. Could you leave a little early? Maybe fly directly from Detroit."

"If things are that serious, then we should be contacting my legal team to provide you with security." The sleep had left her voice completely.

"Leah has this friend that's going to help us, after that I'll be happy to circle the wagons. But could you fly earlier?"

"Sure. I'm to be …" she caught herself, "I'm to be there Tuesday, so I'll just spend a few additional days … at that office."

"Good. I'm sure that I'm overreacting, but it will keep me from worrying unnecessarily. Thank you."

Veronica insisted, "I'm putting Carroll on notice. And we will call him no later than Saturday."

"We should have this behind us by then."

Garron could hear Veronica take a drink from the water glass she always kept by the bed.

She swallowed and then asked, "How are the three of you … getting along?"

Garron thought about that for a moment. "Jay asked Leah to marry him."

Veronica's voice took on a softer edge. "Garron, I'm sorry. That must be tough for you, but you know that Jacob doesn't want to hurt you, right?"

Garron's phone beeped in his ear.

"My phone is dying. Good luck in Detroit. Get some rest, I love you."

"I love you, too. Call me later."

"I will." Garron thought of Wes and the loss of his wife, and he quickly added, "Ronnie, I'm so glad you are a part of my life. Have a safe flight. I love you."

"I'm the lucky …" Veronica began as Garron's cell phone battery died.

Chapter 4

"GARRON, WAKE UP."

Garron felt his foot being tugged and the bed shaking. He sat straight up. His cell phone slid off his chest onto the mattress.

Leah said, "It's time."

"Time for what?" Garron asked as he wiped the sleep from his eyes.

"Our meeting with Patrick," she answered.

"How long was I asleep?"

"Maybe five or six hours. We're to meet the professor at eight o'clock."

"I'm sorry," Garron said as he stood. "You shouldn't have let me sleep for so long. You both needed some rest, too."

As they walked through the RV she explained, "We pulled into the parking lot just after two this morning. I spoke to security and cleared having the RV on campus, so I was able to sleep from about three o'clock until Jacob woke me at sunrise."

When they climbed down from the RV, Jacob was waiting. Garron had to squint in the morning sun. They were in a parking lot that was nearly full, but there were only a few students visible. Garron looked at his watch, and decided that most students would already have made their way to their first class. There were some students visible near the bordering buildings, which Garron surmised were resident halls due to the running or biking outfits that most of the students were wearing as they entered and exited the buildings. Some students were still toweling off from a morning swim.

To his left, Garron saw several baseball and soccer fields. The student body seemed to take full advantage of the South Florida climate.

"Good morning," Jacob said.

"Damn, it's hot already." Garron asked, "Did you get some sleep?"

"No. I couldn't shut my mind down long enough to doze off."

"We have to cross campus, let's get moving," Leah prompted.

The campus was surrounded by ficus, palm, and live oak trees. Crotons, bromeliads, and crown of thorns added splashes of color. The campus was lush and tropical. They passed between buildings onto a small open plaza where a large building dominated the center of the campus. A sign denoted the building as Cor Jesu Chapel. It was a large building in a Spanish Mediterranean revival style with a tall bell tower. They approached from the rear and walked toward the building's entryway. At the front of the chapel was a long, wide mall lined by tall palm trees. The campus' main entrance was visible at the end of the mall. It was a beautiful campus.

Garron said, "This is a beautiful school, do you enjoy teaching here?"

"Very much so," Leah answered enthusiastically.

Jacob said, "She's been courted by a larger school, and the offer was significant, but she's turned them down repeatedly to stay here."

"I enjoy working for the dean, and the School of Natural and Health Sciences is growing. I want to be a part of its continued success." Leah continued, "The overall vision for the school is exciting, and in a few more years this program will be one of the highest rated in the country."

Garron was surprised at hearing Leah's commitment to her new profession. Leah had never shown an interest in teaching; she had even ridiculed Garron for having made that choice after learning of his time at Towson University. Leah thought teachers were underappreciated and overworked, and that only a masochist would choose to be an educator.

From behind them someone called, "Good morning."

They turned to see a large man leaving the chapel and heading in their direction. The man was round and tall, dressed in a lightweight cream-colored suit, including a bowtie. He moved gracefully for a large man, with a lightness in his step that belied his size. His white hair was thin and the wisps were combed straight back from his smooth forehead.

He caught up to them and embraced and kissed Leah warmly.

Leah said, "Gentlemen, I would like for you to meet Professor Patrick Burke."

Leah had her arm under the professor's arm.

"Professor, you remember Jacob."

"Of course, it is good to see you again young man." The professor said with a deep southern accent and a slight chuckle.

"And this is his brother, Garron Shepard."

The professor shook Garron's hand. "Why, you two are the spitting image of one another. It is a pleasure to meet you, Mr. Shepard."

Professor Burke's accent reminded Garron of honey, cigars, and bourbon.

The professor looked puzzled. He looked to Leah. "Garron, that name is familiar to me. I am certain that I have heard it before." Professor Burke's eyes grew wide with recognition. He looked back and forth from Jacob to Garron.

Garron raised one eyebrow and gave a crooked smile.

Leah blushed.

The professor took in Leah's embarrassment and apologized. "Oh, I am sorry. I did not mean to ... well, I mean I am sure ..." He chuckled again and his large frame shook. "I'm stammering. It is rare to find me without the proper words." The professor laughed deeply and it reminded Garron of distant thunder. The laugh removed the tension.

When he regained his composure, he said, "Well now, I believe that you have something to show me."

"Yes, Professor, we have something we would like for you to identify," Leah said.

"Will my office suit our needs?"

"Yes sir," Leah answered.

"Then, if you please." Professor Burke motioned to the building marked Wiegand Hall to his left. "Let us get out of this heat."

Leah and the professor walked arm-in-arm as they made their way to his office on the second floor of the building. Garron was surprised at the old educator's lightness and with the ease at which he climbed the stairs to his office.

In the hall outside the office, Leah asked, "How is Lucy?"

The professor answered, "I'm afraid not too well. She has lost her eyesight. The doctor's prognosis is grave."

"I'm very sorry to hear that." Leah said gently patting the man's arm.

"Thank you, my dear, your concern is much appreciated."

The professor unlocked his office door and ushered the group inside. The office was spacious but every available flat surface was laden with stacked books and magazines. There was a small table just inside the door. On the wall beside the table there was a floor to ceiling bookcase stretching to the only window in the office. The desk faced the door, putting the professor's back to the window. Patrick Burke hung his jacket from a hook on the wall beside his desk.

"Is Lucy your wife?" Jacob asked.

The professor laughed again. "No, no, Lucy is my faithful Scottish terrier." His expression changed, "I lost my wife, Karen, just over five years ago."

Jacob said, "I'm very sorry, sir."

"Thank you my boy. I miss her deeply." The professor took his seat. "I must apologize for not having enough chairs for all, but please make yourselves as comfortable as possible."

Leah and Jacob sat in the chairs facing the desk. Jacob removed his backpack and placed it on the floor beside his chair. Garron leaned against the overloaded book shelves.

Garron looked at the pictures of presidents and key moments in American history on the walls and asked, "Professor, how does a history teacher end up with an interest in the natural sciences? That is, how did you come to teach environmental ethics?"

"History is still my true passion, my first love, but the two studies are not that detached."

Garron furrowed his brow. "I'm having trouble making that connection."

He leaned back in his chair, which squeaked with his body weight. With a wide grin Professor Burke said, "Most people have that same difficulty my boy. But for me the connection is obvious."

He continued, "You see, I grew up on a long established tobacco farm in Virginia. My family had owned that farm for more than one hundred years, and I spent my youth toiling beside my brothers and father. Yes, we were of old money and my ancestors did use slaves to develop that land, something that I am not proud of. But my family had also put their own blood and sweat into the land, as well. So toiling on the farm developed in me not only an appreciation for the generations of people, the history, who worked that land, but also for the land itself, the environment." He interlaced his fingers to illustrate the connection.

"So you see, the study of human history enlightened me to the affect that mankind has had on the environment. And as I learned of the mistakes of previous generations, and of my own, I wanted to teach a future generation to understand our past blunders so as to protect our natural resources."

He smiled. "I apologize, but as you will learn with me, there is no short answer. Did any of that make sense, my boy?"

Garron felt a fondness for the man. "Yes, sir, I'm just sorry that I was too shortsighted to make that connection on my own."

He added a warm chuckle, and then the professor said, "I am glad that I made that connection between the two studies early enough in my life to have made a difference, or at the very least to feel as though I had contributed to society."

Leah reached across the desk and took the professor's hand in hers. "You've made a difference." Leah confirmed. "And not just to me. Your books on the Industrial Revolution in America and the California Gold Rush were groundbreaking. They illustrated the need for environmental responsibility; your books became guideposts for generations to come."

Garron saw the man's eyes and smile soften. The sentiment obviously touched him.

"Thank you, my dear. I'm proud of my accomplishments, but there is still more to do. And at eighty-two years of age, I am running out of time."

Garron was shocked. "Eighty-two? That's incredible, you move with such grace and ease."

This time Patrick Burke laughed loudly. He removed his glasses and wiped the tears from his eyes. "Thank you, my boy. But my days are short, and that is okay. The Lord has blessed me tenfold. Putting me in front of young minds like Leah's has been my reward. They will carry on my message."

Replacing his glasses, he asked, "Now you have something to show me, yes?"

Jacob picked up the backpack from the floor, unzipped the bag, pulled out the book and placed it carefully on Professor Burke's desk.

"My, my, it is beautiful," the professor said.

He slid the book closer to him and massaged the cover.

"I'd say pigskin. This is an interesting blue dye, possibly indigo. Where did you find this?"

Leah answered, "This book was given to Jacob by a close friend who passed away unexpectedly."

"I'm sorry for your loss, my boy." The professor looked out over his glasses at Jacob then went back to his inspection.

He knocked a knuckle against the cover. There was a dull thud.

"Sounds like a wood cover. That with the two Gothic brass latches and corner covers, I'd say that this binding is from the sixteenth century."

"Sixteenth century, does that make it valuable?" Jacob asked.

"The age alone adds to the value, but its true value will be measured by what's inside. May I open it?"

Jacob nodded, excited by the prospect of learning more about the book.

Professor Burke pulled on a pair of white cotton gloves from his desk drawer and then gently pried the two latches and opened the cover. He ran his hand across the books endpapers. "Linen, for the leaves not to be pulp paper is consistent with the sixteenth century, as well."

The professor caught Garron's eye. He said, "The paper is folded only once forming the gathering; we have a folio, in size and style. But the pages are not uniformly trimmed. Some pages are smaller than the others and some appear to be velum."

He slid back from his desk, opened another drawer and retrieved a ruler and a magnifying glass.

Measuring the endpaper he said, "Approximately eighteen inches high. Twelve inches in depth, so the largest pages are roughly eighteen by twenty-four inches in size."

He further examined the pages with the magnifying glass. "This is odd. The pages are only printed on one side of the paper. It seems that we have a collection of material sewn together as a gathering."

Garron asked, "A gathering, Professor?"

"It means simply a collection of pages," the professor answered.

He trained his magnifying glass on the corner of the first sheet. He said, "There is some bleed-through ..." The professor's expression changed as he looked at the page. His hand trembled as he flipped the page and got his first look at what was on the page.

"I can't believe this ... I'm holding ..." He stammered. "This is incredible!"

With a smile Leah asked, "What is it, Professor?"

The professor answered, "Have you heard of the Waldseemüller map of 1507?"

Jacob said, "Yes. My friend, who owned this map, told me a little about it before he died."

"Is that the one that he painted on the wall?" Garron asked his brother.

To the professor, Jacob explained, "My friend painted a mural, recreating a portion of the map."

Professor Burke said, "Well, the Waldseemüller map of 1507 is on permanent display at the Library of Congress. It was once the most sought after map in the world. In 1999, the only known copy of the map became available. In 2001, the Library of Congress and the seller, a German prince, agreed on a price and in 2003, the Library paid ..." He hesitated and removed his glasses. He finally continued with a broad smile, "... ten million dollars for that map."

"Is this a copy of that map?" Leah asked.

The professor smiled broadly. "You have something very special here."

"Are you sure?" Jacob said excitedly.

"I'm sure that this is a copy of the 1507 map. Look at this first sheet, here at the legend." The professor pointed with his gloved finger at the upper corner of the page. "Translating from Latin, it reads,

'Many have regarded as an invention the words of a famous poet that 'beyond the stars lies a land, beyond the path of the year and the sun, where Atlas, who supports the heavens, revolves on his shoulders the axis of the world set with gleaming stars.'

Beautiful words, are they not? Words so beautifully written, that they are impossible for me to forget. And it continues;

'For there is a land, discovered by Columbus, a captain of the King of Castile, and by Americus Vespucius ...'

I have studied the Library of Congress's copy for years. Believe me when I say that this legend reads exactly as that of the Library's copy," the professor concluded, once again removing his glasses.

The professor flipped to a page toward the back of the book and examined it closely.

He said, "This is not part of the 1507 map. It appears to be a portion of a much larger piece; the edges have been clearly cut. The ink has faded. I am not familiar with this piece."

"What does that mean?" Jacob asked.

Professor Burke responded, "Only that this is a collection of resources sewn into the same binding, resources that appear to be between 500 and 600 years old."

"That is amazing," Leah said.

"Yes, it is, my dear." The professor agreed. "And I would love to spend more time with this piece of history if you would allow me."

Jacob responded hesitantly, "I'm not sure that is a good idea, Professor. There are some people looking for this map who are willing to do anything to get it."

"But they don't know where we are, or that we are meeting with Professor Burke," Leah offered. "With a little more time could you verify this map's authenticity, Professor?"

"I believe that I have the needed supplies at my home office to, within reason, authenticate this document," Professor Burke responded.

"Why don't we let the professor do what he can to authenticate this map so that we have a better understanding of what we are involved in? That way, when we do go to the authorities, they won't be able to browbeat us," Leah suggested.

"I don't want to let it out of my sight. No offense, Professor," Jacob said.

"No offense taken my boy." The professor smiled. "It is quite a treasure. Why don't you join me for dinner this evening, and after we will make a closer inspection of the map *together?*"

Jacob looked to Garron. Garron was surprised that his younger brother still looked to him for advice. Garron nodded to Jacob.

Jacob said, "I think that is a wonderful idea."

"Fantastic!" The professor answered. "I have a few things yet to do today, if I can keep my mind off this map." He chuckled. "But I will leave here early, so could we say dinner at four o'clock, if that is not too early?"

"I'm anxious to learn more, so the earlier the better," Garron responded.

Jacob answered, "Four o'clock it is, and we will see you then, Professor."

Jacob picked the folio up with even more reverence than before and placed it in his backpack.

"Would you like for us to bring anything, groceries, wine, anything at all?" Leah asked.

"No my dear, I will have all that we need. Just bring your pretty smile, and all will be well." The professor wrote down his address and handed it to Leah.

"I will see you at four. Please take good care of that treasure until then," the professor said as he escorted his guests out of his office.

Jacob responded, "Believe me, we will, Professor."

***

"I'm hungry, how about you?" Jacob asked.

Leah and Garron agreed.

"Let's grab something at the café," Leah suggested.

"So it seems that $10 million is a strong motive for what we've seen happen to Murphy and Wes," Garron said as they walked across campus and past the chapel.

"*Now* you believe that their deaths were not coincidental?" Jacob said.

"I don't know, but people have been killed for far less, so maybe," Garron answered.

Leah led the way to Thompson Hall and the Buc Stop Café, which was directly next to the chapel in a building they had passed earlier. Leah ordered coffee and bagels, while Jacob and Garron took a seat at one of the small tables. When their order was ready, Jacob helped Leah get the coffees to the table.

Leah set a cup of black coffee and a cinnamon raisin bagel in front of Garron. She still remembered his preferences. Leah and Jacob added cream to their coffees and Jacob let out a sigh of relief after taking a sip of the hot brew.

Jacob said, "So what do we do while we wait for the professor?"

Between bites of his bagel, Garron said, "I don't know about you, but I'm anxious to learn more about this map. Leah, could you get us access to the Internet?"

"I could set you up in the library; I'm sure that I can clear it with the library staff," she replied.

Garron finished half of the bagel. "Where do you think Murphy got this map?"

"I really don't know, but he *was* a collector," Jacob replied finishing his coffee.

"But you would think that if an important historical piece like the only other copy of the 1507 map had come up for sale, then Professor Burke would have known about it," Garron countered.

"Maybe it was a recent acquisition for Murphy, or maybe it wasn't obtained legally. There are other means," Leah proposed.

Jacob did not hide his offense. "Are you saying that Murphy was involved in some kind of antiquities black market?"

Garron weighed Leah's logic. "That would explain why he was being sought by the authorities. But Homeland Security, I can't make that leap."

"What if the map's sellers were somehow tied to terrorism? Then DHS would be very interested in following the money trail," Leah added.

"That makes sense, and that doesn't mean that Murphy was a knowing participant in funding terrorists, just that he couldn't pass up buying the most valuable map in the world," Garron said.

"Listen to you two." Jacob seethed.

Leah took Jacob's hand. "How would you explain Murphy having such a valuable piece of history hidden in his house? And why else would DHS be so interested in him? I'm just talking through a scenario that might explain why Murphy lost his life."

Jacob eased a bit. "I think we can be sure that the map is involved. A ten million dollar price tag is proof of that, but let's not let our imaginations run rampant."

"Fair enough, maybe I let my imagination run a little wild for a minute." Leah acquiesced.

But Garron was not so sure that Leah's theory was far off the mark.

***

After the three had finished their breakfast, Leah introduced Jacob and Garron to a member of the Monsignor William Barry Memorial Library staff, who set them up with two computer terminals within the Bibliographic Instruction Lab on the library's second floor. Leah left the brothers and returned to Wiegand Hall, where she would use her unexpected return to campus to handle her office duties and check that her classes had been properly covered by her teaching assistant.

Garron and Jacob anxiously clicked away on their keyboards searching the Internet for any and all mentions of the 1507 Waldseemüller map. There was a myriad of information available. Garron diligently combed through all the information, occasionally stealing glances towards Jacob's backpack. He was struck by just how significant a find this map would be, if indeed it was determined to be authentic. Garron was also amazed by the story of the copy of the 1507 map held by the Library of Congress.

The map came to be during The Renaissance, a time when classical thought was balanced with new scientific discoveries. Cartography had relied on Ptolemaic teaching for centuries but the world was in need of a new map. Considering the new discoveries of Christopher Columbus, numerous Portuguese voyages around the Cape of Africa, eventually known as the Cape of Good Hope, and the contested westward voyages of Amerigo Vespucci, the globe was becoming much larger than previous cartographers allowed. Two men, Matthias Ringman and Martin Waldseemüller, took on the challenge of redrawing the globe using all manner of collected knowledge to provide the most accurate depiction yet conceived.

One of the most influential sources for the new map was also one that became the most contested, the Vespucci Letters. In 1502 or 1503 a letter began to circulate around Europe entitled *Mundus Novus*. It was supposedly written by Amerigo Vespucci who undertook at least two voyages across the Atlantic, and it was a firsthand account of what was found there. In his letter, Vespucci makes a revolutionary claim that the newly discovered land in the western hemisphere was indeed a continent. This letter, as well as another, had great influence on Ringman and Waldseemüller.

In 1507, using all resources available to them, Ringman and Waldseemüller completed their original sketch and the map went into publication in the small French town of St. Die. The pair's original intent was to produce a new atlas that would bring together all past and current understanding of geography in a single volume, so the 1507 map was created to introduce their audience to the *Mundus Novus*, the New World. The map was quite successful and 1000 copies were printed and sent to academics throughout Europe. Many were used in the classroom to teach geography and cartography, at that time called cosmography.

The true significance of this map was its clearly defined and newly discovered continent across the Atlantic, and naming it America, after Amerigo Vespucci. This was the first time the continent was given a name. In the map's companion book, known as the *Introduction to Cosmography*, the newly found land mass was "to be surrounded on all sides by the ocean." This was six years prior to Vasco Núñez de Balboa catching sight of the Pacific Ocean from a mountain peak in Panama, and thirteen years before Magellan confirmed it with his voyage around the tip of South America. There was no mention in European history of a sailor catching site of the Pacific until 1513. So how did two German scholars working in France create such an accurate map of the American continent? An answer had never been found. And ironically, the map was nearly lost to history altogether.

By the time a few copies of the *Introduction to Cosmography* began to re-surface in the eighteenth century, all known copies of the 1507 map had been lost. The 1507 map was no longer being used in academia. In fact, a latter map also created by Waldseemüller, replaced it in the European class-room. The new map even seemed to take a step backwards; there was no longer a new continent to be found across the Atlantic. Waldseemüller's 1513 map, within his Ptolemy Atlas, eliminated the west coast of South America completely. In fact Waldseemüller renounced using America as the name for the western land mass. In 1513, he called the region "Terra Incognita" or Unknown Land. But in the eighteenth century, the rediscov-ered *Introduction to Cosmography* sparked a hunt for the lost 1507 map. It took someone more than 350 years to pull it back into the light of day.

Garron sat back in his chair. He stretched and then asked his brother, "Can you believe it? Murphy's map is extraordinary."

Jacob did not answer.

Garron looked around the desk's divider and found Jacob sleeping. Garron smiled. He reached over and knocked on the back of Jacob's chair.

Jacob stirred. "What?" Then after realizing who nudged him, he asked, "Everything okay?"

"Jay, go back to the RV and get some rest. You'll sleep more soundly there."

Jacob rubbed the sleep from his eyes. "You'll be okay here?"

Garron laughed. "I don't think that I'll miss your witty conversation, or your study habits." Garron mocked a yawn.

"Screw you. You were the one curled up drooling all over yourself last night, while I was dutifully watching over you," Jacob countered.

"Exactly why you should let me do the research and you should catch some shut eye."

Jacob stretched again and yawned loudly. "Okay, you know where to find me then."

He rose from his chair, and as Jacob reached down to pick up the backpack, Garron said, "Let me keep that. You'll never fall asleep with this laying beside you. I'll keep it right here with me, safe and sound."

Jacob nodded and left the computer room.

Garron turned back to his computer screen and continued to read about the map by scanning multiple web sites devoted to the subject.

In 1901, purely by chance, Father Josef Fischer found a copy of the 1507 map in the south tower of an ancient German castle. Father Fischer was a teacher at a Jesuit school in Austria; he traveled Europe digging through old libraries in scholarly pursuit. With a free summer in 1901 he came to Wolfegg Castle in southern Germany. After viewing many of the castle's treasures, Father Fischer found a folio that contained several extraordinary maps, but the 1507 Waldseemüller map was the true gem. It had been relegated to myth and folklore until Fischer pulled it from the tower.

In 1907, the map came to market at the price of $300,000, but there were no buyers. In the summer of 1914, war came to Europe and the map lay dormant in the castle tower for nearly another century. Finally, in 2003, a deal was made with the owner of Wolfegg Castle, the German government, and the Library of Congress for the sale of the 1507 map. Five hundred years after its creation, the 1507 Waldseemüller map was officially put on permanent display at the Library of Congress.

Garron sat back in his chair and looked down into his lap at the red backpack. He had been holding it close.

The light had become more bronze as it sank to the west. Garron was startled when he looked at his watch and saw that it was nearly three o'clock. He shut down his computer, threw the backpack over his shoulder and headed for the RV.

***

"I left a voicemail for you, letting you know that I was leaving my office and heading for the RV," Leah said a bit too harshly.

"My phone died last night, and I don't have my charger." Garron said as he sat down heavily on the bench seat. He looked at Jacob. "Did you get some sleep?"

Jacob answered, "I slept soundly, so well in fact that Leah nearly caved in the door trying to wake me to unlock it."

They settled into their seats and drove north, leaving the campus behind. The professor's directions were easy to follow.

Patrick Burke's home was just south of Weston, and only 45 minutes from campus. He owned a modest house in a nice neighborhood that was lined with Live Oak trees. Sidewalks interlaced the neighborhood. People could be seen walking their dogs and children were playing on their well-manicured lawns. It appeared to be an ideal community. The professor's lot was located at the end of his street, spanning the width of the city block. The rear of the lot was accessible by a narrow alley. There was a two-car garage at the rear of his property separated by a patio with a small pool. Jacob parked the RV on the street in front of the professor's house. A large blue-green Bismarck palm tree dominated the front yard. The house had a stucco finish the color of warm honey. Terracotta barrel tiles lined the roof. The front door was arched and made of a solid wood burnished with time. Leah rang the door bell.

The professor answered the door with a dish towel over his shoulder. There was a small black dog at his heels.

Leah said, "Sorry that we're late."

"Nonsense my dear, your timing is impeccable. You can help me set the table. Please come in." The professor turned and led his guests down the hall toward the kitchen. "Please watch for Lucy, since she lost her sight she always seems to end up under foot."

The center hall separated the dining room on the right from a living room on the left. The doorways were all arched. The kitchen was well planned with a small breakfast nook and an island overlooking a small den.

The professor pulled a chicken from the oven and spooned the drippings over the bird.

"Is roasted chicken with root vegetables okay with everyone?" He asked.

"Perfect," Garron said as his stomach rumbled. He had spent hours at the computer without eating.

"It smells delicious, Professor," Leah said.

"Please call me Patrick, my dear. No titles or formality allowed in my home."

"How can I help, Patrick?" Leah asked.

"The plates are in the cabinet behind you, the silverware just below. Could you set the table please?"

Leah collected the utensils and dinnerware and, with Jacob's help, set the dining room table.

"Garron, would you do the honors by opening those bottles of wine just behind you?" Patrick asked.

Garron turned to find two bottles of chardonnay, four glasses, and a wine opener behind him on the counter. Garron cut the foil and opened one bottle, filling three of the four glasses.

"Both bottles, Patrick?" Garron asked his host.

Patrick noticed that Garron had only filled three glasses. "You are not drinking, my boy? It's good wine from my own estate."

Garron shook his head. "You have your own winery?"

Patrick continued to plate the chicken and scoop the vegetables from the pan.

He said, "When I was twelve, my mother died of cancer. My daddy tore out the tobacco plants and planted grape vines. The land proved good for grapes, as well. The winery was operated by my oldest brother until he passed ten years ago. Now it belongs to me. We'll open the second bottle later, if we need it. Will you have water then?"

"Water is great." Not wanting to ask for another glass, Garron filled the fourth wine glass with water from the refrigerator's dispenser.

The group sat down at the dining room table in front of a beautiful meal. Patrick sat at the head of the table with Leah to his right, Jacob beside Leah, and Garron to the professor's left. Lucy curled up under the professor's chair.

Patrick extended a hand to Garron and Leah. "Will you join me in saying grace?"

They joined hands as Patrick led them in prayer. He concluded with, "and we thank you Lord for bringing us to this table as friends."

Patrick made Garron feel welcomed and appreciated; it felt as if he had known the man his entire life. Garron, then thinking of Murphy, wondered if Jacob wasn't the only Shepard who could benefit from having a father figure in his life.

"This is delicious, Patrick," Leah offered through a mouthful of chicken.

"And the wine is awesome." Jacob added.

"Thank you both. I do not like the fad in chardonnay these days. Most wineries are making a crisp, clean, un-oaked wine. If that is what you want, then drink a Sauvignon Blanc. I like my chardonnay like my biscuits, buttery." Patrick chuckled.

Garron said, "Patrick, I've learned a bit about the 1507 map today from the internet. Do you think that this could really be a sixteenth century copy?"

"The age of your map seems correct, from what little I've seen that is, but we must see how it holds up under scrutiny. I want to confirm that it is a stamped print."

"Stamped print?" Jacob asked.

"Waldseemüller, or rather Matthias Ringman, created a sketch of the map, and from that sketch wooden blocks were created. The sketch would be recreated in reverse by carving the wood blocks. Raised areas would make contact with the paper, and depressions would create blank space on the map. The blocks would have then been covered in ink and clamped into a press. The paper would then be pressed down onto the block. That way multiple copies could be printed relatively inexpensively. The book that accompanied the map ..."

"*The Introduction to Cosmography*," Garron interjected.

"My, my, you're a quick study my boy. The *Cosmographiae Introductio* spoke of there being one thousand copies created." Patrick pointed his fork toward Garron. "What else did you learn today?"

Garron recited all that he could remember. He spoke of the chance finding of the map by the Jesuit priest in a German castle, the buzz that it stirred at the beginning of the twentieth century, and the ten million dollar deal made by the Library of Congress. Leah, not to be outdone, proved that she had been doing her own research by adding that this was the first map to show the newly found land as a continent and the first in naming it America.

"This is why the Library of Congress was so excited to possess the one and only copy. Or at least the only known copy," Leah concluded.

"You two make my spirit sing!" The professor cheered. "You are both excellent students!"

"Regarding Amerigo Vespucci, did you uncover that Waldseemüller never again listed the New World as America?" The professor asked, with obvious pleasure at the dinner table conversation.

"I did," Garron responded. "A letter that Vespucci had written heavily influenced the map makers and later that letter came under scrutiny, although the reasons were a bit fuzzy from what I had read online."

"Good, well at least I can teach you something." Patrick laughed.

"In the early 1500s two letters were circulated around Europe, one of which was published within the *Introduction to Cosmography*. These letters were said to have been penned by Vespucci. They spoke of voyages across the Atlantic, one of which occurred in 1497, when Vespucci's ship had reached South America. The significance of this letter is that Columbus's third voyage, and the first time he reached South America, did not happen until 1498. So was Vespucci, not Columbus, the first European to have reached South America? If you believe the letter to be authentic, then he was. And Ringman and Waldseemüller believed the letter. They had no reason to believe that the letter was anything but a firsthand account of a transatlantic voyage. But the authorship and authenticity did come into question and Waldseemüller never again used 'America' to name that distant land."

The professor surveyed the table. "And if you have all finished, then we should move to my study where we can view this marvelous treasure."

The group cleared the table; dishes and glasses were cleaned and stacked, and leftovers were covered and refrigerated. They continued to discuss the Waldseemüller map and what a second copy would mean to the academic world. The second bottle of wine was opened and they moved into Patrick's study to examine the map, with Lucy padding slowly behind them.

The study was large, approximately twelve by fifteen feet, with a fireplace on one wall. There were pictures of Patrick and a younger woman on a college campus, a wedding photo of the same two people, and another with a very young Lucy squirming between the couple on a porch swing. Two of the other walls were covered by floor to ceiling bookshelves, leaving only the doorway open. Against the last wall was a large cabinet with a computer niche and a keyboard drawer. There was another desk parallel to the cabinet creating an open work space. The professor's desk chair could roll between the cabinet and the desk; allowing easy access to the work space and the computer with a simple turn of the chair. The cabinetry and shelves were made from unstained cherry, showing off the wood's beautiful grain. Several pendant lights hung from the coffered ceiling illuminating the desk, computer, and two leather chairs near the fireplace. There were three wooden folding chairs positioned in front of the desk.

Jacob opened the backpack and carefully lifted the folio, placing it on the professor's desk. Patrick opened a desk drawer and withdrew a magnifying glass, a transparent ruler, cotton swabs, white cotton gloves, graph paper, and a small flashlight. He handed a pair of gloves to each of his guests.

"They will be a bit big for you my dear, but I'm afraid that I only have gloves large enough to fit these mitts," Patrick said, showing his hands to Leah.

Patrick put on his glasses and slid the folio closer to him. Jacob, Leah, and Garron gathered around the desk, all ignoring the chairs that the professor had provided.

Patrick said, "I know that I should spend time on this folio cover, but honestly the folio could have been re-covered at any point throughout the life of the map. So I'm going to focus on the map, if I have your blessing?"

"Whatever you think is best; I have absolutely no experience with any of this. I leave it in your capable hands, Professor," Jacob responded.

"Excellent. Then let us get started." Patrick ignored the use of his title. He had switched from host to teacher.

The professor opened the cover of the folio gingerly and started his investigation. With the magnifying glass, he carefully looked at the edges and corners of each page, flipping the pages with the ruler and ignoring the images on the pages themselves.

He looked up from the map. "As I thought, the portion of this folio that is dedicated to the 1507 map is rag paper, which is era appropriate." He smiled looking up into the faces huddled around him. "You may want to have a seat. This will take some time."

All three of his guests sat down without taking their eyes from the map.

The professor then began to examine the border illustrations and images on the first page of the map. He then did the same for several more of the pages.

"Do you see how much of the ink has turned brownish in color? That is also to be expected. Iron gall ink would have been used for the majority of the illustrations and land masses and the like. But if you look at some of the text, it is still black, also to be expected because a separate ink was used for typesetting." He smiled broadly. "So far, so good."

He flipped back to the first page, the page that held a portion of the Caribbean and the southern tip of Florida. He spun the folio so that it now sat perpendicular to his chair, and held the opened page suspended in the air. The professor turned on his flashlight and shone it through the page.

After running the light over every inch of the page he said, "Perfect. Here is the watermark," he indicated with a circular motion a spot near the center of the page. "Can you see it?"

Simultaneously, all three stood and jockeyed for a position in which they could see the area of the page the professor was indicating.

"Wait, wait," The professor said with a chuckle. "I'll trace the watermark so you can all see it more clearly."

The professor withdrew a sheet of Mylar and a pencil from a desk drawer. With a delicate touch and repeatedly lifting the Mylar sheet, he traced the watermark. It was a triple pointed crown.

"This is also the watermark that I expected to see. It matches the known watermark for Vautran Ludd and the Gymnasium Vosagense, the St. Die printer known to have produced the map. This would be very difficult for a counterfeiter to fake."

He rolled back from his desk and collected his glass from behind him and took a long swallow of the wine.

"The condition of this map is fantastic. I do not see much degrading of the organic material of the paper or the ink. This truly is fascinating." The professor beamed.

"So is this the real deal?" Jacob asked.

"It looks very promising with my limited resources, but let's not be too hasty." He turned on the computer screen where an image of the Waldseemüller map had already been queued. The professor then wheeled back behind his desk. "Let's look at the content of the map for any inconsistencies."

The professor turned to the fifth page of the folio, the portion of the map covering Europe. He examined the map closely, using the flashlight to illuminate portions of the page.

"The Library's copy originally belonged to Johann Schöner, a cartographer, and he had used the map as a reference guide for the creation of several maps and globes of his own. He is the one who compiled the folio found by the Jesuit priest in Germany, preserving it for prosperity's sake. Schöner created a series of grid lines across Europe to help him with his calculations. Those grid lines are not present on this map, which is as it should be if we are considering this to be an original."

The professor used the ruler to once again flip to the first page of the map, and he began to examine the coastline and islands printed there. He covered every inch of the illustrations on the border of the map. Often he would refer back to the computer screen behind him, comparing the two maps.

While the professor worked at the computer, Garron would move in to examine the map more closely. He saw on the map drawings of round, cherubic faces in the borders. He saw the same image that was on Murphy's bedroom wall, the islands of the Caribbean and the peninsula of Florida. In the upper right hand corner of the page was the legend that was written so beautifully it had imbedded itself into the professor's memory.

The professor slid back to the desk and the map. He carefully flipped to the second sheet and began his examination anew. Garron peered over Patrick's shoulder, captivated by the artistry of the map.

The second sheet prominently displayed a long land mass in its center. On the extreme right edge of the map there was a portion of another coastline and islands dotted the space between. The land mass and islands were labeled in Latin.

Garron asked, "Professor, what are we looking at here?"

The professor ran his gloved finger down the center of the page, indicating the long land mass. "This is Central and South America." He pointed toward a large island at the top of the page. "And this is Hispaniola, or the Dominican Republic and Haiti."

"On the far right of the page, that is what, the coast of Africa?" Garron asked.

"Correct. And these are the Canary Islands," the professor confirmed.

Patrick studied the Canaries carefully with his magnifying glass. He used his flashlight to highlight the archipelago. "Do you see the seams around this island chain? That is consistent with the Waldseemüller map as well. Any corrections to the map would literally have been cut and pasted. Remember that these images had been carved onto a wooden block and then stamped to the paper. It was too difficult to carve a new image, so the correction was made to the paper of the first production prior to copies being made."

The professor flipped to the next sheet. He gasped once as he took in the image. This sheet was a continuation of the last. The southern tip of South America was portrayed. And on the land mass, *America* was printed neatly.

The professor rubbed the page lovingly. "It still moves me to see this. This was the first known use of the name for the newly discovered western lands."

Garron examined the page from over the professor's shoulder. This third sheet equated to the bottom left hand corner of the map. South America, the South Atlantic, and a small portion of the African coast made up the upper right third of the page. The majority of the sheet consisted of border illustrations and a large map key.

Jacob asked, "What do you think, Professor, is this an authentic copy?"

Patrick sat back in his chair and removed his glasses. "Everything that I have seen is as expected." He smiled. "I believe that these few sheets that I have examined are indeed authentic."

Leah said, "That is amazing."

Garron cautioned, "But when we were in your office, Professor, you said that there was a mix of paper material throughout the folio."

"That is correct. And you are right to be cautious." Patrick pushed his glasses back in place and flipped further back into the folio's pages. "This is vellum, which is stretched and scraped animal hide. The material was popular in earlier centuries due to its resilience. Documents on vellum have been known to have a life span of more than one thousand years."

The professor examined the page. The image was faint and difficult to read. The edges of the vellum were cut neatly, and it was of a smaller size than the pages they examined earlier. Patrick passed the flashlight under the sheet; the light shown through the vellum causing it to glow. Faint images came into view. The professor's hand shook and he dropped the flashlight onto the desk. A look of shock and disbelief crossed his face; he looked to be in pain.

"Patrick, are you okay?" Leah was truly concerned. She laid an arm around his shoulders.

"This cannot be," the large man muttered as he pulled a handkerchief from his breast pocket and wiped his forehead.

"What is it, Professor?" Jacob begged.

The professor sat silently for a moment staring at the folio. "I need to examine this more closely." He looked up at Jacob. "May I remove the pages from the folio?"

"Is that safe? I mean, removing the pages won't damage them, will it?" Jacob was concerned.

"By removing the pages it may decrease the value, although, with the pages removed correctly scientists will more easily be able to study this treasure. And when you decide to bring this to the academic world, I don't believe that the removal of the pages will be of the highest concern. My process will be delicate, deliberate, and done with the greatest of care," the professor assured Jacob.

"But what is it, Professor? What are we looking at?" Jacob asked again.

The professor shook his head slowly. "I don't want to guess. I need to comb through this folio to be sure."

Leah and Garron nodded to Jacob.

"Okay, Professor, I leave it in your hands."

"Thank you, my boy. Garron, could you bring to me a glass of water from the cabinet under the sink? The bottle should be labeled as distilled water."

When Garron returned to the study he was carrying a large glass of water.

"I didn't know how much water you might need," Garron said as he handed the glass to the professor.

"This is perfect my boy, just perfect." The professor adjusted his glasses and collected several large cotton swabs from his desk. He dipped one of the swabs into the glass of distilled water, and used it to apply a small amount to the glue in the folio's binding.

"The distilled water will soften the glue. We will then be able to delicately lift the page from the binding. The pages will not be damaged. But this will take some time, hours probably. So why don't you tell me how you came to receive this treasure?"

Jacob explained to the professor Murphy's lifelong passion for maps and the sea. He told him how Murphy had been acting strangely the past few months, and showed the professor the keys that Murphy had asked Jacob to keep safe for him. Garron interjected how he and Jacob found the hiding space behind the mural on Murphy's wall, and the condition of both Jacob's and Murphy's homes. Garron also described the visit that he had with the DHS agents while still in his studio. Leah spoke of Murphy's rotor cuff injury and how he could never have attempted a dive with that injury. And Jacob finally, with a heavy heart, told the professor how his friend's body had been found floating in the bay. Patrick had listened intently while his guests recounted their story, occasionally adding more water to the folio's binding.

The professor said, "I think that we are ready to remove the pages."

He withdrew a small rectangular wooden box from his desk from which he pulled a set of forceps and several other stainless steel implements. The professor handed the flashlight to Garron, who instinctively pointed it at the work area. The professor pulled up slightly on the first page and slowly worked one of the stainless steel tools, a spatula, between the paper and the glue. The page slowly began to pull free. The professor slowly and meticulously continued removing each page one by one until all of the folio's sheets were unfolded and stacked on his desk. With the sheets separated from the folio, Garron finally appreciated the immense scope of their find.

The professor then began to examine the vellum page once again. He moved the flashlight methodically over every inch of the sheet. Patrick began to recreate what the flashlight revealed onto a sheet of graph paper. After nearly an hour, his sketch revealed the subject captured on the vellum. It was another map.

There was an ocean bordered on both sides by large land masses. The water between each land mass was dotted with islands of differing sizes.

Leah studied the graph paper. "That coastline resembles North America." She pointed to the land mass on the left of the paper.

The professor did not answer immediately. He sat wide-eyed, staring at his recreation.

"Professor, what have we found?" Garron asked.

"You are correct in assuming that this is the Atlantic Ocean, but the coastline you see on the left of the page is that of Cathay. That is the coast of China," Patrick finally answered. "When this map was created, the continents of North and South America were not yet known. This map illustrated a possible westward passage to the east."

Garron was taken aback. "How old is this map?"

The professor answered with a smile, "If this is the map that I believe it to be, then it dates to 1474."

The group stood stunned.

Patrick took in the faces of his guests. "I can see that you are impressed, but wait until you hear the story that accompanies this map." He emptied his wine glass and then said, "I believe this to be the Toscanelli map of 1474. It was originally sent to Fernão Martins, a priest at the Lisbon Cathedral, by Paolo dal Pozzo Toscanelli. The map was accompanied by a letter suggesting that a westward passage to the Orient was possible. That original letter and map was lost, but a recreation of that map and a transcription of that letter were later sent to Christopher Columbus. That map accompanied Columbus on his voyage to the New World."

"This map belonged to Columbus?" Jacob asked excitedly.

Patrick shook his head. "The copy that Columbus received from Toscanelli would not have been on vellum."

Garron said, "Are you suggesting that this is the original?"

"It may be." The professor was aglow with excitement.

"This is fantastic!" Jacob cheered.

"There still needs to be some tests completed before we can be sure," the professor cautioned.

"Come on, Professor, we have two of the greatest maps ever, and who knows what else, in one collection. You have to admit that this is awesome," Jacob pressed.

With a laugh, the professor said, "It looks very promising. You have something special here, my boy."

Jacob and Leah hugged tightly, Garron patted the professor on the back. The room was alive with excitement. Even Lucy could feel it; her tail wagged as she turned in circles under the professor's desk.

"I want to walk through each page of this folio. I think that we will need a pot of coffee." He rose from his desk and headed to the kitchen, Lucy close behind him. Even without sight, the dog stayed close to her master.

Garron studied the vellum sheet carefully with the magnifying glass, while Jacob crawled into the leather chair and Leah sat on his lap, excitedly talking about what owning these maps must have meant to Murphy. Garron felt his eyes begin to cross; he pinched the bridge of his nose and then looked across the room to the leather chairs. Jacob rested his hand on Leah's thigh while she ran a finger through his hair. The tenderness between the two caused Garron's chest to tighten. Garron ran a hand through his own hair and then rose from the desk chair to join the professor in the kitchen.

***

The professor turned to see Garron's entrance.

"What can I get for you, my boy?" He asked.

Garron answered, "I just needed to step away for a moment."

Reading Garron's expression, the professor asked, "From the map or from the love birds?"

Garron gave the professor a short smile.

"I do not envy you young man, I am not sure that I could handle myself with such grace as you, considering the situation."

"I'm not so sure that I am handling this so well at all."

"Don't sell yourself short. You put aside your contempt in order to ensure that your little brother was out of harm's way. That deserves praise."

Garron appreciated the professor's kindness.

"I found myself tested a long time ago, and I can assure you that your handling of the situation is admirable. I, unfortunately, embarrassed myself greatly."

Garron was shocked. "Tested, how so?"

"Karen, my wife, was a very free spirit. It was one of the reasons that I fell in love with her. She was one of my students, although nothing ever blossomed between us until after her graduation. I never believed that our difference in age was cause for concern, but when Karen decided that she needed to hike the Alps, I was not physically able to accompany her. She found a hiking companion in an old boyfriend, someone she dated while they were both attending university, someone her own age. At first I encouraged her, believing that intellectually I could deal with my wife spending 60 days with an ex-lover. But no matter how I handled the matter philosophically, emotionally I was just a jealous old man."

Garron said, "I think that whatever you were feeling was natural, and to be expected Professor."

"Karen could be trusted and I should have done just that. But when she returned from her adventure, I treated her with contempt, saying and doing things that required years to repair." The professor was silent for a moment. He shook his head slightly and said, "I lost Karen to heart disease, she died much too young."

To Garron the professor suddenly looked very small and fragile.

"So you see, my boy, I respect how you are handling your situation with maturity and grace." He smiled at Garron.

The professor picked up a serving tray that held a carafe of coffee, cream, sugar, and four mugs.

"Shall we return to our cartographic treasure trove?" He asked, leading the way to the study with Lucy at his heels.

***

He poured everyone a cup of coffee and then returned to his desk. The professor began his re-examination of each of the folio's pages. Often rolling back to his computer and the electronic versions of each of the maps he found on multiple web sites. Garron did his own examination of the Waldseemüller pages. He was in awe of the detail of the map and its illustrations. He appreciated the difficult work of carving the images into a block of wood. Cartography was an art form. It was when the professor inspected yet another vellum page of the folio that he let out a gasp. Leah and Jacob were pulled from the comfort of the leather chairs across the room by the professor's reaction.

"This is amazing!"

"What is it, Professor?" Leah asked.

"This is another document of great value." The professor indicated the vellum sheet stretched out on his desk.

It was larger than the first and the images were brightly painted onto the vellum's surface. It was another map, only on this map there were lines radiating from several points on the page. The coast of Spain and North Africa were recognizable, along with several islands in the Atlantic. Within the interior of the landmasses were castles, a cathedral, and trees.

"It's another map," Jacob said excitedly.

"It's not a map, but a portolan, a sea chart," the professor corrected. "A portolan was created by seafarers who were most interested in the ports and harbors of a coastline. The interior of a land mass was of little importance on a portolan chart. The radius lines equate roughly to the 32 headings of a mariner's compass." The professor used the ruler to point out the lines crisscrossing the page. "This particular one appears to be a portion of a much larger portolan. A vellum chart of this age would have been larger with rough edges; these edges are clean and sharp. It would originally have been fastened to, and wound around, a wooden rod or roller. The roller would then have been stored in a tube for safe keeping while at sea. The artwork and subject matter look very similar to the Albino de Canepa chart of 1489, although that map depicted a much greater area."

Garron said, "This collection must be worth a fortune."

The professor did not respond. He was intently examining the final document from the folio. It was another sea chart that was drawn on paper, not vellum. The images were clear and easily read. This portolan had not been painted, but drawn in ink; the brownness of the iron gall ink was apparent. The subject matter had become familiar to Garron. This was another drawing of the Caribbean; it was nearly identical to the mural Murphy had painted.

Garron said, "That looks similar to the Waldseemüller map, Professor."

Patrick was studying the bottom right corner of the map closely. He quickly flipped the sea chart over and examined the reverse. There was something written on the portolan's edge.

"What did you find, Professor?" Garron asked.

Jacob and Leah crowded the desk.

Patrick handed the magnifying glass to Garron. "Tell me what you see." The professor rolled back from his desk with his brow knitted.

Garron used the magnifying glass to enlarge the script on the edge of the chart. "It looks like this map has been signed by someone." The signature was elegant and embellished with wide loops and broad strokes. "It's difficult to read, but I think the last name is Pinzón. Is that what you saw?"

The professor sat awe-stricken in his chair. After a minute he managed to nod in answer to Garron's question.

"Who is Pinzón?" Jacob asked.

"Martín Alonso Pinzón," the professor answered, "was a Spanish navigator and ship's captain. He was the captain of the Pinta during the voyage of 1492."

Garron was astonished. He said, "He sailed with Columbus."

"As did his two brothers," the professor added. "Vicente Yañez captained the Niña, while Francisco was the Pinta's master. They were all acclaimed seafarers and were an integral part of the first voyage." Patrick stood and refilled his coffee mug from the carafe. "But Martín Alonso is best known for disobeying Columbus and setting off on his own course once the fleet had reached the Caribbean. The Pinta was on its own for more than forty days."

"I don't remember ever learning that in history class," Garron said.

"It was relegated to a footnote in history because of Christopher Columbus's accomplishments. But it is a very interesting side story." The professor took his chair once again. "Columbus's original log was lost, but the first voyage was abstracted in Bartolomé de las Casas's *Diario*. It mentions that Pinzón left the fleet in search of an island that the local Taíno people called Babeque. They told stories about the shores of Babeque gleaming with gold so that one needed only to bend over and scoop the gold from the ground. But Pinzón was unsuccessful and returned to the fleet once he learned of the Santa María's sinking. Columbus was so relieved to have the Pinta back with the fleet after he lost his flagship that Pinzón was never punished for his dereliction. But earlier entries in the log did show that Pinzón was an exceptional navigator and sailor, and that Columbus called on him several times to motivate the crew." The professor paused. "Without the Pinzóns, the voyage may not have been a success."

Jacob said, "Then we have another important piece of history here."

Patrick rubbed his temples. "It may be more important than you think."

"How so, Professor?" Leah asked.

"The signature will need to be verified, but if we consider that this map belonged to Martín Alonso, then it will require rethinking the entire history of sea navigation."

"You've lost me, Professor," Jacob admitted.

"If Martín Alonso owned this document, then it must have been in his possession prior to 1493. He died shortly after returning from that 1492 voyage to the Caribbean." The professor flipped the chart back and pointed to the coast of South America. "Yet sighting of the South American coast by a European was not documented until 1498. How could a map of that area predate 1498?"

"Sounds like you're talking about the Waldseemüller map again," Jacob joked.

Patrick leaned over the desk and inspected the coastline of South America. "The continent's east coastline is detailed and similar to the Waldseemüller map. The scope is smaller, it is as if this is just the first sheet of the 1507 map." He sat back in his chair. "Could this be source material for a portion of the Waldseemüller map?"

"That would explain why the 1507 map was so accurate," Leah added.

"Or the map's not as old as we think. The Waldseemüller map can be dated to 1507, fourteen years after Martín Alonso's death. It seems more likely that this map did not belong to Pinzón at all. The signature could be a forgery, or maybe one of the other Pinzón brothers signed Martín Alonso's name," Garron said, examining the map.

"Possibly; it is a fascinating collection. But the documents do seem unrelated. I need more time with these documents." The professor continued, "I am going to reexamine every inch of this folio to see if anything stands out. While I do that, would any of you like to take a shower or lay down for a while? The guest bedrooms and bath are upstairs. You are welcome to use them."

Jacob and Garron stood silently looking down on the portolan.

"A shower sounds good, Professor, thank you. Sleep's out of the question with the way my mind is racing," Leah said. She kissed the professor on the cheek and left the study heading toward the stairs at the front of the house.

The three men continued their examination of the folio's pages. They passed the pages around the desk without saying a word. Finally, Jacob moved his folding chair to the computer and began his own research on the Waldseemüller, Toscanelli, and the Canepa maps, as well as on Martín Alonso Pinzón. Patrick continued to play his flashlight and magnifying glass over the documents. Garron turned from the desk and removed his gloves. He poured himself another cup of coffee. While holding the mug in one hand, Garron ran his other hand over the folio's leather binding.

It was well tailored and a beautiful shade of blue. The front cover was rigid and the leather was moderately worn. The condition was amazing for being more than 500 years old. The spine's cover was creased with slightly more wear. There was an intricate cross and a small bird embossed on the folio's spine. The rear cover was bowed as if the board was warped. Garron laid the cover open on a corner of the desk and pressed down on the rear panel. He could feel the cover give under his fingers. He did the same to the front cover, but it did not flex. Garron set down his coffee mug and then carefully examined the seam where the rear cover flap met the spine. It had loosened, as the pages had, when the professor applied the distilled water. Garron pulled at the edge of the raised seam. It opened slowly revealing the bowed birch wood board underneath. In the void created by the crescent shaped bowing of the board, something caught Garron's attention.

"May I borrow your forceps, Professor?" Garron asked.

"Of course you may." Patrick handed the forceps to Garron. "Have you found something?"

"I'm not sure," was his response.

Garron used the forceps to grasp the corner of something tucked between the board and the cover. With some effort, he pulled out a folded sheet of paper from the void.

The professor said, "My, my, what have you there?"

Jacob turned away from the computer to see Garron use the forceps to place the sheet of paper into the professor's gloved hand. The professor used the forceps and the ruler to unfold the paper.

"This is pulp paper, and it appears to be of a contemporary formula," he said, examining the newly found sheet.

Garron looked over the professor's shoulder and saw what appeared to be a letter. It was addressed to Ian, and dated October 9th, 1989. The letter was signed, "Your Loving Uncle."

Without reading it, the professor folded the letter and removed his glasses.

"I think that you should read this, my boy," the professor said as he handed the letter to Jacob.

Jacob read the letter to himself until tears flooded his vision, then he handed the letter to Garron.

Garron read the letter aloud:

Ian,

I believe that I am getting close to solving this riddle.

When I am ready to hand over the archives to you, I hope to have completed this puzzle so that you have a full understanding of the importance of what we are safeguarding.

I've removed this from the collection to keep it safe. Someone has been snooping around the archives and I don't want him to find this, so keep it with you, don't bring it to Augustine.

I'm proud of you. I will see you soon.
Your Loving Uncle

Leah entered the study with her hair tousled. She surveyed the room and stepped close to Jacob.

"What did I miss?" She asked.

Jacob handed Leah the letter. She read it and then asked, "Was this in the folio?"

"It was hidden behind the cover," Garron answered.

Leah asked Jacob, "Do you have any idea what Murphy's uncle is talking about in this letter? What are the archives? What puzzle?"

"I have no idea." Jacob stood, wiped the tears from his eyes, and straightened his back. "But, I'm going to find out."

Garron was rereading the letter. "The letter mentions, 'a collection' and 'safeguarding,' I think that we can assume, especially after seeing this folio, that the 'collection' is a library of rare maps, charts, portolans or something like that."

Jacob asked for the letter once again. He read it and then handed the letter to Leah.

Garron asked, "So what's next?"

"I think that we're heading to St. Augustine."

Leah looked up from the letter. "Jacob, I think that it's time to go to the police."

"No, it's time to get to the bottom of this. I still don't know what this is really about. There are still too many questions. Maybe we can find the answers in St. Augustine," Jacob countered.

Leah moved her penetrating stare from Jacob to Garron.

Garron said, "Don't look at me, I agree with Jay. I can't quit now."

Garron could see that Leah was seething.

"Professor, please tell these two that the smart thing to do is go to the authorities with the map," Leah pleaded.

"I believe that to be the smart choice, but ..." Patrick hesitated, then continued, "... then you may lose your only chance of solving this riddle."

Leah spun on the professor and met his gaze.

"Sorry, my dear, but this may be one of the greatest finds in recent history. I was only being honest," the professor begged.

"That's settled then," Jacob said. "Next stop St. Augustine."

"Well, may I suggest St. Augustine by way of Okeechobee?" Patrick suggested.

Jacob asked, "Why Okeechobee, Professor?"

"I have a colleague living in Okeechobee. He is a dear friend. His name is Dr. Maynard Clayton Smith."

Leah was shocked. "Clay Smith? You're friends with Crazy Clay?"

"Crazy Clay?" Garron said.

"That's what his students called him. He was easily derailed from the lesson plan with a question about aliens building the pyramids, or Atlantians seeding Mesoamerican cultures. I've met him several times in the past, and he is a bit out there," Leah explained.

"Clay is a bit, shall we say, eccentric, but he has a brilliant mind. I taught with him for many years. He and I had many interesting conversations. But genius and lunacy are only a half step apart." The professor continued, "Clay has become a historical revisionist in recent years. He has done some impressive research into pre-Columbian trade routes and he may be able to help with the Pinzón portolan."

"Couldn't we just call him, Professor?" Jacob asked.

Patrick chuckled. "Clay doesn't own a phone. He believes that the federal government has tapped his phone in the past. He has become a bit of a recluse now that he is no longer teaching."

"But you think that it's important to meet with him?" Garron asked.

The professor nodded. "Clay will have information that you could never find anywhere else, even with a lifetime of research."

"Then we should stop ..." Jacob began before being interrupted by Lucy barking incessantly.

"She startled me," Leah said. "I forgot that she was even in the room."

The professor said, "She barks like that when someone comes to the door."

Jacob looked from Leah to Garron.

"Are you expecting anyone, Professor?" Garron asked.

The professor understood; his face fell.

Jacob began to collect the folio's sheets and tucked them back inside the cover. Garron took the folio from Jacob, slid it into the backpack, and slung the pack over his shoulder.

Patrick said, "You should leave through the back."

At the kitchen door, Garron peeked through the door's window onto the backyard. He saw the moon reflected in the pool; all seemed quiet.

"It seems as though you are on a clock, and that you have run out of time. May I suggest splitting up?" The professor said handing Leah two sets of keys. "Use my cars and be sure to visit Clay. He can help."

Leah looked down at the two key fobs, one was stamped with a Volkswagen emblem.

"The Beetle belonged to my wife, she loved that car. She bought it new in 1956. My mechanic keeps it well maintained."

Leah said, "You should come with us, Professor. Whoever is following us is dangerous. You may not be safe."

The two embraced. Patrick said, "No, I will be fine my dear. This is your adventure. You can tell me all about it once you've solved the puzzle. I will aide you by sending your pursuers on a wild goose chase." He smiled. "This is all very exciting."

A knock sounded at the front door.

The professor said, "Now you must go!"

Jacob shook Patrick's hand. "Thank you, Professor."

Patrick looked from Jacob to Garron and said, "Now you two take good care of my favorite young lady."

Garron nodded. "We'll let you know what we find. You can have the book rights."

The professor chuckled.

Garron ushered Leah out the kitchen door, with Jacob close behind.

***

Garron pushed Leah gently onto the patio. He watched her skirt the pool en route to the garage. He looked over his shoulder for his brother, but movement in the shadows beside the professor's house caught his attention. A bearded man wearing the uniform of a Florida Power and Light technician stepped briefly into the light that came from the back door. Jacob saw him, as well. Garron stopped and turned. He watched his brother take a step toward the technician, then drop and roll with the grace of a gymnast. With great speed, Jacob delivered an upper cut to the man's bearded chin, knocking off his hard hat. Garron was shocked at his brother's viciousness, but he quickly understood when the man staggered and raised his hand; he was holding a gun. Jacob extended his left arm and grasped the gunman's wrist. In one fluid motion, Jacob dropped to one knee and with his right fist delivered a devastating blow to his adversary's groin. Jacob turned slightly and stood up quickly, pulling the man's wrist downward as he rose. Jacob brought his right shoulder up sharply under his opponent's elbow. Garron heard the man's elbow pop loudly, and saw Jacob remove the gun from the man's loosened grip. His brother struck the man in the center of the forehead with the butt of the gun. The man toppled backwards, unconscious. When Jacob turned to meet Garron's gaze, Garron was startled by the rage on his brother's face.

Garron stood unmoving. Leah pulled Garron by the arm, uprooting him.

Inside the garage there was a black Cadillac Seville and a blue Volkswagen Beetle.

Leah said, "I'll take the VW and drive to Dr. Smith's house. I'll meet up with you in St. Augustine."

"No," Jacob said. "I don't want you out of my sight. Get in the Cadillac."

"The professor believes that Clay can help. You two can uncover something in St. Augustine while I talk with Clay. We should split up, no one will know that I'm going to Okeechobee, I'll be perfectly safe."

"Then we will all go to Clay's together," Jacob insisted.

Garron interjected. "I think that Leah is right."

Jacob turned on his brother, "What?"

"These guys are tracking us down way too quickly. Splitting up will help us to stay ahead of these assholes," Garron argued.

Jacob said, "I can't believe this."

"You two go to St. Augustine, I'll visit the professor's friend," Garron offered.

"No Garron, Clay won't even answer the door if you show up. He and I have met before. I'm going," Leah countered.

Jacob insisted, "We don't have time to argue."

Leah kissed Jacob quickly. She threw the Cadillac's keys to Garron. "Right, so go and be careful." She opened the Beetle's door and climbed inside.

Jacob hesitated for an instant, but then gave the pistol he had taken off of the man in the yard to Leah. He then joined Garron in the Cadillac. Garron pressed the automatic garage door opener on the visor above his head. Leah quickly backed the VW into the alley and pulled out of Garron's view through the rearview mirror. Garron backed out of the garage. He paused just a moment, thinking of the professor. He hoped that they had not brought trouble to the gentleman's door. A chill crawled down his spine. Garron put the Cadillac in drive and pulled away in the opposite direction from Leah.

Chapter 5

THE SEVILLE'S CLOCK read twelve fifteen. Garron had been driving for roughly two hours, and neither he nor Jacob had spoken a word. Traffic was light, and the highway looked more or less the same for miles. Palm trees and Slash pines lined the roadway in developed areas. The unpopulated areas were dark and wild. Garron momentarily took his eyes off the road to look at his brother. Jacob sat with the backpack in his lap, staring straight ahead.

"I thought that you must be sleeping. After you got me to I-95, you haven't made a sound," Garron said, breaking the silence.

"You need me to drive?" Jacob asked.

"No, no, it's not that I need the company," Garron stumbled. "I mean, that I'm not tired. I was just wondering if you were okay."

Jacob took a moment to answer, "I'll be fine."

Garron caught Jacob looking his way.

He said, "It's just that back at the professor's, in the yard, I went to a dark place that I haven't been to in a while."

Garron didn't understand immediately. He asked, "You mean the guy with the gun?"

"Yeah, I haven't hurt someone like that in a long time."

"Well, I don't think that he was a DHS agent or a cop."

"That doesn't matter Gar, I just never wanted to be *that* guy again. I've tried to put all of that behind me, far behind me."

Garron had never before seen his brother so conflicted.

"I, for one, am glad that you were there. It's because of you that we were able to get out of there safely."

"It's because of me that you, that everyone, is involved in this in the first place." Jacob turned toward Garron.

Garron stole a glance to see the deep pain on his brother's face, and the tears in his eyes.

"Listen Jay, none of this is your fault. You've been keeping a promise to a friend, and you've been defending his honor. Leah and I are here because we love you. You are not responsible for this mess."

"But the professor, I led them right to the professor ..." Jacob trailed off.

It was true that they had pulled Patrick into this, and Garron had trouble reconciling their decision to leave him behind.

"We don't know that anything happened to the professor," Garron said with little conviction.

The words did little to assuage Garron's guilt; he was sure that Jacob felt the same. They were both silent again.

After about twenty minutes Jacob asked, "What should we do when we get to St. Augustine?"

Garron had been thinking about their next step. With Murphy's ties to real estate, Garron was hoping they could find land titles in Murphy's name at the court house. But with it being Saturday, he had to rethink that tactic. Maybe they could track down Charles Murphy's home and see if he still had family residing at that address.

"I think that maybe you should try Charles's home and see if you can get anything from there. And we have the library," Garron said.

"The library, you mean the public library?"

"Yeah. I can start with Charles's obituary and see if it names any next of kin. Then I can see if I can put some names to Murphy's real estate buddies."

"I don't know where Charles lived. I've never been to St. Augustine. Murph just invited me to join him on his next trip, sometime in October."

"Again, we can get that from the library, or maybe just a simple perusal of a phone book could point the way."

Garron attempted to stay positive, but he wasn't sure that this would be so easy.

Jacob's cell phone rang.

He read the screen, "It's Leah."

"You really shouldn't have that phone on, they could be tracking it," Garron cautioned.

Jacob answered the call.

Garron listened to the one-sided conversation.

"Okay, I love you. We have maybe three hours. I'm glad you're safe. Text me when you get to St. Augustine. I'm going to turn my phone off, but I'll check it periodically for messages. I love you, too. Bye."

Jacob ended the call and turned off his cell phone.

"I didn't think of the cell phone thing, do you think that's how they found us?" Jacob asked.

"I think that it depends on who 'they' is. Besides, I'm not exactly up to date on my man hunting procedures. I get all my knowledge from books and movies." Garron laughed.

Jacob offered, "Leah has made it to Dr. Smith's house. She's going to wait until morning to see if he has any information that can help us."

"Not waking *Crazy Clay* at midnight seems wise." Garron circled his right index finger over his temple.

This time they both laughed.

"You said that we have another three hours ahead of us, why don't we pull over and get some sleep? We can't do anything before sunrise anyway."

"Okay, but let's not use a rest stop. Let's pull off the highway and find a residential street to blend into."

Garron exited the highway and found an older condominium community without security patrols. They both reclined and attempted to sleep.

***

Leah woke at dawn. The sun was still low on the horizon. She tried to massage the kink from the right side of her neck. She was surprised that she had fallen asleep so quickly, but her exhaustion had outweighed the worry.

She had pulled her legs up and rested her feet on the passenger seat of the Beetle. The interior of the car was quite spacious and in pristine condition. Leah understood why the professor's wife loved this car so much, it was fun to drive. However the little car was quite slow and Leah was constantly worried about running out of gas because there was no gas gauge. She also wondered about the time, she didn't wear a watch and had turned off her phone. It was certainly too early to wake the retired professor. Leah looked across the street to Dr. Maynard Clayton Smith's house.

The house was a small concrete block home that was typical to the area, but this home was in need of a coat of paint and some maintenance. The roof rippled with age. The walls were a faded yellow, with visible flaking and rust stains from the yard's irrigation system. There was more dollar weed than grass in Clay's lawn. It certainly wasn't Leah's idea of a retirement dream home.

Leah studied herself in the rearview mirror. She looked tired and run-down, much like Clay's house. Her short blonde hair looked dull and lifeless, and she had a tuft near the back that wouldn't lie down. The shower she had at the professor's seemed like a distant memory. Leah was worried about her mentor; she thought it had been a mistake to leave him behind. Maybe she could call him from inside Clay's house, just to make sure the professor was unharmed.

A light came on in the house.

Leah watched as the front door opened and a thin man stepped out wearing a brown bathrobe. He shuffled toward the newspaper lying in his front yard. He looked every bit the moniker that the student body had given him while teaching chemistry at Barry University, Crazy Clay. Leah wasn't sure why, but she felt the need to slip the pistol Jacob had given her into the waistband of her jeans before stepping from the Beetle and hurrying toward the little man. She adjusted her blouse to conceal the gun.

"Dr. Smith, good morning," Leah called out.

He bent over and picked up his paper. He stood, adjusted his oversized plastic-framed glasses and took a moment to take in the woman coming his way. Leah watched as Clay studied her carefully.

"Ms. Preston, why are you here?" Clay pointed the bagged paper at Leah.

"I'm glad you remember me." Leah smiled. "Professor Burke thought that you would be able to help me solve a puzzle that I'm working on," Leah added quickly.

The mention of Patrick's name had the desired effect and Clay relaxed, lowering the paper.

"It's quite early, Ms. Preston. Maybe you could come back later." The little man tugged his bathrobe tightly around himself.

"I'm afraid that's just not possible. I apologize for showing up unannounced, and at such an early hour, but I am under some time constraints." She applied her best smile.

Clay did not budge, obviously not wanting to invite Leah into his home. She tried another tactic.

"You see, sir, I'm being followed. I have nowhere else to turn." Leah spoke just above a whisper.

That worked. Clay's head swiveled from side to side scanning the street.

"Quickly Ms. Preston, come inside."

Leah smiled inwardly as she followed the man into his home. What better way to win over a paranoid individual than to invite him into a conspiracy.

There was only a narrow gap between stacks of newspapers and magazines to navigate through the house. The house smelled of damp paper. Leah followed closely fearing that she might get lost among the piles of periodicals, never to be heard from again. The kitchen at the rear of the house was paper free, but the kitchen had been turned into Clay's office. There was a desktop computer and a laptop on the kitchen table. A printer was on the chipped laminate countertop near the sink. The walls were painted a hideous shade of pink and the majority of the cabinet doors had been removed.

"I have coffee," Clay said, laying the wrapped newspaper on the table.

He sat and sipped from a mug of coffee near the laptop.

"That would be wonderful," Leah replied.

Clay pointed to a cabinet. "The mugs are there beside the refrigerator. The coffeepot is by the sink."

Leah had begun to sit down, but then quickly realized that if she wanted coffee she would have to pour it herself. Leah pulled a mug from the cabinet and peered inside to see if it was clean. It was clean enough. She filled the mug.

"Do you have cream?" She asked.

"Nope, I don't drink the stuff. And you shouldn't either. Milk's estrogen levels contribute to the influx of hormone-dependent cancers such as testicular, breast, and prostate cancer."

Leah took a sip of the coffee. It was awful. She took a seat across from the professor.

"Milk can cause cancer?" Leah asked.

Clay clarified, "The estrogen from the pregnant cows contributes to cancer."

Clay studied Leah's expression. "You're thinking that people around the world have been milking cows for centuries."

Leah nodded.

"The risk comes from the modern-day practice of milking the cows nearly 300 days a year. The hormone levels are abnormally high due to the cows being milked so late into pregnancy. If you must have it, then purchase it from a local farmer who only milks his cows a few months of the year." He took a sip of his coffee. "I had a guy who provided me with milk, but he has been deported."

Leah smiled. "Thank you doctor, we should always watch what we are putting into our bodies." Leah shifted in her chair. "Dr. Smith, Professor Burke said that you might be able to help me with ..."

He interrupted, "Who's following you?"

"I'm not sure exactly."

"Then how do you know you're being followed?"

Leah decided that she would employ tactics to win the doctor over to her cause. She moved to a seat closer to the man. She dropped her voice, "Well there was this guy with a gun last night dressed like an FPL tech."

He leaned in closer to Leah, "Sounds like CIA."

"Could it be?" She asked.

"They claim that they don't work within the US borders, but that's a laugh. In 1969 there were ..."

Leah interrupted to keep the conversation directed. "The professor said that you know a little about pre-Columbian trade routes."

Clay paused with his mug to his lips. He sat the coffee down without taking a sip. "What else did he share with you? I expressed clearly to Patrick that our conversations were to remain private. I have to be very careful with my research." He hurriedly closed the laptop that sat to his left and shoved some papers under the table onto the seat next to him. "I think that you should go." He rose from the table.

Leah attempted to recover. "Dr. Smith, Patrick only sent me here because he believed that with your comprehensive knowledge of the subject, you might be able to point me in a direction with my ... own research."

Clay pushed his thick glasses up the bridge of his nose and shook his head. "No, I don't think so. I'm on the precipice of a great discovery and I don't want you stealing my data."

Leah felt things spiraling out of control.

She blurted out, "What if a map turned up from the fifteenth century that could prove your thesis?"

The little man stared at Leah with his magnified eyes. "You've seen the map?"

"Yes sir, it predates all others that have been previously uncovered."

Clay Smith retook his seat, checked his coffee mug and then stood to refill it. "Would you like more coffee, Ms. Preston?"

Leah wasn't sure if she could finish her first mug, but she didn't want to offend the curious little man. "Thank you."

He brought the carafe to the table and refilled her mug. "How did you come across this map?" Clay asked.

"It was recently found with other maps, all collected into one folio."

Clay eyed his guest suspiciously. "Do you have the folio with you?"

Leah shook her head. "I left it with a colleague."

"And you've had the map dated?"

"We just discovered the map yesterday. We haven't had time for a chemical analysis. But the paper and ink appear to be age-appropriate," Leah explained.

Clay sat quietly. He narrowed his gaze and watched Leah carefully. He said, "Without the map, I do not see how I can help you, Ms. Preston. I think that maybe you should leave." He rose from his chair yet again.

Leah spoke quickly. "The map included the coastline of South America, Africa, and the Caribbean islands."

The little man walked past Leah toward the hallway.

"On the back of the map was a signature. It was signed by Martín Alonso Pinzón." Leah spit out the name.

Clay stood motionless at the kitchen's threshold. He turned slowly and shuffled back to his chair. "Is the signature legible?" he asked.

Leah nodded.

Clay adjusted his glasses once more. "What would you like to know?"

"Anything that you can share," Leah answered after she breathed a sigh of relief. "I need to know more about Pinzón, in particular. I only know what Professor Burke shared with me, that he was the captain of the Pinta and that he had left the fleet after reaching the Caribbean."

"So then you are unaware of Martín Alonso's first trip to the Caribbean in 1488 with the French navigator Jean Cousin?"

Leah took a sip of the terrible coffee that was now cold. "You're saying that Europeans discovered the Caribbean Islands four years before Columbus?"

"Why do academics insist on using the term discovered, when there were civilizations living in the western hemisphere for tens of thousands of years before white Europeans desecrated these continents?" He continued, "Yes, I am saying that other European vessels had reached the Americas prior to Columbus. Isn't that why you are here?"

"And you have proof to support that claim?" Leah asked.

Clay set his mug down with such force that the coffee spilled over the brim. His magnified eyes glared at Leah. "Not in my house, Ms. Preston! I will not be ridiculed in my own home. I know what you all called me on campus, and I allowed it, but not here. You came to me for help."

Leah had not intended to insult the man, but it was obvious that the doctor was sensitive concerning his research. "I'm very sorry, Dr. Smith. You are correct. You do deserve more respect than I have shown you now or in the past. Please forgive me."

Clay just continued to stare at Leah. Then finally his eyes softened, and he took a sip of his coffee. He asked, "Have you heard of L'Anse aux Meadows?"

Leah took a deep breath. She had to walk a fine line with this man. "It sounds familiar."

"It is the Norse settlement in Newfoundland dating from 980 CE to 1020 CE. That is direct proof of Europeans visiting the New World prior to the Columbus voyage." The doctor watched Leah closely for a reaction. "Europeans were not the only people to visit the Americas prior to 1492."

Leah was determined not to display her impatience with the doctor's departure from her initial question.

"What of the Chinese stone boat anchors found off of the coast of California, or the Polynesian influences in South America? Then there are the Olmec colossal stone heads in south-central Mexico with their African facial features. And what of the presence of cocaine, a New World product, found in Egyptian mummies? Or the spear tips from Haiti which contained the same ratio of base metals as those from Guinea, Africa? All of these examples predate 1492." Once again Leah could feel Clay judging her reaction before continuing. "Crazy Clay," he pointed to his chest, "is still a scientist, and a theory is simply that until substantial proof supports it. I just want academics to keep an open mind. We need to remember that oral history, folklore, and myth are usually based in fact. New discoveries are made every day that require us to rethink our historic timelines."

Leah wondered if she had misjudged Clay Smith, and she was intrigued with his theories, but she wasn't here to discuss the errors created by scientific prejudice.

"So Doctor, is there proof of Pinzón's earlier voyage to the Caribbean?"

Clay looked stupefied. His tangent had led him too far away from the initial question. Leah could see his eyes working behind his glasses, attempting to reconnect his thought processes. He found his path and his focus rested on Leah once again.

He cleared his throat. "The only proof exists in French oral tradition. But a previous voyage may help to explain Martín Alonso's skill at sailing across the open sea of the Atlantic."

Leah was happy to have Clay back on track.

"It is known that without Martín Alonso's navigational skill, his ability to motivate his men, and his knowledge of ship building and refitting, the voyage would have been less successful, or possibly a flat out failure." He continued, "When the tiller of Martín Alonso's ship, the Pinta, broke on route to the Canary Islands at the start of the voyage, he expertly sailed the damaged ship safely to harbor. As the voyage wore on, Columbus had difficulty in motivating his men. Martín Alonso was able to stave off a mutiny by the crew. And it was Martín Alonso's course changes that enabled the fleet to make landfall. Each of these examples was part of the *Diario* of the voyage written by Bartolemé de las Casas, supposedly using Columbus's original log. So, in essence, Columbus himself spoke to Martín Alonso's vital importance to the voyage."

"Professor Burke mentioned the *Diario*," Leah cut in.

Clay barely paused, "But what we do not know is how Pinzón felt about the admiral. There has been speculation that Martín Alonso was jealous of Columbus's celebrity, or that he felt betrayed by the admiral who did not honor their agreement for shared recognition of the discoveries. The separation of the Pinta from the fleet has been used as proof of that discord."

"What do you believe, Doctor?" Leah asked.

"I believe that Martín Alonso wanted a slice of the pie for himself. And who could blame him? After all, Pinzón had a great deal of money invested into this undertaking. And I believe that Martín Alonso did not respect Columbus. Columbus needed praise. In Columbus's letters to Ferdinand and Isabella, he juxtaposed his intention not to be boastful with his self-proclaimed heroics. He claimed to have single-handedly negotiated with the natives, and to have saved the peaceful Taínos from the hostile Caribs. This brazen attitude would have been evident to Martín Alonso. Columbus had been trying to sell his competency as a sailor for a decade to the Spanish Court. Martín Alonso knew that Columbus had made a career out of self-promotion. I believe he wanted to be sure that the voyage was profitable, not just for Columbus but also for himself."

"Do you know if Pinzón found anything of value during his time away from the fleet?" Leah attempted to keep the conversation on track.

"I first need to spin the tale. On or about November 11th, the Pinta sailed away from the fleet searching for an island mentioned by two natives aboard the ship, where gold was so plentiful that it could be picked up by the handful from riverbeds. It wasn't until January 1st that the Pinta rejoined the fleet, after Martín Alonso heard that the Santa María ran aground. Did you know that Martín Alonso had two brothers on the voyage, as well?"

"Professor Burke mentioned Vicente and Francisco when I met with him," Leah responded.

"Vicente was captain of the Niña. After Columbus ran the Santa María aground, and with the Pinta on its search for the island of Babeque, the island with the rivers of gold, the Niña was the only ship Columbus had remaining of his fleet. Columbus decided it was time to limp home with his one ship, but in answer to his prayers, the day after raising anchor, the Pinta rejoined the Niña. And I believe he returned because Martín Alonso wanted to aid his brother, not the admiral, on the voyage home. I believe that Martín Alonso had been keeping an eye on the fleet for those forty-something days that he had isolated himself. When he heard of the misfortune of the Santa María from the islanders, he rejoined his brother, allowing cargo to be transferred to the Pinta to afford both ships the best chance of making it back to Spain."

Clay's voice had grown raspy. He went to the sink and filled his coffee mug from a water filtration system and took a long drink.

He sat back down and continued his tale. "But on the voyage home, the Pinta and Niña were separated again. This time they were separated by a great storm, possibly a hurricane. Adding to the level of intrigue, Pinzón reached Spain first, but the monarchs would not meet with Martín Alonso. The contract the monarchs created was with Columbus and they decided to see if their admiral would make it home before allowing Pinzón an audience. The Niña did not reach Spain for an additional fifteen days. The unhealthy Pinzón went home to Palos to die, while Columbus limped into the Spanish Court to be praised for his accomplishments. But some say that Columbus traveled first to Palos to speak with Pinzón on his deathbed."

"He wanted to say goodbye to his dying friend," Leah offered.

"Or to find out what Pinzón had found while absent from the fleet."

Leah speculated, "You think that he found Babeque."

"Yes I do, and I believe that he wanted to keep the wealth of the island for himself and for his family. Understanding Columbus's nature as he did, Pinzón knew that his only chance for wealth and prestige was to carve his own piece from the New World."

"But how could an island of such wealth be lost to history?" Leah asked.

"Did you know that Vicente is credited with being the first European to discover an estuary of the Amazon River? And that he made several trips across the Atlantic?" Clay asked.

Leah shook her head.

"I believe that Babeque was an island like no other in the Caribbean, and that the Pinzón family exploited it fully. On each trip across the Atlantic, Vicente would stop at Babeque and collect its treasure. And I believe that Pinzón wanted an audience with Ferdinand and Isabella to lay claim to his Caribbean treasure."

Leah had to admit that it was a fascinating theory, but it would be nearly impossible to prove.

Clay looked down at the mug in his hands. Leah could see his lips moving, but there was no sound. He seemed to be struggling with something internally.

He finally asked, "Patrick didn't mention the nature of my other research?"

Leah shook her head slowly, confused. "He only sent me here because of your knowledge of Pinzón."

"When you inspected the map, did you see any strange symbols that you could not account for?"

Leah thought that a strange question. She eyed the man quizzically.

Clay took a deep breath and let it out in a huff. "Mention of a map has turned up in my alchemical research."

Leah was startled. "You're studying alchemy?"

***

The Cadillac pulled into the old city center of St. Augustine. Garron parked the car on a street near a park with a long covered pavilion that looked as if it could be used for a farmer's market. The streets were quiet. There were only a few joggers and dog walkers at this early hour. Jacob had spotted a coffee shop, so Garron and his brother climbed from the Caddy, Jacob pulling on the backpack. They made their way across the park and halfway down the block to grab something to eat.

The weather was changing; it was slightly cooler and breezy. The sun had not been above the horizon long, but there were some heavy, dark clouds visible. It felt like it could rain.

The coffee shop was nearly empty. There was a young redhead paying for her frappuccino at the long counter to Garron's left.

"Hey, I'm going to use the men's room. Can you get me a cup of coffee and a croissant?" Jacob said as walked to the back of the shop.

Garron approached the counter. The barista was a twenty-something woman with dyed jet black hair and a sleeve of tattoos on her left arm. She had the look of a 1940s pin-up model, with circular curls and defined eyebrows, and what must have been fake eyelashes. She was quite attractive.

She had already pulled a croissant from the case, overhearing Jacob's order on his way to the bathroom.

"Do you think he'll pay you back?" She said, nodding toward the back of the store.

Garron smiled, "Probably not. Could you make that two croissants and two cups of your house blend?"

Pin-up pulled a second pastry from the case.

"Do you need room for cream?" She asked.

"His will, mine's black, thank you." Garron looked around the empty shop. "It's quiet in here for a Saturday morning."

"That's thirteen," she said, punching some keys on the register. "The rush will start in about an hour. People get up a little later around here."

Garron paid her and took a seat near the front window of the shop. Jacob soon joined Garron at the table, carrying a phone book.

"This shop still has a pay phone," Jacob said placing the phone book on the table.

"Cream's over there, hon," Pin-up called from behind the counter, pointing toward the corner of the shop.

"Thank you." Jacob smiled as he crossed the room.

He added cream to his cup and returned to the table. He took a bite of the croissant and then flipped to the "M" listings in the phone book.

"Here's a listing for Charles I. Murphy. Murph told me that he was named after his uncle, so I'm guessing the 'I' stands for Ian."

Jacob jotted the phone number and address onto a napkin.

"Do we call first? Or do we just stop by?" Garron asked.

Jacob turned to Pin-up, "Excuse me, could you tell us where the library is?"

"Sure, it's just five minutes from here, out on Ponce de León Boulevard."

Jacob stood and showed her the napkin with the address he had copied from the phone book. She gave Jacob directions. Jacob reclaimed his seat and finished his croissant in one bite.

"I think that we should split up. I'll take the car to see if this is the right Charles Murphy, and you hit the library. It's a short walk," Jacob proposed.

"I'm sure that the library doesn't open for a couple of hours." Garron read the clock behind the counter, seven thirty-four. "Why don't we check this address out and then hit the library together?"

"This address is about 30 minutes from here. With all that's happened I'd like to use our time wisely, divide and conquer."

Garron nodded. "Someone may be watching Charles Murphy's house so you'll need to be careful. Be patient, and check things out before you stroll up to the front door to ask for Murphy's uncle."

"I'll meet you back here at noon." Jacob stood and slung the backpack over his shoulder.

Garron said, "Good luck."

Jacob gave his brother a weak smile. "Yeah, you too."

Garron finished his croissant. Just behind him, near the front door, was a display with brochures of area attractions. Garron pulled a street map from the rack and spread it over his table.

"Did he pay you back?" Pin-up asked from behind the counter.

Garron laughed. He said, "It didn't even come up."

"Would you like a refill?" She asked holding the coffee pot.

Garron looked into his empty cup. "Sure, thank you." He rose from his seat.

"Don't get up; I'll bring it to you." She stepped around the counter.

Garron studied the map.

"The library's not on that map," she said as she filled his cup.

She set the pot down and pointed to an area of the map. "It's just about two or three blocks north of where this map ends." She made a circular motion just off the edge of the map.

"Thank you. You wouldn't know when it opens would you?"

"Ten o'clock, the library opens at the same time Monday through Saturday. I spend my fair share of time there during the week."

Another customer, a well-dressed black man, walked into the shop carrying an umbrella and a newspaper. Pin-up said hello and took her place behind the counter. The man placed his order and she went to work on the espresso machine.

As Garron looked out the window and wondered how he would spend the next two hours, the sky opened up. An awning covered the window, but the rain beat on the street with such ferocity that water splashed from the street onto the window. He hoped that it was just a passing storm. He had heard that rain would come and go unexpectedly in Florida.

Garron studied the map and the advertisements for local attractions like an alligator farm, the Fountain of Youth museum, and a local winery. St. Augustine looked like a nice vacation town, but with the summer heat Garron couldn't imagine walking through the otherwise pedestrian friendly streets.

Pin-up approached and sat at Garron's table and asked, "Did you know that we were expecting rain today?"

"Passing over quickly, I had hoped," Garron responded.

"It's expected to last most of the day. You're not planning on walking to the library, are you?"

"That was my plan."

"You have an umbrella?" She asked.

"Nope."

"I heard your brother say that you'd be meeting back here at noon, so why don't you borrow my umbrella and return it then?"

Garron's brow must have furrowed in confusion.

"You two are brothers right? You look nearly identical."

Garron looked out the window at the pounding rain. He smiled. "I think I'll take you up on that umbrella offer. I promise to return it."

The other customer rose from his seat and walked through the front door, springing open his umbrella and turning left. Garron watched as the water soaked the man's leather loafers. Garron realized that it was going to be a long walk.

Pin-up picked up the newspaper that the man had left behind and tucked it under her arm as she wiped down the table.

"You want this paper to kill the time?" She offered.

"Sure, thank you."

She said, "You should see the stack of newspapers that are in the back. There must be four or five month's worth. I'm running out of room. The newspaper company used to collect the old issues with each delivery, but now the new copies are just waiting outside my door each morning. Who reads the paper anymore, anyway? I get my news from the Internet."

She handed Garron the paper.

"I contacted a recycling company, but they're understaffed during the summer months," she said taking the seat across from Garron once again.

Garron set his cup down. "Do you think that you have any papers from May?"

"I bet that they go all the way back to Christmas, why?"

"That's why I was heading to the library. I need to find an obituary from May. You might be able to save me a trip through this monsoon."

She stood and said, "Come on back."

***

"I've been reading George Starkey, Robert Boyle, and Newton. And in a journal, whose authorship is uncertain, I have found mention of a map that was of interest to alchemists of that time. It was deemed *The Map of the Great Work*."

Leah asked, "Newton? As in Sir Isaac Newton?"

Clay smiled. "You are surprised to hear that the Father of Physics and Calculus was also an alchemist. You should not be, alchemy helped to establish many of the modern sciences. Alchemy provided procedures and equipment, and it helped to identify many base substances used in modern chemistry."

Leah was surprised. She believed alchemy to be a pseudoscience of quacks and con artists.

"Newton spent more than a decade trying to create the philosopher's stone. Some say that he was successful. And it was this success that earned him the position of Warden and then Master of the Royal Mint of England, using his ability to hunt down counterfeiters. At one point eleven percent of the Royal Mint's coins in circulation were counterfeits. Newton was tasked with finding and punishing the offenders."

Clay continued. "I've done a great deal of research in this field, but this anonymous journal is the first source that mentioned a map."

"How could a map be connected to alchemy?" Leah asked.

"I don't know, but if I were to guess, information was hidden in the map." He explained. "Remember, alchemy was illegal in the seventeenth century and considered heretical by the Church. Alchemists had to practice in secret. Newton kept many of his notes in code."

"So a code may be hidden in the map?" Leah asked.

"That's my theory." Clay nodded. "If I could see your map then …" He let the request trail off.

"Sorry, Doctor." Leah shrugged and opened her hands.

Clay was obviously disappointed. "If I could see the map, then I might be able to help you more, Ms. Preston. But I don't blame you for not sharing your research, I would do the same."

"It's not that I don't want to show you the map. I truly don't have it with me."

The disbelief was obvious on the doctor's face. Leah may be holding something that could vindicate the man's professional career. But even if she had the map with her, she couldn't risk the man's life by sharing it with him. However, she could point him towards the Library of Congress's copy of the Waldseemüller 1507 map and the Canepa portolan. Those maps exist in the public record. Dr. Smith might find his answers within those copies. She felt sorry for the man that no one took seriously.

"Dr. Smith, may I use your bathroom?"

He removed his glasses and wiped the lenses with his bathrobe. "It's midway down the hall and on the right."

***

Jacob drove the Cadillac over the Bridge of Lions following A1A south and the directions that the coffee shop girl had provided to Summer Haven. The area looked like many other sea towns. The ocean was to his left, and Jacob could see large houses set on deep lots. Then he passed multiple condominium complexes. Then the development began to yield back to nature, with houses fewer and farther between. It was a beautiful drive, and Jacob hoped that the local government took the necessary means to protect this sea shore from further development.

Jacob pulled up to the gated driveway that matched the address he pulled from the phone book. A large white concrete wall enclosed the property. There was a black iron gate blocking Jacob's path. He pulled up to the call box on his left. The home wasn't even visible from the gate. But if the gate, with its scroll work and shield-shaped crest, was an indicator as to the size of the home, then it must be enormous. And if this was the home of Murphy's uncle, then Jacob thought that Charles must have done quite well with his other investments, because the dive business was never that lucrative.

Jacob noticed a groundskeeper through the gate, so he decided to step out of the car. The man had been digging a narrow ditch; it looked to Jacob as if he were burying a cable or power line. The groundskeeper was a large man with fiery red hair and a full beard. He had paused to take a cell phone call, and was leaning against a shovel. He held up a finger, letting Jacob know that he would be just a moment longer.

Jacob overheard the man say, "Yeah, well I have company … I believe so … I'll call you back." And with that he ended the call.

Jacob smiled as the man approached. "Sorry to interrupt."

The man stepped closer and leaned against the gate. "Can I help you?" He asked in a Boston accent.

Jacob thought that he heard contempt in the man's voice. Helping Jacob was the last thing that this man wanted to do.

"Maybe, I'm looking for the home of Charles Murphy."

"What address do you have?"

Jacob read the address from the napkin in his hand.

"You've got the right address, but there is no one here by that name." The man pushed a button and the gate slid open slowly. He stepped through the gate and rested again on his shovel. He asked, "Murphy you said, right?"

"Charles Murphy," Jacob clarified.

The groundskeeper looked up and down the quiet street. He pointed back over Jacob's shoulder and said, "I think Murphy is the name of the owner of that house down there, across the street."

Jacob turned to look behind him, "Which one?"

The man answered, "The second drive on the right."

Jacob said, "Thanks" as he turned back to face the groundskeeper.

There was a loud snap when the shovel's handle cracked across Jacob's left shoulder. Jacob fell to one knee from the blow. He barely had time to process the pain in his shoulder before the man caught him with a heavy right hand to the base of the skull and all went black.

***

"Dr. Smith, I was thinking about it, and I truly don't have the map with me, but I'm willing to tell you all that I know," Leah said as she re-entered the kitchen.

Clay was sitting where Leah had left him before using the bathroom, but something had changed. Something was wrong.

"Dr. Smith, are you okay?"

She noticed the morning's newspaper unfolded and spread out on the table.

"You're willing to tell me everything, about the map and Pinzón, and why you needed my help?"

Leah's brow knitted. "I thought about it, and I think that I have something that could help with your research. But what's wrong? What changed since I went to the bathroom?"

"Everything, you're willing to tell me everything? You'll share your research?" The man's eyes were wide behind his lenses.

"Damn it Clay! Quit repeating yourself and tell me what's wrong."

He stood so quickly that he nearly knocked over his chair. He said, "You have to leave, you have to leave right now!"

"What? Why?" Leah's body tensed; she felt the need to run.

"I called the police, Ms. Preston."

Leah noticed the phone in Clay's hand for the first time.

"I saw the gun in your waistband, and there's this," he pointed to the table. "Patrick was murdered last night. It's in the paper."

Leah touched the gun at her back instinctively. Her blouse barely covered the weapon. She stepped closer to the table. Patrick Burke looked up at her from the front page of the newspaper.

"The article said that the police were looking for your boyfriend, his brother, and you as people of interest in the investigation. And with the mention of Karen's VW Beetle being stolen from Patrick's home, I thought that you ..." He trailed off.

Leah whimpered. "And you thought ..."

"I'm sorry. Patrick was a dear man, and I thought ... so I called ..."

"You thought that I could have killed my mentor, a man that I loved ... for what, a map?" Leah shook with anger. Tears filled her eyes.

"I'm sorry. I should have given you an opportunity to explain. But now you just need to go!" Clay backed away from Leah.

"Why give me the chance to run? Why the change of heart?"

The little man shrunk into himself. "You were going to share your research with me. Your research ... with me ..."

Leah wiped her eyes and started for the front of the house.

"No, not that way," Clay cautioned. He opened the back door. "They're looking for the Beetle. Here is the key to my motorcycle. It doesn't look like much, but it will get you wherever it is you are going. Do you know how to ride?" Clay held the key out in front of him.

"I do." Leah took the key from Clay and rushed out into the backyard.

To her right she found an early model Yamaha. It was battered and beaten. The red gas tank had long ago lost its luster and the black leather seat was worn and cracked.

She hadn't ridden a motorcycle since Jacob taught her to ride when she was just 19 and still married to Garron. It had been fun tearing around the cornfield behind the Shepard's home while Garron and Jacob watched. They had both cheered as she sped by. That was a long time ago.

The age of Clay's bike benefited her. She was familiar with the clutch and transmission, as well as the kick start. The old Yamaha turned over immediately.

Behind the house was a canal that ran parallel to the street. Leah let out the clutch and sped off across Clay's backyard to the berm of the canal. She accelerated up the incline, then raced along the canal. The sound of sirens echoed from a distance. Once she was ten or twelve houses away from Clay's she came to a cul-de-sac on her right, which ran perpendicular to the canal. Leah took the down slope slowly and eased the bike onto the black top. She accelerated gradually while her mind raced. She was tortured by the guilt of bringing the professor into harm's way and of leaving him behind last night. But through the tears filling her eyes and the torment in her soul, she found her way to Route 70 and headed east. She reached I-95 without seeing a police car and sped north toward St. Augustine.

***

Garron sifted through the piles of newspapers stacked in the utility room of the coffee shop for hours. Adela, that was Pin-up's name, periodically checked on Garron, filling up his coffee cup on more than one occasion. It would probably have been faster to give up on the stacks and move his search to the library, but the rain had not let up. When his frustration nearly became unbearable, he found a stack of papers from May. His luck changed when he opened the second paper from the May stack. In the obituary section of May 24th, Garron found a listing for Charles Ian Murphy. He took the section back to the front of the shop. The coffee shop was thinning out from the late morning rush that had kept Adela at the espresso machine for an hour. Garron took a seat, and read the obituary.

Charles Ian Murphy
Summer Haven

Charles I. Murphy of Summer Haven, agent and owner of Seloy Realty, died at 2:15 a.m., Thursday May 23rd. He was 73. Mr. Murphy was the

husband of the late Julia C. Murphy. He leaves a nephew, Ian Murphy of
Marathon, Florida. The burial will be 10 a.m. Saturday, May 27th at San
Lorenzo Cemetery.

The obituary was short, but Garron was able to glean a valuable piece
of information from the listing: Seloy Realty. Garron found a listing for the
realty company in the phone book that Jacob had brought to the table
earlier. He jotted down the address and phone number.

Garron waited for Adela to finish with her customers before he asked,
"Are you familiar with Seloy Realty?"

She smiled. "Yeah, they helped me buy a house. Wait, were you looking for Mr. Murphy's obituary?"

"You knew Charles Murphy?"

"My real estate agent worked for him. He was such a cute old man,
with that cute English accent and those big mutton chops, so cute. It was
so sad what happened to him."

Garron let his confusion show. "What happened?"

"The obituary didn't say?" Adela sat at the table with Garron once
again.

She spoke just above a whisper. "He was killed during a home invasion. The burglar got away with a small fortune and shot poor Mr. Murphy
in the head while he slept. They never caught the bastard either."

Garron felt a chill run down his spine.

"You okay?" Adela asked. "You went snow white on me."

Garron knew that Charles Murphy's murder was related to his
nephew's death and to the folio. Garron was now convinced that there
were no longer any coincidences.

Garron recovered. "I'm okay, it's just that Charles's nephew was a
friend of my brother's. My brother doesn't know about the murder. Can I
use your phone, Adela?"

"Sure hon."

Garron first called Jacob's cell phone and left a message. He then
called Leah, her voice mail picked up, as well. He left a cryptic message for
both to be very careful, and explained that Charles Murphy had been killed
during a robbery.

Garron had a thought, "Adela, is the real estate office nearby? The one Charles Murphy owned?"

"Just three blocks away, on Spanish Street." Adela picked up the sightseeing map and drew an 'x' on Spanish Street near the corner of Hypolita Street.

Garron grabbed the map, laid forty dollars on the counter and headed toward the door. "Thank you, I'll see you later," he called over his shoulder.

Adela picked up the two twenties and said, "Hey, thanks."

The rain was pouring down; Garron remembered Adela's umbrella offer too late. He was soaked just halfway up the block. He crossed St. George Street and took cover across the street under a two-story covered deck at the Government House Museum. Garron pulled out the wet map, ripping it in the process, and studied it once again. Two more blocks north and one block to the west. There was movement on King Street, in the direction from which he came. It caught Garron's eye and held him to the spot. Two men were moving quickly in his direction, which in the downpour was to be expected, but Garron recognized one of the men from the coffee shop. It was the well-dressed black man with the umbrella, the man with him was dressed like a maintenance man with a full red beard. Garron stepped further back under the decking and used the shadows to conceal himself.

Garron wondered if the men were following him, or if he was just being paranoid. The two men slowed at the intersection and paused a moment, and it looked to Garron like they were scanning the streets. Were they looking for him?

The sound of a motorcycle echoed down King Street. Garron felt sorry for that poor soul getting caught in this storm, although, hadn't it been raining for hours? He didn't want to take his eyes off the two men crossing the street, but the motorcycle moved into his periphery and he stole a glance. It was a woman, with her short blonde hair plastered to her face from the rain. It was Leah!

Garron fought the urge to run into the street and flag her down. He turned back to the two men, they had also noticed Leah. Did they recognize her, too? They ducked back under an awning of the building directly across the street from where Garron was taking shelter. Leah passed. The two men conferred, and then Red Beard returned from the direction he had come.

It was obvious to Garron now that the men were looking for him. Garron crouched deeper into the shadows and watched as the man crossed in front of him, without taking notice. Garron studied the soggy map once again trying to find a point to intersect Leah and warn her of the pursuer. He surmised that she would be looking for the Cadillac, because they had not laid out a plan to reconnect. Garron guessed that she would check the streets and the public parking areas. The public parking signs were prominent. Leah would start there. The one-way streets aided Garron in plotting a course to intercept Leah. He stuffed the map back into his pocket and peaked around the building looking for the black man with the umbrella. The man was nowhere to be found. Garron bolted from his refuge, darting north down the walking mall of old storefronts and restaurants. The sound of the motorcycle was fading. The parking area near the Castillo de San Marcos was Garron's destination. Figuring in Leah's direction toward the river, and the one-way streets, Garron determined that the parking lot would be his best bet. It was a wild ass guess, but that was all that he had. Garron came to the end of the walking mall and turned, then headed toward the river. He could see the parking lot just over a block away and could hear the motorcycle approaching. Halfway down the street, he saw Leah turn into the parking lot near the ancient fort. He forced his legs to pick up the pace. The wet pavement would not allow Garron to slow down as he approached the corner. His momentum would carry him into the street. He was able to see that the street was empty to his left, but his vision was blocked by the buildings on his right. He just prayed that a car wouldn't be coming from that direction. He took two more strides and then the collision took Garron off of his feet.

***

Leah rode slowly through the lot looking for Professor Burke's Cadillac. She was soaked through to the bone, she was cold, and she was exhausted. It was a long ride on a motorcycle and her muscles ached from the tension of riding in the rain. When she ran into the heavy, body-chilling rain 45 minutes ago, she wasn't sure that she could make it to St. Augustine. Many times she had considered pulling over to call Jacob and Garron, but she knew that their cell phones were off to protect them from being tracked, and she had the sense that she was being chased.

Leah became frustrated looking through the parking lot. She had no idea where Jacob and Garron might be, and she wished they had formulated a better plan to reconnect. Leah knew that if she could just get dry she could think more clearly and come up with a better plan of attack. She began to cry, although, the tears were lost in the rain. Leah's frustration and exhaustion got the better of her. She decided to get off the motorcycle and take some cover from the rain. She nearly fell off the bike, her legs barely able to support her. She stretched slightly and looked toward the old fort for shelter, but a flash of movement on her left caught her attention. Leah saw two men collide and fall into the street.

***

Garron thought that he must have run into a truck judging by the force of the impact. He was surprised to see not a vehicle, but a man, beside him on the wet pavement. It was the red-bearded man that he had seen with the coffee shop patron. Garron got to his feet as quickly as his aching joints would allow. As Red Beard shifted, Garron noticed that one of the man's pant legs had been torn, and blood was staining the fabric. Red Beard moaned and started to right himself. Garron spun and continued to the parking lot.

Garron yelled for Leah to start the bike, but the distance and rain must have made it impossible for Leah to hear him. Finally just twenty feet away, he yelled for Leah to start the motorcycle once more.

"Where's Jacob?" She asked.

"We have to go now!" Garron insisted.

"Garron, where is your brother?"

"Damn it Leah, start the bike."

"No Mr. Shepard, let me give you a ride in my van. Ms. Preston has been in the rain long enough," the well-dressed man from the coffee shop said from under his umbrella. In his left hand, close to his body and out of the rain, was a pistol. It was pointing at Leah.

"Ms. Preston, please leave your gun in your waistband. I'll remove it for you before you get into the van." Umbrella Man motioned with his pistol to a navy blue van pulling into the parking lot.

As Garron considered his options, a hand clamped onto his shoulder from behind. Garron felt something hard dig into the center of his back. He stole a glance over his shoulder; it was Red Beard.

The man with the umbrella spoke as he slid the van's door open, "Now will you two please join me in the van?"

Red Beard shoved Garron toward the van. Leah followed closely. Red Beard tugged the gun from Leah's waistband. Garron and Leah climbed into the back of the van. Red Beard followed and pulled the van door closed behind him. A young black man was driving and Umbrella Man slid into the passenger's seat beside him.

Leah asked, "Where are you taking us?"

"To reunite you with your boyfriend, of course," Umbrella Man answered.

"Is Jacob all right?" Garron asked.

"Your brother is fine, for the moment, but his future has been left in your hands."

Garron was disconcerted by the familiarity with which this stranger addressed them.

Leah asked, "What do you mean?"

"If you can confirm the story Jacob provided, then all three of you will be," Umbrella Man chuckled, "well, as they say, right as rain."

"Who are you?" Garron demanded.

"There is no need to worry about that right now. If you tell us the truth, then introductions can come later."

Leah saw Umbrella Man pull something off of the dashboard.

He said, "Now put these on." He handed Garron and Leah each a pillowcase. Leah looked into Garron's eyes and saw her own fear reflected there.

Leah spoke, "I'm not going to …"

But before she could finish, Red Beard struck Garron at the base of his skull with the barrel of the gun. Leah watched Garron slump to the floor of the van, unconscious. She and Umbrella Man locked eyes then she slowly pulled the pillowcase over her head.

***

When Garron came to he was still in the van, and it took a moment to realize that the pillowcase had been drawn over his head. The van had stopped and he listened carefully; he could hear sounds from outside the van. Garron felt something binding his wrists together behind him. He squirmed and rose to a sitting position. His head ached. He had no idea how long he had been unconscious.

"Leah," he whispered.

There was no answer.

He sat quietly. It felt as if he were alone. If Leah were unconscious, he thought that he should still have been able to hear her breathing. Garron felt guilty for not protecting Leah. He wondered if he had led their kidnappers straight to her.

The van door slid open, and Garron felt the van shift with the weight of someone stepping into the vehicle.

"Up," a rough voice said as Garron was hauled to his feet.

Garron crouched, anticipating the van's doorway. He was shoved from the van and landed hard on the ground. Garron slowed his breathing to calm the anger and panic brewing within him. He knew that he needed to keep a clear head if he expected to survive. He forced himself to think about his surroundings using his other senses.

It was a hard landing; so it was concrete or blacktop, he thought. The ground was still wet; so they had not driven out of the storm's track, but it had stopped raining.

Garron was hoisted to his feet once again.

His kidnapper stayed to Garron's right side, never releasing his grip on Garron's arm. Garron could hear a conversation taking place in front of him. Garron recognized the voice as that of Umbrella Man. That meant that it was either Red Beard or the driver who was manhandling Garron. The driver was a young man, very thin and, even though Garron only saw him behind the wheel, Garron thought that he was probably rather tall. Considering the strength of the hand holding him and the sound of the man's breathing close to his ear, Garron concluded that it must be Red Beard herding him away from the van.

They were getting closer to the two men in conversation. Red Beard relaxed his grip slightly on Garron's right arm. Garron wondered if the other hand was holding a gun. Is now the time to try an escape?

"Thinking about rabbiting?" Red Beard's Boston accent interrupted Garron's thoughts. "I can feel you tensing up, getting ready to try something stupid. I wish you would. I'll be happy to break your knee. You don't have to be in one piece to answer some questions." Red Beard laughed, and then shoved Garron forward.

Garron's toe caught what must have been a step and he went crashing, unable to protect himself, into a set of concrete stairs leading upward.

***

The pillowcase was pulled from Leah's head. She was in a folding metal chair in the center of a large room. There were heavy drapes over the windows and the walls were lined with folding banquet tables and chairs like the one she was sitting in. Directly in front of her was the black man who had forced her and Garron into the van. He was well dressed in a striped gray suit and purple tie. Verdant emerald cuff links caught the light as he propped his umbrella in the corner near the door. He unfolded his own chair, sat, crossed his right leg over his left, and looked at Leah calmly.

"Ms. Preston, all that I want from you is your story."

Leah studied the man in the chair. He was a slight man with narrow shoulders. His dark skin was smooth, and Leah could not easily judge his age. His eyes were bright and intelligent, and they looked at Leah with anticipation, begging her to speak.

"My story? Where is Jacob?" Leah asked coldly.

"Mr. Shepard is near, and he is safe. Please tell me about the last 48 hours."

"You hold me at gun point, force me into a van, pull a pillowcase over my head; and you just want to chat? Screw you!"

"Mr. Shepard warned us that you might be resistant." The man laughed. He saw the anger flare in Leah's eyes and quickly realized his mistake. "I'm sorry. I do not mean to mock you. I wish that it wasn't necessary to have treated you in such a barbarous way, but I have lost a good friend, and my family is in danger. So I must be cautious. And at times I act in contradiction to my character."

He uncrossed his legs and leaned closer to Leah. He sat silently for a moment and chose his words carefully. "I am … I was, a friend of Ian and Charles Murphy, my name is Malik Qwari."

Leah was stunned.

"All I need is for you to confirm Mr. Shepard's account of the last 48 hours, and then I promise you that I will reunite the two of you. Absolutely no harm will come to either Shepard's brother, or yourself. In fact, if your recounting of the last two days matches Mr. Shepard's, then we will find ourselves on the same side of this … fight."

Leah was confused, but she understood the gravity of her situation. If Jacob had told Qwari the truth, then she had nothing to fear. However, if Jacob had omitted something from the events of the last two days, or if he had spun a tale in order to protect someone involved, then even the truth would doom then all. Leah wondered if Jacob would have trusted this man who sat before her with the truth. What if Qwari questions Garron? How will he answer?

Leah finally said, "Okay, Mr. Qwari, here's what I know."

***

Garron sat with the pillowcase still over his head and his hands bound behind his back. After climbing a flight of stairs, he had been seated in an uncomfortable steel chair. He knew that he was not alone; he could hear someone shifting and pacing from across the room to his left. Garron had asked for some water, but there was no reply. He had also asked for his brother and Leah. He was ignored again. Now he sat silently listening to his kidnapper pacing. Garron believed that the noise was coming from the direction from which he had been forced into the room. The man was pacing near the exit, blocking his escape. Garron wondered if it was still Red Beard tasked with watching him.

"Is that a limp that I hear?" Garron tested.

There was no reply, but the pacing had stopped.

"How's your leg? It looked pretty bad, back there on the street."

Still silence.

"There was a fair amount of blood and from what I could see those pants were ruined," Garron prodded.

"Shut your mouth!" Red Beard replied.

Garron smiled under the pillowcase. Bingo.

"I was wondering. How does your boss feel about you screwing up like that? For hired muscle it was pretty easy surprising you on the street like I did."

Garron didn't share that he was surprised by their collision, as well.

"I bet he's not very happy with you," Garron persisted.

Red Beard exploded, "You son of a bitch!"

Garron could hear Red Beard start towards him. He tensed, listening to the man's approaching footfalls. Garron rose from his chair quickly and rushed toward the sound of the oncoming man. Garron's shoulder collided with Red Beard's midsection, catching the man by surprise. Garron maintained his footing, but now he stood, unable to see with his hands still tied behind his back. He turned toward where he believed the door to be and dashed ahead blindly. Garron tripped over something and fell to the floor, landing painfully on his right shoulder. He struggled to sit up, but he was knocked back to the ground by a shot to the jaw. Blackness threatened from Garron's periphery; he forced his mind to focus.

Red Beard said from above him, "Stay down, asshole!"

Garron felt the barrel of a gun forced into his forehead through the pillowcase. He thought that he was going to die. Garron surprised himself by laughing. He said to Red Beard, "I surprised you again, didn't I?"

"Fuck you!" Red Beard delivered a vicious kick to Garron's side, then he heard a round chambered.

"That will be quite enough, Mr. Mackenzie," someone said from the doorway.

Red Beard snarled, "Please tell me that I can waste this asshole."

"Put the gun away and help Mr. Shepard to his feet."

Garron caught his breath and said from the floor, "Yeah, a little help Mr. Mackenzie."

"Fuck you, asshole."

"Garron?" Leah had entered the room.

Garron could hear her run to him. The pillowcase was pulled from his head, and she was looking down on him with compassion. Behind Leah he could see Umbrella Man holding a red backpack.

Pain in his ribs made it difficult to speak, but Garron asked, "Are you okay?"

Then he watched as Jacob stepped into the room, looked at him lying on the floor, and then walked over to Red Beard and dropped the man on his ass with a right upper cut.

A sharp, hot pain shot through Garron's right side as he tried to laugh.

***

Leah was examining the cut over Jacob's left eye. She dabbed at the cut with an alcohol swab.

Jacob winced. "Leah, I'm fine. The bleeding has stopped."

"The bleeding stopped before you cleaned it. There's a risk of infection," she replied.

Garron held an ice bag to his aching ribs and watched as Leah doted over his brother. They had been moved to a room downstairs and had been left alone to tend to their injuries. It appeared to be an unused office, with mismatched furniture and sealed boxes. Garron turned toward the window. The sun was starting to set. There were no remnants of the storm that blew through earlier. He looked out onto a courtyard formed by a u-shaped building, with each wing connected by a covered walkway. A large Live Oak dominated the courtyard. There were several concrete benches tucked along a concrete pathway. Pygmy date palms and ti plants dotted the area. A parking lot was visible, although there were very few cars in the lot. The building seemed to be a commercial building that was closed for the weekend.

A knock came to the door; Malik Qwari entered. "I'm sorry to have kept you waiting. I needed to be certain that we could relocate you securely. How is everyone?"

"Relocate? You are not taking us anywhere until we get some answers," Garron insisted.

"I'm sorry, Mr. Shepard, but we need to move you to a more secure location. I promise that we will have plenty of time to answer your questions once we have relocated."

Garron stood from his chair, wincing at the pain in his ribs.

"I'm telling you that I am not going anywhere until you tell me what is going on."

"Gar, it's okay. Malik is trying to help," Jacob said.

"The police are looking for us. Malik is going to keep us hidden away until we get this all sorted out," Leah added.

Garron realized that he was not privy to some vital information.

"Why are the police looking for us?"

Jacob and Leah looked at each other. Garron could see tears fill Leah's eyes.

Jacob said, "Professor Burke was killed last night. The police are looking for us in connection with the murder."

Garron slowly retook his seat. Guilt consumed him. He had just met the man yesterday. The depth to which he felt the loss confused him. But innocence when lost is fundamentally devastating. Garron was having difficulty catching his breath and his head began to spin. He managed to ask, "What happened?"

"It was staged to look like a robbery. He was shot and killed," Qwari answered.

Garron muttered, "Just like Charles."

Qwari nodded. "Now you can understand the need for your relocation. We must move swiftly. I have a car waiting, please follow me."

***

A black limousine waited just outside. The driver was introduced as Malik's son, Abram, who was also the driver of the van that plucked Leah and

Garron off the street. Malik assured the trio that Abram would see that they made it to their destination safely; and that he would follow closely behind, after tending to some material that he also needed to relocate. Leah, Jacob, and Garron filed into the darkened rear compartment of the limousine.

Garron sat in the back of the limousine, leaning against the glass. Jacob had tried to speak to him, but Garron was insensate. He could not reply even if he had heard Jacob. Garron did not understand his reaction to learning of the professor's death. It seemed to be affecting him as deeply, but differently, than the loss of his own parents. Garron felt as though he had pulled the trigger and ended the professor's life himself. Garron was still trapped in his thoughts of Professor Burke when Abram opened the car door. Garron nearly spilled out of the car.

***

Jacob took in his surroundings after stepping from the limo. He stood in a wide driveway that circled a large water fountain topped with a copper, three-mast-tall ship. There was a five car garage and at least two out build-ings that Jacob assumed housed gardening supplies and a possible pool house. The pillared façade had a short, brick stairwell leading to the double front doors.

Jacob was concerned about his brother. Garron had been despondent since hearing the news of the professor's death, and even now he just stood in the humid evening air with a glazed look.

Jacob could hear the sound of the front gate opening, and saw a van pull into the driveway. He could see Malik in the van's passenger seat and Mackenzie behind the wheel. Malik stepped from the van.

He said, "Gentlemen, Ms. Preston, will you please follow me into the house?"

Malik placed a hand on his son's shoulder, "Abram, please help Bryan to unload the van."

Malik led them into the house, through the two story entry, and into a lavishly furnished drawing room. They quickly stepped through the drawing room and into an equally lavish but smaller parlor. A large window looked out over the Matanzas River, where heron and egrets were visible by the water's edge. Throughout the room there were multiple seating arrangements, and in the far corner, near the window, was a beautifully carved bar.

Jacob watched as his brother walked directly to the bar and, from the decanter, poured himself a glass of sherry that he immediately drained. Garron poured himself a second glass and then took a seat near the window, looking out onto the river.

Malik asked, "Is there anything that I can get for anyone?"

"I believe we are okay for now," Jacob answered.

Garron spoke from his seat by the window, "The hell we are."

"What can I get for you Mr. Shepard?" Malik said from the doorway.

Garron stood. "You know what I need. I need some fucking answers!"

The outburst surprised Jacob and the anger in Garron's eyes frightened him. "Gar, take it easy. Malik is trying to help …"

"What the fuck is wrong with you?" Garron spit out the words. "What did this guy tell you that has you so calm and amiable? 'Cause I haven't heard shit that has me trusting this son of a bitch."

"Garron, what has gotten into you?" Leah, too, was surprised by Garron's reaction.

"And you," Garron spun to face Leah. "How do we know that this bastard wasn't involved in the professor's death?"

Leah began to cry.

"Garron, that wasn't necessary," Jacob protested.

Malik stepped closer to Garron. "Mr. Shepard, you have every right to be angry, and I am sorry that I have not yet answered your questions, but I have spoken to your brother and provided him with some information. With that information he has decided that he can trust me. So please speak to him while I attend to a very pressing matter. I will be no more than thirty minutes, and then you and I will have a conversation a little later that will provide answers to all of your questions."

Malik turned and left the room, sliding the pocket doors closed tightly behind him.

Jacob watched Garron simmering. He remembered his brother having a temper when they were both children, but, while Jacob struggled with his temper, Garron seemed to have matured beyond those issues. But it seemed that the Shepard temper was something that Garron had not truly conquered after all. Jacob watched Garron step back to the bar and the sherry bottle.

***

Garron rattled the bottle against the crystal glass as he poured another sherry. He knew that his anger had gotten the best of him, but he could not hold his tongue. Being held at gun point, jerked off the street, blindfolded and beaten had caused his blood to boil. And to learn that Jacob and Leah had information that they did not share pissed him off even more. Garron drained the glass.

Leah placed a gentle hand on Garron's hand, the one that held the sherry decanter's neck.

She said, "I'm sorry, we hadn't really had time to tell you about our conversation with Malik. You were so distant in the limo that you didn't even seem to be aware that we were sitting right there beside you." She squeezed his hand. "Please don't drink anymore."

Garron turned to meet Leah's pleading gaze. He was struck by the compassion in her eyes.

She smiled meekly. "Let's have a seat and we'll tell you all that we know."

They had a seat and Jacob brought Garron up to speed. Jacob explained how the address that he found for Charles Murphy was correct, and how Mackenzie had used a shovel to surprise him. When he woke up, he was tied to a chair in the building they had just left. Malik had entered the room carrying Jacob's backpack and promised to untie Jacob if he could confirm some information.

"Murphy, his uncle, and Malik had been friends for more than thirty years. Plus, Malik and Charles were those real estate partners Murphy had told me about."

"And you just took him at his word?" Garron asked.

"Just let me finish Gar," Jacob requested.

Garron nodded.

"I didn't believe him at first. He showed me a picture of the three of them that must have been taken ten or fifteen years ago, Malik's son was just a young boy at the time. That guy Mackenzie and another guy were in the picture, too."

Garron shifted in his seat.

"I know you're thinking that a lot could have happened in fifteen years or the picture could have been doctored, but please just listen and give me some credit for not being a complete moron."

Jacob continued, "Then the conversation turned to the maps. They had taken the backpack from the car after Mackenzie cleaned my clock, and they had looked inside. Only, once Malik learned that what I was carrying was an old folio, they never opened it up."

"They never looked at the maps?" Garron was skeptical.

Jacob nodded. "This is where the story gets weird. Murphy apparently handled old books and such for this group and according to the group's rules no one else in the organization was allowed to handle these things."

Garron's confusion must have been obvious because Jacob said, "Like I said, weird, but Malik has promised to explain later."

"I told Malik that Murphy left instructions for me to keep the folio safe. I left out our cryptic scavenger hunt and the fact that we only stumbled into St. Augustine by chance."

"So because Murphy gave you the map, Malik thinks that we are in on his game, that we're initiated," Garron concluded.

Jacob said, "Exactly, or at the very least that we knew to look for Malik after Murphy's death."

Garron asked, "So you trust this guy?"

"I don't know, but I'm willing to hear him out. There's something going on, and I think that Malik is the guy to fill us in."

"Did your new friend tell you that Charles Murphy was murdered?" Garron asked curtly.

He could tell by Jacob and Leah's expressions that the answer was no.

"He was killed during a home invasion. With the amount of death circling this group, do you think that it's wise to trust this guy? I think that we should be cautious."

The room was silent. Jacob was deflated. Garron wanted to handle this situation logically, but he needed to be more compassionate; his brother was hurting.

Leah spoke up, "We agree, but we think that Malik is our best chance at finding out who might be behind the murders of Murphy, Wes, Patrick, *and* Charles."

A moment passed.

Jacob asked, "What do you think Gar?"

Garron didn't feel as though he had a choice. He said, "We'll see where this takes us."

***

The parlor doors slid open and Malik Qwari stepped in carrying a tray of sandwiches and several carafes of water.

"I thought that you might be hungry. I have some vegetarian sandwiches and water," Malik said as he set the tray down on the central coffee table. "Mr. Shepard, Garron, could I bring you some more sherry?" Malik asked, examining the nearly empty decanter.

Garron could feel both Jacob's and Leah's eyes on him. "No, thank you."

"Very well, then please sit and enjoy the sandwiches."

Garron only hesitated a minute before taking a seat and diving into the sandwiches; he was famished.

Jacob said to Malik, "I've brought Garron up to speed, but we are all still anxious to learn more."

"Like why you weren't interested in the folio," Garron prompted between bites.

Malik sat back in his chair, crossed his legs, and tented his fingers on his lap. He had changed into a pink polo shirt and tan pants with close-toed sandals. He now wore a pair of small round tortoiseshell glasses. Malik sat in thought for a moment.

With a slight nod, he began, "Let me start by saying that this is quite atypical for how our organization has handled its affairs in the past. We have had our … challenges in the past, but this particular trial has stretched our resources to very near their breaking point. We have never before, in our 500 years, had such a ruthless adversary as we now have in Anton Margaux."

With a mouthful, Leah interrupted by asking, "I'm sorry did you say 500 years?"

Jacob questioned Malik as well, "Murphy was a part of a five century old organization?"

"Yes, we are members of *The Brotherhood of the Three Crosses*. And you, Jacob, were chosen by Ian to be his successor as our *Chartophylax*; our archivist. A position that should not be taken lightly and it requires a lifelong commitment. Our entire collection of current and ancient documents was Murphy's responsibility."

Garron said, "Are we talking about some kind of fraternal organization, like the Freemasons?"

Malik shifted in his chair. "I should probably start from the beginning."

"Good idea," Garron agreed.

Malik began, "Our organization was started in 1503 by Vicente Yañez and Francisco Martín Pinzón, a decade after Martín Alonso's death."

At the mention of Pinzón's name, Jacob and Garron looked at one another in disbelief.

Leah surprised the men in the room by asking, "Malik, does this have something to do with Babeque?"

Leah met the men's stares and said, "I wasn't just out joyriding while you boys were getting your heads beat in. I did pick up a few things from Clay." Leah waved her hand for Malik to proceed.

Malik took a long drink of water and continued his story.

He explained how there were three positions within *The Brotherhood of the Three Crosses*. The first was the *Conrector*, or the Financial Officer; that position belonged to Malik. The second was the *Chartophylax*, or the Archivist. And the third was the *Custos*, or the Guardian, Bryan Mackenzie's position. Each of the three positions also required *Vicari*, or Successors. When the time neared for one of the Brothers to step down, he hand-selected a successor and then nominated his choice during a *Congressus*. The nominee would then be vetted by the *Custos*. The Guardian scrutinizes the nominee's past and decides if he is worthy of initiation.

"That's where we were with you, Jacob. Ian had nominated you after his uncle's death and Bryan was doing his due diligence with your background check. That process usually takes six months to a year."

"If you knew that we were friends of Murphy's, then why did you treat us the way that you did?" Garron asked.

Malik lowered his gaze. "We don't know who to trust. Ian's wasn't the only death that our Brotherhood has had to deal with in the recent past."

Jacob asked, "Why didn't you mention that Charles was murdered? You must know that the two deaths are related."

Malik removed his glasses and rubbed the bridge of his nose. "Charles is not the only member that we have lost. We also lost Bryan's predecessor six months ago, his brother Liam. It seemed at the time to have been a horrible accident, but hindsight has proven otherwise. With you showing up unannounced, we were not sure if we could trust you. Please accept my apology for the way that you were treated."

Garron said with a sneer, "It seems that your organization is under attack, so much for being a secret order."

Garron's jab had the desired effect, he watched as Malik withered in his chair.

Leah cast a look on Garron. "Malik, you mentioned a name earlier. Is that who's behind these murders?"

Malik straightened in his chair. "Anton Margaux is the most likely choice. The Margaux family had been members of The Brotherhood for centuries. A Margaux had held the position of *Corrector* for more than 120 years. But in 1958, when Anton was just six years old, his father was discovered stealing documents from the archive, and with an investigation The Brotherhood learned that Anton's father was using the organization's resources for his personal gain. His membership was terminated."

"So you just kick the guy out and say, forget everything that you've learned, have a nice life?" Jacob asked.

Malik shook his head. "The Brotherhood requires a lifelong commitment."

"What are you saying?" Leah asked.

Malik just sat quietly.

Garron answered, "When your membership is terminated, then you are terminated."

"You killed him?" Leah was shocked.

"The Brotherhood took a vote, and it was decided to end the Margaux membership, but a large amount of investments were provided for the Margaux family's financial future. We are not without compassion."

"Compassion, you stole a six-year-old boy's father from him. Do you really believe that compassion played a role in it?" Leah was angry. "I'd hunt you down, too!"

"What can be so important that you would be willing to kill a man? What are you protecting?" Jacob asked.

"Ms. Preston, I know that it may be difficult to understand, but we, as Brothers of the Three Crosses, have accepted our role and understand our responsibility to the organization. Margaux knew the consequences of his actions."

"But I'm sure that his six-year-old son did not," Leah countered. She stood by the window with her arms crossed over her chest.

No one spoke.

Garron broke the silence, "Malik, you haven't told us why The Brotherhood was started in the first place."

Malik hesitated and Garron caught him glancing at Leah.

Garron said, "We are all in this together, Malik. Jacob and Leah have each lost someone they loved because of your Brotherhood. They both deserve to know what's going on here."

Malik said, "This is all highly irregular. There are initiation rites and Ms. Preston …" Malik let his voice trail off.

"Don't tell me it's because I'm a woman," Leah said in disbelief.

"We are a 500-year-old *fraternal* order, Ms. Preston."

"Well, your chauvinistic inflexibility and your outdated rituals didn't save your precious order from one of your own initiated brothers," Leah fumed.

Malik did not respond.

"I'd be happy to leave. The truth is that I don't trust you anyway. I'd give you back the map and wipe my hands of this whole mess. I have a good lawyer, I'd be just fine." Garron stood from his chair and took a step toward the door.

"That won't be necessary, Garron." Malik said, "You are correct, you all deserve to know the truth. Ms. Preston, I apologize. And Ms. Preston you were correct. This has everything to do with Babeque."

Leah turned from the window, slowly crossed the room and retook her seat.

Malik told the trio how *The Brotherhood of the Three Crosses* came to be.

"On November 21st, 1492, more than a month after arriving in the Caribbean, Martín Alonso sailed the Pinta north-north-east and away from the fleet. The rewritten log book of Columbus stated that Martín Alonso deliberately disobeyed an order to follow the fleet to the southwest. It was what Pinzón learned from the Taíno natives that caused him to abandon the fleet.

"Columbus made it common practice to take on indigenous guides to help navigate the island shores of the Caribbean. He had placed two such guides on the Pinta. Those Taíno guides told Martín Alonso of an island that held such a great quantity of gold, one merely needed to bend over and scoop the gold up from the earth with his bare hands. Columbus's log referred to the island as Bohio, while other reference material named it Babeque. Pinzón, in want of wealth and family honor, attempted to find Babeque. According to Bartolomé de las Casa's historical account of the voyage, Pinzón found Babeque to be void of any gold. The truth is the knowledge that *The Brotherhood of the Three Crosses* protects, and it is vastly different than that of the history books.

"When the Pinta arrived at Babeque, Martín Alonso took his brother Francisco, Maestro Diego the ship's surgeon, and the two Taínos ashore to lay claim to the island and to do a preliminary search for gold. As the landing party reached shore, they were met by a group of people from a nearby village who saw the ship approach. The guides translated the captain's interest in the island and so the visitors were delivered to the island's *cacique*, or chief. The villagers and the cacique were most generous hosts and Pinzón found them eager to please. The Spanish explorers were viewed as 'gods from the sky' by the island's inhabitants, and were treated as such. Pinzón was encouraged by the gold jewelry of the villagers. However, he was too quickly disappointed. The cacique, whose name was Garacana, explained that Babeque had no gold, and that the gold that was worn on the noses and necks of his people came from other lands, and must be traded for to obtain. The captain was downtrodden. He took a great risk in leaving the fleet, and to come up empty handed was dispiriting. He immediately set back for the Pinta.

"Garacana, through signs and the translation of Pinzón's guides, pleaded for the captain to remain on Babeque. His village had been under constant attack from marauding Caribs, and he begged the captain for his aid in protecting his village. The Caribs were a warring people known for their battle prowess and savagery. They would strike villages throughout the Caribbean, stealing provisions, and taking slaves. The Caribs would take young women for their brides and kill the young men, in effect, robbing a village of a future generation. Garacana saw the Spanish as his opportunity to free his village from the persecution of the Caribs.

"The winds were not favorable for travel, so Pinzón decided that he would leave a group of men overnight, camped on the shores of Babeque to protect Garacana's people from a possible Carib attack. The captain explained to Garacana that once the winds changed he would be leaving Babeque in search of gold, but while he and his men were anchored off shore he would ensure the villagers' safety. Garacana attempted to delay the captain's departure by collecting anything of value from the island and offering it to the Spaniards. Each morning, Pinzón would wake and view from the Pinta, piles of offerings set out on the beach of Babeque. Bundles of cotton, baskets of fruits and vegetables, and a dried gourd filled with the villagers' gold jewelry. On the second morning the offering consisted of more fruit and dried fish. This continued for three more days.

"On the fourth day the winds had changed. Martín Alonso, Francisco, and Maestro Diego went ashore and walked into Garacana's village once again. The captain expressed his gratitude to the cacique for his generosity, but explained that the winds had changed and that the Pinta would set sail. The cacique was deeply saddened and begged Pinzón to stay. The cacique promised more offerings and, through the interpreter, even offered his own daughter to the captain. Martín Alonso expressed his regret, but insisted that he needed to find more gold and treasure. As the guide translated the captain's words, Garacana seemed noticeably relieved. Pinzón assumed that the translation was misunderstood by the chief. He asked the guide to reiterate to the chief that he and his men were leaving immediately. Garacana left the hut quickly. As the guide assured Pinzón that he had translated the captain's desire to set sail without delay, Garacana returned and presented Martín Alonso with a dried gourd that had been plugged and sealed with a dark resin."

Malik leaned forward in his chair. "The contents of that gourd presented to Pinzón more than 500 years ago are why we are here today."

"What was in the gourd?" Leah asked.

"It was something so valuable that it caused the crew of the Pinta to stay anchored off the coast of Babeque for eighteen more days. When Martín Alonso would not be received by the court of Ferdinand and Isabella, on his deathbed he decided, with his brothers, to create *The Brotherhood of the Three Crosses* to protect what he had found on Babeque."

"But what did he find?" Jacob demanded.

Garron said skeptically, "A treasure so great that it needs to be hidden for centuries fits in a gourd?"

Malik bristled at Garron's sarcasm. "The crew spent those eighteen days hauling baskets weaved from palm fronds onto the Pinta."

Leah said, "So those baskets were holding the treasure, and depending on the size of the baskets, we could be talking about hundreds or thousands of gourds."

"Did Martín Alonso's brothers make return trips to Babeque and collect more of the treasure?" Jacob asked.

Malik settled back in his chair. "During those eighteen days the crew of the Pinta had become quite unruly. One crew member had even raped a woman, and when the rape victim's husband confronted the rapist, the crew member killed him. Pinzón made his condolences and apologies to Garacana, and explained to the cacique that the offender had been put to death. Martín Alonso explained that he thought it best that he take his crew and explore neighboring islands for gold to diffuse the situation. The cacique was distraught. He lived in fear of the Caribs and begged the captain to stay. But the captain could not be persuaded. In order to guarantee Pinzón's return, Garacana said he would continue to fill a basket a day until the captain's return. The Pinta set sail and explored several more islands, but the search proved fruitless. When Martín Alonso returned to Babeque, he was not prepared for what he found. Black smoke was visible as the Pinta approached the island. On the beach where Pinzón expected to find the offerings, he found the cacique's body tied to a stake above a pile of ashes. Garacana had been roasted over the offering baskets."

Leah said, "That's terrible."

"It was written that Martín Alonso wept over the dead chief's body. No one was found alive in the village. It appeared that the Caribs had annihilated the village, burning everything and everyone in a massive blaze. The captain ordered his men to bury all of the villagers. During the long hours of this macabre task, a dugout canoe of Taíno fishermen arrived at Babeque. They offered the captain more bad news. The Santa María had run aground and sank. Martín Alonso knew that he must rejoin the Niña to help Columbus limp back to Spain. The two ships met and evenly distributed cargo between them, so that neither ship was overladen. Then both ships set sail east across the Atlantic, only to be caught in a hurricane and separated once again. But each ship survived the storm, with the Pinta arriving in Spain ahead of the Niña. Martín Alonso made a request for an audience with the king and queen, but they would not respond. Ferdinand and Isabella waited for Columbus's return. They only wanted to learn of the expedition's success from their appointed admiral. Martín Alonso returned to Palos and died just a few days later, after meeting with his brothers."

"What happened to the baskets of treasure that were onboard the Pinta?" Jacob asked.

"Martín Alonso had them spirited away after being rejected by the Spanish sovereigns," Malik answered.

"But they must have spent it, or used it to finance additional voyages or investments, right? That can't be what you are still protecting," Leah suggested.

Malik shook his head. "The Pinzón brothers agreed that the treasure should remain hidden until the time was right for it to be known to the world."

Garron sat forward in his chair. "You don't know what the treasure is, do you?"

Jacob said, "That can't be. You must know what all of this is for. Murphy had to have known what he was giving up his life for."

Malik was slow to respond. "This is not the first time that The Brotherhood has been threatened. About one hundred and fifty years ago, when our country was at civil war, the treasure was nearly lost. After the war, The Brotherhood decided that the only way to keep the treasure truly secure was to limit the amount of knowledge passed on to the next generation of *Vicari*. Since then, no one member of The Brotherhood has the collected knowledge of the past. We each have our piece of the puzzle, with no one having the collective whole. What I have shared with you is the common knowledge of our organization. In our tradition, each *Magister* would then pass down his specific knowledge to his *Vicarius*."

Jacob was stunned. "You're kidding me. You don't even know what you are protecting?"

"It must be difficult for an outsider looking in to understand. Each of my brethren is proud to have been selected to carry on our tradition. Each of us had been groomed from a very early age to understand and appreciate the value of what he had been chosen to do. My father instilled in me a greater sense of purpose, and I am doing the same for my son. We know what is expected of us, and we are willing to give our lives for that conviction," Malik answered.

Garron stared at Malik in awe. "You sound like any number of religious zealots or cult leaders. This is ridiculous. Do you have any proof for any of these claims, or is it just hearsay, oral tradition passed down from one nut to another?"

Malik spat back, "You will not dishonor our traditions or the memories of those men who came before us."

Garron stood. "Proof Malik, do you have proof?"

Malik stood as well. The men faced off. The pocket doors to the parlor slid open and Mackenzie entered, he had obviously heard the two men arguing. Jacob met the man as he crossed the room. The tension was palpable.

Malik raised a hand, signaling Mackenzie to halt his advance.

"Of course it is difficult for you to understand," Malik continued, "Yes Garron, I do have proof." He walked to a wall, opened a panel that was hidden in the wall, and withdrew an overstuffed envelope.

Malik handed the envelope to Jacob. "This is for you. Inside you will find a letter from Ian, as well as the letters from each of the last Archivists

to their Successors over the last 150 years. Of course, this letter substanti-
ates my tale only to a certain point. So if faith is not enough, you should
also remember that as *Chartophylax* you have our entire archive as proof."

Garron knew that the letter would be enough for Jacob to accept the
lunacy Malik had proposed, but the nagging ache at the pit of Garron's
stomach would not abate until he examined the archive.

Garron said, "I need some air."

"Bryan, would you see Garron out, please," Malik said.

"I don't need an escort."

"I'm afraid that I must insist," Malik answered.

Garron knew that he had not given Malik reason to trust him and con-
ceded to the escort. Mackenzie led Garron down the hallway toward the
back of the house. A door stood partially open in the hall. Garron caught a
glimpse of surveillance monitors aglow in the dark room. Mackenzie had
been monitoring the parlor's conversation from within that room. They
stepped through the kitchen and out the back door.

***

Garron stood in the backyard overlooking the moonlit Matanzas River. The
air was still heavy with humidity. Bryan Mackenzie stood just behind him.
Garron felt a festering animosity for his escort.

"You were listening in on our conversation," Garron said over his
shoulder.

Mackenzie did not respond.

Garron spoke without turning to face the man, "So you're the
Custodian."

"I am the *Custos*," Mackenzie answered in his Boston accent.

"Right, the *Custos*. That translates to …"

"The Guardian, I'm in charge of security."

"Security, how's that going for you? Not too well, I'd say."

"How's your sobriety going for you? Not too fucking well either,
huh?"

Garron spun and clinched his fist, but paused when he saw the man's
gun in his left hand. Mackenzie watched Garron's eye take in the gun and

when their eyes met, Mackenzie winked. Garron clenched his jaw and turned back slowly toward the view of the river.

"Malik said that your brother died in an accident."

"He said that he initially thought it was an accident, but I always knew that it wasn't. My brother's truck was found turned over in a canal, he drowned. They said that he had been drinking."

"But you believed …"

Bryan interrupted, "I *knew* that someone staged the accident. Liam hadn't touched a drink in over fifteen years. He was proud of his sobriety."

Garron thought about the sherry he drank while in the parlor. "People slip."

"That's what Malik said, too. He didn't want to think that someone had gotten to The Brotherhood. It wasn't until someone mailed me Liam's fifteen-year AA chip in an unmarked envelope two weeks ago that he finally believed what I knew all along."

Garron had not used Alcoholics Anonymous to quit drinking. Veronica had helped him through his recovery, but he knew the importance of the coins.

Mackenzie pulled the coin from his pocket and flipped it to Garron. "That's a vintage bronze chip that Liam's sponsor gave him when he reached his fifteenth anniversary last November. He carried it with him everywhere."

Garron examined the coin by the moonlight. He could read the serenity prayer and the XV on the coin's faces. The coin was well worn from years of handling. Garron suddenly felt ill. He turned away from the house and vomited.

Mackenzie said, "I knew that you'd understand."

Garron turned back to the man. He could see the pain in his eyes. He approached the man and handed the bronze coin back to him. Garron said, "I'm sorry."

Mackenzie took the coin and nodded.

They went back inside.

***

Mackenzie and Garron joined Malik and Leah in the drawing room. They had left Jacob alone with Murphy's letter. They sat in near silence for forty minutes until the parlor doors slid open.

Jacob's eyes betrayed the smile he set on his face.

"Garron, could you join me?" Jacob asked.

Garron stepped across the room, catching Leah's eye. She nodded slightly. Garron stepped into the parlor. Jacob closed the doors behind him.

Garron held up a hand silencing Jacob before he could speak.

He hugged Jacob and whispered. "There are cameras in this room, I don't know about audio."

Jacob looked around the room. He whispered, "Read the letter on the desk."

Garron read Murphy's letter.

Jacob,

I had hoped to be beside you when you learned of The Brotherhood. It is unfortunate that I had to compress centuries of tradition into a short note.

Please know that I am proud to have you as my Vicarius, and I have never before had a friend as great as you.

You can trust Malik and Bryan, they are good men. But do not share this letter with them.

I have been combing through the archives, which are now yours, but my search is for the whole truth. I have taken a vow to protect the traditions of The Brotherhood, but with Liam's death, I felt that it was time to know exactly what we are protecting. Do not discuss this with anyone inside or outside The Brotherhood. Do not take this warning lightly.

I hope that you found what I had left for you in my home. I believe it to be the key to understanding this mystery. With it in mind, start your own search of the archives and finish what I have started.

Good Luck! Take care of yourself, and know that the work you are doing is extremely important.

It was signed with love, by Ian Murphy. Garron felt tears come to his eyes as he now better understood the relationship that Jacob and Murphy shared. Garron wiped the tears away.

Jacob stepped in close to Garron and whispered, "Will you help me with this?"

Garron asked, "With the archives?"

Jacob nodded.

Garron could now see the determination on his brother's face, and knew that he could not say no. He nodded his assent.

Jacob picked up his red backpack, opened the parlor doors and addressed Malik. "I would like to see the archives now."

"But we are moving them in the morning to our new facility. We will have a state of the art viewing room and sensor protected vault to house the archives. Tomorrow would be better."

"Malik, I am your new *Chartophylax* and I am requesting to view the archives."

Malik hesitated only a moment. "Of course, my brother, we are securing them in the garage for the night, we did not unload them from the trucks."

The group moved through the house and to the garage, which was connected by a service entrance at the far end of the house.

Leah asked, as they made their way through the rooms, "This house is beautiful, who does it belong to?"

"It was my wife's and my home. Since her passing and Abram's start at college, it hasn't felt like home, so I am in the process of selling this property. I've been staying in a small cottage a little further south."

They entered the garage. The limousine and two vans sat in the otherwise vacant garage. Mackenzie unlocked the vans and opened the rear doors revealing the stacks of metal boxes. The boxes resembled large security deposit boxes with electronic keypads.

"With the garage being air-conditioned and the documents secured in the lock boxes, we thought that they would be safe in here for the night," Malik said.

Jacob set his backpack down. "Garron has agreed to become my *Vicarius*. We would like some time alone with the archives. We will have everything ready to be moved by seven o'clock tomorrow morning."

Malik was taken aback and met Garron's eye. "This is most irregular."

Jacob countered, "Yes it is, and it is time for us to adapt so that we can better face this challenge."

Malik stood quietly.

"If we are to help you, Garron and I need to familiarize ourselves with all of this." Jacob swept his hand over the boxes. "Murphy trusted me. I need for you to do the same. And don't worry about Leah. I don't keep any secrets from her anyway."

Garron watched Malik look to Mackenzie, and to Garron's surprise, the man nodded his approval. Then Garron thought he saw through the man's thick red beard the semblance of a smile. Malik and Mackenzie turned and left the garage and the contents of the archive to their new Archivist.

Jacob began to unload the boxes from the van. "Garron, it's going to be a long night. Did you see that patio furniture we passed on the way to the garage?"

Garron understood Jacob's meaning and said, "I'm on it."

After several trips from the service entrance to the garage, Garron finally slid the table and chairs into place near the van. Jacob had already opened several of the boxes and had pulled out multiple vinyl folios. The folios were all identical, except for the label displaying the years covered by the documents inside. Beside the date, the folio also had an elaborate cross and small bird stamped on the cover. Jacob handed a folio to Garron.

"How did you know the code to enter into the keypad?" Garron asked his brother.

"It took several tries. I started with Murphy's birthday, his address, his phone number, even his social security number."

Garron raised an eyebrow.

"I did a lot of the paperwork for the dive business," he said in explanation. "Then I tried the year he entered The Brotherhood according to the letter he left for me, nothing. And then 1507 for, well you know why, and I still struck out. Now don't be offended, but then I thought of you."

"What do you mean?"

"I thought of Murphy's favorite drink," Jacob said with a stiff smile.

Garron soured slightly, "Yeah, what a man drinks is important to him."

"Exactly, and I was thinking about the last couple of years when Murphy would usually end his day with the same drink. And that was also when he would start rambling on about old maps and such. Only he wasn't rambling, he was trying to teach me something. Murphy said that he and his uncle used to have similar conversations over the same glass of bourbon."

"What bourbon?" Garron asked.

"1792 Ridgemont Reserve, and it worked."

Garron said sarcastically, "Glad that I could help, but I was a scotch man."

Garron asked for the envelope containing the string of letters from Jacob's predecessors. Except for Murphy, each Archivist had written relatively the same introduction to The Brotherhood's archives. Murphy seemed to be the only one to have suggested discovering the true nature of the treasure that Malik had discussed. Murphy understood the danger The Brotherhood was facing; the extermination of the brethren meant the loss of the treasure for eternity.

Garron set the letters aside and opened the first of his metal lock boxes. Inside were neatly filed vinyl folios approximately five inches thick and a pair of white gloves. Each folio was labeled with a date range, and each had the same elaborate cross and a small bird on the cover's upper right corner.

Garron was examining a folio labeled, 1640-1655. Each document was embossed with the same cross and bird that adorned the folio's cover. The documents were in Spanish. Garron's Spanish was poor at best, but he determined that the contents consisted of letters, passenger manifests, cargo manifests, and land holdings. He said, "With these being in Spanish, this will be slow going."

Jacob said, "There should be an English translation at the end of the folio, at least there were in these two."

Garron turned the folio to the last page and found an English translation of a cargo manifest from 1655. He read each line carefully, twice, and then realized that he had no idea what he was looking for. Garron looked over the number of boxes stacked near the van and beside the table. He sighed. English translations or not, Garron knew that it was going to be another very long night.

***

After three hours of research, Leah stood and stretched.

"I need something to drink, do you boys need anything?" She asked.

Garron rubbed his eyes. "Coffee would be great. I'll come along, I could use a break myself."

"I'll take a cup," Jacob said without looking up from his folio.

Garron followed Leah into the kitchen. To their surprise there was already a hot pot of coffee waiting on the kitchen counter. So they began to search the cabinets for mugs. Mackenzie entered the room from the video screen room, holding a mug of coffee.

He said, "Can I help you?"

"Bryan, hi, we were wondering if we could have some of your coffee. We all need a little pick-me-up," Leah said.

Without a word he walked to a cabinet near the refrigerator and pulled out three coffee mugs and set them next to the coffee maker.

Garron asked, "Do you have surveillance cameras in the garage, too?"

Bryan grinned and said in his heavy accent, "Just overlooking the entrances, don't worry I'm not watching you. I'm just keeping an eye on the grounds, watching the perimeter."

Garron wasn't sure if he believed him.

Leah handed Garron a mug of coffee while she went to the refrigerator for cream. On the side of the mug were the same elaborate cross and small bird that adorned the folios.

"What's with the cross that resembles a green snowflake?" Garron asked Bryan.

"It's our insignia, the emblem of The Brotherhood. It's an eight-pointed cross."

"But it's only two intersecting crosses, not three," Leah said, examining her mug.

"The significance is in the eight points. It resembles the green Avis Cross of the Knights of St. Benedict of Aviz, an order from the twelfth century in Portugal. The Pinzóns liked the wordplay when they adopted it for our Brotherhood."

Leah asked, "Wordplay?"

"In Latin, avis means bird," Bryan answered.

Garron was perplexed. He knitted his brow.

"So foreign languages are not your strong suit? Pinzón is Spanish for chaffinch, a small songbird," Bryan explained.

"So, you're not just muscle, you surprise me Mackenzie." Garron laughed.

Bryan smiled. "I have to get back to the monitors. There's more coffee in the pantry if you need to make another pot."

***

Back in the garage, Leah handed Jacob a coffee mug.

"That was fast," Jacob said, sipping from his mug.

"Mackenzie had a pot waiting for us," Garron said.

Jacob was surprised, "He didn't seem so hospitable earlier."

"He's not so bad. His anger is understandable, considering the loss of his brother. He's just not sure who to trust, sound familiar?" Garron punched Jacob lightly in the arm.

"Are you making friends, big brother?"

"I'm just saying that this is much more complicated than I might have thought originally."

"And Bryan's more complicated too; did you know that he's familiar with Latin and Spanish?" Leah added.

Jacob smiled. "Maybe he could help us make sense of some of this." He pushed a folio across the table. "I mean, this is all very interesting, but it pretty much looks the same."

Leah and Garron joined Jacob at the table and discussed what each had read so far. Cargo manifests were common to all of their folios. It seemed that The Brotherhood first set up shop in Jamaica in 1509, believing that they should be near the treasure and at a distance from the Spanish Monarchy. The Brotherhood had created its own smuggling network of trade ships from its base in Jamaica. The monarchy attempted to account for every item loaded onto a Spanish ship crossing the Atlantic, but smuggling was common. Anything of value was taxed by the Spanish crown, so The Brotherhood mastered the art of smuggling to secure great wealth for their future. In the financial reports Leah had read, The Brotherhood had amassed a fortune with an overall worth near 100 billion dollars.

"Even the most recent reports, written by Malik, show financial growth in a shaky global economy. It seems that Malik knows how to make money," Leah said.

Garron said, "Maybe that's the real treasure, maybe that's what Anton wants to get his hands on."

They all sat quietly for several minutes considering Garron's suggestion.

"I found a few letters that reference the search for a map dated between 1504 and 1506. The correspondence was between an un-named Guardian in Jamaica and an Italian named Gianotto Niccolini," Jacob said.

Garron emptied his coffee mug. "One of our maps?"

"I think so. It was finally discovered in St. Die, France. The Guardian at the time hired ten men to search Western Europe for a map that was said to have been stolen by Dutch privateers. The map was said to have vital importance to The Brotherhood, and that it had once belonged to Martín Alonso Pinzón. The letters are cryptic, but with the map being found in the same city where Ringman and Waldseemüller were creating their map, I'd say that the two maps are related."

"Maybe Pinzón's portolan *was* used as a reference guide in creating the 1507 map. Waldseemüller seemed to have created a map that was ahead of its time, maybe that's because he used a map of the Caribbean created by Pinzón that was yet unknown," Leah proposed.

"That makes some sense. The correspondence I read from Jamaica specifically said that the map was drawn by Martín Alonso's own hand," Jacob confirmed.

Garron stared at the eight-pointed green cross on his empty mug. There were two maps of interest now: the Pinzón portolan and the map referenced in the Jamaica letters, a map drawn by Pinzón. The map that they had examined did not point to the location of a treasure, but maybe this newly mentioned map would.

Garron suddenly shouted, "A map drawn by Pinzón!"

Leah and Jacob were startled by Garron's outburst.

"Earlier I read a cargo manifest for a vessel sailing from Jamaica that referenced something that caught my attention." Garron found the 1640–1655 folio.

He continued as he flipped the pages, "It didn't make any sense at the time, but maybe it's what we're looking for."

Garron read through several of the translated cargo manifests until he found the one he wanted. He scanned it and then smiled; he handed the folio to his brother.

Garron said, "This is a cargo manifest from a ship sailing from Jamaica to Cuba in 1655. Read line 16."

Jacob read aloud, "Bird drawing."

Jacob looked at the smile on Garron's face and said, "Bird drawing? I don't understand."

"I could be wrong, but you have to agree that it is an odd item to warrant a line on a cargo manifest, right? That's why it stood out when I read it earlier. I think this might be it. I think this might be what we are looking for." Garron was excited.

"I'm not following you Gar."

Garron's smile grew. He lifted his mug and tapped the green cross, looking directly at Leah. She thought back to Mackenzie explaining the significance of the cross while she was pouring coffee in the kitchen. Suddenly her eyes opened wide.

"Pinzón is Spanish for chaffinch, a small songbird." Leah's enthusiasm matched Garron's.

***

Garron saw the confusion on Jacob's face. He said, "Bird drawing; pinzón drawing; a drawing made by Pinzón."

Jacob said, "Okay, but a drawing is not a map. Don't you think that's stretching it a bit?"

"Maybe it's a poor translation, or maybe it's a code so that the uninitiated reading the manifest wouldn't know that the drawing was really a map," Garron argued.

Leah asked, "Any idea why it was moved from Jamaica to Cuba?"

Jacob answered, "According to some of the letters I read from the early eighteenth century folios, The Brotherhood set up their headquarters in Havana, Cuba. There was mention of Jamaica falling to the British."

"So our brethren were holding the treasure map in Jamaica until the British come knocking, then they moved the map to Havana and set up shop there," Garron said.

"But not for long," Leah said holding a translation of a letter in her hand. "According to this letter, Havana fell to the British in 1762."

"Is there mention of the map?" Garron asked.

"Not in this letter, but it mentions a ship leaving port just before the British take control of the city, a ship named Sprightly."

Garron knelt beside Leah and asked over her shoulder, "Do we have a cargo manifest for the Sprightly?"

Leah quickly paged through the translated pages. She said, "Yes we do."

She read down the list. The items listed were consistent with the period: cotton, lumber, tobacco, bolts of fabric, slaves and so on. Then she reached line twenty-two.

"Here it is. Line twenty-two is our bird drawing. And look at the destination port."

Garron read aloud, "St. Augustine."

"It must be our map. Murphy must have found it," Jacob said.

Garron smiled. "I don't think that we can make that assumption until we scour the rest of these archives. You've examined Murphy's map, it doesn't point to a treasure." Garron surveyed the pile of documents that lay before them. He said, "At least we have a better idea of what we're looking for. We have a few more hours before sunrise, let's get busy."

They were now able to concentrate on letters and manifests dated between 1762, the arrival of the map in St. Augustine, and 1865, the conclusion of the Civil War, because the map was not known to exist in the modern Brotherhood.

After twenty minutes, Jacob said, "I found a letter, dated 1763, that says The Brotherhood decided not to relocate after Spain lost Florida."

Jacob explained that in an attempt to regain control of Havana, Charles III, king of Spain, traded his holdings in Florida to the English crown to regain Cuba. With Spain in bankruptcy and England becoming an empirical powerhouse, The Brotherhood decided to remain in St. Augustine. *The Brotherhood of the Three Crosses* left behind its Spanish roots.

"That sounds promising," Leah said joyfully.

The trio dove back into the archives with added fervor. After another hour they had combed through every document between their target date ranges. They did not discover a map hidden in the folios.

"I think that this points strongly to our map being the right map," Jacob said.

Garron was frustrated by his brother's fixation with Murphy's map. He laid the map out on the table for further review. They discussed how the Pinzón portolan appeared to be source material for the 1507 map; the likeness was uncanny. But there weren't any indicators pointing to where the treasure could be found.

Garron said, "I think we have to consider that there is still another map yet to be found. Our map is historically valuable, but it is not unique. Pinzón's portolan is identical to the same geographic region on the Waldseemüller map. Neither map hides the existence of Babeque. The island is easily located on both maps, and neither map points to the treasure."

Leah and Jacob nodded.

"We have to keep looking," Garron suggested.

With regret, they expanded their date ranges. Garron began reading a folio dated to the Civil War, Jacob opened a folio dated prior to 1763, and Leah looked through a modern folio. The early morning sky had begun to brighten.

***

The door leading to the house opened and Malik stepped into the garage. He paused just inside the door.

"I have breakfast started, will you join me?" Malik called across the garage.

The researchers all murmured their agreement, pried themselves from their chairs, yawned and stretched. They moved, heavy-footed, toward the kitchen.

Garron went directly to the coffee pot and poured himself a mug of coffee. The smell of sausage tickled his palate. Malik had prepared a heaping stack of pancakes, and Garron wasted no time forking a few on a plate along with several links of sausage. On the table he had his choice of honey, maple syrup, or blueberry jam. The pitcher of syrup was warm, so he dosed his short stack and then dug in.

Leah decided on blueberry jam. She took the seat beside Garron.

She said to Malik, "Thank you, this looks delicious."

"It is delicious. Malik, thanks," Garron added between bites.

"You are very welcome." Malik smiled graciously. "Jacob, you are not having breakfast?"

Jacob was standing near the kitchen window sipping from his coffee mug and looking out over the river.

"Looks like a beautiful morning to be on the water," he said in response.

Malik stood beside Jacob and rested a hand on Jacob's shoulder.

"Ian would have loved to have been the one to have introduced you to the archives. He was proud of his work and would have liked to have you there to share his discoveries and his passion for our history."

Jacob met Malik's eyes. "Thank you."

Malik nodded and patted Jacob's shoulder. "Now eat some pancakes before they get cold."

Jacob fixed himself a plate, topped off his coffee, and took a seat next to Leah at the table.

"Has your study of the archives been rewarding?" Malik asked.

Garron pushed away his empty plate and sat back in his chair rubbing his stomach. "That was just what I needed." Garron continued, "I'm reading the diary of the Archivist who was stationed at Fort Marion during the Civil War."

Malik nodded. "Those were trying times for, not only our country, but also for our Brotherhood. The Archivist was the only Union sympathizer in The Brotherhood at the time. Of course, I have not read the diary, but that era in our Order is legendary. That is when our Brethren decided to change the initiation rites and segment the Order to protect the treasure and each other."

"So the division of our country caused a rift in The Brotherhood as well?" Jacob asked.

Malik smiled. "Sometimes we forget because of the number of northerners moving into the state, but Florida is part of the south. And Florida did indeed secede from the Union. Our poor Archivist was left completely alone to hold Fort Marion for the Union."

"Is Fort Marion still standing?" Garron asked.

"Yes indeed. It is the fort that you saw near Old City. It is known by its original Spanish name, Castillo de San Marcos."

"They left one Union solider to hold an entire fort on his own?" Leah asked.

"The way I understand it, those men who did not desert the Federal Army when Florida seceded were called into service further north. Florida was not an immediate threat to the Union. But they did not want to leave the fort completely unmanned, so they left our poor Brother there to man the gates, alone," Malik answered.

Leah asked, "So you do discuss, between Brothers, what is in the archives?"

Malik set to brewing another pot of coffee.

"We do, but the Archivist is the only one with access to the documents. When Charles or Ian would come across something of historical significance during their cataloguing or preservation of materials, they would share it with us."

Garron said, "I want you to know that I'm in this until the end, but I am still having trouble understanding why you do what you do, without knowing what the treasure is."

"And you mentioned that it was decided that when the world was ready, then the secret would be revealed. If you don't know what the treasure is, how can you know when the world would be ready to receive it?" Jacob added.

Malik finally took a seat. "That is something that every one of our Brethren has had to struggle with for more than 140 years."

"So how do you justify it?" Garron asked.

"Faith, Garron, I simply have faith that in time all will reveal itself."

"Blind faith can be dangerous," Garron reflected.

Leah said, "How do you know that now is not the right time? With the challenges that you have had to face recently, couldn't you argue that now is indeed the right time?"

"That is something that has crossed my mind. I have always believed that the Archivist is the key to The Brotherhood's existence. The answer has to be in the archives, but it remains hidden."

"So Archivists have pursued the treasure?" Jacob asked.

"How could they not? They have The Brotherhood's entire archives at their fingertips, it would be tempting. Although, that possibility has never been discussed, so if Murphy was looking for the treasure in our archives I would not know. And I do not want to know."

"You wouldn't want to know?" Leah was concerned.

"Consider this; every Archivist since 1865 pursued the treasure, and when he discovered the secret to the treasure in his research, he decided not to share his find with anyone. There must be a valid reason for keeping it a secret, right? Or maybe there has never been an Archivist yet to discover the treasure. Then, in that case, it must not yet be time for the treasure to be revealed."

The table reflected on what Malik had said.

"Strangely enough, that makes sense," Garron acknowledged.

"Be careful, Dad might have you drinking the Kool-Aid next." Abram walked into the kitchen.

Abram was a tall, lean young man who carried himself with the grace of an athlete. He resembled his father, although he was more handsome.

Malik stood and asked his son, "Would you like some pancakes?"

"No, Mackenzie and I are going snooping to see if we can learn if Anton is in town," Abram answered, pouring himself a mug of coffee.

Mackenzie now entered the kitchen. "With all that muscle that Anton is sure to keep around him, it should have caught some attention."

"Are you sure that is wise?" Malik asked Mackenzie.

"He knows too much about us, Malik. I'm not sitting around waiting for his next move."

Abram added, "Besides you have your new Archivist, he and his friends can help you move the documents to their new home."

"I'm just not sure that we should stray too far from one another with Anton hunting us," Malik argued.

"You trust me as Guardian to keep us secure, right?"

Malik nodded.

"Well then, let me do my job. And don't worry, I'll keep your boy safe." Bryan punched Abram in the arm. He said, "Come on kid."

Mackenzie and Abram left the kitchen. Garron heard the front door open and close a minute later.

Leah said, "Your son is a very determined young man."

"That stubbornness translates well in his studies, but it does test my patience," Malik admitted.

"What's he studying?" Leah asked.

"He's studying medicine at Duke University."

"You must be proud."

"I am, but recently it is not only physical distance that separates us. He has been quiet and elusive as he prepares to return to school."

Garron said, "But it seems that those two are close." He nodded toward the front door.

"Bryan seems to understand my son quite well, which is more than I can say for myself," Malik answered.

"I'm sure that every father in America can say the same about his own son," Leah offered.

"Maybe, but since Charles's death, Abram seems to have lost faith in The Brotherhood, and in me."

"I can see how that could affect a young man. He is probably worried about your well-being as a result," Garron said.

Malik reflected, "If I had to be honest, the misunderstandings between Abram and me began while his mother was ill. He believed that I was spending too much time with The Brotherhood and not enough time with my wife." He paused. "He may have been right."

Jacob rose from the table.

"Malik, I would love more time with the archives, when do you plan to move them?"

"I have a property in Jacksonville that has been prepared to hold our archives. It is a relatively short drive." Malik bowed slightly. "How much time would you like *Chartophylax?*"

Jacob smiled at the gesture. "As long as you can give me. In a few hours I will have finished the folio I started earlier."

"Then go, I'll clean up here. Afterwards, I have several phone calls to make. I'll come to you when I have finished."

"Thank you Malik." Jacob rinsed his mug in the sink and made his way towards the garage.

Leah said, "Why don't you join your brother? I'll help Malik here in the kitchen."

Garron nodded. "Thanks again for breakfast."

Malik smiled and bowed again.

Garron followed his brother into the garage.

***

Garron had not told Malik that the diary of Ordinance Sergeant Horatio Douglas had been notated in another hand. Someone had read the diary and noted pages of interest in the diary's front cover and had written notes in the margins. Garron picked the next date on that list and continued reading the diary. He believed that he was following clues left by Murphy.

The diary spoke to troubled times in St. Augustine. There was a true division in the community over the discussion of secession: Federalist vs. Secessionists. Many of St. Augustine's well-to-do had acquired their wealth from material trades with the northern coastal states. Florida at the time was very much a frontier state. An embargo by the north left the settlers wanting for basic amenities such as textiles, lumber, kitchen implements, guns, and ammunition. The threat of losing those supply lines resulted in an exodus from the city.

Sergeant Douglas's diary covered a period of seven months: July 1860 to January 1861. The entries of interest to the diary's previous reader were those dated after December 14th, 1860.

15 December 1860

An assembly gathered today at the Court House to decide who should be sent to the State Convention. This Christmas is overshadowed. Secession seems imminent. I am without my family for the first time since Willie came into our world. Claret has taken him to Trenton to stay with her people.

There is tension between our men. There are men who do not know whether to stand with their State or their Country. I will pray of a concession that will keep our Country united.

24 December 1860

Mr. Solana and Mr. Mays were selected to go to Tallahassee. I am afraid that secession is a part of each man's character.

I miss my wife and son. Claret has sent word that she made it to Trenton safely. She writes of unrest and the talk of war circulating in Trenton. I pray tonight for peace. It seems that it is cold in Trenton; Claret has grown accustomed to the warm Florida winters.

30 December 1860

I have volunteered to stay behind. Our men have been ordered elsewhere. I am all alone in the fort tonight. It took my full intelligence to convince the Lt. to have me stay behind; I could not tell him of the true reason. I will begin work tomorrow to secure the drawings.

3 January 1861

In Tallahassee, delegates meet today to discuss secession. How would I vote? Free coloreds would dissolve the way of life for so many. Quite a bit of coin is made on the backs of the coloreds. But they are men, even if they are not the same as us.

I remember my friend Waldo at these troubled times. I was surprised to receive a copy of his book yesterday. Dockt. Brady told me that supply lines have not yet been cut. There is an understanding in Waldo that exceeds most men. I still recall our visits with Achille as young men, discussing all matters over wine. '26 seems so long ago. How I enjoyed those days of promise.

8 January 1861

I feel as though God himself has saved me! The Secessionists marched on the fort last night. A group of men I know marched armed as I slept. There was a threat of violence. I was left with little option but to surrender. But I did require Col. Craig to provide me with a receipt for the fort and the contents.

I pray that the plaster has dried in the Gate where I hid the drawings.

Dockt. Brady gave me shelter; we are of like mind.

10 January 1861

Florida has seceded. There was great celebration by many in town today. Word of secession reached us quickly. The National flag of Florida is flying in the square. Many of my like-minded friends have left town. I still stay with Dockt. Brady.

I continue to read Waldo's book. It gives me reprieve. Its subject reminds me of talks we had in '26. We discussed Nature supplying us with all that we needed. We spoke of Nature having an order and balance that man needs to understand. I believe that he would have made an excellent Brother.

I quote him; "If, in the least particular, one could derange the order of Nature, who would accept the gift of life?"

"Jacob, I think that you should read this." Garron handed his brother the diary then joined him; looking down over his shoulder he pointed to the entries dated 30 December and 8 January.

"Do you think that these entries are referring to the bird drawing mentioned in the manifests?"

Garron said, "I can't be sure, but it's possible. I've read the majority of the diary and it seems that we have a member of The Brotherhood hiding drawings in the fort with concern for their safety. It could be our map."

Jacob reread the diary entries and flipped the page to see that the last entry was dated 10 January. He thought for a moment.

He asked, "Do you think that the map could still be in the fort?"

"I don't know, but this sergeant was part of the last generation of Brothers who knew the secret. Maybe they literally left it buried." Garron shrugged his shoulders. "Or maybe he returned to the fort and dug it up, although there is nothing in the remainder of this folio that mentions that."

Jacob held up the diary and said, "And there won't be mention of it in more recent documents because this is when they changed the rules of the game."

"What if the sergeant died in the war and that's why the location of the map was lost? That could be the real reason that later generations lost track of the treasure."

Leah entered the garage. "You two look like the cat that swallowed the canary."

Jacob said, "We might be onto something."

Jacob and Garron discussed their theory and showed Leah the diary entries. She sat contemplatively for a long moment.

Finally she said, "I never really believed that the earlier generation of the Order was acting solely out of altruism. I just don't have that kind of faith in people. It makes more sense to me that it was lost as a casualty of war."

"What if …" Garron was interrupted by the garage door opening.

***

Bryan Mackenzie ducked under the opening garage door. He quickly surveyed the garage. He was wild eyed.

"Where's Malik?" Mackenzie spat the question.

Leah answered immediately, "He was in the kitchen."

Mackenzie rushed toward the kitchen with Leah, Jacob, and Garron close behind.

In the empty kitchen Mackenzie called out, "Malik!"

Malik stepped from the hall. With a glance at Mackenzie, he knew something was wrong.

"Have you heard from Abram?"

"Why would I hear from my son, he was with you?"

"Anton has him."

Malik was stunned. "Bryan, tell me what happened."

"I dropped Abram off at the Gypsy Cab Company to talk with that hostess he was dating. He wanted to see if she had noticed anyone poking around. I went over the bridge to see if the guys at the pub knew anything.

I had a quick bite to eat and talked the boys up a bit. When I went back to pick him up, Chloe said that Abram had only been inside for a couple of minutes when some big guys who were eating at a corner booth noticed him. They all went out front, without saying a word to her, and then they left in a dark SUV."

Malik fell into a kitchen chair. He pulled out his cell phone and dialed Abram; the call went straight to voicemail. Malik withered in the chair.

Leah asked, "What do we do?"

Mackenzie stepped into the room with the security monitors. He withdrew an automatic rifle.

"I'm going to find him."

Jacob said, "I'm going with you."

Mackenzie nodded his thanks to the new Archivist.

"Where do we start?" Garron acknowledged his desire to help.

The three men headed toward the door.

"Wait. I think that you need to think this through," Leah pleaded. "Come up with a plan of attack before marching off."

The men did not respond.

"Jacob, wait!" Leah screamed. "What if they are just trying to separate us so that we are left vulnerable?"

They stopped inches from the door.

Malik's cell phone rang.

Chapter 6

MALIK FUMBLED WITH the phone, he seemed to have lost all fine motor skills.

He finally held the phone to his ear and answered quickly, "Abram?"

The voice on the other end of the phone said, "Mr. Qwari, we have not met as of yet, but I knew your father. My name is Anton Margaux."

Malik held a finger to his lips to silence the room, and then hit the speaker button on the cell phone.

Malik asked, "What have you done with my son?"

"Your son is fine Mr. Qwari. He is with me right now. Would you like to speak with him?"

Abram's voice came over the phone, "Dad? Dad, I'm very sorry."

"Abram, are you alright? Have they harmed you?"

"No, I'm okay. I'm just real sorry Dad."

"It will be fine son. Where are you?"

Anton's voice came back on the line, "Mr. Qwari, I would like to return your son to you, but there is something that I need in return."

Malik trembled. "If you hurt him, I swear …"

Anton interrupted, "That is completely up to you Mr. Qwari, and if you follow my instructions to the letter then all will be as it was."

"What do you want?"

"You know what I want Mr. Qwari, I want The Brotherhood's archives."

"I can not …"

"Malik, is your pledge to The Brotherhood more important than the life of your only son?"

Malik struggled with his answer. He began to speak several times. He finally said, "Tell me where and when."

"I knew that you would make the correct choice. I have a farm in Volusia County. I believe that you know the place. The Brotherhood gave it to my mother after they killed my father. I guess that I held on to it for nostalgia's sake, sentimental I guess."

"When?" Malik bit his lip.

"By the end of the day. How much time do you need to gather all of your material? And please remember that I want it all."

Malik answered, "Nine or ten hours."

"Then let us say at sunset, which gives you more than eleven hours to collect everything, load it onto those vans of yours, and deliver it to my farm." Anton paused. "Have all of your brethren who are listening help you with your delivery. I want them all there. It can be the final meeting of *The Brotherhood of the Three Crosses*. It will be quite an historic event, don't you think?"

Then the phone went dead.

"We're not handing over the archives," Mackenzie said.

"I don't know what else to do Bryan. I cannot leave my son in that madman's hands," Malik countered.

"He mentioned a farm. Let's go get Abram," Jacob offered.

"Exactly, let's go get the kid back!" Mackenzie slapped the stock of his weapon.

"I will not put my son at risk by riding in there like some cowboy with guns blazing," Malik said.

Leah was the voice of reason. "Let's just take a step back and gather our thoughts."

Jacob said, "Giving up the archives is not an option."

"Jay, you've been a member of this fraternity less than 24 hours. Malik and Bryan need to weigh all of their options."

"Fuck you, Gar! Murphy gave his life for those documents in that garage. I am not loading them on a fucking van and handing them over to Murphy's killer."

Garron pointed at Malik. "Please tell me that you're not saying that it's okay for this man's son to die for those papers in the garage."

"Malik and Abram are both members of this Brotherhood. They know the risks," Jacob argued.

Leah was shocked, "Jacob, what are you saying?"

Malik asked, "Garron you mentioned options, do you have a suggestion?"

Garron sat down with Malik at the table.

He said, "The purpose, the *true* purpose of The Brotherhood is to protect the treasure, correct? What if giving up the archives *is* going to protect the treasure?"

Jacob said in disgust, "I can't fucking believe you."

Leah said, "Hear him out, Jacob."

"During our research last night and this morning we found an item mentioned in several documents that caught our attention. We tracked this item's movements through a number of documents spanning several centuries." Garron paused. "I think what we found is a map pointing to the treasure."

Mackenzie insisted, "Let me see these documents."

"Not a chance," Jacob turned his anger toward Bryan.

Malik ignored his brethren, "Garron, do you have a plan?"

"I haven't thought it through yet, but what if, before we hand over the archives to Anton, we find the map ourselves? We hold up our end of the deal Anton proposed, and now the map provides leverage to ensure our safety. It will take Anton some time to research the archives and eventually find mention of the map as we did, giving us the time to decide what to do with the treasure."

Jacob said, "That's not much of a plan, brother. Anton will never let us walk away tonight. I am sure that he plans on killing us all. And even if he did let us live, he would eventually hunt us down once he learns of the map."

"Not if we've already used the map to find the treasure and tell the greatest secret ever held."

"You're saying that we just throw away 500 years of tradition without a fight?" Mackenzie asked.

"No, I'm saying that it is time for the world to learn of the work The Brotherhood has accomplished. Now is the time for the treasure to be found. The Order has been compromised, and even if it is not Anton who wins this battle, someone else will follow. There is nothing left to protect. The writing is on the wall, and it is clearly written." Garron looked Malik in the eye. "You told me yesterday that The Brotherhood has never faced a greater challenge, I admit that I am new to this, but I believe that it is time."

Malik sat quietly.

"Malik, you cannot be considering this," Mackenzie said.

"Do you have a better idea?"

"We kill Anton and grab Abram!" Mackenzie answered.

"He's well armed, well organized, and he seems to know our every move. He has already proven that he is ready to kill anyone who stands in his way. This is not a man who will let us catch him off guard," Leah said.

Malik asked, "So the map is here in St. Augustine?"

Garron nodded, "It's in the Castillo de San Marcos."

"It's in a fucking national park! What's your plan for that hot shot?" Mackenzie scoffed.

"Jacob, what do you think?" Malik asked.

"It seems like possessing the treasure is our only play." Jacob nodded as an apology to his brother.

Mackenzie was shocked. "Malik, this is not the answer. We can't hand over the archives to Anton."

"If we have the location of the treasure, then we have leverage. Nothing else will ensure my son's safety." He continued, "Garron, I am trusting you with my son's life. Find us that treasure map."

The group discussed their plan of action.

Leah and Garron would search for the map at the Castillo de San Marcos while Jacob, Malik, and Bryan loaded the vans with the documents from the archive. If Leah and Garron were not able to find the map quickly, then the three remaining would begin the trip to Anton's farm without them. Malik would explain that neither Leah nor Garron were willing to be initiated into The Brotherhood, and that they left town before Anton had made his demands. No one believed that he would accept the lie, but they hoped that Garron would call shortly after the others arrived at Anton's with good news and the leverage they needed to get out alive.

They also came up with a backup plan. Malik had Bryan wire the vans with explosives that could be remotely detonated. If it became necessary, Malik could detonate a bomb in one of the vans destroying half of the archival material. They could then ransom the remaining material for their lives. Jacob protested risking the documents, but Malik convinced him that Murphy would have understood their dilemma.

They all wished each other good luck and set about their tasks.

Malik shook Garron's hand and said, "Godspeed."

"I'll call you once I've found the map. I will find it!" Garron responded.

Jacob and Leah lingered away from the group. They said their tearful goodbyes and embraced tightly. Jacob handed his red backpack to Leah. They had decided that Murphy's folio could not be handed over with The Brotherhood's archives. Garron had also retrieved the Ordinance Sergeant's diary from the archives to aid them in their search of the fort. Leah joined Garron and they climbed into Abram's BMW X5 and pulled away from the estate. They drove north on A1A and eventually came to the Bridge of Lions without saying a word. They could see the Castillo de San Marcos from the bridge.

Leah asked, "So what's our plan?"

"I have no idea," Garron answered and smiled feebly.

***

Leah and Garron paid their admission and crossed the drawbridge into the fort. There were a number of park rangers walking the grounds. Garron knew that his search was going to be difficult. The fort was a hollow square with four diamond-shaped structures at each corner called bastions. They passed through the thick walls and entered the central courtyard. They found stairs to their right that led to the fort's upper deck. From one of the bastions they could look down into the central courtyard and the surrounding grounds.

Leah asked, "Where do we start?"

Garron looked around. There were very few visitors at the fort on this hot August day. St. Augustine is certainly better enjoyed in cooler weather. He pulled up his shirt and tugged the diary from his waistband. He flipped to the January 8th entry.

"The sergeant who was left to man the fort wrote that the wet plaster that he used to cover the map's hiding place was near a gate. The only gate that I saw was the one we entered near the drawbridge."

Leah turned and pointed to the corner of the bastion where the sentry box overlooked the river. "There are gates at each one of those tower thingies on each corner."

They walked to the nearest sentry box and examined the gate. The walls were made of coquina, a type of limestone rock formed by small shells, like the majority of the fort's structure. The gate was black-painted iron. There were signs of repair, but to Garron they looked too recent to be that of Sergeant Douglas. Leah and Garron walked around the upper deck and inspected each sentry box and the watchtower. Each had an iron gate much like the first sentry box, but all appeared to have been refitted in recent years. Garron worried that someone repairing the old fort might have stumbled across the map in modern times.

After finding little of interest in the upper deck, they moved their search to the courtyard area of the fort.

Leah asked, "Do you think Douglas could have been writing about the main gate near the drawbridge?"

"Absolutely, but I was worried about attracting too much attention from the park rangers by starting there. Let's eliminate all other possible locations before we move to the drawbridge."

Leah looked around the courtyard. She said, "There are gates on many of these rooms surrounding the courtyard. It could be anyone of them."

They split up. Leah moved clockwise around the square, with Garron moving in the opposite direction. They spent nearly two hours investigating every doorway before they finally met back at the front of the fort. Garron had been temporarily interested in a room that had once been hidden. At some point in history a cannon collapsed through a floor, uncovering a room hidden behind a wall. Garron investigated the room, which he had to crouch to enter, but did not uncover anything that pointed to The Brotherhood or Sergeant Douglas.

"That leaves the main gate," Garron said.

"We are bound to draw attention, what's your plan?"

"I'm going to ask a ranger for help."

"What?" Leah asked, but Garron was already approaching a young lady dressed in a park ranger's uniform.

"Excuse me," Garron said to the ranger.

Her name tag read Tanya. She was tall and lean with light brown hair and a dark complexion. Garron would have guessed that Tanya had an American Indian branch in her family tree. She may have been pretty. It was hard to tell in the uniform.

"Yes sir." Tanya responded in a clear voice that resonated to the Midwest.

"Could I ask you a question about this fort, specifically regarding its time during The Civil War?"

Leah grabbed Garron's arm.

"What are you doing?" Leah forced a smile. "Leave this young lady alone."

Ranger Tanya interrupted, "No, that is quite all right. I am happy to help. That's why I am here."

Garron gave Leah a look.

"Thank you." He smiled at the ranger.

Tanya said, "The Castillo was known as Fort Marion at the time and the Union Army held the fort for the majority of the war. The Confederate Army had taken the fort without a shot in 1861, but only held the fort for a little more than a year. The Union Army found the fort unmanned in March of 1862 and held it for the duration of the War."

Garron smiled again. "I was interested in how the Confederates gained the fort in 1861."

"That is an interesting story. When Florida was threatening secession in the late months of 1860, the soldiers in Fort Marion were deployed to parts further north; that is, all but one man. When secession was adopted in early 1861, a small civilian militia marched on the fort and demanded that the poor man surrender the fort. He had very little choice, but in handing over the fort he did demand that the militia write him a receipt for the fort and its contents." Tanya shook her head. "You know, sometimes that Ordinance Sergeant gets a bad rap for not making a stand, but I don't believe that he really had a choice." She snickered, "I picture an angry mob carrying guns and torches, like something out of a version of Frankenstein."

Garron and Leah laughed politely.

Garron said, "I was actually interested in the ordinance sergeant in particular."

"Well, let's step out of the sun and I'll share what I know," Tanya said, leading Garron and Leah over the drawbridge and into the shade of the fort's shadow. The dipping sun left long shadows across the battery.

"What are your names?" Tanya asked.

"I'm John and this is my wife, Irene." Garron used Leah's middle name, which he knew that she despised.

Tanya asked, "Where are you from?"

Leah answered, "Maryland."

"I'm from Ohio, we are practically neighbors," she laughed.

Tanya pulled off her wide brimmed hat and wiped her forehead. "I'm still getting used to this Florida humidity." She continued, "Ordinance Sergeant Horatio Douglas was rumored to take great pride in his job as caretaker of the fort. Letters that I have read from residents of St. Augustine dating to the Civil War period said that Douglas had great difficulty in handing over the fort to the militia. It wasn't that he was concerned with the politics involved. He was concerned with the upkeep of the facility. Although the militia did not see it that way initially, Douglas was seen roaming around the walls of the fort daily. The militia members were worried that Douglas might try to gain access to the fort to spike the cannon, rendering them inoperable. They eventually decided that he meant no harm and even consulted with him when repairs or maintenance were needed within the fort."

Tanya replaced her hat on her head. She asked, "Why the interest in Douglas?"

Garron hesitated only a second, and then said, "I've been doing some digging into my family history. I caught the genealogy bug, and I might be related to Horatio Douglas through my mother's side of the family."

"Genealogy has become quite popular these days." Tanya nodded. She continued, "One of the letters that I read endeared me to the man."

Leah asked, "How so?"

"Well, it spoke to the fact that Horatio had so much trouble relinquishing his duties that he would often sleep near the fort so he could still keep an eye on things. The letters said that his light could be seen near the sentry post in the Old City Wall each night." She pointed back toward the city at two stone structures.

"What are those structures?" Garron asked pointing in the same direction.

"Those are the Old City Gates."

**

Garron looked at his watch while he impatiently waited for a young couple to finish taking pictures of the Old City Gates. Two coquina towers supported two black iron gates. On the western tower was a gated sentry box, which was a small covered alcove that allowed the guard to shelter from bad weather. Two sections of coquina wall extended from each tower. The young couple walked through the gate and down St. George Street. Garron stepped closer to the sentry box.

Leah said, "Nice job back there with that ranger. The genealogy angle worked nicely."

"Thanks, but you helped to sell it."

Then Leah punched Garron solidly in the upper arm.

Garron rubbed his shoulder, "What's that for?"

"Don't ever call me Irene again," she laughed.

Garron laughed, too.

Leah said, "This sentry box looks promising."

"I wish we could see inside," Garron said, looking at the sentry box's padlocked gate.

Garron peered through the gate's bars trying to see anything that might hold promise. "The sun is getting low, I wish that we had a flashlight," Garron said.

Something on the wall behind the padlocked gate caught his eye.

"Can you see that?"

Leah pushed in beside him. "What?"

"On the right wall at about eye level, tell me what you see."

Leah let her eyes adjust to the low level of light. She peered into the darkness of the sentry's box. "I see something carved into the stone." Her eyes grew wide. "It's a cross!"

"We have to get in there," Garron said and looked around for something to pry the lock.

They searched on opposite sides of the wall for something to help them gain entry to the sentry box. Garron came up empty handed. Leah returned to the gate with a length of steel pipe approximately five feet long.

"Where did you find that?" Garron asked her.

"It's a stanchion. It was over there. It slides into a hole drilled in those cobblestones to prevent cars from getting any closer to this gate."

"We're going to make a lot of noise with that."

Leah countered, "We don't have time to be subtle." Leah positioned herself in front of the padlock and raised the pipe like a spear.

"Let me do that," Garron suggested.

"I can do it," Leah argued.

In a two handed stabbing motion, Leah brought the end of the pipe down onto the padlock. The shock of the strike ran up her arms causing her to drop the pipe on the stone walkway. The steel hitting the stone was cacophonous; the sound reverberated down St. George Street.

Once the ringing subsided in his ears, Garron said, "I don't doubt that you are physically fit, but maybe I should give it a try."

"Don't be a smart ass," Leah said, as she tried to shake the tingling from her hands.

Garron picked up the pipe and took the same stance that Leah had used. He thrust the pipe downward, striking the lock solidly. The padlock gave way. He tried to hide the discomfort in his arms with a short laugh, but the fact was that Garron was just lucky. He set the pipe down gently with numb fingers. The gate opened smoothly. And they both squeezed inside the sentry box. Garron used his fingertips as much as his eyes to look at the eight pointed cross carved into the coquina. He felt other graffiti as well, and supposed that the gate was added to stop such vandalism.

"What's this?" As Leah crouched to see the stone floor she grabbed Garron's thigh to steady herself.

The touch caused Garron's breath to catch in his chest. He felt his face flush.

He regained his composure and asked, "What do you see?"

"It looks like a repair to the floor. It's chipping badly near the wall."

Garron said, "Let me take a look."

Leah had to stand to make room for Garron. She grasped his thigh more tightly as she stood. Garron staggered slightly; the top of his head collided with the jagged coquina.

"Shit!" He rubbed his head.

Leah placed her hand gently on the back of Garron's neck.

Garron felt his pulse race again at her touch.

She asked, "Are you okay?"

He stammered, "Yeah, I'm fine."

Garron crouched to examine the spot where a small stone met the base of the wall. He dug at the joint and felt it crumble beneath his fingers.

"This stone is loose. Give me some room."

Leah stepped out of the sentry box. Garron continued to dig at the joint.

"This is taking too long, hand me that pipe."

Garron took the pipe and raised it above the stone.

He asked, "Do you see anyone?"

Leah looked around, the light was low but she didn't see anyone nearby. She shook her head.

Garron brought the pipe down on the center of the stone. The sound was deafening in the enclosed area. Garron's ears rang. His hands went numb, causing him to drop the pipe, but the stone gave way. He knelt and pulled the stone free to reveal a small chamber below the wall. Garron reached into the dark niche and pulled out a small leather wrapped rectangle. He looked up to see Leah smiling. Garron untied the leather wrapping and uncovered a book entitled, *The Conduct of Life* by Ralph Waldo Emerson.

Leah asked, "Is this another clue? We don't have time for another clue."

From outside the sentry box, a voice called out, "Hey, what are you two doing?"

Leah and Garron wasted no time running in the opposite direction from the voice, straight to the X5 in the Castillo's parking lot. Garron slipped behind the wheel and started the engine. He raced from the parking lot toward I-95. The coordinates for Anton's farm were preloaded into the GPS, and a voice prompted Garron to turn right.

"Where are we going?" Leah asked from the passenger's seat while holding the Emerson book in her lap.

Garron sipped from a water bottle he had brought from Malik's and then answered, "To Anton's."

Leah took a second water bottle from the vehicle's console and took a long swallow. She adjusted Jacob's backpack between her feet on the X5's floorboard.

Leah said, "But we don't have the map."

"And we are out of time. But we have something. Open that book and give it a once-over."

Leah examined the book, opening the cover carefully. It was a first edition from 1860. The book was in extremely good condition for being buried in the ground for more than 140 years. Written on the end leaf was an inscription:

I was shaped profoundly by the experiences that we shared in '26. I remember those days fondly.
    Waldo

Leah said, "This book was given to Sergeant Douglas by Emerson himself. They were friends."

Several folded pages slipped from inside the book and fell into Leah's lap. The paper was old and darkened with age. She carefully unfolded the pages.

Garron said, "What is it?"

Leah stared at the brown ink and delicate lettering written in Latin.

"I'm not sure."

***

The two vans came to a gate, where they were met by four heavily armed men. Jacob tensed as one of the men shone a flashlight into his face through the window. The gate was swung open and the guard slapped the hood of the van and motioned for them to pull through.

Malik put the van into gear and eased through the gate. Jacob watched in his side view mirror as Mackenzie followed closely behind them in the second van. The setting sun had trouble penetrating the scrub pine forest that surrounded the farm. The lane the van followed was barely wide enough to accommodate the vehicle; saw palmetto scraped at the doors. Nature had reclaimed this land.

"Could you check to see if we have cell service, Jacob?" Malik nodded toward his BlackBerry that lay on the center console.

Jacob inspected the phone, the display showed full service.

Jacob nodded and then said, "Garron will call, Malik."

"I must have faith that he will."

The farmhouse and barn came into view. It looked to be a typical early twentieth century cracker style home. It was small and was elevated on concrete pilings to allow for air circulation and to help battle the Florida heat, although several of those pilings had been overturned by vegetation. The buildings were in a desperate stage of disrepair. A portion of the barn roof had collapsed and the entire building sat canted to the left. The front porch of the farmhouse slanted at a severe angle, and a chimney had collapsed and lay in rubble, stretching toward the trees. In front of the decaying porch of the farmhouse stood eleven armed men watching Jacob's van come through the trees. Malik pulled forward slowly and stopped the van parallel to the house. Jacob watched the men through his side window and then turned to Malik on his left.

Malik looked Jacob in the eye and said, "Here we go."

Malik stepped from the van and walked around the front to join Jacob. Jacob looked over each of the men standing before him. The weight of the gun in his waistband did little to comfort him. Jacob saw the group's attention shift to Mackenzie's van as it pulled up about twenty feet from his own van. Mackenzie slid across and opened the passenger's door. He used the door to shield him and raised the barrel of his M4 and pointed it at Anton's henchmen.

Anton Margaux stood out from his small army, dressed impeccably in a smartly cut suit with a pocket square to match his tie. Anton was a tall handsome man with long features, who looked much younger than Jacob expected. His dark hair was combed straight back from his forehead, accentuating the length of his features.

Jacob felt a surge of rage seeing the man responsible for his friend's death. He wanted to pummel the man and choke him to death with his tie.

Malik sensed Jacob's tension and gently laid a hand on his shoulder. He said in a whisper, "Please remember why we are here."

In a louder voice directed toward Anton, Malik said, "Where is my son?"

Anton spoke, "Thank you for being punctual. But we seem to be missing a couple of your new friends. Where are Garron and Leah?"

"They will not be joining us," Malik responded.

Anton hesitated. "That is disappointing. I thought that we had a deal."

"And we do. We three are all that remains of *The Brotherhood of the Three Crosses*. Neither Garron nor Leah accepted our invitation to join the order."

Anton smiled. "Jacob, you would like for me to believe that your brother has abandoned you now in your greatest time of need? He flew to your side days ago after years of silence out of concern for your well-being. And what of your lovely Leah, she has joined you from the moment she knew of your loss. Now she turns her back on you? You must take me for a fool."

"You asked for our archives and they are in the vans," Malik acknowledged. "I ask again, where is my son?"

"Ah yes, the infamous archives. The reason we are all here." Anton continued, "Please step away from the vehicles so that my men can inspect the contents."

"Not until I see my son."

"Malik, you are in no position to make demands. You are out-numbered and out-gunned. Step away from the van."

Malik smiled. "We are indeed outnumbered." He called back to the second van, "Mr. Mackenzie, how many men did Mr. Margaux bring with him tonight?"

Mackenzie answered, "There are fifteen. Besides the assholes standing in front of you, there are two men over my left shoulder in the tree line and three that are trying to improve their position behind me. I seemed to have parked my van in their sightline." Mackenzie smiled wryly.

"Very good Bryan, thank you. And Bryan, if things take a turn for the worse, could you be sure that your first shot is in the center of Mr. Margaux's chest, please?" Malik said, without his eyes leaving Anton. "We three are willing to die tonight, if need be. Can you say the same Anton?"

No one spoke. The trees were filled with the sound of frogs and insects waking up to the night.

Finally Anton called out, "Abram, join us please."

The young man came into view from behind the corner of the farmhouse. He approached slowly with his head down.

"Right here my boy," Anton said as he clasped both hands on the young man's shoulders and positioned Abram in front of him. Anton said, "See, here he is, safe and sound as promised."

"Son, are you all right?" Malik asked.

Abram answered without looking up, "Yes."

Anton said, "There you are, so let's see what's in the vans."

Malik called out, "Mr. Mackenzie, please join Jacob and me by our van."

Bryan slid back through the cab of his van, exited the driver's door and moved to the shelter of Malik's van. He put the van between him and Anton's men and took aim over the van's hood.

"Anton, you may have your men check the contents of that van," Malik instructed.

Anton nodded to two of his men. They moved around to the back of the second van and opened the doors. They slung their weapons over their shoulders and began to rummage through the cardboard boxes that held the archives. Malik, Bryan, and Jacob had transferred the documents from their steel boxes to cardboard before loading the van earlier in the day.

Jacob's heart was pounding. Sweat dampened his brow. Jacob wondered why Garron had not called as of yet. He felt vulnerable.

"It's here, Mr. Margaux," a man called from the back of the van.

Anton smiled. "I must say that I am surprised."

"You took my son. You left me with no choice."

Abram looked up for the first time and met his father's gaze.

"Now that you have what you want, let my son go and ensure our safe passage."

Anton seemed to contemplate the request, "I would like to, really I would, but I am not convinced that you could let all of this go Malik. I'm not sure that you could walk away from this life. You said yourself, you are willing to die for your precious Brotherhood, but are you willing to let The Brotherhood die?" He paused. "I think not. Before too long you will be hunting me and I just cannot let that happen."

"So you intend to kill us all," Malik confirmed.

Anton nodded. "And now I will also have to spend resources in chasing Leah and Garron down as well, which is unfortunate but necessary. I cannot have any loose ends."

Abram spoke up, "You said that if you got the archives then no one would be hurt."

Anton chuckled and tightened his grip on the young man's shoulders. "For you being such a smart boy, you sure are gullible."

Abram dropped his gaze to the ground and shook his head, "What have I done?"

Anton clarified, "You see Malik, I contacted your son two months ago with a proposition, and honestly he agreed much more quickly than I expected. I believe that Abram resents The Brotherhood, and possibly even you for how his mother's last few months were handled. I promised an end to The Brotherhood if he would just deliver the archives."

Abram interrupted, "I didn't know that anyone would get hurt. It's just that … you weren't around … when Mom needed you … when I needed you. And after Mom died, you submersed yourself even deeper in The Brotherhood." Abram began to cry.

Malik's voice was tight with remorse. "He exploited your pain, Son. I am very sorry."

Jacob's heart broke at the pain that both father and son felt. He thought of his own father.

Malik controlled his anger. He said, "I was hoping that you might have surprised me, Anton. But you have forced my hand. I must make a difficult choice."

Anton responded, "Choice? You have no options here."

"But I do, Anton." Malik forced a smile. "Mr. Mackenzie, will you explain to Anton our options."

Bryan pulled the detonator from his pocket and showed it to Anton over the hood of the van. "I wired both vans with an incendiary device. Our choice is whether to burn one or both." He smiled, "And before you start shooting, I should tell you that this is a dead man's switch. If my finger releases this switch, they both burn."

"So in essence you were correct, Anton, it is not my choice. It is actually yours," Malik said.

Anton grabbed Abram by the back of the neck and drew a nickel plated gun from inside his jacket in one fluid motion. He screamed, "I will shoot your son. He will die in front of you." Spittle flew from Anton's mouth.

Malik shook his head. "You've already confirmed that you intend on killing us all. You have played your hand. No more threats Anton."

Jacob could see the short barreled revolver shaking in Anton's hand.

Malik continued, "I still have cards to play. Garron and Leah are moving the treasure as we speak. Even if we die here today, and you and the archives manage to survive, you still will have no hope in finding the treasure."

Anton screamed vehemently, "You are bluffing! You don't have any idea where the treasure is hidden. Hell you don't even know what the treasure is!"

"So then, call my bluff. Pull the trigger. Or better yet, let me raise the stakes." Malik slapped the van's hood.

Mackenzie released one of the triggers of the detonator. A quick white flash was visible through the windshield and the open rear doors of the second van. The fire spread quickly following the accelerant throughout the back of the van. The cardboard and documents ignited rapidly.

Malik and Jacob both drew their weapons from their waistbands.

Anton screamed, "You son of a bitch!"

Anton's men widened their stances and took ready aim at their targets.

One of the men asked, "Sir, what is your command?"

Anton whispered, "Don't shoot."

The man asked again, "Sir?"

"Don't shoot! Don't shoot!" Anton said more loudly.

The roar of the fire could be heard. The insects and frogs fell silent. Black smoke poured from the open rear doors of the van.

Anton tightened his grip on Abram's neck and forced him to his knees. He held the barrel of the gleaming revolver to the back of Abram's head.

Anton demanded, "Tell Mackenzie to disarm that second incendiary!"

"Bryan," Malik said, "if Anton pulls that trigger, please be sure that the second van burns."

Anton and Malik stared at each other for a full minute. Finally, Anton released his grip on Abram's neck and slid his pistol back under his jacket. He raised his hands in a gesture of surrender, "Okay, okay Abram join your father."

Malik said, "Come to me, Son."

To Jacob, Abram looked like a small boy who had been caught disobeying his father as he walked slowly to the van. Malik embraced his son.

Anton asked, "So what is your proposal?" He had regained his composure and straightened his tie and adjusted his jacket.

Malik unwillingly released his son. "Garron will be calling me momentarily with the new location of the treasure. You release us and once we are safely away, I will call you with that location."

Anton clasped his hands behind his back and rocked on the balls of his feet. "So I am to trust that once you are out of harm's way you will call and just hand over the treasure? Sorry Malik, you must think me a fool."

Malik's cell phone began to ring nearly on cue. He pulled the cell phone from his pocket and confirmed that it was Garron. He answered the call, "Hello Mr. Shepard, were you successful in your endeavor?"

"Malik is everyone okay?" Garron asked.

"Yes, we are all just fine. Did you have any trouble in your quest?"

Garron responded, "I am sorry Malik, we didn't find the treasure map."

Malik forced a smile. "Good, very good, and were you able to relocate your find?"

Garron was confused, "What? No. Malik the treasure map wasn't there."

"I understand and that is excellent news. You have done very well. And please thank Ms. Preston for me."

Then it dawned on Garron that Malik was speaking not for his benefit.

"Anton is listening and you are in some trouble."

Malik answered, "That is correct, and he is contemplating our deal now. I will ask him for his decision. Please hold."

"Anton, Mr. Shepard would like your response."

Anton smiled broadly. "May I speak to him?" He extended his arm toward Malik. Anton added, "Malik, you must let me speak to Garron to broker this deal. That is the only way to make this work."

Malik hesitated, but stepped forward and handed Anton the cell phone.

Anton took the phone and spoke into the receiver, "Garron, this is Anton Margaux. We need to come to an agreement to ensure that everyone remains happy and healthy. But first, could you describe the treasure?"

"Is everyone there safe?" Garron asked.

"Yes, yes of course. Everyone is fine, father and son are reunited. But please, I must insist that you describe the treasure. Is it beautiful?"

"It is the most beautiful thing that I have ever seen. It is incredible: silver, gold, rough cut emeralds, and intricately crafted jewelry. You've never seen anything like it," Garron lied.

"Excellent. Could you hold on just a minute while I tell Malik the good news?"

Garron sighed with relief.

Anton asked his men to extinguish the burning van.

Then Anton spoke to Malik, "I am very disappointed in you. Did you really think that such a ruse would work?"

Speaking back into the phone, Anton said, "Garron you can keep your treasure, but I am afraid that your brother will have to die."

"What? Wait, I don't understand, I will give you the treasure if you let them go!" Garron pleaded.

Anton said, "Tell your ex-wife that her boyfriend says goodbye."

Garron admitted the subterfuge, "I'm sorry. I lied, but I will give you what we found at the Castillo in exchange for their lives."

Anton said quizzically, "The Castillo, huh? You have my interest. What did you find at the Castillo?"

"A copy of an old Emerson book that once belonged to a member of The Brotherhood who was stationed at the fort during the Civil War."

"Interesting, and besides the book, what did you find?"

"We haven't had a chance to fully examine it yet, but you can have it."

Anton sighed, "Garron, you are a terrible liar. What did you find in the book? And please test my patience no further. I do not want for your brother to pay for your dishonesty."

Garron hesitated before answering, "I'm not quite sure what we've found, there were some old papers folded into the book."

"Describe them," Anton prompted.

"They are drawings of some plants and such, labeled in Latin."

Anton's voice took on a new tone, "How far are you away from my farm?"

Garron answered, "Ten, almost eleven miles. We're close."

"Very good, bring me the book and the sketches and I will let your brother and his new friends go unharmed."

Anton ended the call.

***

Garron and Leah saw the smoldering van near the farmhouse as they drove into the clearing. He stopped the BMW X5 when he saw *The Brotherhood of the Three Crosses* facing a line of heavily armed men. Neither Garron nor Leah had a weapon and he felt extremely vulnerable. He pulled a little closer, but kept a safe distance from the smoldering van. Garron opened the driver's door and stood on the X5's running board.

Garron called out, "Anton, I have the book and the papers. Let them go and I will bring you what I have."

A voice called back, "Garron, could you please shut off your headlights?"

Garron reached back inside and turned off the lights.

"Thank you. Now I am going to have someone come over to you and examine what you have found."

"Not until I know that my friends are at a safe distance."

Anton answered, "I first need to verify that what you are trading is worth the lives of your friends. If they check out, then everyone is free to go."

Anton said something to one of his men that Garron could not hear. He watched the man walk over to one of the black Lincoln Navigators that was parked near the barn and open a rear door. A woman stepped from the vehicle and received directions from the man. She began to walk to the X5. She was an Asian woman who, with her hair pulled back, looked very young. She wore a white blouse and jeans and moved with urgency.

Garron reached back inside and pulled his bottle of water from the cup holder.

He shouted, "Stop right there, if you take another step then I soak these papers with this bottle of water."

Garron's threat had the desired effect. The woman stopped in mid stride.

She pleaded, "No please, the water may destroy the paper."

Anton said, "Mr. Shepard, you once again test my patience. If that is rag paper, then the water will not harm it. Allow Dr. Ng to examine those documents and then we can discuss the next course of action."

Dr. Ng took a step toward the X5.

"What if it's not rag paper? Are you willing to take that chance? You release my friends and then we discuss these documents, which judging by the doctor's reaction must be extremely valuable."

Dr. Ng looked back toward Anton for instructions.

After a moment Anton said, "Very well Garron, but your brother stays with me."

Garron countered, "No deal. They all leave or so help me God I will soak these papers!"

Jacob spoke, "Gar, it's a good deal. I'll stay with you while Abram, Malik, Bryan, and Leah get to safety. But The Brotherhood takes what remains of the archives with them."

Anton weighed the offer. "It is a deal. There you have it Garron. Your brother knows how to broker a deal. What do you say?"

"Agreed, but Malik and the others leave before your doctor examines the papers."

Leah spoke for the first time since arriving, "No, I'm staying here."

"Leah, don't be stubborn, you must leave with Malik," Jacob insisted.

Leah said, "I'm not moving from this spot."

Garron pleaded, "Leah, please."

"No!"

"It seems that Ms. Preston is quite loyal and stubborn. I'd like for her to stay anyhow. This relationship between the three of you is entertaining, it will be nice to have her around. Malik you are free to go. Take your son and your Guardian and leave. Don't turn back. I do not want to ever see you again. If I do, then it won't end so well for you next time." Anton waved them away.

Malik turned to Jacob and grasped the man's hand. Jacob could see the torment behind the man's eyes. Malik said, "Thank you. I am very sorry, but I must keep my son safe. Please forgive me for leaving you."

Jacob answered, "There is no need for forgiveness. Take care of Abram, he needs you. If everything goes well, then I'll catch up with you a little later."

Mackenzie caught Jacob's eye and with a short nod climbed behind the wheel of the van. Malik guided his son into the van. Abram looked fractured; he kept his eyes on the ground. Malik nearly had to lift him into the van. Jacob hoped that the young man could heal. The van's door closed and Mackenzie turned the van away from the farmhouse. It slipped from view behind the trees lining the lane.

Garron looked at his brother standing alone in front of Anton and his men. He began to doubt their chances of making it out alive.

Anton prompted, "Dr. Ng, if you'll please examine those papers."

Anton's doctor quickly approached the X5 and took the book from Garron. She laid the book on the vehicle's hood, withdrew a flashlight and examined the papers that were tucked inside.

"Dr. Ng, what do you think?" Anton asked.

"They're perfect! We've found them Anton. Ten years and now here they are."

Garron said, "So there you are Anton. Your doctor has verified the documents, now let Jacob join me and we'll be on our way."

At the last second Garron caught movement from his left side. He side stepped a blow from one of Anton's men who had been concealed in the darkness of the night. Garron countered with a heavy left cross that connected with the man's chin. The man staggered, but recovered quickly. Garron threw another punch that missed his adversary. He had committed too heavily to the punch and fell against the front quarter panel of the X5. The man took advantage of Garron's mistake and fell against him, pinning his arm behind his back and forced Garron down onto the hood. Garron saw Leah across the hood of the SUV with a gun to her head. The gunman had the red backpack slung over his shoulder. Garron stopped struggling.

The man with the gun to Leah's head winked at Garron. "Good boy. Now walk to the farmhouse or I'll shoot this bitch in the face."

The gunman handed the backpack to the doctor.

Garron and Leah followed Dr. Ng over to where Anton was standing. She handed him the book.

As they approached, Garron said, "We had a deal. You have the papers now let us go."

Anton said to Jacob, "Please put down your weapon or I will have you choose whether my men shoot your girlfriend or your brother first."

Jacob shook with rage, but eventually dropped his gun. Two of Anton's men moved to secure him.

Anton said, "I will also need each of your cell phones."

Anton motioned for one of his men to collect the cell phones.

"And as for our deal Garron, I do not trust you or your brethren so you should just be satisfied to know that three of your new friends still have their lives. And I think that I will keep you around for leverage, because if I know Malik he will not give up so easily." Anton smiled.

He turned his back and moved toward the Navigator. Anton called over his shoulder, "Now, if you will join us, we have a plane to catch."

Leah asked, "Where are you taking us?"

"Why to Bimini of course," Anton said with a smile.

Chapter 7

THEY DROVE A few miles north of St. Augustine to the Northeast Florida Regional Airport and boarded a Gulfstream G650. The majority of Anton's security force stayed behind, but three of his men did board the plane. Anton called them Smith, Jones, and Taylor. Taylor seemed to be Anton's chief of security.

Taylor was a solidly-built black man the color of onyx. His features were sharp, with a prominent chin and jaw. Taylor was not a tall man, but his strong physique and confident posture made him look like the biggest man on the plane even though Smith and Jones were each a full head taller than the man. Smith and Jones appeared to be carved from granite, but each moved with a fluidity that belied their size.

Garron, Leah, and Jacob sat on a divan near the center of the passenger compartment. Smith and Jones sat directly across from the trio in two armed seats separated by a small table. The interior of the cabin was spacious and comfortable. It was an example of modernity with its white leather upholstery and the clean lines of its maple cabinetry. The compartment was lined with oval windows that would have allowed natural light to flood the plane if they had been flying earlier in the day.

Now it was late, and Garron felt exhausted after crashing from the adrenaline rush that spiked through his body earlier. Jacob and Leah held hands beside him on the divan; they looked as fatigued as Garron felt. Deeper into the cabin, Dr. Ng sat at a table bent over the drawings that Garron had found buried in the Old City Gates. She was taking notes while examining the papers with a lighted magnifying glass. Dr. Ng, with her diminutive size, looked out of place among Anton's minions. Garron thought that she was quite beautiful. She lit up when she saw the drawings, and her smile was captivating, contrary to everything else that Garron had experienced since arriving in Florida three days ago. Anton had looked over Dr. Ng's shoulder for a moment as he removed a shoulder holster that held a nickel plated revolver, and then he had disappeared behind a pocket door into the stateroom at the rear of the plane with the red backpack. They had been in the air for twenty minutes.

Anton stepped from the stateroom.

Dr. Ng looked up from the documents and smiled widely. "They are fantastic, well drawn with an attention to the smallest detail. The final ingredient is here, but I do not recognize it."

Anton looked towards the divan and said, "Now, now Gracie, let's not reveal all of our dirty little secrets to our new guests just yet."

Gracie Ng's smile faded as she looked across the plane's cabin. She had been so immersed in her work that she had forgotten about the new passengers on the plane.

Anton continued, speaking to the trio on the divan. "We will be on the ground shortly. I have arranged for your accommodations. I am sure that you will be comfortable."

***

When they landed on South Bimini, there was a long van waiting to take them to the water shuttle. Bimini was an island chain, with the largest of the islands being North and South Bimini. Bimini sat only 53 miles east of Miami, which made it the closest point in the Bahamas to the U.S. Jacob had fished in the fertile waters off of Bimini in the past.

The night was cool with a steady island breeze that brought chills to Garron's bare arms on the boat that carried them to North Bimini. The boat ride was short, and the group boarded another van that swiftly traversed the quiet early morning streets of Alice Town. North Bimini was a mere seven miles in length and they came to their final destination at the north end of the island quickly.

The van pulled up to a small, gated guard house and was waved in immediately by the man stationed there. Palm trees ran along a wall blocking a view of the property beyond the gate house, but as the van pulled through the gate a large resort compound came into view. There were parking lots to the right and the left, both lined with more palm trees. Directly in front of the van was a large porte-cochere, like that at the entrance of a fine hotel.

Anton spun in his seat to meet his guests' eyes. "Welcome to the resort. I bought this place three years ago when we moved our operations from Oslo. I acquired it from a defunct developer who falsified the project's initial scope, putting the island's infrastructure in jeopardy. The lawsuit destroyed the developer. His loss is my gain."

The resort's west wing was dark. It had been buttoned up with hurricane shutters. But the east wing and main entrance were brightly lit. The resort's three stories were painted sunshine yellow and trimmed in tangerine orange. A small pond, including a bronze mermaid, was accented with landscape lighting, revealing koi fish swarming near the pond's edge.

They entered the building. The reservation desk was to the right; it was unmanned. It was when they entered the lobby that the building no longer looked liked a resort. It was completely empty. The furniture that one would expect to see in the lobby of a high-end resort was missing. The walls were lacking art work and the shelves of the small library, which was near the rear of the lobby, were empty. The wide open space with thirty-five foot ceilings and gleaming marble tile looked more like an empty dance hall than the lobby of a resort.

Near the library was another set of automatic double doors opposite the front entrance that led to a courtyard and a large empty pool. Beyond the pool were a croquet court and a putting green. In the distance beyond the putting green, was a beach where the moonlight reflected off of the ocean.

Anton said, "These men will escort you to your cottages on the beach. There, Chef Eddie has left you a fruit plate and a few sandwiches. You must be hungry. You should find everything that you need in your cottage to keep you comfortable. Breakfast will be served at seven o'clock. I will see you then. Please make yourselves at home."

With that said, Anton, Dr. Ng, and Taylor continued to the lighted wing of the resort. Smith and Jones signaled the remaining three to follow them toward the beach.

They walked along a pathway lined with ferns, palms, and bromeliads with the beach on their right. Hammocks were strung between towering almond trees. The group followed the path until they reached ten cottages that lined the beach. Each was painted a different color that reminded Garron of the bright colors of Front Street in Bermuda. When they came to the first cottage, Smith signaled for Leah and Jacob to step inside. Jones led Garron to the second cottage, the one painted orange. Garron looked over and made eye contact with his brother before Jacob stepped inside his cottage. Smith offered Jones a cigarette, and then both men took positions on the pathway in front of each of the cottages.

The cottage was spacious. There were three rooms; a living room, a bedroom, and a bathroom. A kitchen was missing; Garron supposed that meals were meant to be taken in a common dining room, but there was a small bar and mini-fridge just inside the front door. On the bar top was a plate of sliced fruit and two wrapped sandwiches, as well as a liter bottle of water. The bedroom had been made up with fresh linens and someone had provided turn-down service; there was even a mint on the pillow. Garron found the adjoining bathroom stocked with fresh towels, a bathrobe, soap, shampoo, and a shaving kit.

Garron returned to the living area, unwrapped one of the sandwiches and opened the bottle of water. He sat down on the small couch and made quick work of both. As he sat on the couch deciding whether to take a shower, he fell asleep.

***

Garron woke to a pounding on the door. His neck was kinked from sleeping on the couch, and his breath tasted of onions from the sandwich he ate before falling asleep. Garron could hear Jacob calling his name. Garron stood unsteadily and opened the cottage door.

"Shit Gar, I thought that something might have happened to you overnight," Jacob said in relief.

Jacob stepped through the door carrying a garment bag like those from a dry cleaners shop.

"Sorry, I apparently was dead to the world. I fell asleep on the couch. What's that?"

Jacob answered, "They were on your door. Leah and I had one on our door this morning, too. It's a change of clothes."

Garron took notice of the linen shirt and khaki shorts that Jacob was wearing.

"What time is it?" Garron asked.

"Breakfast is in five minutes."

Garron took the garment bag from his brother and then said, "I'm going to grab a quick shower. I'll meet you there."

Garron turned and headed for the bathroom.

Jacob left Garron's cottage, locking the door on the way out.

Leah was standing on the pathway outside the cottage.

She asked, "Is everything okay?"

"He's getting in the shower, he'll catch up."

Jacob looked around, "No sign of our guards?"

"I haven't seen anyone." Leah reached out and took his hand. "Let's get something to eat. I'm hungry."

The sun had risen and the air was beginning to warm. The surf rolled gently on their left as they made their way back toward the resort's entrance. Once past the empty swimming pool, they entered through the automatic doors into the lobby. A staff member, a young black lady with closely cropped hair dressed in the uniform of waitstaff, directed them to the right and into a dining hall.

Like the lobby, the dining hall was sparsely decorated. There were only six long banquet tables, with chairs, set up in the middle of the room. There was no other furniture. But the tables were elegantly set with china, crystal glassware, and white linens. The waitress held the chair for Leah, and directed Jacob to take the seat beside her. She left the room without a word.

Anton, Dr. Ng, and another man entered the hall. They walked quickly to the table and took their seats. Anton sat at the head of the table with the man on his left. The man looked to be in his sixties, with a full beard and gray-blond hair. He had broad features and wide shoulders, and stood about six feet tall. Dr. Ng took the seat beside the man. They were all smiling widely.

Anton asked, "Will Garron be joining us for breakfast?"

"He's running a little late. Apparently he slept well," Jacob replied.

"That is good to hear. I see that you received the clean clothes that Mira arranged for you. They seem to fit well. How are your accommodations?"

"They're just fine, but this is a bit surreal. First you kidnap us, and then you treat us like your houseguests. Are we your prisoners or what?"

"Sorry that I'm late," Garron called out as he entered the dining hall.

"Welcome Garron. We have not yet started, so you are just in time. Please take a seat," Anton cheerfully welcomed the newcomer.

Garron surveyed the table and located the only open table setting beside Dr. Ng. He hesitated and then sat beside the doctor.

Anton said, "Let me make introductions. Jacob, Garron, Leah, I would like for you to meet Drs. Ng and Hansen."

The doctors both smiled.

"Of course you remember Dr. Ng from last night. She comes to us from Stanford University. Gracie is the botanist on my team. Dr. Hansen hails from Oslo, Norway. Ole is an anthropologist and an expert in the ancient runic alphabet."

Dr. Hansen smiled more broadly and welcomed the newcomers.

Anton spoke to Garron, "Your brother just asked if you were my prisoners. That is a difficult question to answer." He folded his hands in his lap. "I am sorry that I treated you as I did last night. I was holding your affiliation with The Brotherhood against you unjustly. You were brought into all of this unpleasantness and forced to make a decision on which side to take without having all of the available information shared with you."

Jacob bristled, "Did you say unpleasant? My friend's death is more than just unpleasant."

Anton raised his hands in a gesture of surrender. "I am sorry. I did not mean to depreciate the loss of your friend. I just want you to know that I had nothing to do with Murphy's death."

Jacob and Anton met each other's gaze.

"I can see your anger Jacob, and I do not blame you, but please give me a chance to show you that I am not the evil villain that The Brotherhood has made me out to be."

A short black man entered from a door opposite the entrance to the dining hall. He was dressed in chef's whites and carried a carafe of coffee.

Anton looked over his shoulder to see the man approaching.

"Good morning Chef Eddie!" Anton greeted the man enthusiastically.

In a heavy Bahamian accent Chef Eddie replied, "Good morning, sir. I trust that you had a good night."

"It started out a little shaky Eddie, but it turned out to be one of the best nights of my life." Anton waved a hand over the table. "Let me introduce our guests. This is Jacob and Leah, and beside Gracie is Garron."

Eddie bowed slightly. With a warm smile he said, "Good morning and welcome. Would you all like some coffee?"

Coffee was poured to those who wanted it and then Eddie said, "Breakfast will be served shortly. But let me ask, do any of our new guests have any food allergies?"

Leah, Jacob, and Garron shook their heads.

"Very well, I will be right back." Chef Eddie smiled and left the room.

Jacob drank his coffee. "So Anton, do you expect me to believe that Murphy's death was an accident?"

Anton leaned into the table. "I do not. But I want you to ask yourself who else may have wanted Murphy dead." He paused and then asked, "Did Malik share my story?"

Jacob nodded slightly.

"So you know that my father was killed by The Brotherhood when I was six years old? And did Malik tell you why my father was killed?"

Jacob answered, "For attempting to steal the treasure."

Anton shook his head slightly. Anton clarified, "He was killed for digging through the archives in an attempt to share the treasure with the world."

"Your father wanted the treasure for himself," Jacob argued.

Anton nodded as he said, "And I am sure that Malik believes what he told you, after all, his father was his source. And it can be argued that I am biased for the same reason. But ask yourself this, if my father was killed for investigating the archives, then what would happen to a member of *The Brotherhood of the Three Crosses* who stole something from those same archives?"

Jacob thought of the red backpack and the folio it contained. He thought of Murphy's search through the archives and the telltale trail that he had left behind. Jacob wondered if what Anton was telling him could be believed.

Chef Eddie appeared with the waitress that had seated them, carrying their breakfast.

After everyone was served, Eddie described what he had prepared, "This morning I will be serving half of a pink grapefruit, eggs Florentine, and salted fish with butter and capers. The eggs come from my chickens at home, and the grapefruit was plucked from my tree this morning. Please enjoy."

Anton said, "Chef Eddie, it looks fantastic. Thank you very much."

Eddie bowed slightly and then left the room.

Anton smiled. "I got lucky with Eddie. He is a very talented chef. He's lived on Bimini all of his life and when I found him he was cooking at another resort on the island. It wasn't hard stealing him away. Eat up."

The food was delicious.

Garron said, "Anton, this is all very strange." He wiped his mouth with his napkin. "I appreciate the hospitality, but this reminds me of an old James Bond movie. The evil mastermind discovers that Bond is a secret agent and then invites him to dinner, provides the tuxedo, a fabulous meal, and then the death ray or tank of sharks." Garron smiled. "Thanks for the new clothes by the way."

The table laughed heartily, even Jacob cracked a smile.

Anton smiled. "I assure you that I have no death ray, but don't swim too far out because there are plenty of sharks in nearby waters. And let me remind you, you were the ones initiated into the secret organization with its own global agenda." He laughed again. He continued, "In all seriousness though, I understand that we initially found ourselves on opposite sides of this thing, but I hope that once you learn of our research and my goal you will see that I am not the evil mastermind that you were expecting."

Leah asked, "What is your goal?"

"I am trying to finish what my father began. I hope to liberate mankind's most important discovery from a cult who appointed themselves gods. My father wanted to give mankind back a gift that was stolen in antiquity, robbing later generations of a treasure that God intended for us all."

Dr. Ng said with a smile, "Easy now Anton, remember that you are sitting at a table with an Atheist and a Buddhist and you have new guests."

"My apologies, I do not mean to offend anyone. It is just that I feel very passionate about this."

Leah sat forward. "What is the treasure?"

Anton smiled. "We have almost found it. We are closer than ever before to the treasure's final rediscovery. And I intend on having you by my side as we unveil it to the world."

Garron looked across the table at Jacob's expression as it changed. The anger and determination that was so easily read from the intensity in his eyes and from his furrowed brow were gone. A look of confusion and concern now covered his brother's face.

"I must apologize, but I have a conference call in five minutes," Anton said as he stood from the table. "When everyone has finished breakfast, I will have Dr. Hansen show you his research and recent discoveries. Then we will all meet in an hour at Dr. Ng's lab and discuss our latest finds. I will see you soon." He stepped from the room.

***

After everyone had finished breakfast, Dr. Hansen asked the group to follow him to his laboratory. Dr. Ng promised to see them later and headed toward the lobby. Dr. Hansen led the trio further down the east wing's hall and out into the morning light. They stepped into a small courtyard encircling a dry fountain. On the opposite side of the courtyard was a two story building similar to the two wings of the main building.

As they approached the door, Dr. Hansen said, "I've never seen Anton so excited. We may actually be close to solving this riddle."

The man's voice had a heavy Norwegian accent. It was deep and warm in tone.

"Why are you here Dr. Hansen?" Leah asked.

"Please call me Ole. I've been working with Anton for twenty-three years, ever since I found the first rune stone. I had been working for UiO at the time, in the Runic Archives of The Museum of Cultural History in Oslo."

"What is UiO?" Garron asked.

Ole answered, "The University of Oslo. But shortly after finding the stone, my funding ran out and my colleagues thought my hypothesis too crazy for another grant. That is when Anton walked into my lab and offered to fund my research."

The automatic doors opened and the group stepped inside. The lobby of this building had been converted into Ole's lab. It had been furnished with a desk, bookcases, and several laboratory tables.

"No one else is in this building, so I converted the space so that I could enjoy the view." He pointed to a window overlooking the beach and the ocean.

Leah said, "I don't blame you at all, it is beautiful."

"Dr. Hansen, I'm afraid I don't know much about rune stones. Why was Anton interested in your research?"

"A rune stone can truly be any stone that has been carved in the runic alphabet, but most describe a great battle or voyage, and sometimes they may tell of an important expedition, or sometimes of an accomplished ruler or warrior. Many will include prayers to a god like Thor. A typical stone will mark where a tribe's hero fell in battle by stating his name, his family name, and that he fought bravely. The runic alphabet is sometimes difficult to interpret, and we cultural anthropologists often argue over the translations proposed. We never seem to translate an inscription the same way twice."

Ole Hansen motioned toward a table. "Let me show you these."

He flipped a switch under the end of a laboratory table and two lights came on highlighting two glass boxes on the table's surface. Under the protective glass were two large stones inscribed with runes. One stone was very dark in color; the other was much lighter and more porous.

"The dark stone is the first that I found, and the one that interested Anton. The inscription is written in short twig Younger Futhark, which dates the stone after the ninth century and tells me that the author was from either Sweden or Norway."

Garron looked at the stone carefully. It was nearly black in color, and without the box's lighting, he wasn't sure that he would have noticed the inscription at all. It was oblong in shape, being narrower at the top than at the base. The stone was about six inches thick.

He asked, "And you translated this inscription?"

"Well, many of my contemporaries believe this stone retells a tale of Old Norse mythology. They believe the stone describes a mythical journey to the Hvergelmer Well. The Hvergelmer is a river that pours from Niflheim, which is similar to the Greek's underworld or the Christian's hell."

"But you believe it translates differently?" Leah asked.

"I believe that it describes a real voyage undertaken by a father and his son between 1100 and 1200 CE."

Jacob said in disbelief, "A real voyage to hell?"

"Well of course not, but a voyage that could have inspired the Old Norse myth of Niflheim."

Garron asked, "The myth doesn't predate the stone?"

"It does, but I believe that this stone is a marker for just one voyage of many. I believe that expeditions like the one inscribed on this stone were occurring for generations." Ole smiled broadly. "I can see the doubt on your faces."

"Sorry Ole, this is just new to all of us," Leah apologized for the trio.

"There is no need to apologize," He said with a smile.

"So what does the stone say?" Jacob asked.

Ole translated from the stone:

Olaf and Olafson travel to the source of darkness. Here they retrieved ice from the ice wall and covered it in animal hides. The ice is loaded aboard a ship that holds no men. That ship is pulled behind Olaf's ship for a four moon journey to the land of Odrerir. Let Thor protect their voyage.

Ole pointed to a drawing of a figure on the stone. "This represents Thor, who was often called upon to protect sailors on other rune stones. And down here near the bottom is a date. It has been obscured, but it reads either 1121 or 1171."

"What is the significance of this inscription, Doctor?" Garron asked.

"You must please call me Ole. It is important because of the length of the journey." Ole explained, "I found this stone on an island in the Arctic Circle, Jan Mayen. It is a remote island covered by a glacier that is also home to an active volcano."

"There is a glacier as well as a volcano on the same island. That must be rare," Jacob said.

"Not as rare as you might think, but it is an interesting geological region."

Garron recaps, "So Olaf and his son sail to Jan Mayen and take ice from the glacier and bring it back home."

Ole shook his head. "Not back home. The journey took four moons, that is, four full moons or four months."

"Four months?" Leah was astounded, "How far did he tow that piece of ice?"

"That is why this rune stone is significant. Four months on the Atlantic would put these men either in Africa or the Caribbean."

Jacob had a revelation, "That's why you're here on Bimini."

Ole smiled again.

"So you're suggesting that Vikings were in the Caribbean before 1200 AD," Leah offered.

"That was my theory, and my white stone helps to substantiate this theory," he motioned to the lighter stone in the second case.

He translated the short inscription:

Olaf who died at sea on his voyage to deliver the ice wall ice.

"This is dated 1122," Ole finished.

"That's all that it says?" Jacob asked.

Garron smiled and asked, "Ole, where did you find this stone?"

Ole chuckled, "Right here on Bimini."

"So there is your proof. Vikings were in the Caribbean in 1122, hauling ice from the Artic circle." Leah patted the doctor on his shoulder.

Garron asked, "But why Bimini? How did you know to look here?"

"That is where Anton was able to help. He said that he had collected folktales from several cultures around the Atlantic basin that described voyages to the Caribbean centuries before the Spanish. And he said that one of those stories mentioned ice. Anton led me to Bimini. We discovered the stone just off the coast less than one mile from here. It was submerged. It seems that water levels were lower at the time of Olaf's death."

"How does this tie in with The Brotherhood's treasure?" Jacob asked.

"You will have to ask Anton," Ole responded. Ole looked at his watch. "And you can ask him now. We are to meet at Gracie's lab right now."

***

When Jacob, Leah, and Garron were led into Dr. Ng's lab by Ole, Anton was looking over Gracie's shoulder at the sketches Garron recovered from the Old City Gates. Garron saw Jacob's backpack lying on the floor. The Pinzón portolan and the Waldseemüller 1507 map were on Gracie's desk.

Like Ole, Gracie was using one of the resort's rooms for something that it was not originally intended. She had set up her lab in what would have been the resort's most spacious two story suite. The lower level of the suite had a bathroom and one large room that overlooked the ocean through a pair of French doors. The upper level held the bedroom, and looked over the large living space with an open balcony. Dr. Ng was using the large first floor for her laboratory.

Anton looked up from the drawings and smiled. "I hope that you found Ole's research interesting. He has done some really excellent work."

Ole beamed with pride.

"Gracie has been working on the sketches that you found for us Garron. They seem to have been drawn by the Pinta's surgeon, Maestro Diego. No doubt Malik told you of Diego joining Pinzón's landing party when they went ashore on Babeque. But I don't want to steal Gracie's thunder, so Dr. Ng if you will?"

Gracie looked at Anton speculatively. "How much do you want me to tell them?"

Anton put a reassuring hand on her shoulder. "There is no need to worry. These folks are not like the other members of The Brotherhood. We can trust them. Once they see what we have found and understand our intentions, they will see the errors of their brethren."

Gracie Ng hesitated a moment longer, removed her glasses and then explained what she had found. "Maestro Diego's sketches have eluded us for some time now, and at one point I doubted their existence, yet here they are. We had identified five of the seven items from other sources, but without these sketches we never would have identified the final elements. Look at these drawings."

Gracie replaced her glasses and called up the images on her computer screen. Jacob, Leah, and Garron stepped closer to the computer. The first image was of a tree with beautiful purple flowers. Included in the sketch was a pod of the tree that resembled a string of beads.

Gracie said, "This is Lonchocarpus violaceus, or the balché tree."

Gracie brought up the next slide.

"This is Diego's best rendering of ice."

The sketch showed a rough block of ice melting; a vessel collected the melt water.

Referring to the sketch on the screen, Gracie said, "This had given Anton some trouble. I mean, how do you identify where the ice was harvested? The ice sketch coupled with the next one," she opened another image, "confused us for a while, but that's when Ole found the second rune stone." She smiled at her colleague.

The new image was that of the same vessel being filled with water. The water was labeled in Latin.

Gracie translated, "The water from a pool on this island, Babeque water."

She advanced to the next slide. A rendering of a bee and a honeycomb filled the screen.

"This is Meliponini beecheii m. yucatanica, or the Royal Lady Bee of the Yucatan. Or more precisely, it is the honey that is of interest. It was the rendering of the little man in the corner of the page mixing the honey in a canoe that helped us identify this little guy. The Maya use this particular honey in their fermenting of Balché, an intoxicant like mead."

The next slide popped up on the screen. It was a tree with large pods hanging from its branches.

"This was easily identified. This is Theobroma cacao, where chocolate comes from."

Gracie advanced to the next slide.

"This is one of our new items. I was able to identify it easily due to Diego's attention to detail. This plant is Ikarisou. It has been used for centuries by Japanese and Chinese herbalists. The dried leaf and stem are powdered and then used as an aphrodisiac."

Gracie removed her glasses once again. She spun in her chair and looked at Anton. "Finding Ikarisou means that this trade system is even more global than we thought. We are rewriting history with each advance."

She then advanced the slide. "But this little sucker is difficult to identify. It is well drawn, but still elusive. I do not, nor does the algorithm that you provided, recognize it. It appears to be part of the Alcalypha family, but it is a species with which I am unfamiliar."

The sketch was of another plant. It looked to be a woody shrub or tree with red stringy flowers hanging from the thin limbs.

Anton smiled widely. "You'll find it, my dear, I know that you will."

Garron spoke up, "I'm more confused than ever, what do these sketches have to do with the treasure?"

Gracie stared at Garron for a long moment. "You really don't know, do you?"

Garron heard the anger in her tone. "That's why I'm asking."

She shook her head. "How do you make a pledge to a cult like The Brotherhood that keeps such vital information from you? A cult that kills a six-year-old boy's father for asking the same question that you just posed."

Anton placed a gentle hand on Gracie's shoulder. "Gracie, that is how The Brotherhood recruits its members. They perpetuate ignorance and exploit relationships. Our guests were told very little, only that I had a part in the killing of their friends. Of course they chose to side with The Brotherhood under those circumstances. We would all probably do the same."

Anton met Jacob's eye. "It is time for you to know the whole truth. I'll explain as I show you the rest of my facility. I believe a tour will help to answer your questions."

Leah, Jacob, and Garron followed Anton into the hot morning sun. Ole and Gracie stayed behind to continue their work. They followed the path behind the cottages in which the trio was staying. The sound of the surf and shorebirds was carried on the wind. Palms rattled as they swayed.

Anton asked, "So you know the story of Martín Alonso Pinzón coming ashore on Babeque, and you know of his meeting with Garacana?"

"We do. Our story left off with Garacana offering the captain a sealed gourd," Garron responded.

Anton nodded. "After Pinzón received the gourd from Garacana, he immediately attempted to break the resin seal and peer inside, but Garacana would not allow this. Garacana wretched the gourd back from the captain. Pinzón drew his sword. The scene must have been chaotic. Garacana pleaded with the interpreter to convince the captain that he meant no disrespect or harm. The cacique and the interpreter began to argue. Garacana was desperate for the captain to understand him, but the interpreter seemed unwilling to translate the chief's wishes. Finally, Garacana pulled a short spear from the wall of the hut and drove it into the interpreter's side. Pinzón raised his sword to strike the chief, but Garacana dropped the spear and began to unseal the gourd."

The group continued walking past the lobby entrance and the dining hall. They walked beyond the west wing of the resort and came to a series of large domed buildings. They appeared to be greenhouses.

Anton continued his tale, "Garacana poured the contents of the gourd onto the wound of the writhing interpreter. Maestro Diego pushed the cacique away from the wounded man and applied pressure with a piece of clothing he found in the hut. Pinzón demanded that the interpreter explain why Garacana attacked him. The wounded man spoke of Bimini."

Jacob stopped suddenly near the pathway leading to the greenhouse entrance.

He said, "That's what was in that gourd? That's what Pinzón discovered? That can't be."

Garron saw the shock on his brother's face.

Anton said, "That is exactly what it is!"

"But that's just a myth, sought after by fools for centuries," Jacob argued.

"Yet I have a letter in Francisco Pinzón's own hand explaining what he witnessed that day. A letter addressed to his Brethren, pleading for them to continue to guard their secret even after his death."

Jacob mumbled, "It can't be, it just can't be."

Garron demanded, "What is it? What are you two talking about?"

Anton replied, "As your brother obviously knows, Bimini in the Taíno language means *life of the spring waters* or the Water of Life."

***

The group was still in shock as they followed Anton into the greenhouse. Just inside the door, they were met by a forceful blast of air from overhead. Then a second interior door opened and they entered. Inside were dozens of trees planted neatly in rows stretching the length of the building. Each tree stood about twenty-five feet in height. The dense canopy of the trees was in bloom with beautiful lavender flowers; the air was thick with a sweet fragrance.

Garron said, "So you're telling me that Pinzón found the Fountain of Youth? That's ridiculous."

"What he found was the Elixir of Life," Anton corrected. "The myth led many adventurers astray. They began looking for a fountain or spring, when they should have been looking for the ingredients that made up the elixir."

"You're saying that whatever Garacana poured from that gourd was the Elixir of Life?" Leah asked.

"The elixir that Garacana poured from the gourd healed the wound of that poor interpreter right before Diego and Pinzón's eyes. After only an hour, the wound was invisible and the man no longer felt any pain. I have a letter from Maestro Diego to Vicente verifying that fact."

"And those Diego sketches were of the ingredients to the elixir," Garron said.

"Exactly, and I've spent my life hunting them down and collecting them. My father copied many of the drawings from the archives, which is why he was murdered, but two of the ingredients had eluded us until now."

Anton turned to face the trees and raised both arms into the air.

"These are the trees from the drawings," Leah acknowledged.

"These are the balché trees. And if you look closely at the flowers, then you will see the royal lady bees diligently at work creating our second ingredient, the honey."

Garron could see the bees dancing from flower to flower on nearly every tree throughout the greenhouse.

A short man with brown skin and a khaki uniform stepped out from between the trees.

Anton waved enthusiastically at the man, who waved back. "That is Alejandro, my beekeeper. We were very lucky to find him and his bees. The royal lady bee is endangered. Although their production of honey was valuable to the ancient Maya, current generations have supplanted the native species with the more productive Africanized honey bee. Tending these bees is nearly a lost art form."

Garron watched as Alejandro moved between stacks of cut tree limbs.

Anton followed Garron's gaze.

He explained, "The royal ladies make their hives in hollow logs and limbs. The Maya simply find the bee colony in the forest, cut the section of the limb containing the hive, seal the cut ends, and then bring it home. Alejandro insisted on not transplanting the hives to more modern box hives. And who am I to argue with tradition?"

They watched as Alejandro carefully uncapped one end of a tree limb that he selected and scooped out some honey. He placed the honey into a small glass vial and resealed the hive.

"Alejandro makes it look so easy, but believe me, there is a true art to harvesting the honey from the hive without damaging the comb. If a comb is too severely damaged, the colony will abandon the hive. Our previous beekeeper lost three hives due to his heavy handedness. Alejandro was a godsend."

Garron said, "I'm hung up on something Anton. I can't figure out why the Pinzóns or The Brotherhood would want to keep the elixir from the world."

"Imagine a world without disease. Cancer, heart disease, blood disorders, all eliminated. Cellular degeneration and senility, the effects of aging halted. A person could essentially live forever. To *The Brotherhood of the Three*

Crosses this possibility was sacrilege. Life was a gift from God. The act of living was simply a means to reach a promised heaven. But if life was everlasting here on earth, what did that mean for Christ's promise of an afterlife? This is a noble argument for keeping the elixir hidden, but to me it seems too altruistic."

Anton led the way to the second of the greenhouses. The second greenhouse, too, was filled with trees, although these were cacao trees.

Anton continued his argument, "I have difficulty believing that a captain so interested in capturing his own gold would pass up on arguably the most valuable product ever created. His greed drove him to find Babeque, or rather Bimini, in the first place. Because of the total annihilation of Garacana's village, no one was left to pass on the secrets of where to harvest the ingredients for the elixir. I think that it is likely that The Brotherhood wanted to 'patent' the process before making the discovery known. A great deal of wealth was at risk."

Garron asked, "Didn't Pinzón die shortly after returning to Spain from an illness?"

Anton nodded, "My father explained in a letter he had left in his personal effects, that The Brotherhood would reveal the elixir once the world was converted to Christianity, which at the time seemed possible. In spite of the Muslim victories in the Holy Land, Isabella and Ferdinand had finally pushed out the Moors from Granada, the final Muslim stronghold in Europe. And with the Catholic Monarch's Inquisition, it seemed as though the path for Christianity was being paved. The discovery of the New World was proof that the monarchy was blessed by God. It is possible that Pinzón believed that finding the elixir was divine intervention, saving him from a life driven by greed. And the fact that he chose to die of his illness contracted on the voyage adds credence to this argument."

Garron argued, "If Pinzón was protecting Christianity by not releasing the elixir, then why wait for the conversion of the world's souls? There seems to be contradictions in that argument. It seems like Pinzón stole an opportunity from the Catholic Church, if indeed he kept the elixir secret to protect Christianity. Who wouldn't convert to a religion that could literally baptize you with the Elixir of Life?"

Anton nodded. "You have captured it perfectly." Anton had led the group to the end of the greenhouse. "What ever you choose to believe about Pinzón's intentions, the fact is that The Brotherhood did manage to keep the elixir hidden, and that no one profited from the find."

Anton motioned to the trees that they had just passed. "These are my cacao trees. Just another of the elixir's ingredients that we have gathered here on Bimini. Just behind this building is a custom freezer unit where we house our Jan Mayen glacial ice."

"Why gather all of the ingredients here?" Garron asked.

"Yes, it certainly would have been easier for those ancient mariners to bring the other ingredients to the ice," Leah added.

"We know that the Vikings brought the ice here, which was not an easy task, and we know that the Maya traveled to Bimini as well, bringing their balché. So we extrapolated that Bimini's water is somehow at the literal center of the elixir's manufacturing process."

"But what's so special about this water?" Jacob asked.

"The water contains high levels of magnesium, lithium, and sulfur, but other springs around the world contain much of the same minerals. We believe that it has something to do with the microbial life within the water here. If the water is transported for great distances, then we believe that something within the water sample changes, rendering the ingredient useless. It is still a mystery. So we bring everything here just like the ancient mariners did."

Garron clarified, "So centuries ago travelers would descend on Bimini from across the seas. They would bring with them specific endemic ingredients from their home ports and add them to the elixir's recipe. A tribal chief would mix the ingredients together and reward the mariners with eternal life."

Jacob asked sarcastically, "Why don't we have 500-year-old Vikings and Maya still sailing the seven seas?"

"I don't know. But my theory is that the chief understood the power of the elixir, and was able to control the solution's concentration. He would make the elixir just powerful enough to keep his mariners returning for more, and providing the needed ingredients."

Jacob said, "It seems unlikely that the elixir died with Garacana."

Anton asked, "Does it?" He continued, "The elixir would have been a tightly guarded secret among a very select number of individuals. With the destruction that the Spanish and then other Europeans brought to the New World, is it really hard to believe that all who held the sacred knowledge were lost?"

Leah countered, "But they had the Elixir of Life. Disease should not have decimated the native population like it did."

"That is a strong argument, and one that I have trouble countering. But consider that some of the native population did survive the introduction of the new epidemics. And remember that other ceremonies and social behaviors were exterminated by the Spanish onslaught. So with the loss of the Bimini elders, then the elixir may have been lost to the local populations as well."

"But all of this is still speculation. Until now you haven't known the ingredients in order to test your theory," Garron said.

"You are correct. I have spent my life trying to find those ingredients, and now we are just a short step away from providing the world with its greatest gift."

Anton led his guest out of the greenhouse. "I must leave you; I have some business to attend to. Please make yourselves at home, enjoy the sun and surf." Anton beamed.

"Anton, I need to call my wife," Garron interrupted the niceties.

Anton nodded. "She must be worried about you, but I cannot involve anyone else in what we are doing here. My success thus far is due to a high level of secrecy." He seemed to consider his options and then said, "May I contact her in your stead, and ask her to join us?"

Garron smiled. "You don't know my wife Anton, she's not that pliable. If you called on my behalf, then she would never let you off the phone without complete disclosure."

"Then may I ask that you leave a scripted message for her at one of her offices? Then I will make my invitation after she understands that you are safe and sound."

"Couldn't you just monitor my call to be sure that I do not divulge anything of importance?" Garron proposed.

Anton weighed that option. He said, "You, yourself, said that she will not let you off the phone without full disclosure; so I cannot allow it. I am sorry."

Garron considered Anton's offer. "Okay, we'll do it your way. But remember that trust is a two way street, Mr. Margaux."

Anton smiled and bowed slightly.

***

Garron called Veronica from Anton's office. He read from a script that Anton had written, which said very little, but should help waylay Veronica's anxiety. Anton would have his work cut out for him once he makes his invitation.

Leah and Jacob had returned to their cottage, with the intention of joining Garron for lunch at noon in the dining hall. It was eleven-fifteen. Garron strolled on the pathway that led to the cottages; he had enough time to freshen up before lunch. As Garron passed the building that housed Dr. Ng's lab, he saw the doctor smoking a cigarette in a small patio near the building's entrance.

Garron surprised her when he said, "Hello Dr. Ng."

She jumped at the sound of his voice.

"You startled me." She looked at her cigarette. "It's a dirty habit, but I only smoke two or three of these a week, just when I've hit a road block."

"So you're having trouble with that final ingredient?" Garron asked.

She nodded and extinguished her cigarette.

"It seems familiar, but I just can't pin it down." Her eyes went out of focus.

They stood in silence for a long moment.

Garron said, "Okay, well maybe I'll see you at lunch."

As he started to walk away, the doctor said, "Mr. Shepard, I am sorry about my outburst earlier in my lab. Anton explained that circumstances pushed you toward The Brotherhood."

"There is no need for an apology, and please call me Garron, we just found ourselves on different sides of this difficult situation. I still don't know where I stand in all of this."

Dr. Ng extended her hand. "Please call me Gracie. You're different than I expected. Anton told me that you're an artist, and yet you seem pretty analytical in the way you are gathering the facts and reserving judgment."

Garron graciously took the doctor's hand and shook. "Well, this is the first time since this all began that I've been given the opportunity to truly weigh my options. These last few days, I've been caught in an emotional whirlwind."

Gracie asked, "May I walk with you?"

They followed the path toward the beach at a leisurely pace. The air was hot, but it was different than the Florida heat. There were towering cumulus clouds rising in the blue sky. A number of pelicans floating on the air currents passed in and out of view between the trees.

"So why are you here Gracie?" Garron asked the doctor.

"Anton was in need of a botanist, and he made me an offer that I couldn't refuse. My mom suffers from ALS. It is a horrible disease and it attacked Mom quickly. So I am sure that you understand the implications of my research."

"For your mom's sake, I wish you luck with your search."

"Thank you."

Garron squinted against the sun. "Do you get to see your mom often?"

Gracie nodded. "Anton flies me back to San Francisco once a month. He has paid for my mother's medical expenses and at-home care since I joined the search."

She continued, "If it wasn't for Anton, I don't know what I would do. My father died when I was a senior in high school. He was the sole bread-winner at the time, we had to scrape bottom to survive. I was lucky enough to earn a scholarship to Stanford, but I still needed loans to cover other expenses. Plus, Mom was diagnosed when I was a sophomore in college. Anton has taken care of it all, my loans, Mom's medical expenses, even housing for my mother. He's a good man."

Garron had to admit that Anton did not seem to be the villain that Malik had made him out to be.

They now stood in front of Garron's cottage, looking out toward the sea.

Garron could see Leah and Jacob swimming just beyond the breaking waves. Leah wrapped her arms around Jacob's neck and kissed him gently.

Gracie said, "I guess Anton provided some swim suits. Those two seem to be a sweet couple."

Garron could hear the swimmers laughing, and then he saw Leah force Jacob under the water playfully.

"I'm going to get cleaned up for lunch." He turned and walked into his cottage.

***

Anton was speaking in a low voice to Taylor, his head of security, when Leah, Jacob, and Garron entered the dining hall. They were the only two in the room. Taylor then left the hall with a slight nod as he passed by the newcomers.

Anton said, "Please come in and have a seat. Gracie will be joining us shortly. Ole is at his archaeological dig site up the beach, he rarely stops for lunch."

The trio took their seats.

Leah asked, "Ole is still digging on the island?"

"I can't get him to stop. He is determined to find the original site of Garacana's village. You should ask to join him. He loves to show off his work."

Gracie entered the hall carrying Jacob's red backpack. She smiled at the group and handed the bag to Anton.

Anton said, "Jacob, I would like for you to have this back."

Jacob took the bag and was surprised at its heft. He unzipped the zipper and looked into the pocket. He said, "It's the folio. You're returning the folio?"

"I have no use for it, and the letter inside was addressed to you," Anton answered.

Garron watched as Jacob pulled the folio from the bag and ran a hand gently across the binding. He opened the folio and examined several pages.

Jacob came out of his reverie and asked, "If the map is of little importance, then why did Murphy go to such lengths to hide it?"

"The portolan that you have there, the one drawn by Martín Alonso himself, is one of the source materials for the Waldseemüller map. Historically, it is a treasure. Pinzón did a masterful job of noting the coastlines of several Caribbean islands and the coast of Florida while he was separated from the fleet. It is rumored that his source for the South American continent's coastline was Garacana himself. Apparently he had made the voyage through the Straits of Florida and across the Caribbean frequently. His village traded with the Maya regularly." Anton leaned over the table and tented his fingers. "It is a significant piece of history, but it is not relevant to my research. So I would like for you to have it back. It belongs to you."

Jacob took a sip from his water glass. He said in a low voice, "Thank you."

Chef Eddie entered with their lunches. They would feast on Caribbean lobster, shrimp salad, and a slice of mango.

Speaking to Jacob, Anton continued, "Your portolan marks a significant milestone in the history of The Brotherhood." Anton looked around the table to see that he had everyone's attention. "During the late fifteenth and early sixteenth century, information regarding the newly discovered territories was highly sought after, so much so that some European countries or monarchies would pay spies to smuggle information to gain the latest in intelligence. Your portolan was a part of that espionage." Anton paused and sipped his water. He continued, "In 1502, a member of The Brotherhood stole several maps from the archives and sold them to an Italian spy, Alberto Cantino. Alberto was hired by the Duke of Ferrara to monitor Spain and Portugal's western discoveries. The sale of the maps led to the first murder of a Brother within *The Brotherhood of the Three Crosses*. The *Vicarius* that was murdered was not a member of the Pinzón family. It was after 1502 that the selection process for members was strictly enforced, and that family was always given first priority when new brethren were considered." Anton kept his gaze on Jacob; he had obviously chronicled the story for Jacob's benefit.

Jacob clutched the folio in his arms, with his gaze somewhere in the distance. Leah squeezed Jacob's shoulder bringing him back from his thoughts. He smiled at her weakly and replaced the folio in the backpack.

"Anton, how did you uncover what The Brotherhood was protecting?" Leah asked.

Anton's face clouded for a brief instant. He said, "My father never had the chance to tell me of his involvement with The Brotherhood before his death, but he did leave papers in a safe deposit box that I recovered. My father left instructions with my mom to hold the papers until I turned thirteen. That was the day that my life changed." Anton's gaze drifted and he sat silently for a moment.

He refocused, "To answer your question Ms. Preston, the single most valuable clue to finding the elixir was the Diego drawing that my father removed from the archives." Anton sat back in his chair. "Martín Alonso spoke through his translator with Garacana for hours the night before leaving Bimini. He wanted to know where the exotic ingredients of the elixir could be found. Garacana could only describe the pilgrims who delivered the ingredients to his village. Diego drew those pilgrims from Garacana's description. I have studied those drawings since I was thirteen years old. They are masterfully done, like the botanical drawings that you found in St. Augustine. Diego paid great attention to every detail including skin color, type of dress, hair style, and the type of boat in which the pilgrim arrived. It was through those drawings that we were able to locate the geographic regions in which the ingredients could be found." He paused. "Garron, I am sure that you would enjoy the artistry of those drawings." Anton looked to Dr. Ng. "Would you allow Garron to view them Gracie?"

Gracie nodded. She turned and smiled brightly. "Just let me know when you would like to see them."

Gracie's smile was captivating. Garron nodded and smiled back.

Chef Eddie returned to clear the table.

"Chef, you once again outdid yourself. Thank you."

"As always, it was my pleasure Mr. Margaux." He nodded to the group and asked, "Can I be expecting everyone for dinner this evening? I'm heading into town to pick up some beautiful duck that I had brought over this morning."

Everyone agreed that duck sounded delicious, and that they would all return to his dining room at seven o'clock.

Anton rose from his chair. "Thank you for your wonderful conversation, I am looking forward to getting to know you better at every meal. Enjoy your afternoon."

The group said their goodbyes. Anton and Gracie moved toward her lab, and Garron followed Leah and Jacob to their cottage.

Chapter 8

"WHAT DO YOU think?" Garron asked his brother.

After lunch, they had returned to Leah and Jacob's cottage and they sat outside under the cottage's veranda in teak Adirondack chairs.

Jacob shook his head. "I don't know what to think. I have to admit that Anton is not at all what I expected."

Leah said, "He has been gracious and his willingness to share has caught me off guard."

"Even the script that he had me read to Veronica was rather forthcoming. He allowed me to use his name and to give our location," Garron agreed. "I was talking to Gracie earlier and she told me that Anton was covering all of her mother's medical expenses, her mom has ALS. Plus he paid off her family's debt."

"That makes it difficult to see him as the villain," Leah said.

They sat quietly for a minute.

Garron asked, "Do you think that Murphy was having second thoughts about The Brotherhood as well?"

"He was obviously digging through the archives looking for something," Leah added.

Garron said, "His trail seemed to prove that he was looking for the treasure, or as we now know, the elixir, and I think that he was getting close."

The trio sat silently looking out over the surf for several minutes.

Jacob finally asked, "Do you think that The Brotherhood could have killed Murphy?"

Garron and Jacob made eye contact.

"I know that's what Anton wants us to believe. He could mean to misdirect us," Leah offered.

Garron answered, "To what end? And if Anton is the villain in all of this, then why keep us alive?"

They sat in silence once more. On the beach, shorebirds fed quickly between the lapping waves.

Jacob said, "I just keep thinking about Dad and how painful his last few months were, and how this elixir could keep families from suffering like that." Jacob's back straightened. "I intend to see this thing through to the end, but Gar, maybe you should fly home to Veronica. If this thing turns sour, I don't want you and Veronica to end up in harm's way."

Garron considered his brother's advice. If Anton was manipulating them, then he did not want to leave Jacob alone in this fight. But he also did not want to bring Veronica into Anton's web. And he knew that if he stayed, then his wife could not be kept away. But if Anton was being honest, and the dissemination of the elixir was his true goal, then Garron wanted to help in anyway that he could to reach that end.

Garron thought of his father, Gracie's mother, and Veronica's pilot Joe and his wife. He decided, "I'm staying."

Jacob nodded. "Then we enjoy Anton's hospitality, but at the same time we should keep our eyes and ears open for trouble."

Leah smiled. "I really would like to be a part of bringing the elixir back to the world."

Garron climbed out of his Adirondack and stepped off the veranda. He agreed with Leah, "I would, too." He looked out to sea. "I'm going for a swim. I'll catch up with you later."

Jacob rose as well. "I need to stretch my legs." He smiled at Leah.

Leah knew that Jacob meant that he needed some time alone. She nodded. "If I can catch him, then I'm going to ride into town with Chef Eddie. I'd like to find some snorkel equipment."

***

Jacob walked the grounds of the resort, following the footpaths that meandered along the beach and through lush vegetation. He thought about Murphy's search through the archives in an attempt to identify the treasure. Jacob wondered if the fraternity to which Murphy had pledged his life could have killed him. What would Murphy have thought about the treasure actually being an elixir? Jacob thought about his father as well and the pain he endured at the end of his life. Jacob felt the loss of those men deeply.

Jacob heard three quick gun shots coming from further down the path. He stepped cautiously between palms and sea grape that blocked his view. Three more shots froze him in his tracks.

Jacob heard men laughing. He eased around the vegetation and saw Anton with two of his men shooting at coconuts set up for target practice on the beach. Anton's nickel plated pistol gleamed in the afternoon sun.

Anton turned when Taylor motioned toward Jacob on the path.

He said, "Hello Jacob, come and join us."

Jacob approached the three men cautiously as Anton reloaded his revolver.

In explanation Anton said, "This is my way of releasing some tension. I hope that I didn't startle you."

Jacob said, "That's a beautiful gun. Is it a Colt?"

"You know your weapons. Yes, it's a Colt Single Action Army revolver. It's an 1882 Storekeeper model with a four-inch barrel." Anton beamed.

Jacob asked, ".45 caliber?"

"Exactly. It is powerful and easily concealed."

"Here take a shot," Anton suggested.

Anton closed the chamber and handed the gun to Jacob. As Jacob took the weapon, he saw Taylor tense slightly. Jacob looked down the beach at the palm stump holding the coconut. He cocked the hammer and took aim.

Anton said, "Remember that it has quite a kick."

Jacob squeezed the trigger slowly. The gun sounded like a cannon and kicked toward the sky, jarring Jacob's elbow. The coconut exploded sending water into the air.

Anton laughed. He commended Jacob, "Nice shot!"

Jacob's ears rang slightly. He handed the pistol back to Anton. Once he had relinquished the Colt, Taylor relaxed.

Jacob said, "That is a powerful weapon, powerful and beautiful."

"Thank you. This gun belonged to my great grandfather. I cherish it."

"I can understand why. Thanks for letting me take a shot."

"We will have to do it again. Just not today, I have an understanding with the local constable. I am aloud nine shots a day. I am actually not allowed to have the weapon on the island, but I let the constable handle the Colt occasionally and, like you, he appreciates its beauty, so he looks the other way."

Anton asked, "Where is your lovely companion?"

"She went into town with Chef Eddie. She's going to get us some snorkel gear while Eddie gathers some things from the market." Jacob looked at his watch. "I should check to see if she's back." Jacob turned back toward the path. He said, "Thanks again, that Colt really is a magnificent weapon."

"You are most welcome. Enjoy your snorkeling, have fun," Anton replied.

***

As Garron stepped out of the ocean after his swim, he found Gracie holding his towel. She was wearing a visor, sunglasses, and a running outfit that hugged her body tightly. Ear buds hung around her neck. Her legs and arms were well-toned. Gracie Ng was obviously a runner. Her petite frame was well sculpted, but still feminine.

She held the towel out for Garron. "You looked very comfortable out there."

Gracie nodded toward the water.

Garron toweled himself dry. "I like it better than running."

"When I get stuck, I either smoke or run. I figure running is the better choice."

Garron said, "It's been a long time since I swam in the ocean. I like feeling that buoyant. I'm glad Anton supplied the trunks."

Gracie eyed him from head to toe. She smiled sheepishly. "It looks like you swim quite a bit."

Garron blushed and wrapped the towel around him.

Gracie laughed. "I'm just saying that you look pretty fit."

Garron smiled at the compliment. He said, "I was thinking about those drawings by Diego while I was swimming. Do you think that I could take a look at them?"

Gracie did not hesitate, "Sure, I'll meet you in my lab in 40 minutes. I want to grab a quick shower."

She pulled off her visor and ran her fingers through her raven black hair.

Garron caught himself admiring the way her hair shone in the sunlight.

He stammered slightly when Gracie noticed his gaze, "I need a shower, too. I'll see you later."

He headed for his cottage without looking back.

***

In Gracie's lab, Garron took a seat on a stool pulled closely to a leather bound notebook placed under a work light. Gracie's hair was still wet from her shower, and Garron could smell the sweetness of her shampoo as she stood above him and handed him a pair of white cotton gloves.

Drawn in ink on the page open before him was a broad man with long hair and a long beard. The man in the image wore a three-quarter length coat held by a wide belt. The lapel and the front were intricately ornamented. A conical helmet with nose guard adorned his head, and long boots covered his feet and calves. The sketch was exquisite.

Garron flipped to the next sketch in the notebook. A man wearing a short shirt or tunic wrapped with a length of cloth around the waist was the subject of the second drawing. The shirt had an elaborate woven pattern near the neck. The man's facial characteristics were interesting; he had a sloped forehead and narrow eyes. Diego had drawn two round stones protruding from the bridge of the nose representing a piercing. It was obviously the Mayan pilgrim represented on the page.

Garron looked up from the notebook and said, "These are beautiful. They are so detailed."

"These sketches helped a great deal in tracking down the ingredients," Gracie acknowledged.

"But you are still having difficulty with the last ingredient," Garron stated.

Gracie nodded and flipped to another drawing in the notebook. "I believe that this guy must be the source of the final ingredient, but I am still missing something."

The pilgrim on the page was a black man heavily adorned with jewelry: bracelets, rings, and a necklace with a large pendant. The man wore flowing robes and a small round cap on his head.

Gracie said, "I've been able to identify the man as someone from northwestern Africa; either from the Mali or Songhai Empires. And we've searched that part of the continent for any plants that have been rumored to have health benefits. There were many, and we had a few contenders, but none match the drawing that you found for us." Gracie laid a hand on Garron's shoulder and smiled.

Garron returned the smile and felt a rush of pride. He could see the pages that he and Leah found in the Old City Gates spread out on the table to his right. He took in the sketch of the Ikarisou and said, "Don't lose track of the size of this trade network. Maybe the African acquired the final ingredient through trade. The plant may not be indigenous to the African continent."

Gracie pulled a stool up beside Garron. "That is my new working theory. So I have expanded my search globally. But the algorithm has not yet identified the plant."

"How does the algorithm work?" Garron asked.

"It functions much like facial recognition software. It compares the plant's most distinguishing features to those in scientific databases across the world. Many nations have catalogued their indigenous plants in a hope to fight the extinction of endemic species."

The sketch of the bees and honeycomb caught Garron's eye. He thought of the threatened royal lady bees. He asked, "Does your algorithm cover extinct species?"

Gracie nodded slowly and slid the drawing of the woody plant in front of her. "That is my greatest fear, that the plant is extinct."

Garron took in the artistry of Diego's sketches once again. "Can your algorithm check the plant against other artwork?"

Gracie cocked her head to the side and asked, "Other artwork?"

"I'm probably way off base here, but could it be possible that our mysterious plant has been captured in other works of art? Maybe not necessarily the subject of the painting, drawing, or even the photograph, but possibly the plant could be a part of the landscape or background of the piece," Garron suggested.

Gracie nodded slowly. She leaned over the drawing and examined the plant's features carefully with a lighted magnifying glass. After several minutes of examining the drawing, she looked up and met Garron's eye. "I think that I need to adapt the algorithm. Please don't be offended, but would you excuse me while I work?"

Garron was excited. "You think that it's possible? Could the algorithm do that?"

She rubbed her eyes and then turned toward another desk and found her glasses. She placed them on the bridge of her nose and smiled slightly. Gracie answered, "You may very well be onto something." With her attention already back on the sheet in front of her, she said, "I'll see you at dinner."

Garron did not want to leave on the verge of making a breakthrough, but he wanted to respect Gracie's request for privacy. He decided to leave Gracie to her work and left the lab.

***

Garron entered the dining hall well before seven o'clock, anxious to see if Gracie had made any progress since he had left her in the lab rewriting the algorithm. Anton stood in the room speaking to Chef Eddie. No one else had yet arrived.

Anton said excitedly, "Garron, I have some excellent news."

Garron smiled widely and said, "What did she find?"

Anton was taken aback. "I'm sorry, what did who find?"

"I thought that you were speaking of Gracie. I'm sorry, what were you going to say?"

"Gracie will not be joining us for dinner. Apparently she wants to work through dinner this evening." Anton paused. "The good news is that your wife will be joining us in two days. She will be flying into Miami from overseas the day after next."

Garron was still torn about having Veronica involved, but he said, "Fantastic. Thank you for allowing her to join us."

"Of course, I look forward to meeting her. I am a bit in awe of how successful your wife has been over the past decade. Everything that she touches seems to turn to gold. I could probably learn a thing or two from her." He laughed.

Garron smiled. "I am very proud of Veronica, thank you."

Leah and Jacob entered the room, followed closely by Ole Hansen. Leah was in a beautiful printed strapless dress that showed off her well-toned arms, shoulders, and her long neck. Jacob was wearing a linen shirt and pants with a pair of leather sandals. They both looked quite nice.

Dr. Hansen stood in stark contrast to the couple. He was wearing a dirty khaki shirt and filthy jeans. He had removed his wide brimmed sun hat and was mopping his forehead with a red handkerchief. Ole said, "I am sorry for my appearance. I just returned from my dig site. Please apologize to Eddie for me. I am not comfortable with sitting at his table looking such a mess." Ole looked down at the front of his shirt and shook his head. He turned and left the room.

Chef Eddie served a strawberry salad when his guests took their seats.

Anton said, "You two look like you enjoyed the day."

Leah said, "We did, thank you for your hospitality."

Jacob added, "And the clothes."

Leah and Jacob told Anton of their day snorkeling and swimming in the warm water. And they spoke excitedly of their hike on one of the island's nature trails. Jacob explained his excitement at seeing a Bimini boa along the trail.

"What have you been up to this afternoon?" Leah asked Garron.

"I spent some time with Gracie in her lab."

Leah shook her head slightly and stabbed her fork at the salad, spearing a strawberry.

He said, "What?"

Leah stabbed the air with her fork. She said, "Gracie's a pretty girl."

"What's that supposed to mean?" Garron asked defensively.

She pulled the strawberry from the fork with her teeth. "When we came back from snorkeling, I saw you two on the beach today after your swim. You seem to be hitting it off nicely."

Garron felt a familiar feeling rise within him. It was an anger that only Leah could stir in him.

"Just be careful, Garron, she is obviously smitten with you," Leah said as she put down her fork, having finished the salad. She wiped her mouth with her napkin.

Jacob said, "Leah, stop."

"What? It's true. I saw the way that she was looking at him. I just don't want him to do anything that he'll regret," Leah countered.

Garron felt flush. His hand shook as he took a sip of his water, the ice cubes clinked against the glass. He saw Anton looking away, obviously uncomfortable with the conversation.

"Leah, you know that Garron would never …" Jacob let his thought trail off.

Garron exploded. He pointed at Leah across the table. "You have no right to judge me, none whatsoever."

Leah stammered, "I didn't … I only …"

Garron cut her off, "You did, and you always do. Everything that you say is orchestrated, it always has been. Don't try to manipulate me. You don't have the right to tell me who I can and can't spend time with, neither of you do." Garron stood and tossed his linen napkin on the table. He strode quickly to the door.

***

Garron walked out onto the beach, breathing heavily. His arms were ridged at his sides; his fists were clenched. Garron paced across the sand trying to regain his composure. He could not understand why Leah held such power over him. Her words were as sharp as a scalpel and she wielded them with a surgeon's precision.

"Garron, are you okay?" Dr. Hansen asked from the pathway behind Garron.

Garron spun quickly, startled. "Ole, what?"

Ole had cleaned up. His hair was still damp from a shower, and he had changed into fresh clothes.

"I noticed that you were pacing, you seem agitated. Is everything all right?"

Garron did not answer.

"I am sorry to have bothered you," Ole apologized and turned to go.

"Have you had dinner?" Garron asked with a smile.

"I am heading into town now for just that reason. Would you like to join me?"

"That would be great. Thank you."

Ole led the way to a Jeep in the parking lot near the resort's front entrance. They made the five minute drive into Bailey Town, which was a small village of mostly locals. The town was quaint with Bahamian charms. The houses were small and the streets narrow. Ole parked the Jeep on the curb in front of a restaurant. Garron followed Ole into the small red building to a round table at the end of the bar.

A short man with round features and a broad smile approached their table with an exaggerated limp. In a heavy Bahamian accent the man said, "Hello Mr. Ole, you doing good today?"

"Mr. Johnny, this is my new friend, Mr. Garron," Ole said by way of introduction.

"Nice to have you, Mr. Garron," Johnny said. "Will you both be having the same?"

Ole smiled, "Yes sir. It is the best on the island."

"It's the best in the Bahamas," Johnny corrected as he disappeared into the kitchen.

A large lady in a lightweight, printed cotton dress came to the table with two bottles of Kalik Gold beer. She set the two bottles on the table. She squeezed Ole's shoulder. "Good evening, Mr. Ole." Her face was round and pleasant, and her tone welcoming.

"Hello Ms. Beth, this is Mr. Garron." Ole squeezed the hand on his shoulder affectionately.

Ms. Beth reached over and pinched Garron's cheek. "He is a cute one, where have you been hiding him?"

"He flew in just a couple of days ago," Ole answered. "You're not in the kitchen tonight?"

"My youngest is cooking. Don't you worry, she's almost as good as her momma," she answered as she went back behind the bar.

Garron said eyeing the beer bottle, "These are nice people."

"I am going to miss them when I return to Oslo. They are warm and gentle people who are generous and sincere." Ole raised his beer in a toast. He said, "To the people of Bimini."

Garron hesitated only a second and then raised his bottle in salute. The beer was cold and he drank half of the bottle in two long swallows.

Mr. Johnny returned from the kitchen with two bowls and set them before Ole and Garron. He hobbled to the bar and collected two spoons, napkins, and two more beers. The bowl was overflowing. Garron recognized corn and tomatoes, but he had no idea what else was in the bowl.

Ole saw him examining the dinner. "This is the best conch salad that you will find on the island," Ole said appraisingly.

Ms. Beth called out from behind the bar, "The best in the Bahamas."

Ole laughed.

Garron stuck his spoon into the bowl and took a tentative taste. The conch's flesh was dense, the slightly pickled taste melded nicely with the sweet corn and the acidity of the tomato. Garron quickly took another bite. With the beer, it was one of the best meals that he had ever eaten.

Ole laughed. "Ms. Beth, I believe that my new friend enjoys your conch."

She laughed robustly. To Mr. Johnny she said, "Papa, I think he'll need a second bowl."

***

Jacob and Leah walked along the beach after dinner. The sky was nearly clear of clouds and the moonlight made it almost as bright as day.

Jacob asked Leah, "What was that about?"

"What?" She asked.

Jacob responded, "Riding Garron about spending time with Gracie."

"I just don't want him to do something that he would regret."

"You know Garron almost as well as I do, and you know that he would never cheat on Veronica."

They stopped and looked out to sea.

Leah said, "I just don't like that girl clinging onto Garron."

"If I didn't know better, I would say that you are jealous."

Leah turned sharply and met Jacob's gaze. He was smiling.

Jacob took her in his arms. "Listen, I think that I understand a bit of what you are feeling. I mean when I see you with Garron it bugs me a little, so why wouldn't seeing him with another woman bother you too?"

He kissed her on the top of the head. "Just go easy on the guy. He's not going to do anything stupid."

They held hands and stuck their toes in the surf.

***

Garron enjoyed Ole's company. He was a kind man with interesting stories, but he did not dominate the conversation; he was truly interested in what Garron had to share. Throughout the evening their table was visited by many different locals, all eager to say hello to the Scandinavian. Ole knew everyone by name and inquired about family members where appropriate. Quite a crowd had gathered in the small building. It seemed odd for a Sunday night, but it was a cheerful atmosphere that everyone was enjoying. Garron lost track of the number of beers that he drank, but the table top was filled with empty bottles. He could remember precisely the number of bowls he had had of Ms. Beth's delicious conch salad; he had three.

A gentle hand grasped Garron by the shoulder and a voice raised above the din of the room asked, "Having fun?"

Garron looked up to see Gracie Ng smiling down on him and Ole.

Ole stood and hugged his colleague and said, "My dear, you look ravishing."

Garron stood as well. He had to agree that the doctor looked beautiful. Gracie was wearing a strapless lightweight cream-colored dress accentuated by a wide brown belt. She was wearing her hair down; it fell fluidly over her bare shoulders. A beaded turquoise necklace hung delicately on her chest. She was even wearing makeup.

She turned and hugged Garron, as well.

Ole went to the bar to bring the newcomer a drink.

"So, how did your research go?" Garron asked.

She shook her head, but smiled. "Later, we'll talk about it later."

Ole returned and handed Gracie a bottle of Beck's Dark and gave Garron another bottle of Kalik Gold. He then made his way over to a group of patrons and struck up a conversation.

In a voice loud enough to be heard over the crowd, Gracie said, "Ole has shared his favorite spot on the island with you. You should feel privileged."

"I do. Have you had the conch salad?" Garron responded.

Gracie laughed. "Everyone on Bimini has had Ms. Beth's conch salad."

She looked at the number of empties on the table and said, "You two have been here for awhile. If I knew that you were going out with Ole, then I would have warned you not to try to keep up with him. The man never shows any sign of intoxication."

Garron nodded that he understood. "He keeps bringing me beer. I tried to protest, but he would have nothing of it," Garron said, slurring his words.

Gracie looked Garron in the eye. She shook her head slightly and set her own unfinished beer on the table. She grabbed Garron by the arm. "I'm getting you out of here while he's distracted."

Gracie pulled Garron into the street and the warm night air. The moon was nearly full and exceptionally bright.

"Is it okay to walk?" Gracie asked. "I had someone drop me off, so I don't have a vehicle. Besides, I think the night air might do you some good."

They began walking up the street, back toward the resort. Garron had to concentrate on placing one foot in front of the other, but he agreed that the fresh air was helping to clear his head. Gracie put her arm under his and squeezed gently. The warmth and softness of her skin felt nice.

"So tell me about your research," Garron prompted.

"Your suggestion of adapting the algorithm was brilliant." Gracie squeezed his arm tenderly. "I was able to include in our search the databases of art museums around the world. The true bonus is that most museums have digitized their collections, so seeking out the source material won't be necessary."

Garron weaved into the street. He felt Gracie gently guide him back to the side of the road.

She said, "With that said, there is still a plethora of material out there. It will take a great deal of time for the algorithm to do its job, but I am still certain that we will find it."

Garron staggered into the street once more.

"Should we take a break?" Gracie asked.

"I think that it's better if we keep walking. I'm actually feeling better."

Gracie went around to Garron's other side, placing herself between him and the street. A car had not passed since they started their walk, but Garron appreciated the sentiment nonetheless.

They walked quietly for a few minutes. The lights of the resort came into view.

Gracie broke the silence, "I heard that you had an argument with Leah earlier."

"She still thinks that she owns me." Garron's inebriation became clear to him when he realized that he no longer was able to filter the thoughts spinning in his head.

Gracie said, "I don't understand. How can your brother's girlfriend own you?"

Garron compensated for his outburst and considered his response carefully.

"Leah is my ex-wife *and* my brother's girlfriend."

Garron's arm was tugged slightly as Gracie suddenly stopped beside him.

"Were they together before …" She let the question trail.

Garron shook his head slowly. "Leah and I had been divorced before they got together."

Gracie said, "Well, that's a relief." But she then qualified, "Don't get me wrong, either way it sucks."

"I'm trying to be open-minded and understanding, but it does suck," Garron agreed.

Gracie squeezed his arm and they began their stroll once again. They walked past the gatehouse. Gracie said hello to the guard. They passed the front entrance and followed the pathway to Garron's cottage.

He said, "Here we are. Thank you for rescuing me from the evil clutches of Dr. Hansen."

Gracie laughed. She stretched up and kissed Garron on the cheek. "Get some sleep," she said.

Garron watched as she walked away and her dress was caught by the light ocean breeze. He turned and stepped into his cottage closing the door behind him. He started to unbutton his shirt when a knock came to the door. Garron opened the door to find Leah standing on the veranda. She had changed from her dress into a tank top and shorts. The top was form fitting and accentuated her heavy breasts.

Leah caught Garron's gaze and folded her arms over her chest.

She said, "I couldn't sleep, and I just heard you come in. I wanted to apologize for earlier."

"You were out of line," Garron scowled.

"I agree. It's just that sometimes you are oblivious."

"What's that supposed to mean?"

"You've never known how you affect the women around you. You can be charming without even trying. I just didn't want you to find yourself in the middle of something uncomfortable." Leah turned to walk away.

Garron reached out and took her arm gently. "Did you just pay me a compliment?" Garron smiled crookedly.

Leah pulled away gently. "Good night, Garron."

Garron closed the cottage door and laughed quietly on his way to the bathroom, pulling off his shirt as he went.

***

Garron laid in bed. The cottage was warm; he had turned off the air conditioning earlier in the day and opened the windows. He used only the light sheet to cover him. The moonlight shone through the cottage's large windows. He considered getting out of bed to close the blinds more tightly, but decided that sleep wouldn't come easily either way.

Garron heard the bedroom door latch disengage and looked down to see the moonlight filtering in as the door opened slowly. He could see someone framed in the doorway. It was Gracie Ng. He just lay there, unable to move; he watched her approach the bed slowly. The moonlight caused her raven black hair to look nearly silver. She still wore the cream-colored dress from earlier, only now it looked white in the moonbeam. Gracie undid her belt and let it fall to the floor. She shrugged her left shoulder from the strapless dress and then the right, exposing one breast at a time. Then the dress slid to the floor at her feet. Garron could see her in profile as she stepped in front of the window and closer to the bed. His eyes took in the roundness of her breasts and then the cup of her tight bottom in the moonlight. For the first time he thought of protesting, but when his mouth opened, Gracie bent over and kissed him deeply. He felt her soft tongue against his. She sat down on the edge of the bed and ran a hand across his bare chest, circling his nipples. She leaned in and kissed him again. Only this kiss lasted longer and seemed somehow familiar to Garron. When the kiss finally ended, she pulled away and Garron recognized Leah for the first time. Leah slid her hand slowly down Garron's quivering stomach. Lower under the sheet, and lower still until she touched his …

Garron woke suddenly and sat up in bed. His heart was racing and his breathing was rapid. He swung his legs over the side of the bed and ran a hand over his face. He gazed around the room and peered into every corner. He was alone. He had fallen asleep.

"What the hell was that?" He said out loud to the dark room.

He climbed out of the bed and went into the living area. He checked the front door and found it locked. He felt uneasy and guilt gnawed at him. Garron went to the bar and poured himself two fingers of Scotch. He drank it quickly. He looked at the empty glass in his hand.

He asked himself, "When did I start drinking again?"

Garron went back to bed, closing and locking the bedroom door. He pulled the blinds tight to keep out the moonlight.

Chapter 9

GRACIE AND ANTON did not join the group for breakfast. Ole said that something in Gracie's research kept them away. They ate a delicious meal of dried fruits, yogurt, and an omelet filled with ham, peppers, and onions. Throughout breakfast, Garron had trouble making eye contact with his ex-wife. Ole seemed untouched by the previous evening's events, while Garron's head felt like it was stuffed inside a kick drum. Garron's hangover must have been apparent, for Chef Eddie brought Garron some ibuprofen without being asked. Garron nodded his thanks and swallowed the pills quickly.

After breakfast, while Leah and Jacob walked hand-in-hand from the dining hall, Ole asked Garron if he would like to join him at his archaeological dig site for the day. Garron agreed and followed the Norwegian back to his room to borrow a change of clothes.

Dr. Hansen's room was on the top floor of the same building that held his laboratory. He was staying in the luxury suite that overlooked the ocean. It was enormous by hotel standards. The furniture was of a modern wicker design with dark warm tones. There was a small kitchen, two bedrooms, a small den, and a long wide balcony that was filled with deck chairs and a love seat.

Ole stepped into his bedroom and returned with a pair of khaki pants and a denim shirt.

"They might be a little short, but I think that they will serve your needs."

Garron held the pants to his waist. The legs were about three inches too short.

"I can make them work."

After Garron changed, he and Ole climbed into the Jeep and drove up the beach about three hundred yards. Ole's dig site came into view. There were piles of sand roped off with yellow caution tape.

Ole parked the Jeep and led the way around the piles of sand. A clearing had been made in the trees. Several long rectangular holes had been dug. A large number of white plastic buckets lined the holes. Shovels, trowels, and brushes were piled near large plastic drums holding water. Protruding from the walls of the holes were a number of colored flags that Ole explained denoted where he had found layers of carbon, indicating remnants of camp fires buried long ago.

"What have you found so far?" Garron asked.

"I moved the majority of the artifacts back to my lab, but just yesterday I found something very exciting."

Ole moved over to a tarp that was covering a waist high workbench. He removed the tarp to reveal a small collection of items, including bleached white fragments and a few charred sticks.

"I found absolute proof of cooking fires, and the location of a refuse pile, including fish bones, vegetable seeds, and fragments of dried calabash that were undoubtedly used as carrying vessels."

Ole picked up one of the white fragments and held it in the palm of his hand.

"But this is the most exciting of my finds. These are the second and third metatarsal bones of a human foot. I uncovered these yesterday."

Garron asked, "What does that mean? What have you found?"

Ole turned and pointed to a hole that was only three feet square. "This is where I found the bone fragments. I just started this grid yesterday. I hope to find more bones today. But, to answer your question, I hope that I have found Garacana's village."

Garron was drawn in by the man's enthusiasm. He said, "How can I help?"

"I'm going to hand you buckets of material to sift at that table." Ole pointed to a table covered with wire screen. "The large material will be captured on the screen and the smaller material will filter through to the table's lower level." Ole hefted a bucket. "We'll work the first bucket together."

The hose ran to one of the water drums. The water pressure was controlled by a foot switch under the table, which operated similarly to the gas pedal of a car. Ole poured the contents of the first bucket onto the table. He pulled out any carbonized wood and set it in a black tray to his right. Ole then depressed the foot pedal, and rinsed the sand and earth away. He rubbed his hand through the material turning over any large items between his fingers. He sorted through rocks, twigs, and shell to find any material of interest.

He said, "The first few buckets will yield very little, but if you come across anything that you can't identify, just set it aside in that empty gray tray. Just be sure to pull the carbon from the material before you turn on the water." Ole asked, "Do you have any questions?"

"I'm worried that I'll miss something of value," Garron said taking the hose from the doctor.

"The oddities will show themselves, don't worry." Ole smiled broadly.

Ole climbed into his small hole and began to scrape away with a trowel at the walls of the hole. Garron watched as he slowly filled the first bucket. Once it was full, Garron took the bucket to the table and began the process that he had been shown. Garron worked slowly and diligently and when he had finally finished the first bucket, he turned to find three more waiting for him near the hole.

"Sorry Ole, I'm a little slow," Garron apologized as he picked up the second bucket.

"Take your time, I would not want you to hurry and miss something because you were not thorough. Anton has not enforced a timetable as of yet. The only concern is that we have entered hurricane season, but so far the forecast is favorable."

"What happens if a storm comes?" Garron said as he picked several pieces of charcoal from the pile of earth.

"Worst case scenario, I would fill the dig site. I have the GPS coordinates well plotted. I would just start over."

Garron ran his hand through the wet sand and pulled out a piece of a conch shell. He thought of Ms. Beth's salad and smiled.

Garron said, "I guess Mother Nature often challenges you in your business."

"When I worked on Jan Mayen we were limited to the summer months. During the winter in the Arctic Circle we could see the temperature reach minus thirty degrees Celsius."

Garron whistled at the thought of working in freezing conditions. A thought occurred to him, "I wanted to ask how you found the rune stone on Jan Mayen."

Ole hefted another bucket of material out of the hole. "Have you heard of the Landnámabók?"

"I certainly have not," Garron responded as he gathered another bucket from the rim of the hole.

Ole pushed himself out of the hole and sat on the rim. "It is a manuscript that dates back to the ninth or tenth century CE, and describes the founding of a settlement on Iceland. The tale mentions a land named Svalbaro, which I believe was Jan Mayen. I went to Jan Mayen to prove the connection to Svalbaro, and found the rune stone on the Beerenberg volcano purely by accident. It has changed my life."

Garron pulled more charcoal from the table. "It is amazing that you stumbled across the rune stone purely by chance. Looking back on that day, are you glad that you found the stone?"

"It could be the greatest discovery in archaeological history. I am proud to have my name associated with the find."

Garron turned on the hose and began sifting through the sandy material. "You mentioned a Norse myth that the rune described. What made you think that the stone was anything more than a jotting down of that tale?"

"The myth that my colleagues wanted to connect the rune stone to was the tale of Kvasir and the Meade of Poetry. The myth says that Kvasir, a son of gods, was very wise and traveled far and wide teaching and spreading knowledge. The tale says that he met his end at the hands of two dwarves, Fjalar and Galar, who mixed his blood with honey and created the Meade of Poetry. The mead imbues the drinker with exceptional knowledge. The rune stone mentioned Óðrerir in its inscription. This is thought to either be the mead or the vessel in which the mead was made."

Garron brought another empty bucket back to the rim of the hole.

He said, "Well you and your colleagues could both be right. There is an obvious connection between the mead and the elixir. I would also assume that to Norsemen, the Caribbean islanders would look like dwarves. Maybe there is some truth hidden in that myth."

"That is my belief." Ole hopped back down into the hole. "That next bucket is near the layer in which I found the calabash fragments, so be conscientious in your screening."

Garron did find some large pieces of interest as he examined the material from the bucket. He set aside pieces that looked similar to the gourd fragments that Ole had found yesterday. One piece was quite large. The bottom tray of the table had collected a great deal of runoff, so Ole helped Garron to pour the tray's contents onto another nearby table that had a solid top. Ole scoured the runoff contents while Garron continued at the first table with another bucket from the dig. After an hour, Ole called Garron over to his table to share what he had found.

Ole laid out several small white cylindrical pieces on a flat wooden board.

"These are more foot bones. This large one is a proximal phalange. And these are lateral and medial cuneiform bones. We have a few duplicate bones."

Garron asked, "Which means?"

"It could mean that we have found two feet, possibly from the same body. We have much more digging to do, but I believe that I will move us south on the grid with the next hole. Are you hungry?"

Garron nodded.

"I have a cooler in the Jeep with sandwiches. Shall we clean up a little before lunch?"

The two men scrubbed their hands thoroughly before enjoying the vegetarian hummus and bean sprout sandwiches that Chef Eddie had prepared for them. They washed them down with mango iced tea and watched a large pod of dolphins play in the distant blue green water. After lunch they immediately went back to work. Ole worked with a determination that Garron had not yet seen. Two hours passed with little found and little conversation passing between the men.

Then Ole called out from his hole, "Here it is!"

Garron turned off the water and joined the doctor.

Ole was carefully scraping away earth from a long object at the same level of the dig that the foot bones had been found. Ole used a bottle of water to rinse the item and Garron could see the gleam of white surface from under the sand and earth.

"What is it?" Garron asked.

"The better question is what are *they*? It appears to be two tibias crossed slightly one on top of the other." He continued with a smile, "I believe that we have found a grave site."

Garron looked down into the hole. The two long bones were crossed just above the ankle. It looked as if the body had been buried in the fetal position.

"This is really exciting! Congratulations, Dr. Hansen," Garron said as he shook the man's hand vigorously.

"Easy, there is still a great deal to be done, but it looks promising," Ole cautioned.

"Who could it be? I mean, how old is this grave?"

"Well, when I began to uncover charcoal from this site, I had it radiocarbon dated. The results stated that we are working with a site dating between 1480 and 1530."

"You found a site that could have potentially been active when Pinzón set foot on Bimini, fascinating."

Ole wiped his forehead leaving a trail of light mud from his dirty hand. "Thank you for understanding my excitement, and thank you for your effort today."

Garron could not take his eyes off of the leg bones protruding from the soil.

He said, "Thank you for inviting me. This has been exhilarating."

Ole began to recover the bones with material in his bucket.

Garron was shocked, "What are you doing?"

"We have to call it a day and I do not want to leave the site exposed. Don't worry, you can join me again tomorrow if you like, and we will un-cover them once again."

Garron watched as the bones vanished under the dirt.

"Thanks for the invitation Ole, but I don't think that you could keep me away tomorrow if you wanted to."

They covered the dig site with a tarp, put lids on the buckets of mate-rial that still needed examination, and climbed into the Jeep for the short ride back to the resort.

***

Garron walked back to his cottage after leaving Ole at the entrance to his lab. It was just before five o'clock when he stepped onto his veranda and found another garment bag waiting for him on the chair. A note was pinned to the bag.

Festive wear for a festive occasion. See you at 6:00, Mr. Bond!

It was signed by Anton.

Garron pulled off his mud-caked boots and left them outside the cot-tage's door. He stepped inside. Garron was filthy from the day's dig and handled the garment bag carefully. He laid the bag across his bed and un-zipped it to find a tuxedo and a pair of brightly polished black dress shoes. He laughed and hurried to the shower.

***

As Garron approached the dining hall, Gracie came up behind him and locked her arm in his.

"I'm glad you waited for me. I hate to walk into a party all alone." She winked.

Gracie looked incredible in a short backless black dress with spaghetti straps. Her hair was pulled up and adorned with a yellow hibiscus flower.

Garron said, "You look amazing."

"That's just because I'm with you. Shall we?"

The dining hall was beautifully decorated. Tall vases ornamented the center of the table, holding yellow heliconia, red ginger, and white birds of paradise. In addition to the standard table setting, there were silver chargers and crystal champagne flutes. But the most striking piece in the room was the enormous mahogany dining table that sat twelve. The wood was highly polished and pleaded to have the linen table cloth removed.

Garron and Gracie were the last to arrive. All of the men wore tuxedoes and, like Gracie, Leah wore a black dress. Her dress had a revealing neckline and delicate sleeves. A large diamond necklace accentuated Leah's neckline. Ole looked a far cry from the man with whom Garron had moved dirt just an hour ago. He smiled at the late arrivals.

Anton welcomed his guests, "Ah Gracie, Garron, welcome. Please join me in a champagne toast."

He poured them each a glass of champagne.

Garron stood beside Ole. He asked, "How did he find out about your discovery so quickly?"

"We are not celebrating my discovery." Ole tilted his glass toward Gracie.

Garron's mouth dropped as Gracie winked at him once more.

Anton raised his glass and said, "To the pursuit of dreams, to the long days and longer nights, to never losing another loved one before their time, and to vindication."

Everyone raised a glass.

Garron emptied the glass in two long swallows. Anton immediately began to refill the empty glasses. Garron stepped over to where Leah and Jacob were standing.

Garron asked, "You know anything about this?"

"We got back after a day on the water and found the new clothes waiting in our cottage. We had no idea," Jacob answered.

Garron said, "Could they really have found it?"

They watched Anton, Gracie, and Ole laughing. Anton never letting his guests' glasses remain empty for long.

"You two made quite the entrance," Jacob said with a smirk.

Garron met Jacob's eye and saw that he meant no harm.

"Are you sure that's wise?" Leah asked.

"Are you serious? We already went over this. I am not going to cheat on Veronica," Garron responded.

Leah said, "I meant the drink."

"Oh," he looked down at the champagne flute in his hand, "it's probably not the best idea, but we are celebrating." Garron blushed and walked away emptying the glass. He set it on the table as he approached Anton and his doctors.

"Where's your glass?" Anton asked as he lifted the third bottle of champagne.

"I'm fine for now, thank you," Garron answered.

To Gracie he asked, "So how did you find it? You did find it right, that's what this is all about."

"I tried to talk Anton out of this fête, but he insisted." Gracie smiled shyly. "The algorithm kicked back a match. It found a watercolor in the Napoleon Museum."

"So the final ingredient is in France," Garron concluded.

Gracie smiled. "The Napoleon Museum is in the Prince of Monaco's Palace."

Garron snickered, "Okay smart ass, Monaco. But, come on, that may as well be France."

Gracie smiled again and shook her head. "The watercolor is in Monaco, and the painting belonged to Napoleon, but it has nothing to do with France."

Garron furrowed his brow. "Are you trying to be cryptic?"

"Just having a little fun," she confessed. "Napoleon received the watercolor as a gift from a young girl while he was exiled on her island." Gracie paused for effect, "The final ingredient is on an island in the South Atlantic, St. Helena."

Gracie placed an arm around Garron's waist and pulled him toward her. She smiled up at him and said, "And if it wasn't for you, we may never have found it."

Anton said, "I did not know that. Well then, you deserve another drink."

Anton poured champagne into an empty water goblet and handed it to Garron. Garron accepted the glass reluctantly.

"So what is the last ingredient?" Garron asked.

"Well, before you get too excited, that's the reason I didn't want to do this yet." She motioned to the champagne and the table. "I think that this is premature, we should have waited until we put our hands on it before popping the champagne."

Anton retorted, "Don't be silly. We know where to look, and we will have our hands on it very shortly."

"But Anton, no one has seen this plant in more than 200 years," Gracie cautioned.

"We are too close to forfeit. The road has always been rough, why should we expect this last leg to be any different?" Anton responded.

Garron was flabbergasted. "Wait, you are celebrating the fact that you've identified your final ingredient to be an extinct plant?"

Jacob asked, "The last ingredient is extinct?" He and Leah had moved closer to Anton's circle and overheard the conversation.

Anton answered, "I thought that you might all be skeptical, and concerned with our odds of finding the final ingredient, so I have several samples to share with you, which should help to put your minds at ease." He pointed to the new dining room table. "Let's sit and eat. I will share what I have found over dinner. Chef Eddie has pulled out all of the stops this evening."

The group took their seats and Chef Eddie immediately appeared with their appetizer of garlic buttered escargot.

Garron asked again, "But what *is* the final ingredient?"

Gracie answered, "The string tree of St. Helena, or more precisely, its sap."

"And no one has seen this tree in 200 years?" Leah asked.

Anton said, "We found it, the final ingredient. Remember the trials and tribulations that led to this threshold, and do not lose faith."

He pulled a sheet of paper from inside his jacket and continued, "And when we are disheartened, we need to only remember the Catalina grass of Catalina Island. It had not been seen since 1912, but was then rediscovered on March 30, 2005. And on May tenth of the same year, Mount Diablo buckwheat was seen in Mount Diablo State Park for the first time since 1936. The last sighting of Rhaphidospora cavernarum was in 1873, and the last sighting of Teucrium ajugaceum was in 1891. Both were seen again in 2008, in Australia."

Chef Eddie cleared the first course and delivered conch chowder for their next course. Garron excitedly dug into the chowder remembering Ms. Beth's conch salad.

"And, if those were not enough, let us look at the neglected tuft sedge. This plant is endemic to the very island in which we are interested, St. Helena. The sedge was last spotted on St. Helena in 1806. Botanists found multiple distinct populations of this plant in 2008, totaling roughly 4000 plants, 4000 plants that were thought to be extinct."

The group sat dumbstruck.

"And I'm not a scientist, I just pulled those examples from the Internet," Anton said humbly.

Garron said, "So there is still a chance."

Leah added, "This is all fascinating."

Gracie raised her glass to Anton. "Nice work Anton. You've even convinced me."

Garron asked, "So what's next?"

Anton smiled, "We go to St. Helena and find ourselves an extinct tree."

Chapter 10

ST. HELENA WAS not an easy island to visit. It lay 1200 miles from the southwest coast of Africa, and 1800 miles from the coast of Brazil. There was no airport on the island; the average tourist would visit St. Helena by personal yacht or the Royal Mail Ship *St. Helena*. The *RMS St. Helena* traveled from Cape Town only once per month and the trip lasted seven days. The mail ship made port in Cape Town, Walvis Bay, and Ascension Island. But if one had a personal jet, other options were available.

Anton's jet touched down at the Wideawake Auxiliary Airfield on Ascension Island. Wideawake Airfield was officially the Royal Air Force Station Ascension. The airfield was managed by the RAF, while also being home to a number of USAF personnel. This was the closest airport to St. Helena, an incredible distance of 703 miles from the island. The remainder of the trip would be done by boat.

The airfield had only recently been opened to private flights. Permission to visit the airfield had to be granted by both government agencies, and the approval process normally took more than 21 days. Anton made a few calls and obtained permission in a single day. Anton had convinced Garron to make the journey with his team. Garron wanted desperately to see his wife, but the temptation of finding the final ingredient to the Elixir of Life was too great, plus Anton invited Veronica to make the journey, as well. Anton had given permission for Garron to share all that he knew with Veronica to convince her to join him in St. Helena. If Veronica had difficulty in obtaining approval for her own flight to Ascension Island, then Anton would make other arrangements for Veronica to join them if she so chose.

Anton's plane would return to Miami and then fly Veronica to Windhoek, Namibia. Anton had purchased a large vessel to act as his floating laboratory while on the island. It would be waiting for Veronica in Walvis Bay, Namibia, the closest port city to St. Helena. The voyage from Walvis Bay would take four days.

Anton had returned Garron's cell phone so he could make the difficult call to Veronica. Unfortunately, Garron must have attempted to call Veronica while she was in the air and had to leave her a voicemail. He gave her assurance that all was well, and that she needed to return his call before leaving Miami. Garron supplied Veronica with multiple phone numbers by which to reach him; including Anton's satellite phone.

The group was whisked to the dock to meet the waiting boats. Anton had flown in a large number of men on an earlier flight from Miami. They were waiting at the two yachts Anton arranged to sail them to St. Helena. Anton was using his security force to aid in the search for the string tree. He wanted to increase his chances for success by putting as many men as possible into the field, no matter their training. The security team, with the exception of Taylor, sailed on the second ship.

Leah, Jacob, and Garron joined Gracie, Chef Eddie, and Anton on the first ship. Anton allowed Ole to remain in Bimini after learning about what he and Garron had found at the archaeological dig site. Ole was certain that the site would yield its secrets quickly, and that those secrets would only help Anton in his quest.

The yachts were enormous. Each stretched nearly 90 feet in length. On the main deck there was a salon with white leather couches lining the hull. A dining room table that could seat eight was separated by a 30-inch plasma TV that could be retracted into a cabinet. On the lower deck there was a master cabin and two twin bed cabins, as well as a VIP cabin in the ship's bow and each cabin had an en suite bathroom. There were two additional cabins on the lower deck for the crew.

Leah and Jacob were set up in the VIP cabin in the bow of the ship. Garron and Gracie each settled into one of the twin bed cabins near the bow. And Anton took the master cabin near the stern.

A knock came to Garron's cabin door. Anton stood on the threshold holding a satellite phone.

He said, "I hope that you will be comfortable in your cabin."

"This is a beautiful vessel," Garron responded.

"We got lucky. These two yachts were already anchored off of Ascension Island waiting for other fares. Some corporation's management team will be unhappy when they arrive and find that I've absconded with their ride." Anton held up the phone. "I received a call from your wife. She was not able to get through on your phone. She is anxious to join you in St. Helena. I gave her some names that I hope will get her permission to use Wideawake, so hopefully we will see her sooner rather than later."

Garron smiled, "Thank you Anton, you have been most generous."

"Not at all my friend, I am glad that you have joined us." Anton turned to go, "Remember dinner is at eight on the main deck. Now enjoy the voyage."

"Anton, how long is this voyage?"

"Just over two days." With that, Anton climbed the spiral stair case at the stern of the vessel.

After dressing for dinner in a polo shirt and khaki pants, Garron climbed the stairs to the main deck and then went out to the open stern of the ship, nodding to Chef Eddie as he passed the man setting the dining room table. He found Gracie looking out over the ocean. He stepped beside her and leaned on the railing.

"Ever been at sea before?" Garron asked.

She shook her head. "Not in the open Atlantic. How about you?"

"I've been on a few cruises in the Caribbean, the Mediterranean, and once I sailed to Bermuda, but I've never been this far from land."

Gracie snuggled in closer to Garron. "It's colder than I imagined it would be and the sea is a little rough. I hope I don't get sea sick."

Garron wanted to wrap his arm around Gracie to help keep her warm, but remembered the dream that he had had and decided against it. He felt too comfortable with this woman who was not his wife, but he told himself that he could handle it.

Garron asked, "So what do you think of our chances?"

Gracie smirked, "Well you'd have a better chance if you put your arm around me."

Garron flushed. "No, I meant with finding the string tree."

Gracie laughed. "Relax Romeo, I know what you meant. I don't know. The odds are certainly not in our favor, but Anton's optimism is contagious."

Garron recovered from his embarrassment and asked, "Is it optimism, delusion, or is Anton just so used to getting what he wants that he won't take no for an answer?"

"It is true that Anton doesn't hear 'no' very often, but Anton does believe that he will find the elixir. He honestly believes that it is his destiny. You heard his toast last night. He believes that he was meant to vindicate his father."

Garron thought of the pain that a young boy must have felt learning that his father was killed by people that he considered family.

Garron asked, "Do you believe in destiny?"

Gracie laughed again. "That was better, but you'd still get farther with the arm around my shoulders."

This time Garron laughed as well and put his arm around the woman.

Gracie said, "You're asking because I am a scientist. And, would a scientist believe in the prearrangement of the Universe?" She paused. "It seems likely that there is a higher power at work, but was it just to set the world in motion or does it watch our progress on a daily basis? I cannot say. When I consider the elixir, I do not believe that its power derives from pure chance. It seems more likely that there was a plan for the elixir all along, a plan that humanity disrupted. It is my hope that we put it back on track before it is too late, if it isn't already."

"Do you think that a higher power would want us to live forever?"

"Wouldn't it give us a better chance at getting it right? It may help us to reach Nirvana. Let's face it, we don't do very well with the short time that we have on this planet, maybe with more time we could figure out how to live life more resolutely."

Garron considered Gracie's answer. He decided that he liked it.

"I hope that we find the string tree."

Gracie said, "I hope so, too."

Gracie looked inside and said, "The others are starting to take their seats. Shall we join them?"

Garron removed his arm from Gracie's shoulders and turned. He saw his brother and Leah enter the salon and stand near the dining table. Garron caught Leah's eye in the salon and saw the disapproval on her face.

Garron, bowing slightly, asked Gracie, "May I escort you to dinner Dr. Ng?"

Gracie smiled and locked her arm in his. She said, "I would be delighted, Mr. Shepard."

They entered the salon arm-in-arm and strolled directly to the table.

***

After dinner the conversation continued late into the night. Chef Eddie served a flourless chocolate cake and coffee for dessert, then, after several hours of checking on his guests, finally retired for the evening.

Leah asked, "Anton, after finding the elixir, how do you plan to release it to the world?"

Anton poured another cup of coffee from the carafe that Chef Eddie had left behind. "I've spent the last three years establishing an arm of one of my corporations for just that purpose," he answered. "I intend on making my announcement through media outlets directly. I do not want governments interfering with the distribution process. Of course, agencies will want to regulate the consumption and dispersal of any product made available for human consumption, but if I announce the development of the elixir directly to the public, then delaying the approval process will result in a public outcry."

"Don't you think that making the public aware of the elixir before it is ready for distribution would cause chaos and upheaval?" Garron reasoned.

"It would, but I will not wait for government approval before distributing the elixir. The day after I make the announcement, I will make the elixir available worldwide, with or without the approval of a country's government." Anton smiled proudly. "I know that I will be facing lawsuits and backlash, but I figure at that point it will no longer be of any relevance. A lawsuit will never hold up in court, and there are enough government leaders with health issues or with family members that have health issues that I will be able to avoid real prosecution."

Jacob said, "Of course you plan on testing the elixir first."

"Absolutely, we will test the elixir thoroughly before we make it available to the public at large."

"And everyone will have access to the elixir?" Garron asked.

Anton nodded. "It will not be easy, and I know that. Even with intensive forethought there will undoubtedly be glitches in the system. I cannot plan for every anomaly, nor can I stop some from trying to corrupt the process. But I am determined to make this work."

Anton leaned into the table with arms extended and hands folded. "I have already set strategic distribution points around the world. I have also purchased large offices that will be used as clinics to disperse the elixir. I have a database of doctors who are willing to volunteer their time. I will work with healthcare professionals to ensure that individuals who are most at risk will receive the elixir first. This will be difficult, but I have some of the best minds in the world working on a solution as we speak."

"You've invested a great deal in this already. I guess you plan on making some serious profit from the elixir," Leah said.

"There is a great deal of money to be made, but that is not what it is about for me. I hope that you know that. This revelation will change the world. The healthcare industry will be turned upside down overnight, an industry that is worth more than two trillion dollars in the United States alone. The money that will be made must make it back to the doctors and the companies and institutions that are dedicated to healing the sick; otherwise economies around the world will plummet. It would be like suddenly making the automobile obsolete. Markets and industries would falter or fail, putting people out of jobs and straining governments in the process. What we are about to do has its consequences."

Everyone was quiet for several minutes while they contemplated those consequences.

Garron thought of the underdeveloped countries and the looters who would no doubt make an attempt to control the elixir for financial gain. He thought of the pharmaceutical companies and their rush to patent a version of the elixir for their own gain. He thought of religious fanatics who would argue the morality of eternal life. And he thought of the people rioting outside of hospitals and clinics desperate to obtain the elixir before a loved one died. Could Anton's production keep up with the demand? Would a black market arise out of the inability to sort the truly deserving individuals from those who just wanted the elixir to ensure their odds? Garron had his first glimpse of a world that was on the threshold of irreversible change.

Anton broke the silence. "It would be impossible to work through every scenario in advance, but I have faith in the people that I am working with. There will be inevitable change that I hope will put mankind on a course of self revelation, allowing everyone to transcend the life they currently live."

***

The following day, over lunch, the group discussed its course of action upon arrival in St. Helena.

Anton had created a cover story to ensure that the team would have easy access to the remote areas of the island. Anton was visiting the island under the guise of a wealthy environmental steward who wanted to determine if the British government's attempt at reversing the environmental destruction of St. Helena's unique habitat was having the desired effect. If the project was making a difference, then Anton had money to help the cause.

The Peaks Protected Area Plan began in 2007 and was funded by OTEP, the Overseas Territories Environmental Programme. The Peaks Project was put into place to examine the extent of the human influence on the island and to see if actions could be taken to save what was left of the endemic species of flora and fauna. When the European sailors first imported livestock, fruit trees, and vegetables shortly after the island's discovery in 1502, they changed the island's natural rhythm. The new livestock trampled and ate endemic species of flora; land was cleared of endemic

forests and replaced with orchards and gardens. St. Helena was once heavily
forested. Mariners of many nations used the island's lumber for ship repairs. The island was then nearly overrun with goats and an unintended im-
port: the rat. These two newly-introduced species destroyed the recently
planted orchards and vegetable gardens. With the loss of endemic species,
and the loss of the newly introduced gardens, soil erosion devastated the
landscape. The hot southwesterly winds battered the unprotected land, and
the once cloud forest of St. Helena was transformed into a semi desert. The
Peaks Project was created to see if the island could reach a natural harmony
once more, with the help of conservationists.

To the authorities of St. Helena, Anton's team was made up of hired
environmental specialists that were to evaluate the Peaks Project's work so
far. If Anton's team of doctors found promising results, then Anton would
donate a large sum of money to the island's national trust for further
conservation.

Anton said, "Please study the documents in each of your envelopes as
we make our way to St. Helena. You will find a complex cover story that
will include degrees held, schools attended, and the specific objectives for
your visit to the island. Please remember to stay in character for the duration of our stay on the island. You are all members of a scientific team that
I am using to measure the success of St. Helena's environmental
programs."

Garron flipped through his documents. He found in his name a passport, insurance card, faculty badge, and several sheets of paper that explained his supposed role as the evaluation team's entomologist.

Garron held up a Stanford University badge that identified him as Dr.
Garron Shepard. He said, "Why entomology? I don't know the first thing
about insects."

"Don't tell me that you are afraid of bugs," Gracie chided.

Garron responded, "Real funny."

Anton smiled. "There are more than 200 endemic species of inverte-
brates on St. Helena, Dr. Shepard. And you are very excited for the opportunity to study these unique creatures in the wild."

"I am?"

Anton laughed at Garron's response.

"These documents look authentic. I would swear that this is my real passport," Leah said.

"I have my resources and for the right price, nothing is out of reach."

Leah studied the badge carefully. It looked identical to her Barry University identification, but the Leah Preston on the badge had already earned her doctorate. "When we reach the island, we'll split up into multiple teams, allowing us to search a larger area more effectively. We will work in a grid system that Gracie will explain to us after lunch. It will guarantee that we cover every square inch of the island. We intend on starting with the elevations above 1900 feet. This will put us in the Diana's Peak National Park, allowing us the most freedom to begin our search away from prying eyes."

After lunch, Gracie explained how to set up and use a grid system using graph paper and some rough drawings. When Gracie finished her lesson, she handed out a botanical drawing of the St. Helena string tree.

She explained, "This drawing was made by John Charles Melliss in 1875. After Garron helped to identify our final ingredient, it was not difficult to find additional reference material for the string tree. Melliss's work had not yet been digitized, so my original algorithm would not have found his research." Gracie smiled up at Garron. "I was able to pull documents from Melliss's survey of the island, which were part of his 1875 published work of St. Helena. This is a well drawn interpretation of the plant." Gracie added, "Please pay attention to not only the drawing of the mature plant, but also to the seed and sapling stages depicted as well. The red flowers that look like dangling string will be the easiest way to recognize the plant, but that should not be your only means of identifying the string tree. Notice the ovate shape, smooth edge, and the branching venation of the leaf. The stem of the plant should be woody and brown in color."

Gracie looked at her audience and saw the discouragement on their faces.

She said, "It may seem like we are looking for a needle in a stack of needles, but if we stick to our grids then we have a real chance at finding our specimen."

Anton concluded the meeting with, "I would like for all of you to remember that, although others have looked for the St. Helena string tree in the past, none have been so well-funded or as highly motivated as we are. We will find our final ingredient."

The group disbanded leaving Garron and Gracie behind as the others returned to their cabins.

Garron asked Gracie, "Let's say that we find our tree, what happens after that?"

Gracie squinted in the bright sunlight as she studied her topographical map of St. Helena.

She said, "It depends on the conditions under which we find the specimen. We need to examine the health of the population and the sustainability of that population in the wild. We will take soil samples and samples of neighboring vegetation to determine those variables. We will also collect seed samples for propagation of the plant in our labs. And, of course, we will collect a sample of the sap to begin our testing of the elixir."

Garron looked out into the open sea; being at sea beyond the sight of land made him feel uneasy. The sky was clear with only a few clouds near the horizon. The seas had calmed and were relatively smooth.

Gracie stood and said, "I have a great deal of research left to do. I better get back to it. I'll see you later."

As she stepped back into the salon, Leah and Jacob came out onto the deck wearing their bathing suits.

Garron said, "You two are making yourselves right at home."

Jacob responded, "Why not? There's a perfectly good Jacuzzi dying to be used."

"Besides, even on this gorgeous yacht, a person could still go stir crazy," Leah said.

Garron watched as Jacob turned the jets on in the tub and stepped into the water. Leah removed a thin cover up, revealing a tiny black bikini underneath. As she bent her leg to remove a sandal, Leah caught Garron's gaze. Garron smiled shyly and looked away quickly. When he looked back she was submerged up to her shoulders.

Garron asked, "What do you think about all of this?" He held up his packet of information.

"I think that we have our work cut out for us. That plant is not going to be easy to find," Jacob answered.

Garron shielded his eyes with a hand and looked back out to sea. He said, "I was thinking about what Anton was saying over dinner last night; I'm worried about the chaos that the elixir may cause."

"I've been weighing the good the elixir can do for those who need it with the fallout from its discovery, too," Leah said.

"And what's your conclusion?" Garron asked.

Leah shook her head slightly. "I just keep thinking of the lives that can be saved and the families that can be spared the pain of losing a loved one to an untimely death."

Jacob said, "Just think of a world without cancer."

"But what happens to our society when life is no longer finite? Does life become less valuable?" Garron asked.

"The elixir doesn't necessarily mean immortality," Leah offered.

Garron nodded. "Which is why I still want to be a part of this search. I want to know the potential of the elixir's power."

The trio sat quietly for a moment.

Then Garron stood and said, "I'm going to catch a nap while the sailing is smoother than it was last night. I'll see you for dinner."

***

On the way down to his room, Anton stopped Garron and told him of an email that he had received.

"My assistant back in the States received a call from your wife. Veronica is in Miami and she has her jet on standby until she receives approval to land at Wideawake," Anton explained.

Anton also assured Garron that he would do everything in his power to help her with that approval process.

Garron thanked his host and made his way to his cabin clutching a copy of the email that Anton had given him. He removed his shoes and climbed into bed and read the message. Anton's assistant had included a message to Garron from Veronica. It read that she loved him and looked forward to seeing him soon.

Veronica was more than a wife and friend to Garron; she embodied rebirth and a chance at happiness. If thoughts of loss and inadequacy challenged Garron's reason and darkness threatened to overpower him, then he sought out Veronica to talk through his feelings. He understood that his dependency on Veronica was not necessarily healthy, but he argued that understanding the dependency made it acceptable.

Garron reread the message from his wife and then fell asleep.

***

Garron woke from his nap, showered and dressed for dinner. When he entered the salon, Garron found Jacob studying his copy of the string tree drawing.

"Where's Leah?" Garron asked as he sat down beside his brother.

"She's getting ready for dinner."

Jacob asked, "What did you do this afternoon?"

"I slept," Garron answered.

He added, "Veronica is going to join us in St. Helena. She's attempting to gain access to Wideawake, but she may have to sail from Walvis Bay. Either way she'll catch up with us on the island."

Jacob grinned mischievously. "Leah will be happy to hear that. She's afraid that our doctor will be too great a temptation."

Garron clenched his jaw and felt his temper rise, but saw that Jacob was just goading him and forced a grin.

They both laughed.

Garron said, "So you seem at peace. Are you no longer concerned about Anton's intentions?"

Jacob shrugged slightly. "He seems like a decent guy and he's treated us well."

"Do you think that Murphy made a mistake in trusting The Brotherhood?"

Jacob sat back on the couch and ran a hand through his hair.

"He may not have been given a chance. It's hard for me to say, but maybe Murphy knew that he was on the wrong side of things and that's why he started to dig into the treasure."

Garron hesitated before asking, "Do you think that The Brotherhood had Murphy killed?"

Jacob didn't answer.

Garron said, "We can answer that one later. I'll *help* you to answer that one later."

They sat in silence for a moment.

Jacob said, "I'm sorry for some of the shit that I've said to you over the last few days."

"Don't worry about it; we've both lost our heads recently."

"I just want you to know that I'm glad you came looking for me."

Garron saw the honesty in his brother's expression and was touched by the sentiment. Maybe they could make amends. Maybe Garron could forgive his brother.

Garron heard voices climbing the stairs from the lower deck. Gracie and Anton appeared out of the stairwell. Gracie waved when she saw the two brothers sitting in the salon. She was wearing a floral printed dress with a square neckline and cap sleeves.

Jacob said, "But if you weren't married …" He waggled his eyebrows.

Garron stood and slapped his brother in the back of the head.

"Come on, dumb ass, let's have dinner."

***

Garron borrowed some books from Gracie and spent the remaining day at sea reading about the history of St. Helena.

St. Helena was discovered in 1502 by Portuguese sailors. With the island's close proximity to the currents wrapping around the Cape of Africa, it became of interest to trade ships returning from Asia to Europe as a victualling station. The Portuguese introduced livestock and vegetables so that food was available on their return trip from Asian trade ports. The Portuguese never established a permanent colony on St. Helena and soon the English and Dutch started to use the island as well. The British, through the East India Company, finally laid claim to St. Helena and began England's second oldest colony in 1659. Fortifications were built and settlers established permanent quarters.

In as early as 1715 ecological problems began to plague the colony. Deforestation led to severe soil erosion. Goats and rats thrived on the island and were devastating the crops, both domestic and wild. Actions were taken to save the colony and strict growing practices helped to save the domestic plantations of the island. However, the endemic species of the island were discounted and continued to dwindle. Nonetheless, the colony began to prosper.

Napoleon's exile on St. Helena was the subject of a number of the borrowed books that Garron read. Emperor Napoleon Bonaparte arrived on the island in 1815 and moved in with the Balcombe family until his permanent residence, known as Longwood House, was renovated. Napoleon befriended the Balcombe children, but he was particularly taken by the young Betsy Balcombe. Betsy and her siblings brought light to the exiled 47-year-old former emperor's darkest days. He was separated from his own children, so the Balcombe children helped to mend his heart. Betsy was the artist behind the painting held in the Napoleon Museum of Monaco.

Napoleon's presence on St. Helena caused quite a stir. When he landed on the island, the garrison that was sent to guard him was equal to the number of free white men on the island. The island's residents lined Main Street to catch a glimpse of the little man as he made his way through Jamestown, St. Helena's capital city. Napoleon had arrived with furniture, dinnerware, and trunks of books and clothing. The procession made quite the spectacle.

Napoleon spent the remainder of his days on St. Helena. He died in 1821 at the age of 51. He was buried on St. Helena, but his remains were later removed with great majesty and returned to France. Napoleon was finally laid to rest at Les Invalides, in Paris, in 1861. His place of exile on St. Helena, Longwood House, was converted into a museum and now hosted guests from around the world.

Garron was amazed at the part St. Helena played in history. He could not ever remember hearing of the island before Gracie mentioned it the day before. The island hosted many prominent historical figures: astronomers, Edmond Halley and Neville Maskelyne; ship's captains, Cook and Bligh; and naturalist, Charles Darwin.

Gracie had included recent articles in the material she lent to Garron. The articles captured the recent struggles of the island's inhabitants. St.

Helena's remoteness was charming, but that isolation also hindered the island's economy. Tourism was having difficulty taking root due to the lack of an airport, and without thriving commercial ventures residents were forced to leave their island in search of employment. But there was hope for the future and the Saints, as the residents of St. Helena had named themselves, were proud of their heritage and their island.

The capital city of Jamestown was the island's only accessible port. Garron read that the climate of Jamestown was arid, but because of the city's location near the ocean the temperatures were promised to be cool and dry, averaging in the low 70s. His material told him to expect slightly lower temperatures in the higher elevations where he would be making his search for the string tree. Garron was looking forward to the southern hemisphere's cooler winter temperatures.

***

The next morning when Garron awoke he could not feel the rhythm of the yacht that he had grown accustomed to over the last two days. He saw that they had stopped sailing when he drew back the curtain from his cabin's window. Garron quickly dressed and made his way to the upper deck.

Garron was astonished when he stepped out onto the deck and squinted against the brilliant morning sun. The view from James Bay was amazing. The steep cliffs towering over the sea were both foreboding and captivating. Jamestown sparkled with color and lay in contrast to the stark barren cliffs enclosing the city. Many other small sailing vessels and small yachts dotted the bay. A sea wall protected the low-lying city from the ocean's waves.

"Good morning," Gracie greeted Garron as she stepped on deck.

She handed him a pair of sunglasses. "I'm sorry that I didn't think of these earlier; if you don't mind wearing a pair of ladies glasses, then they can save you from wrinkling that pretty face."

Garron looked at the large DG on the arms of the glasses. He hesitated only a second before sliding them over his ears.

"Thank you, that is much better."

"Where were you hiding yourself yesterday?" She asked.

"I could ask you the same thing."

"I was studying recent data pulled from the St. Helena National Trust concerning the replanting of the endangered endemic Bastard Gumwood tree."

Garron was truly shocked. He asked, "Another nearly extinct tree?"

"And like the sedge that Anton mentioned, the Bastard Gumwood was thought to have been extinct until it was rediscovered in the 1980s. And just this year a second adult specimen was found in the wild."

Garron thought of the similarities to their own search and said, "That's hopeful."

Gracie nodded. "This island is a wonderful study of isolated species and the part of human interference within a microcosm."

They both waved as a small fishing boat sputtered past.

"I was doing some reading, too. I looked through that material you loaned me. I learned a lot. I'm surprised that I didn't recall ever hearing of St. Helena before the other day."

Anton stepped onto the deck. He looked out into the bay.

"Here comes our ride," he said pointing at a small craft approaching quickly.

"Garron, Gracie, if you could gather your things, we will be leaving shortly."

Garron and Gracie nodded.

Anton asked, "Garron, could you also let your brother know that it is time to go ashore?"

Twenty minutes later everyone gathered on the rear deck of the yacht. All were dressed in the heavy khaki pants, white cotton duck shirts, and ankle high leather boots that Anton had supplied.

Anton spoke to his team.

"Now that you all look the part, be sure to remember to stay in character while on the island. Keep to yourselves and try not to draw too much attention. There are other scientific teams on the island. If at all possible, try to avoid them. It would not take long for a true entomologist or zoologist to spot our ruse." Anton smiled. "No offense Drs. Shepard."

He continued, "I have taken care of registering our team with Port Control and St. Helena Customs. We are cleared to step ashore." Anton passed out the travel documents to each of his team members standing before him. "Now, let us climb aboard the tender and begin our voyage into history," Anton said with a broad grin.

The tender bounced across the bay and came to the seawall. They filed from the boat, climbed a short set of stairs and stepped through the city's arched gate onto Grand Parade, a wide courtyard that met up with Main Street and ran through the center of town. The group waited for Anton while he collected their drivers from the customs building.

Garron watched as the tender went back to retrieve Anton's men from the second yacht. There were three minibuses parked opposite the customs building, but the drivers were not with the vehicles.

Garron asked Gracie, "What's the plan?" He indicated the buses.

"We split up into three teams. One bus will head for a house that Anton secured in the countryside. One will head to Diane's Peak and the last bus will head to Peak Dale to begin our search."

The streets were relatively quiet, with only a few cars passing through town and a few people ambling down the sidewalks. Looking up the street, Garron could see a picturesque Georgian town that was inviting and full of charm. The buildings were painted in bright blues, clean whites, and warm neutrals. The cliff peaks surrounded the town, looming over the buildings lining the street. A long steep staircase climbed the west cliff wall. The cut of James Valley was even more dramatic from the street than it was from the deck of the yacht. Garron was captivated.

Anton stepped from the building and smiled broadly. Three men followed Anton closely.

Anton looked at his watch. He said, "It is eight-forty local time and sunset is expected at six-sixteen today. This will allow us nearly an entire day to spend in the field."

Anton introduced his escorts, "These gentlemen will be our guides and drivers while we are on St. Helena. George Benjamin and Chris Yon both work for the Forestry Division of the Agriculture and Natural Resources Department."

The two men nodded in greeting.

"And this is Dr. Maxwell Peynaud from the University of Oxford. He is with the Edward Grey Institute of Field Ornithology and has been studying St. Helena for the past ten years."

Everyone shook hands and then moved toward the minibuses.

Anton said, "Leah and Jacob please join Dr. Peynaud in the second bus. Gracie and Garron you are with me in the first bus. We will see you at the Country House later this evening. Are there any questions?"

"Yes," Leah replied. "Why is Garron riding with you?"

"I am sorry. If it is a problem then we can shuffle the teams," Anton responded.

"There is no problem," Garron insisted as he eyed Leah.

"Very well then, good luck," Anton said as he opened the rear door of the minibus for Gracie.

***

George Benjamin drove the minibus out of Jamestown and climbed out of the valley on winding streets. Garron was taken by the narrowness and length of the city sandwiched in the valley between the cliffs. The cliff tops were covered in dense clouds. The landscape was dramatic with its lush greens, shades of browns and reds, and blues.

George Benjamin spoke from the driver's seat on the right side of the van.

"Mr. Margaux, thank you for coming to our small island. I look forward to not only sharing with you the work we have done thus far on the island, but also the beauty that St. Helena has to offer."

George's accent was unique. It was not like the dialects of the Bahamas or Bermuda. There were influences other than the Queen's English.

"We are glad to be here," Anton responded.

George turned in his seat and looked at his guests in the back seat of the minibus. He said, "This must be your first time on St. Helena."

He pronounced it, "'Tis mussie you first ime on Sant Heleena."

"You are correct," Garron answered looking down into another deep valley.

"It is beautiful." Gracie smiled at the driver.

He said proudly, "Thank you and we hope to keep it that way." It came out, "Tank you an us hope to keep it tat way."

Still talking to his passengers in the back, George said, "You are both from the States. We don't get too many visitors from the States. Our island is too remote for as few days as you get in the States for holiday." He continued, "I hope that our airport project will change that."

"You're having an airport added to the island?" Garron asked.

"That is the hottest topic on the island. The project was initiated and then postponed and now it is back on track. Nothing is sure in this economy."

Anton said, "Airport or not, we made it."

George smiled. "And we are very excited to have you. We are lucky to have you interested in our island Mr. Margaux."

"I love our planet Mr. Benjamin, and I want my efforts to make the greatest possible difference. I want to see the fruits of my labor, and with the unique ecosystem on St. Helena I believe the results will be dramatic. Your island has the opportunity to become a beacon of environmental stewardship to the world."

As the minibus entered the national park, visibility was reduced to about twenty feet by the excessive cloud cover. Garron was glued to the windshield, watching the narrow road in front of them winding into the clouds. If another vehicle came through the cloud toward them, then there would be little time for George to react. However, the low visibility did not seem to affect George in the least. He still worked the transmission with ease and sped through the twists and turns of the country road never pausing in his description of the work his team had completed in the Millennium Forest project.

"To date we have more than 8,000 trees planted, and the saplings are doing well. We have to watch them closely. We keep the new saplings watered and free from pests. Conditions are not ideal. The island is dry and the wind is relentless, but when the forest takes root it will start to change those conditions."

George pulled the vehicle behind a gatepost marking the entrance to Diana's Peak and engaged the parking brake. "We are here."

"Mr. Benjamin, I am very interested in learning of your techniques, successes and failures, but we have a short timeline, so may I make a suggestion?" Anton asked as George opened his door.

George paused.

Anton continued, "I would like for you to show me the work that you have done in the Millennium Forest while Drs. Ng and Shepard do some fieldwork here at Diana's Peak."

George hesitated and then said, "If you think that is best, then I …"

Anton interrupted, "Excellent George, thank you. Doctors, we will return for you at five o'clock sharp. Please be thorough."

Gracie and Garron climbed out of the minibus and slid the door closed behind them.

"Mr. Benjamin, I am all yours," Anton said with a smile.

The minibus pulled away with a grinding of gears. Gracie and Garron picked up their over-stuffed backpacks and made their way down a trail that was clearly marked.

***

Dr. Maxwell Peynaud handled the minibus expertly through the cloud cover and up the narrow winding roads of the island's peaks. He said very little on the drive, chewing on his long mustache as he concentrated on the road.

Jacob thought the man to be in his late 40s. He was of average height and weight with a hooked nose and close set eyes. The man's brow furrowed as he watched the road intently.

They came to a sign post marking a path that led to High Peak. Peynaud pulled the minibus off the road and shut off the engine. Jacob heard his sigh as he engaged the parking brake.

He said, "Sorry that I was so quiet on the ride, it's just that these bloody clouds and the winding road puts the wind up me."

"No problem, Doctor, thanks for getting us here safely," Leah said.

Leah and Jacob grabbed their backpacks and followed Peynaud up the marked footpath.

Dr. Peynaud explained his work as they walked. "My work with OTEP brought me to St. Helena ten years ago to study the island's wirebird population. For an ornithologist to have an opportunity to study an endangered species in its natural environment is extraordinary, but to do your work in an ecosystem that is full of species seen nowhere else on the planet is a dream."

He looked over his shoulder at his guests and smiled.

He continued, "But I am afraid that I am the most unpopular man on the island."

Jacob said, "Why is that, Doctor?"

"The wirebird feeds on insects in the grasses of the island's plains. One of the healthiest populations of wirebirds is found on Prosperous Bay Plain, the future site of the proposed airport."

"The airport will destroy the feeding area of the wirebird," Leah concluded.

Peynaud clarified, "The feeding area, the breeding grounds, and the nesting grounds." He added, "Plus the necessary access road. The main artery from the coast for equipment and supplies is proposed to cut through yet another nesting ground."

"So your desire to save the wirebird …"

Jacob was unable to complete his thought as he stepped out of the fern forest and saw the view in the opening along the ridge. The view was awesome. The wind kept the skies clear on this side of the ridge and he looked down over spiraling rock formations stretching to the sea. The formations were jagged and barren with a red and orange tinge.

Dr. Peynaud turned back to see that his guests had stopped on the trail. He smiled. "It is breathtaking, isn't it?" He walked back and joined Leah and Jacob.

"This is amazing!" Leah said.

"They call that formation there," Peynaud pointed to a large jagged rock towering over a valley, "Lot, and the smaller one on the next ridge is Lot's wife."

Jacob squinted against the wind. "I'm not a geologist, but I'm guessing that the wind is the cause of this dramatic landscape."

Peynaud nodded. "It never stops blowing."

They stood admiring the view a moment longer. Then Peynaud suggested that they continue on the path. They traveled another fifty yards before turning off the path and re-entering the fern forest.

"We'll start here," Peynaud said. "This is the farthest southwest extreme of highest altitude on Peak Dale. We can work our way back toward the northeast if that is okay with you."

"Sounds like a plan," Jacob said.

They unpacked their tape measure, stakes, and line to mark their grid. It took nearly thirty minutes to setup the grid, but they finally began their search.

"What are we looking for exactly?" Peynaud asked.

Leah followed the script that Anton had provided on their voyage to the island. "We need to list any endemic species of flora or fauna that we uncover and its exact location using our GPS unit."

Dr. Peynaud frowned. "Being an ornithologist, I'm not sure that I can identify every living thing that covers this peak. Dr. Preston, are you not a marine biologist?"

"Don't underestimate yourself." Jacob continued by changing the topic, "By the way, I believe that I interrupted you earlier. You were mentioning the airport."

Peynaud shrugged and began to search the forest floor. He said, "I'm not completely opposed to adding an airport to the island. As a matter of fact, as an English taxpayer I believe that the island needs an airport to stabilize its economy. Right now the island receives millions of pounds from Parliament to support the territory. The airport would allow for the tourist industry to grow and for supplies to arrive on the island more affordably. It would benefit the Saints immensely. We did a study with the RSPB and determined the best sites for placement of the airport and support facilities, as well as the access road. Some of the island residents took that to mean that we did not support the project. I've worked hard to change their minds. I want what's best for both Saints and wirebirds alike, but I am still unwelcome in some circles."

Leah studied a plant carefully, then stood and stepped to her right. "The important thing to remember is that your study was considered, and options were weighed. We live in a time where ecological consequences are now considered. It wasn't long ago that the wirebird nesting grounds would have been of little consideration to a developer building a new airport or shopping center. We've come a long way."

"You're an optimist, that's hard to find in an environmentalist these days," Peynaud said and continued, "good for you."

Jacob hoped that some of Leah's optimism would rub off on him as he examined another green leaf that looked just like the last green leaf he had just inspected. This would be a long day.

***

Gracie and Garron continued their search only pausing to eat the lunch that Chef Eddie had packed for them. The groundcover was thick, and it was easy to turn an ankle on a covered limb, but they had made relative progress in their grid search. Now the sun was getting low on the horizon.

Garron stumbled on something hidden beneath the cover. He said, "This island is crazy. Some parts are dry and brown, others green and wet."

"We are in the tropics, but the Benguela Current and the South Atlantic High Pressure Cell keep the island at a moderate temperature. As a result, there is always a chance for rain at these higher elevations, while the lower areas stay pretty dry. And once we cross over to the windward side of the island you'll better understand why very little vegetation can survive on the steep cliff sides."

Garron laughed, "What, you're not only a botanist but also a weather girl now?"

"We prefer meteorologist," Gracie laughed as well. "I did a lot of reading on the boat."

"So then, tell me Ms. Meteorologist, what's with this mist?"

Gracie answered, "Warm air and cold water; when the current shifted a century ago the fog moved in."

"Currents shift?"

Gracie nodded, "Yup, currents are affected by many things. The earth is in constant flux: warming, cooling, tectonic shifts, even shifts in the axis. Climate change is more than just greenhouse gases building up in the atmosphere."

They finished their grid and began packing up their bags.

Gracie stood and stretched.

"Don't get me wrong, mankind plays an enormous role in global climate change and fossil fuels are an unsustainable resource. But there are many factors that are being overlooked or outright ignored because they don't fit into someone's campaign platform. And shareholders are too concerned about eroding profit margins to care how their decisions effect the environment. So instead of putting the world's greatest minds on the pursuit of an answer, the media, who happen to be the politician's cronies, pin those minds against one another on the evening news. Then we leave it to the corporations to solve the problem or rather treat the symptoms and make a buck in the process."

Garron smiled wryly and then said, "I hope there's not another one of those things hiding under this groundcover, I might have missed it. Working in teams is helpful, at least you found it."

"Found what?"

"That soap box that you were on. I probably would have tripped right over it."

Gracie put her hands on her hips and gave Garron an evil look.

He laughed. She joined him.

Gracie said, "You should never ask an environmentalist about climate change."

"I don't think I did, but I'll be more careful in the future."

They both laughed again.

Gracie looked at her watch and said, "It's time to head back." She shoved Garron in the direction of the trail head where Anton would be waiting.

***

Anton had purchased a hotel on St. Helena to act as his center of operations. The building stood on 17 acres. It was located on a quiet plain twenty-five minutes from Jamestown. The building was constructed in 1740 and was originally a plantation house. There was a wide, two-story porch that wrapped around the front of the building stretching along the east side to the rear of the house. Four chimneys climbed the outside walls and peaked above the metal roof. It had been owned by an English investor who was counting on the airport being completed on an earlier timetable. He had been happy to receive Anton's call and happier to accept the man's offer.

When the minibus pulled up to the Country House Hotel, Chef Eddie was sweeping the porch and waiting to welcome Anton, Gracie, and Garron back from a day in the field. All of the hotel's windows and doors stood open.

In his Bahamian accent, Eddie said, "Welcome home. I will be serving dinner at seven-thirty."

Anton said as he stepped onto the porch, "Thank you Chef Eddie. I am glad that you made this trip with us."

Eddie looked around. "It is certainly different than my island. I've never seen mountains like these." Eddie made a sweeping motion with his hand toward the door. "Mr. Shepard and Ms. Ng, your rooms are on the second floor at the back of the house. You'll find that I've put your things away for you. Ms. Ng, you are on the right," Eddie handed her a key, "and Mr. Shepard, you are on the left."

Garron took the key from Eddie and smiled.

"I've opened your windows to help air them out. I hope it's not too cold in there."

"Chef Eddie, you are the best." Gracie kissed the man on the cheek.

Garron said, "I agree, but I'm sure that you'd rather have me shake your hand."

Eddie smiled and gripped Garron's hand.

Garron entered a wide hall. The hotel had wood floors throughout. The walls were white plaster and were in need of repair. On the first floor were the common areas of the hotel. There was a guest lounge with a fireplace to the right of the entrance. The furniture was mismatched, but looked comfortable. A dining room with a long table was to the left. Directly in front of the entrance was a staircase with a worn stairway runner leading to the second floor.

Garron climbed the stairs behind Gracie and found seven rooms staggered on opposite sides of the second floor hall stretching the depth of the building. He followed Gracie to the end of the hall. Her room was directly across from his.

She said, "I'll see you at dinner."

"See you then." Garron used his key to enter his room and closed the door behind him.

The room was fairly large. The four poster bed was adorned with a bedspread that looked like it belonged to his grandmother. There was an oval braided rug on the floor that had seen better days, but the room had potential. There were two large windows, one looking over the backyard and the other looking over a large floral garden that was overgrown. There was a beautiful view of the ocean in the distance from the back window.

Garron saw that his boots had left a trail of dirt across the room. He sat in an old rocking chair near the window and removed them. Tomorrow he would leave them on the porch. He noticed the dirt caked to his pants and decided that the shower would be the best place to undress.

In the bathroom he found an enormity of white tile. The floors were tiled, the walls were tiled, and the shower stall was tiled. There was a white pedestal sink, white toilet, and white bathmat and towels.

Garron looked at the dirt caked under his nails and stepped directly into the shower.

***

The teams discussed their time spent in the field over dinner. Chef Eddie had apologized before the meal had begun for the lack of ingredients that he was able to procure from the markets in Jamestown. He was told that the RMS St. Helena was due in port in three days, and until then the selection would be limited. They dined on tuna steaks and boiled potatoes.

The consensus was that the search was going to be difficult and that with the limited resources available, it would be lengthy, as well. Anton promised that he was expecting more manpower to arrive shortly, and he asked that everyone stay positive and enthusiastic. He explained that he was going to train his security team and place them in the field to double their efforts until another science team arrived on the island. Anton had Eddie bring two bottles of Duval-Leroy at the end of the meal. They popped the champagne and toasted to the promise of a new day.

***

The morning of their second day was dampened by rain. Thankfully, Anton had supplied rain gear. Chef Eddie had a bag lunch waiting for everyone in the kitchen. George Benjamin and Chris Yon were waiting outside the hotel for Leah, Jacob, Gracie, and Garron in their minibuses. George explained that Dr. Peynaud had a previously scheduled meeting with his peers from OTEP in Jamestown and would not be joining them. Gracie and Garron climbed into George's minibus, while Leah and Jacob joined Chris. They were on the road shortly after six o'clock.

The rain had stopped by ten and the sun had warmed Garron so that he now clawed through the damp underbrush in his t-shirt. He and Gracie had spoken very little since beginning their search. It was awkward with George joining their hunt, but George's knowledge of the endemic species of St. Helena was valuable. He had pointed out three endemic plants since they started their search that morning. But still they had not found the string tree.

The team stopped for lunch. Garron removed his boots and wrung the water from his socks. He asked, "George, were you born and raised on St. Helena?"

"Yes sir, I have lived my whole life, all 53 years, on St. Helena. I've never even been off the island," George responded.

"You've never left St. Helena?" Gracie was stunned.

"The cost is too high, but I hope to take my granddaughter to visit my daughter in Cape Town this year."

"Your granddaughter lives with you, while your daughter is in Cape Town?" Garron asked.

"Many of our island's young people have to leave their homes and children to make a living. She sends money home with every RMS delivery."

Garron thought of a conversation that he had had with Jacob after dinner. He asked, "Would an airport make a difference?"

"It would make all of the difference. I believe that the tourist industry would save our island. When we are fortunate to see cruise ships in our bay, shopkeepers in Jamestown earn more in one week than in an entire month without visiting tourists. Our young people might not have to leave just to earn a living. And if they did, it would be much easier for them to get back home. I haven't seen my daughter in two years."

Garron reluctantly pulled his wet boots back on and continued the search.

***

The sun was setting and the air was laden with moisture. It was going to be a chilly night; the clouds had cleared from the sky allowing what heat had been trapped to radiate into the darkness above.

When Gracie and Garron returned to the Country House Hotel, they found Leah and Jacob on the front porch pulling their mud caked boots from their tired feet. The group returned less exuberant from their second day of searching through the forests than the first. Everyone looked tired. Mud was not only caked to their boots, but also on their pants. Leah even had mud in her hair. After a brief greeting, everyone hit the showers.

Anton was absent at dinner that evening. Eddie apologized once again for the meal that he provided. He cursed the lack of produce the island had available for him.

Dinner conversation was light, and the mood was somber. The pure scope of their search was overwhelming. The group's optimism had waned.

Gracie had anticipated the change in mood and brought a newsletter from the St. Helena National Trust concerning the Bastard Gumwood tree. She read it aloud during dinner. The tree was thought to be extinct, with the last sighting occurring in the 1890s, but the tree was discovered in the wild in 1982. In the recent past there was believed to be only one specimen of the Bastard Gumwood tree in the wild. But recently a second specimen had been found by one of Dr. Peynaud's OTEP horticulturists on one of the island's cliffs. Gracie explained that the recovery effort for the gumwood tree was successful in planting more than 100 seedlings in the past year. The second adult wild tree would only help with the propagation of the species.

The article had the desired effect and the mood lightened. A current and relevant example of a successful ecological recovery effort helped to brighten the table's outlook.

After dinner Garron helped Chef Eddie to clear the table. The kitchen was in the back of the building directly behind the dining room. Like the rest of the house, it had not been updated since the late 1950s, but was large and well designed. There was an enormous wooden island in the center of the room; there were dirty dishes and glasses on the island where it appeared someone had eaten. A long span of cabinets stretched along one wall. There was an antiquated, oversized range and an extra wide refrigerator in the room. A deep cast iron sink sat on the back wall just under a window looking out over the backyard.

Garron asked, "Did you eat in here this evening?"

Chef Eddie nodded as he took the plates Garron was carrying and placed them in the sink. He said, "George and Chris joined me for dinner."

"I'd love for you to join us in the dining room," Garron said.

"You're very kind, Mr. Shepard."

"And you really should call me Garron."

The two men shook hands.

Garron said, "That should be the last of the dishes. Would you like some help washing up?"

"No thank you. The one update this kitchen does have is a dishwasher, but I appreciate your offer."

When Garron stepped back into the dining room, the room was empty. He heard voices coming from the hall. The voices were muffled but the conversation seemed heated. Garron peered into the hall and saw Gracie and Anton standing near the foot of the stairs. Gracie looked down the hall to see Garron standing on the threshold of the dining room and abruptly ended the conversation. She turned from Anton and strode past Garron and out the front door.

Anton turned and smiled weakly at Garron. He walked down the hall.

"I learned of a downturn in Gracie's mother's condition," Anton said in way of explanation.

Garron said, "She sounded angry."

"She wasn't happy to learn that transportation off of the island was impossible for at least three days. She is obviously anxious to return home to her mother." Anton looked down at floor. "She blames me for dragging her so far from home, and to such a remote location."

Garron looked at the front door where Gracie had exited the house.

He said, "Don't be too hard on yourself. She's obviously in a great deal of pain and she must feel helpless and stranded."

"Thank you." Anton grasped Garron's shoulder. "I have some good news for you; Veronica will be joining us in three days time. She joined my crew in Walvis Bay; she will be coming in by ship."

Garron smiled. "That's excellent news. Thank you, Anton, for getting her here."

Garron could feel a tightness set into his throat; he choked back the tears. He missed his wife terribly. Anton squeezed his shoulder once more. He seemed to understand Garron's pain.

Garron regained his composure and said, "I think I'll check on Gracie."

As Garron walked through the front door, he saw Leah and Jacob wrapped in a blanket and curled up on a high backed bench at the far end of the porch. Garron stepped off of the porch and away from the house. He found Gracie standing near the minibus speaking to George.

Garron said, "Hey, are you doing okay?"

Gracie looked surprised. "What did he tell you?"

"Anton said that your mother had a setback."

Gracie shook her head slightly. "Right, well I feel like a drink. George here has offered to take me into town. Do you want to come along?"

***

Jamestown was fairly busy. The center of the wide street was used for parking, and George took the last empty spot for the minibus. A cruise ship was visible in James Bay. A small crowd had gathered around one building, the Continental Hotel. The two story façade was adorned with a double porch. The ground level porch was filled with people enjoying cocktails and beer from the bar.

George led Gracie and Garron to the bar greeting people on his way. They found the only empty table in the room and took a seat. George excused himself and returned a moment later with drinks in hand. He handed Gracie an empty glass and a bottle of beer.

"For you, my lady, this is the world's finest lager," he said as he filled the glass from a bottle of Tafel.

"And for you, sir, a taste of our island's finest spirit." George poured a shot of clear liquid from a unique angular bottle. "And I believe that I should join you because it is never good to drink tungi alone." He poured another shot.

"What is tungi?" Garron asked.

"It is a prickly pear spirit," George answered and raised his glass.

He said in a toast, "God save the Queen."

Garron took the shot down expertly, feeling the warmth of the alcohol coursing through him immediately. It was a smooth spirit that Garron found difficult to describe.

"This is very tasty. Thank you, George."

"Would you like another taste then, Dr. Shepard?" George asked raising the bottle.

"Please call me Garron. I would love another."

George poured and raised the second glass, "Cheers."

The second tasted better than the first, and Garron slid his glass toward George for a refill.

George rose from the table. "I think before we have another we should have a beer." He inspected Gracie's nearly empty glass, "Would you like another, Dr. Ng?"

"Yes, thank you George."

George bowed slightly and made his way to the bar across the room.

Gracie said to Garron, "Pour me a shot of that liquor, unless you think it unladylike for me to drink that hard stuff."

"You really should try it, it's very good." He smiled. "But you should go easy there, little lady."

Gracie laughed, then drained the glass effortlessly.

She said with a slight grimace, "Damn that is potent."

"But it's good, right?"

"Actually, it is delicious."

George returned with three Tafel lagers and two glasses. He poured them each a beer. He said, "There are two gentlemen at the bar that I would like you to meet. May I ask them to join us?"

Garron felt the good cheer perpetuated by the tungi spirit take hold and replied, "The more the merrier."

George returned from the bar once again with the two men in tow. He made introductions.

"Drs. Ng and Shepard, please let me introduce Dr. Sherwood and Mr. Mills."

Garron rose and extended his hand toward the elder of the two men. He was tall with broad shoulders, thinning hair, and a wide smile with kind, blue eyes.

"I'm Garron Shepard."

The man replied, "Wayne Sherwood."

Garron shook hands with the younger man, who introduced himself as Phillip Mills. He was a handsome man with a boyish grin and mahogany skin.

Garron gestured to the empty chairs. "Please join us."

Everyone took their seats.

Dr. Sherwood asked, "You are both doctors. What are your areas of expertise?"

Garron hesitated.

"Mine is botany and Dr. Shepard's is entomology," Gracie answered. "We are here to study and document the health of the island's endemics."

"This is such an interesting island. Dr. Sherwood and I are part of the archaeological dig in Rupert's Valley." Phillip smiled proudly.

George explained further, "Rupert's Valley was the chosen location for the airport's access road. When they began the road, the crew uncovered a burial site."

Dr. Sherwood said, "The valley was used as a burial site for liberated slaves. After slavery was abolished and outlawed, the Royal Navy would house the men, women, and children liberated from the slave ships on St. Helena. Many of those liberated, especially the children, died on St. Helena due to illnesses contracted while they were crammed into the ships' holds. The dead were buried in Rupert's Valley." He sat back in his chair. "Since the access road required the removal of the skeletons, we were called in to handle the excavation."

Garron recalled reading about the Liberated Africans Depot on the voyage. Between 1840 and 1849, the island became a refuge for 15,000 Africans who were liberated from slaving ships. After slavery was abolished, a British Naval Station was established in 1840 to battle the Atlantic slave trade. The victims of human trafficking were held in the Liberated Slave Depot in Rupert's Valley until transport could be given back to Africa. However, British officials did not speak the many languages of their guests and many of the liberated slaves were relocated to parts of Africa that would have been as foreign to them as any destination in the United States or Brazil, but they did have their freedom.

Phillip said, "This dig is a wonderful opportunity to learn more about the slave trade of the nineteenth century and the victims of that enterprise."

Gracie asked, "How many graves have you uncovered?"

"Ten that fall within the scope of the airport access project," Phillip answered. "The ten graves have yielded more than 300 skeletons, but the valley may hold as many as 20,000 burials."

"Ole would have loved to take a look at their find," Garron said to Gracie.

"Ole?" Phillip asked.

"He's an anthropologist with our team. He was unable to make the trip," Garron responded.

Gracie kicked Garron under the table causing him to spill his beer. Garron read the warning in Gracie's expression and recovered. "Sorry, I'm a bit clumsy."

Dr. Sherwood's smile faltered. He asked, "Why do you have an anthropologist as a member of an ecological study?"

Gracie smiled at the doctor. "Our benefactor usually travels with an anthropologist to help disarm tension when we find ourselves up against indigenous peoples who don't quite understand why we are traipsing through their jungles or deserts."

Gracie followed quickly with her own question, "How long have you been working your site?"

"Ten weeks," Phillip answered.

Garron asked, "Have you found anything that stood out?"

Dr. Sherwood smiled again and leaned into the table.

He answered, "We recently uncovered the grave of a fetus that was laid to rest with great care. The slavers had taken anything of value from their prisoners as they were forced into the holds. So all we typically find in a grave are skeletal remains, although occasionally we will find cowrie shell jewelry or a beaded necklace. But with this infant we found a beautifully woven blanket that was lovingly wrapped around the child's remains."

"That's a magnificent find. You've done well for only ten weeks in the field," Gracie said.

"Thank you. The graves were shallow, so we were able to work quickly. And once we determined the large scope of the project, we were joined by some colleagues," Sherwood responded.

Phillip added, "Plus we had many volunteers who were eager, dependable, and conscientious."

Phillip stood, raised his glass, and looked around the room. He said loud enough to be heard out in the street, "To the Saints of this beautiful island!"

The room responded by raising their glasses and saying en masse, "Cheers!"

***

The next two days were much like the first. Each team expanded their search field and each group came up empty. The work was tedious and slow. At the end of each day, the teams would update Anton on their progress through the island's peaks, noting GPS coordinates on a map of the island laid out before him.

Anton said, "We are just not covering enough ground."

"We are using every minute of daylight," Gracie responded.

"We haven't seen Taylor's team since the first day, have they had any luck?" Leah asked.

"I've been meeting with them separately. I've put them up in another house on the opposite end of the island. They've had the same results as you." Anton continued, "I'm expecting my ship in the next ten hours. There will be eight additional men on board."

"Anton, I know that secrecy is of the utmost importance, but I have a suggestion," Garron said.

"What do you have in mind?"

"We have a strong cover story, so why don't we include some locals in our search efforts? That archaeological team in the valley has been using Saints as a part of their excavation, and from what one of the scientists told me, they are quite resourceful."

Anton looked to Gracie. Garron had trouble reading the look on Anton's face.

Gracie said, "We bumped into a couple of archaeologists a couple of nights ago. They could not praise the work ethic of the Saints enough. I think that it is a good idea."

Anton considered the suggestion as he looked over his map of the island.

"That might work. But I do not want to draw the attention of the archaeologists by pilfering their labor force."

"Their dig is coming to an end. Besides, there are many Saints not working on the Rupert's Valley dig who would be eager to volunteer." Garron added, "If you would be willing to pay a small wage for their help, even better. There is not a single Saint who would not benefit from a little extra money."

Anton nodded.

Garron said, "Let me speak to Dr. Sherwood, or better yet his graduate student Phillip, to ask about their timeline and see if I could get a list of their volunteers."

Anton stood. He clapped his hands enthusiastically. He said, "Excellent! Garron please head into town after dinner and see when they plan on shutting down their dig."

Garron borrowed a car from Chris, who would catch a ride with George later after finishing his meal, and drove into town. At first he had difficulty adjusting to driving from the opposite side of the car, but his time spent on the island as a passenger on George's minibus helped him to acclimate quickly.

Garron knew from their first meeting at the Continental Hotel that Sherwood's team was headquartered somewhere along Main Street. Garron started with the small blue door just east of the Continental. The windows were dark and no one answered Garron's knock on the door. He continued to the building directly beside the hotel. No one answered that door either. A small crowd had spilled out of the hotel's bar onto the porch and then the sidewalk. Garron stepped into the street to skirt the bar patrons. Garron heard someone calling his name from just inside the bar.

Phillip staggered through the crowd, "Dr. Shepard, hello, it's Phillip, we met the other night."

"Of course, Phillip. I was actually looking for you."

Phillip sloshed beer as he switched his glass to his left hand in order to take Garron's extended one.

Garron asked, "Are you celebrating, Phillip?"

"Yes, I am!" Phillip answered a bit too loudly.

Phillip leaned closer to Garron while glancing conspiratorially from side to side.

He raised his right hand to cover the side of his mouth and in an exaggerated whisper said, "We found something extraordinary." Then his brow knitted and he asked, "Did you say that you were looking for me?"

"Yes, I did. I was wondering if you were finished with your dig in Rupert's Valley. I wanted to use your volunteers in our efforts, but if you just found something then I wouldn't want to deplete your numbers."

"No, no, we are finished in the valley. Our find is outside the scope of the airport project. Let's go next door and I'll give you the list of names and numbers for our volunteers."

Phillip weaved as he led the way to the two-storied building west of the Continental. He unlocked the door, swung the door inward, and stepped into the dark. Garron waited for a light to come on before following.

The first floor was one large room that covered the entire width and depth of the building. Center support columns ran the length of the room. Two large windows faced Main Street and on the back wall was a wide barn-type door that hung from a track. It appeared to have been a warehouse that had been converted into Sherwood's laboratory. Eight long steel tables sat in two rows on the concrete floor. The front row of tables held many cardboard boxes; each box was labeled on the front panel with its contents.

Phillip walked past the tables to a desk in the far corner of the room and turned on a desk lamp. He opened a drawer and withdrew a manila folder.

"What's in the boxes?" Garron asked from across the room.

"Skeletal remains mostly, there are still discussions about where to inter the remains, so they wait here in their boxes."

Phillip met Garron in the center of the room and handed him the folder.

"Here is the list of volunteers. They come cheap." He laughed. "It only cost us two good meals a day to keep the most efficient labor force I have worked with coming back day after day." Phillip added, "I've placed an 'X' by the names of a few because I'll be keeping them for my new project."

Garron said, "Thank you, Phillip, I should let you get back to Dr. Sherwood and your celebration."

"Dr. Sherwood has left the island. He's headed back to Cambridge to try and secure more grant money for our new dig," Phillip responded.

As the two men headed for the door, something caught Garron's eye on the back row of tables and caused him to stop short. Something glinted in the low light.

Garron stepped closer to the table and asked, "Phillip is that gold?"

Phillip stumbled as he made an effort to pull a sheet of canvas over the table.

He stammered, "Dr. Shepard, please … if Dr. Sherwood knew that I let you in here … I shouldn't have let you in."

Garron attempted to reassure the young man. "Phillip, relax. I don't want to cause you any trouble, and I don't want to interfere with your research, or scoop your find."

Phillip relaxed noticeably as he met Garron's eye.

He said, "Dr. Sherwood is concerned, and rightly so, that someone will leak our find and start a media frenzy. Or worse than that, have treasure hunters start to pull this island apart."

Garron was shocked at the mention of treasure hunters swarming to the island. He asked, "Is there gold on St. Helena?"

"No, not at all, that's not what would draw the attention of the world."

"Then what is it?"

Phillip considered his response.

He said, "Dr. Shepard, I must have your word as a scientist that you will not share what I'm about to show you with anyone."

Garron felt a tinge of guilt. He hated misleading the young man. "You must call me Garron. Of course, you have my word."

A wide smile came across Phillip's face. With the flourish of a magician, he pulled the canvas sheet back revealing a skeleton and several artifacts, including a spear, a dagger, a small clay vessel, some pottery shards, and fragments of long fabric. There were photographs surrounding the items displaying the position of each item as it was found in relation to the skeleton. The gold that had glinted in the light and caught Garron's eye was woven into the fabric.

Phillip seemed to sober quickly as he began to explain the articles on the table in a tone characteristic of an academic.

He said, "Obviously this was not the grave of a freed slave. These artifacts attest to that fact. In fact this was not found in a grave at all."

"What do you mean it wasn't a grave?"

"This poor man was caught in a rockslide."

Garron could see a fracture in the skull, and the broken long bones of the legs and arms.

Phillip continued, "I literally uncovered him purely by accident about ten meters above Rupert's Valley. I had climbed the valley walls to take some bird's eye pictures of our completed work. I saw his spear head under some rocks that I was standing on."

Garron clapped the young man on the shoulder. "Congratulations Phillip, what a fantastic find."

Phillip's smile grew even wider.

"Thank you." Phillip continued, "Some academics spend their whole lives in the field and never get this lucky."

After a moment of examining the items on the table, Garron asked, "So do you have any idea who this guy is, or rather was?"

"We have some clues." Phillip swept a hand over the artifacts. "But they create more questions than answers. It is quite a puzzle."

Garron stepped closer to the table. "How so?"

"Well, take a look at the fabric. It is silk, and although a great deal of it has disintegrated over time, we have enough of it to attest to the quality of the weaving process and the style of the garment. The length of the gold trim in the fabric shows the height of the garment. It is nearly as long as Rupert was tall. He was wearing a robe."

Garron smiled. "You named him?"

Phillip smiled. "I was the one who suggested Rupert." He continued eagerly, "If you couple the fact that Rupert was wearing a robe with the traces of fabric that was found on the skull, then we can recreate the ensemble."

"Which will point to Rupert's origins, right?" Garron asked.

"Plus, if we look at Rupert's weapons, a tamba and a sheru, we can positively identify his geographical origins."

Phillip paused for effect.

"Rupert hails from Africa."

Garron did not understand the young man's exuberance. "Finding an African so near the African Liberated Slave Depot seems a bit underwhelming."

Phillip frowned slightly and then said, "This man was not a slave. Look at these artifacts, there is no way that a slaver would allow these on his ship."

Garron nodded. "So, he's definitely not a slave."

Phillip added, "Also, you should remember that we are 2,000 kilometers from the African coast, but there is something else that compounds the importance of this find."

Phillip returned to the desk from which he had pulled the list of volunteers and unlocked a drawer. He pulled yet another manila folder from within and brought it to the table.

Before he opened the folder, he reminded Garron, "Remember that you gave me your word."

Inside the folder were photographs of a single piece of gold jewelry beautifully adorned with precious stones. Phillip spread the photos out across the tabletop. It looked like a pendant on a gold chain. The items were photographed beside a ruler for scale. The pendant was approximately 12 centimeters in diameter, almost five inches, and the chain measured 60 centimeters, nearly two feet in length.

Phillip said, "We found this under the skeleton."

"It is beautiful. The color of the stones looks a bit muted. Are those emeralds and rubies?" Garron asked.

"That is what makes this find so extraordinary. The amulet is made from amber, jade, and cinnabar."

Phillip handed Garron a lighted magnifying glass to inspect the photos.

Phillip said, "Amber is found around the world, and cinnabar is even more readily available. But the blue and green stones are jade, and not just any jade, it is jadeitite. Jadeitite is known only to exist on the Pacific coast of South America, in Guatemala. So there is yet an unknown source for Jadeitite in the eastern hemisphere, or the amulet crossed the Atlantic. We will know more when the chemical analysis of the stone has been completed. We will be able to pinpoint the exact mine location."

Garron studied the photograph more closely.

The amulet was round with the bottom of the circle being dominated by the rich brown tones of amber. The top half was pieced together with the blue and green jade. It looked to Garron like a depiction of land, sea, and sky. He studied the small red pieces of cinnabar on the amulet. Garron's stomach dropped and his heart raced. He set down the magnifying glass.

"Phillip, I have a proposition for you, but first I need a drink."

Phillip went back to the desk once more and pulled a bottle from a drawer.

"I have a bottle of tungi," he said.

Garron smiled. "That will do nicely, now let's talk."

Chapter 11

"GOOD MORNING, DR. Ng."

"Good morning George," Gracie said as she approached the minibus.

"George have you seen Garron this morning? He wasn't at breakfast."

George opened the door for his passenger.

"I spoke to Dr. Shepard last night and he asked that we meet him in town this morning."

Gracie paused with one leg in the vehicle. "Did he ever come back last night?"

George shook his head. "Dr. Shepard called me last night and asked that I bring Chris into town to retrieve his car. Dr. Shepard met us near the Continental, gave us the keys and asked that we pick him up in the morning."

Gracie looked at her watch. "Well then, we had better get moving. Jamestown is a bit out of our way."

George closed the minibus door behind Gracie then climbed behind the wheel.

Garron was standing in front of the Continental Hotel. He waved as the minibus approached. Then he made what he hoped to be the international sign for roll down the window. George lowered his window as he pulled the minibus alongside the curb where Garron was standing.

Garron said, "George, would it be too much to ask for you to wait while I show Dr. Ng something?"

George surveyed the busy street. "I'll park near the waterfront and wait with the van. How long will you be?"

"Not too long. We will find you when we have finished."

Gracie slid the door open and stepped out onto the sidewalk.

She said, "We really should get going, we're losing daylight."

"I know, but I have something that you must see."

Garron led the way to Phillip's lab. Gracie studied Garron.

"You look like hell. Did you sleep last night?"

Garron answered, "Not much."

"What were you doing all night?"

With a huge grin Garron said, "You'll see." He opened the door to the warehouse.

Phillip stood over the covered table in the center of the room.

"Phillip, you remember Dr. Ng."

"Of course I do." Phillip waved as his guests made their way into the room.

Gracie saw the same tired expression in Phillips eyes that she had seen in Garron's.

"You two look like shit, neither of you slept last night. What's this all about?"

Phillip responded, "Garron and I had a great deal to discuss last night. It seems that I may be able to help you find what you are looking for."

Gracie turned on Garron and with steel in her voice asked, "What did you tell him?"

A shiver ran down Garron's spine as he looked into Gracie's eyes. Garron turned away and winked at Phillip.

"Phillip, could you please introduce Dr. Ng to Rupert before you have to add my body to the rest of the remains in your lab?"

"Who's Rupert?" Gracie asked.

Phillip uncovered Rupert and the artifacts that were found on the steep valley wall. Phillip explained to Gracie the circumstances under which he had discovered the items laid out before her on the steel table. He identified the spear as a tamba and the dagger as a sheru. Phillip let Gracie examine the clothing remnants with their intricate gold detail.

He said, "So far everything points to Rupert originating from somewhere in northwest Africa. The boubou and kufi, the robe and cap, suggest that Rupert was Muslim. The tamba and sheru help date him to the height of the Mali Empire in the thirteenth century. Of course, we will have to wait for the results of the carbon 14 dating and the strontium isotope analysis to be certain of the age of our artifacts."

"This is a fantastic find Phillip; congratulations." Gracie turned to Garron, "But what does this have to do with our research?"

Garron grinned. "All in due time, Dr. Ng. Phillip, please show her the pottery."

Phillip nodded. "Like I said, Rupert died in a rockslide and under his remains I found these fragments of pottery and this vessel."

Gracie looked down on several pieces of simply decorated shards and a small clay vessel that was still intact.

Phillip said, "From his body position, it appeared that Rupert was cradling the pottery like a rugby ball when the rockslide took his life." Phillip pantomimed holding an object with both arms drawn tightly to his abdomen. "It seems as though he was trying to protect the pottery with his body. The small vessel survived and the contents of one of the larger vessels remained trapped in the cupped fragment. The vessel held soil and plant matter. It seems that Rupert was an early botanist collecting plant specimens from St. Helena."

Gracie looked at Garron who nodded slightly and smiled.

Garron said, "Now Phillip, let Gracie view the photo."

Phillip placed a photograph of the amulet under a magnifying lens supported on a frame.

He said, "This is why Garron told me of your search for the string tree."

Gracie studied the photograph carefully. The amulet was round and its surface was made of small cuts of blue, green, and red stones. The stones were placed together like a mosaic to create a landscape. The darker blue stones were laid in the upper part of the circle creating the sky. The green-blue stones created a sea meeting the sky at a horizon line. The bottom third of the circle was covered in dark brown shades of amber, creating land. From the amber, a small tree made from the green stones rose up into the blue sky. Tiny, red rectangular cut stones hung from the limbs like blossoms. Gracie was looking at what was possibly a representation of the St. Helena string tree. She looked up from the photographs to see Garron's broad Cheshire cat grin.

"Do you know what those blue and green stones are? They're jade," Garron asked and answered his own question. He continued, "And not just jade, but a specific jade that can only be found in South America, a jade that the Maya used in their art."

"Not just the Maya, but the Olmec before them," Phillip clarified. "But we can't rule out another source of the jade without further chemical analysis."

Garron said, "I don't think that this is a coincidence. I believe that this goes a long way in proving a pre-Columbian trade route existed between the Old and New World. A trade route that I explained to my buddy Phillip was the true reason for our visit to the island."

Gracie began, "So you told Phillip ..."

Garron interrupted, "Yup, I told Phillip of the ancient oral tradition on Bimini that spoke of the St. Helena string tree. But Phillip, like us, can't figure out why this plant would have any significance to a culture half a world away."

"And Phillip was willing to share his find with you because ..." Gracie trailed off.

Phillip answered, "Garron can be very convincing."

"Phillip realized that proving a pre-Columbian trade route across the Atlantic was far more beneficial to his career than simply finding the remains of an African man 120 miles from Africa."

"Like I said, he can be very convincing." Phillip laughed.

"Garron does have his talents," Gracie agreed.

Garron beamed with pride.

He said, "But there's more to the story. Phillip and I knew that nothing could be salvaged from our broken antique flower pot, but we wondered if something of value could have survived in the smaller still sealed vessel."

"What do you think?" Garron posed the question to Gracie.

Gracie gently lifted the small clay vessel and examined the seal. It appeared to have been sealed with a plant or tree resin and there were no cracks visible in the clay.

"It's possible. Have either of you heard of the Methuselah Tree?"

Both men shook their heads.

Gracie continued, "The Methuselah Tree is a Judean date palm that went extinct in the first century. During excavations in Masada between 1963 and 1965, 2000-year-old seeds were found preserved in an ancient jar. The seeds were held in storage until 2005 when efforts were made to germinate them. It worked and the tree is over five feet high today."

"Two thousand years old, that's amazing!" Phillip was overjoyed.

"But we can't open the vessel here. I need optimal conditions if we expect to recover the tree. I'll need to soak the seeds in a hormone-rich bath and then add an enzymatic fertilizer fortified with nutrients. Success counts on the type of conditions in which these seeds were stored over the last 700 years. That's assuming that this little vessel holds anything at all."

"It had to have been sealed for a reason," Garron suggested.

Gracie examined the condition of Rupert's remains.

She said, "I'd say with the amount of hair and remnants of skin on that skull, there is a good chance that the environmental conditions are favorable to us finding something sustainable in this vessel."

Gracie beamed. "Gentlemen, I'd say that this calls for a celebration. How about a drink?"

Both men turned a little green and answered in unison with a resounding, "No."

***

"Garron wake up," Gracie said as she nudged Garron from sleep.

He had fallen asleep in the minibus shortly after leaving Jamestown.

Garron muttered something incoherent as he wiped his eyes and attempted to take in his surroundings.

Gracie said, "We're back at the Country House. Go inside and get some rest. I'll go to Anton's search site and give him the good news. You and I can talk more at dinner tonight."

Garron said, "Okay, just make sure that Phillip gets the credit for the find."

"I'll be sure that he does. Now go. Get some sleep."

"See you tonight. Thank you," Garron said as he dragged himself from the minibus and made his way to his room.

To George, Gracie said, "I'd like to make the drive on my own, if you don't mind."

"Are you sure? I would be happy to take you to Longwood, Dr. Ng."

"That's okay George. May I take the minibus?"

"As you wish. I'll catch a ride back into town and help the wife at her shop. With the cruise ship tourists in port, it should be a busy day for her."

"Thank you, George. I will see you later."

George left the minibus running as he slid out of the driver's seat. He watched as Gracie climbed behind the wheel and smoothly put the vehicle in gear. George was confused as Gracie turned right onto the street and headed south. Longwood District was in the opposite direction.

***

The drive to the old fortifications at Sandy Bay, where Anton had setup his true headquarters, took nearly thirty minutes. At one point near the shore, the minibus had to leave the paved road to reach an area just west of the fort. Gracie parked the minibus in a clearing and made the remainder of the trip on foot. The wind was incessant. The fort was perched on the steep cliff of Sandy Bay Barn, overlooking Powell Point.

Sandy Bay Fort was in decay, but a large portion of the fortifications were still standing, including the dry moat, drawbridge, storehouses, and tower. The top of the fortress was made up of a circular military building holding magazines, barracks, storerooms, and secured with a portcullis.

Gracie was met at the drawbridge by two armed men that she did not recognize. They only permitted her entry after radioing her presence to someone unseen. Gracie was surprised to see the high level of activity within the outer wall. The courtyard had become a city of tents stretching to the tower at the far end of the compound. Most of the men were busy lifting boxes or running cables or wiring cameras; all were armed. Gracie estimated their number at thirty. She made her way through the tent camp to the south end of the courtyard where she was met by yet another pair of sentries before she was allowed to enter the inner courtyard through the portcullis. Gracie could see Anton standing in the inner courtyard supervising the unpacking of equipment. He waved her past the guards.

"What is all of this?" Gracie asked.

"Our men and supplies arrived today. I'm having your lab set up in the tower building, it is the most secure."

"I meant all of the guns," she clarified.

Anton met her gaze. "It would benefit you not to forget that we are still at war, Gracie. The Brotherhood's resources are greater than mine, and once they find me, they will come for me. I will be ready for them, they will not steal this from me."

The look in Anton's eyes frightened Gracie. She understood his pain, but something had changed in Anton in the last few days that caused her to second-guess her alliance to the man.

Anton asked, "Why were you and Garron Shepard not within your designated search area today?"

Gracie was startled. "Did you have me followed?"

Anton did not respond.

"We were with one of the Rupert Valley archaeological team members in Jamestown."

"I had Shepard followed last night. I knew that he never left Jamestown."

Anton turned his attention back to the men handling the oversized crates.

He said, "Do not forget, Gracie, that he is a member of The Brotherhood."

"Garron believes in our cause, Anton. We can trust him."

Gracie was distracted by two armed men carrying a woman whose head was covered by a black bag. The woman was bound at the wrists and ankles and she hung lifelessly in the men's arms.

"Who is that?"

"Veronica Shepard. She is our insurance policy."

"Anton, have you harmed her?"

"She is fine. She is a pompous bitch with a tongue that can cut, I had her drugged to quiet her, but she is fine."

Gracie watched as the men laid Veronica on a cot inside one of the magazine stores and then padlocked a steel gate behind them, leaving her bound and blindfolded. Gracie knew that this had gone too far. She worried what might happen to the Shepards and Leah.

Anton asked, "Have you slept with Garron?"

Gracie was snapped out of her reflection by the question.

She answered through gritted teeth, "No, I have not. You asked me to get close to Garron and to earn his trust, I have done that. I didn't need to sleep with him for that to happen."

Anton asked, "Did you accomplish anything today?"

"We secured a number of locals to help in our search effort." Gracie's gaze bore into the back of the man's head.

"And it took Shepard all night to broker that deal?"

"No. You know of his drinking problem, he and the archaeologist spent the night emptying a bottle. The archaeologists are leaving the island today. They were celebrating and asked Garron to join them."

Anton eyed Gracie skeptically. He nodded. "Very well, but in the future there will not be another single day in the field lost. Is that clear?"

Gracie only steeled her gaze.

Anton said, "Since you are here, help my men to set up your lab equipment. Generators are in place, you should have electricity in mere moments."

Anton stepped away from Gracie and strode out to the courtyard.

Gracie had arrived at Sandy Bay with the intention of telling Anton about the small clay vessel, but now she was concerned that she had aligned herself with someone dangerous. She thought of her mother. Gracie knew why she was here, but had she misjudged Anton's intentions? She turned to tend to her lab equipment.

***

Garron awoke with barely enough time to shower before dinner. As he made his way toward the dining room, he felt lighter, rejuvenated and he had a spring in his step as he descended the stairs. Garron knew that finding the Elixir of Life would change the world, and even though he was concerned with the elixir's potential for good being corrupted, he was proud of having had a hand in introducing it to the world.

Garron was late. Everyone was already seated and had begun their first course. To his surprise, as he surveyed the table, the mood seemed somber.

His smile faltered. "Hello everyone, I am sorry that I am late."

"Sorry that we started without you, but we were not sure if you'd be joining us," Anton said.

Garron took his seat next to Gracie. He looked around the table at the serious expressions on his companion's faces.

"Why does everyone look so glum?" He asked.

Anton sipped his wine. "Your brother and Leah were giving their daily report, and unfortunately it is nearly identical to the reports of the last few nights. We are all frustrated. It's tough trudging through the forest day after day with nothing to show for your efforts but torn pants and mud-caked boots."

Garron was surprised.

He looked at Gracie and said, "But that's all over now. Gracie, you told them the news, right?"

"Not yet," Gracie answered.

Leah asked, "What are you so excited about?"

Gracie explained, "Garron had a great meeting with the archaeological team that was working in Rupert's Valley."

Garron sat back in his chair with a big smile.

Gracie continued, "We will be able to add 15 members to our search. The Saints are eager to help."

Garron waited for Gracie to continue. When he realized that Gracie had no intention of telling the table about Phillip's find, he looked at her quizzically. Under the table she tightly squeezed his thigh. She shook her head almost imperceptibly as she sipped from her glass.

Anton said, "Yes, that is good news. Garron, let me thank you for the suggestion and for making it happen. Now our numbers have more than doubled."

Still confused, Garron answered, "You're welcome."

Gracie squeezed Garron's leg once again and smiled at him.

"Now, Jacob please continue with your report on the progress of your search of Peak Dale," Anton prompted.

Garron drank his wine slowly, not hearing his brother's response. He had no idea what had just happened. He managed to stifle his curiosity through dinner. The table was cleared and everyone bid one another a good night. Garron followed his brother and Leah onto the hotel's front porch. Leah sat beside Jacob on the bench. Garron paced the porch deflecting their questions until Gracie finally joined them.

Garron asked, "What the hell is going on?"

Gracie held a finger to her lips and whispered, "I know that you are confused, but listen to me. Have George take you," she indicated Leah and Jacob as well, "to Phillip's and retrieve the vessel. Phillip may protest, but you cannot take no for an answer. Then have George bring you to the fort."

"What fort?" Garron asked.

"The one at Sandy Bay, he will know the one I mean."

"Garron, what is she talking about?" Jacob asked.

Gracie said, "There is no time for that now. Garron can tell you on the way to town. You must go now."

"I don't understand," Garron whispered.

"Listen. Anton will be on a conference call for the next hour. We don't have much time." Gracie clasped Garron's hand between her own. "Please trust me. You must hurry."

"Will we see you at the fort?" Garron asked.

"I'll be there setting up for the test. You must bring me the sample."

Leah asked, "What sample? What is this all about?"

Garron nodded and turned.

He said, "I'll explain on the way. Let's go!"

Chapter 12

THE MINIBUS WEAVED down the mountainside into the valley. George had the group into Jamestown in record time.

"So you really think that this guy, Phillip, found the seeds of the string tree?" Jacob asked as they spilled from the vehicle.

Garron said, "There's a good chance that's what's inside the vessel he found."

They stepped up to the warehouse door and knocked loudly.

"But why does Gracie want to keep it from Anton?" Leah asked.

"I do not know." Garron knocked again more forcefully.

The building was dark and the street was empty. Garron could not hear any movement from the other side of the door.

Jacob said, "There is no one here. Step aside."

Jacob inspected the lock and the door's jamb. He took a half step back and then kicked the door mightily just above the lock. The wooden jamb splintered and the door swung inward. There was just enough light streaming through the large windows for Garron to make his way across the room and to the metal desk in the corner. The desk drawer was locked. He found a steel ruler atop the desk and attempted to pry the drawer open. The ruler bent and twisted in his hands. In a dark corner he saw a pile of tools. He found a shovel and slipped the blade into the drawer. With a pop and twisting of metal, the drawer opened. Garron pulled the file from the drawer and checked the material within. Satisfied with the file's contents, he went to the table holding Rupert's remains and took the small sealed clay vessel that he hoped held the seeds of the extinct St. Helena string tree.

He looked at his brother and Leah and said, "Let's go."

Leah stood with mouth agape at the remains and artifacts on the table. Jacob grabbed her by the arm and pulled her to the door. After the trio filed into the minibus, George spun the vehicle around and began to climb out of the valley.

***

The trip across the island took nearly forty minutes. George drove expertly and pulled the minibus into the clearing just west of the fort. There were several other vehicles in the clearing; including Chris Yon's minibus. Chris stepped from his vehicle when he saw George approaching.

Chris said, "Dr. Ng asked for you to meet her in the fort's tower at the south end of the courtyard. The men at the gate are expecting you. She asked that you hurry, but she doesn't want you to draw too much attention from the men inside the fort."

George handed Garron a flashlight. They decided that it would be best for him to stay behind with the minibus in case they needed to make a quick get away. Leah, Jacob, and Garron climbed the dark ridge toward the well lit fort. Garron thought that he heard generators running in the distance over the scream of the wind. They were on the windward side of the island and the trio had to shelter their eyes from blowing sand and debris.

Two men stood on either side of the drawbridge. Each man was holding a small automatic weapon.

Garron said to the guards, "Dr. Ng is expecting us."

One man nodded and said, "You are to join her at the far end of the compound."

The threesome made their way through the courtyard that was filled with crates and equipment. Tents lined both sides of the footpath leading to the tower. Some men were visible on the walls high overhead, but otherwise the fort was quiet. The trio stepped into the inner courtyard beyond the portcullis. Gracie's laboratory was brightly lit. Garron could see her silhouetted through a window covered with heavy translucent vinyl sheeting. The door to the lab was covered in the same material. Garron pushed it aside and let Jacob and Leah enter ahead of him.

Gracie looked up from her lab table. She was wearing safety glasses and had her hair pulled atop her head.

She asked, "Did you get it?"

Garron nodded and handed her the small vessel.

"Phillip was not there, so I didn't have to use my negotiation skills. But I owe him for some repairs to the front door and desk."

Jacob asked, "What's with the militia outside?"

Gracie moved toward a table and set the vessel under a bright light.

"Anton insists that *The Brotherhood of the Three Crosses* will attempt to find the string tree," she answered as she took a seat on a metal stool in front of the object.

"The Brotherhood knew nothing about the string tree," Jacob said.

"He believes that it is just a matter of time before they track him down." Gracie continued, "That's why I wanted to inspect this pottery to-night, without Anton; I want to diffuse this situation before it goes any further."

"Then let's take a look," Garron urged.

Gracie flipped down a magnifying lens that was attached to the frame of the safety glasses that she was wearing. She examined the small pear shaped jar closely.

After a moment she said, "The seal looks solid. There is a good chance that the contents remained dry."

Gracie used a very thin, sharp scalpel to slice carefully through the resin that sealed the vessel. She pulled the blade smoothly around the mouth of the jar. Gracie set the knife aside and tightly gripped the plug with her right hand. She twisted the plug while spinning the base. In a slow twist the plug pulled free of the vessel. Gracie poured the contents slowly onto a sheet of white, acid-free paper. The group looked down on 15 to 20 seed pods, seed pods that looked very much like the Melliss drawing of 1875.

Gracie removed her safety glasses and said, "I think that we have found our string tree."

The group stood around the table, stunned, looking down on the tiny pods.

Leah asked, "Can you really grow a plant from 700-year-old seeds?"

Gracie said, "It is difficult, but not impossible."

Gracie lit a burner and swiveled a graduated cylinder over the flame.

She said, "I have been preparing an acid solution rich in hormones while I was waiting for you to arrive. But first, I need to soak the seeds in warm water to soften the seed coat. I need this water to boil for ten minutes, then after it has cooled slightly, I will add the seeds and let them soak. We will have only a few chances to get this right. Even if we get lucky, the germination rate will be miniscule, at best."

"How long will it take for the plant to germinate?" Jacob asked.

"Germination will begin in months, and it will take a year or more before we can harvest the sap needed for the elixir," Gracie answered.

"A year, I'm not sure Anton will be able to wait a year. It sounds like he's fallen over the edge," Garron said.

"But we are very close and with the knowledge that these are indeed string tree pods, I believe that Anton will step back from the brink. He can continue his search knowing that he has a specimen back in the lab."

Gracie continued, "And I'll keep him busy. I need a better equipped lab. Once I seal these seeds in the hormone solution, I will need to keep the specimens free from contaminates. This is obviously not the best choice for a sterile environment." She raised a hand into the air, signaling the makeshift lab. "And once I have potted the seeds, those pots will need to be secure from airborne contaminates. I don't want a wayward prickly pear seed rooting itself in my pot."

Gracie smiled reassuringly. "I am sure that Anton will regain his perspective once we begin to plan for the longevity of these seeds."

The vinyl over the door parted. Phillip stepped into the lab followed closely by Anton and one of his armed guards. The guard had an automatic rifle slung over his neck and held tightly to his broad chest. His hand remained on the gun's grip as he surveyed the room.

Anton spoke. "Phillip tells me that he found something of interest during his excavation of Rupert's Valley, but when he took me to examine his find, we discovered that someone had broken into his warehouse. The thief removed the one item that I was interested in. But I told Phillip not to worry, for I was confident that we would find the thief."

Gracie spoke quickly, "Anton, we found it."

Anton eyed her intensely. "Gracie, may I speak to you outside."

Gracie followed Anton out of the lab. The guard stayed behind blocking the door.

Garron said, "Phillip, I am sorry. Are you okay?"

"That wanker is scary." Phillip nodded toward the door. "What exactly is going on here?"

Garron shook his head. "Honestly, I am not sure."

Garron tried to see through the vinyl sheet covering the window. The backlight allowed him to make out the silhouettes of several people in the courtyard. But the vinyl obscured his view. He was able to identify Gracie by her frantic hand gestures. Garron pulled back the vinyl to get a better look.

There were five people in the courtyard. Anton and Gracie were the closest to the lab. Three more figures stood in partial shadow. Garron was able to identify Taylor by his square frame; there was an additional man who Garron assumed was another member of Anton's security force. He was a large man who looked somehow familiar. Garron studied the guard as he shifted in and out of shadow, but he was unable to get a better look at him. The fifth person stood between the two hulks, and was tiny by comparison. Garron believed it to be a woman, but there was an unnatural shadow over her face. It was as if she were wearing a veil.

Garron saw Anton quickly raise his hand and bring it down heavily across Gracie's face. She fell to the ground. Anton's nickel plated Colt caught the light as he drew it from under his jacket and pointed it at Gracie on the ground.

Garron stepped quickly away from the window and in a hushed voice said, "Leah, put the seeds back in the jar."

Leah did not hesitate; she saw the look in Garron's eye.

To Jacob, Garron said, "Get ready to move."

The guard tensed as he watched Leah collecting the seeds. Garron protected his hand with an apron lying on the lab table and quickly hurled the graduated cylinder, containing the boiling water, at the distracted guard. The container found its mark. The glass exploded as it hit the man in the face; the scalding water and glass shards blinded him. He instinctively grabbed his face. Garron hefted the heavy metal stool and swung it, knocking the guard unconscious.

Jacob, although surprised by his brother's actions, reacted rapidly and made quick work of the lights in the room. The lab was bathed in darkness, the only light coming from the flame of the burner.

Garron removed the guard's rifle and handed it to Jacob. Garron found a large pistol at the small of the man's back.

Garron nodded to Jacob. Jacob made the weapon ready to fire.

Garron called through the vinyl sheeting, "Anton, we have the seeds and if you don't want them to be burned to ashes, then you'll leave Gracie alone."

Anton called to the guard that was guarding the door.

Garron answered, "He's in need of some medical attention."

For a moment the only sound was the hum of generators and the hiss of the burner in the lab.

Finally Anton said, "Ok Shepard, let's talk this through."

"This seems all too familiar Anton. Didn't we have a similar conversation just a few days ago? I hope that you remember that I do not bluff."

"And it would behoove you to remember how that last negotiation turned out, as well," Anton said sarcastically.

Garron felt his blood boil. He breathed deeply to keep his cool.

After Garron regained control, he said, "If you raise another hand to Gracie, then I swear that you will watch your life's work go up in flames."

"Garron please, I think that this is all just a misunderstanding. We should talk."

Garron sat with his back against the wall under a lab table. Leah sat between him and Jacob.

Garron said, "Sure Anton, let's talk. I have a question for you, how many of the murders over the last few weeks have you been responsible for?"

Anton took a moment to reply, "They were all in my way."

Garron saw Jacob shift under the table. The look in Jacob's eye frightened Garron. He reached across Leah and squeezed his brother's ankle. Garron whispered, "Stay cool."

Jacob nodded in reply.

Anton said, "Garron, there is still room for negotiation, talk to me."

Garron called out to Anton. "You killed four people, two of whom we loved." Garron thought of Murphy and Professor Burke. "You turned a young man against his father, and then you held him for ransom. After that, trusting you was our fault, but that's for us to live with. You promised Gracie that you would save her mother from a slow painful death, but now you're holding her at gunpoint. And you've assembled an army on a remote island to protect something that you *hoped* to find, from a fraternity that you've already ruined. Let's count it off: murder, treachery, deceit, and paranoia. Did I miss anything?"

"I should have a grenade thrown through the window. Then I could pick the seeds from your blood," Anton spit out the words vehemently.

Garron forced a laugh. "Now, now, you should mind that temper of yours. You shouldn't be so hasty." Garron looked around the room. "I'm sure that Dr. Ng could name off a number of flammable chemicals in this well stocked laboratory that could ignite easily, and flames would swallow these seeds before you had a chance to save them."

Garron added, "We've managed to surround the seeds with a bottle of alcohol and hydrazine. Now I don't know what hydrazine is used for, but I can read an NFPA label and hydrazine is rated as a Class II substance. That means it will go boom."

Garron looked at Jacob and Leah and shrugged. He winked at Leah who cradled the small clay vessel in her lap. She smiled wearily.

Anton did not reply.

Garron said, "Anton, you can hurl a grenade and start the fire yourself or if I hear the report of a gun, then I'll start the fire for you. Are we clear?"

There was silence.

Garron screamed, "I said, are we clear?"

"Not entirely," Anton responded. "There is something that you haven't taken into account. But you can't be blamed. Gracie hasn't told you everything. You see, I have a new guest on the island, someone that you should meet. Tell Garron who it is Gracie."

Gracie wept as she sat on the ground with her hand to her face. Her cheek had begun to swell.

"Tell him!" Anton insisted.

Gracie cried out, "He has Veronica. I'm so sorry. I didn't think …"

As Gracie's voice trailed off, Garron thought of the veiled figure he had seen from the window standing between the two guards. Instinctively he knew that it was his wife. His breath caught in his chest. His heart fluttered like a moth caught in a spider's web.

It was Jacob's turn to console his brother. He whispered, "Easy Gar, take it easy."

Anton called into the lab, "So you see Garron, we each have something the other wants. Give me the seeds and I'll let your wife go."

Garron wiped the tears from his eyes. He saw Jacob shake his head. Leah laid a hand on the gun shaking in Garron's hand.

Garron breathed deeply in an attempt to control his anger. He nodded to reassure Leah and his brother. Garron said in an even tone that belied his contempt, "Anton, you are a lying son of a bitch. You'd never let us go."

Anton laughed. "You could try and shoot your way out, but you are severely outnumbered and outgunned. And I promise that my first bullet will take the top of your wife's skull off."

"And I assure you that my bullet would stop that black, dead heart of yours." Garron countered.

Anton laughed again. "Then neither of us would get what he wants."

"There is another option," Garron suggested.

"I am listening."

"We all walk out of here together. At the front gate you will let my family go. When they are away freely, then I will give you the seeds."

Jacob begged, "No Gar. You can't trust him."

Leah added, "We are on an island Garron. It won't be that hard for him to track us down before we can make arrangements to get out of here."

Garron said, "I know, but I prefer our chances outside of this fortress. But I'm listening if you have a better idea."

Leah and Jacob could offer no other options.

"That sounds like a deal that I can live with," Anton called to the lab.

Leah, Jacob and Garron crawled out from under the table. Garron chambered a round in the pistol and then took the jar from Leah.

Garron called out, "We're coming out. Remember, if any shots are fired then either Jacob or I will place our first shot square in your chest Anton."

Jacob nodded his understanding.

"Agreed." Anton called to his men, "Hold your fire; no one fires!"

Before they stepped through the doorway, Garron said to Jacob, "When we get to the drawbridge, you take Leah and Ronnie directly to George's minibus. Don't wait for me. Don't hesitate. Have George hide you somewhere, you can trust him. I'll catch up with you later."

Jacob's chin quivered. He fought to suppress his tears.

Garron added, "You have to keep our girls safe Jay. I'm counting on you. Promise me, Jay, that you will listen to me."

Jacob wiped at his eyes with the back of his hand. "I promise."

Garron nodded. "You're out the door first. Keep the gun trained on Anton. Leah follows you."

Jacob parted the vinyl and led Leah out into the courtyard.

***

Garron found himself in a situation from which he could see no hope of survival. On the walls above him, he sensed movement even if he saw no one. A coordinated attack could kill Leah, Jacob, and himself before he would have a chance to fire a single shot. For that reason he stayed close to one wall as they moved north through the fortress. Anton kept pace with Garron but moved down the center of the courtyard, keeping his distance. Gracie followed Anton with her head hung low. Jacob and Leah were just a step behind Garron. Jacob keeping the automatic rifle trained on Anton with each step. Garron could hear Veronica mumble from under her hood as she staggered between Taylor and the other guard.

Garron recognized the other guard as Agent Whitlock. He said, "So you even have your men impersonating government agents?"

Anton smiled. "Money can get you nearly anything. You've seen my false credentials firsthand."

Garron was awed by just how easily Anton manipulated him from the start.

"Take that hood off of my wife's head," Garron insisted.

"She hasn't been harmed. I will remove the hood once we have reached the drawbridge," Anton replied. "She is a spirited woman. She'll stay calmer with the blindfold in place."

They were just a hundred yards from the fort's entrance. Garron could see more men at the gate.

Garron asked, "Why are you doing this?"

"Veronica is my insurance policy, and you must agree that it has proved invaluable," Anton responded.

Garron shook his head. "I meant, why devote your entire life to finding these ingredients, the elixir can't bring your father back."

"But it will honor his name. And now I can spend eternity basking in that glory. Eternity, Garron, I will be a god walking among mere men."

Garron asked, "Did you ever plan on healing the sick?"

Anton laughed. "Only if they could afford it."

The tents in the courtyard were dark. But Garron knew that Anton's men were out there in the shadows waiting for the signal to open fire.

Garron felt a sense of relief after making it to the drawbridge. The relentless wind battered them as they stepped from the security of the fortress walls. Garron turned to face Anton.

He said, "My brother will take the women to the minibus. After they pull away, I will give you the seeds."

Anton shrugged nonchalantly. "That is the deal to which we agreed."

"Now take that hood off of my wife's head," Garron insisted.

Anton signaled for Taylor to remove the black hood.

Veronica squinted against the stark glare of the flood lights Anton's men had placed around the perimeter of the fortress. She slowly focused on Garron. Her eyes went wide, but she lifted her chin proudly. Taylor untied her hands then Veronica removed the tape from her mouth.

Garron felt the tears welling in his eyes, but steadied his voice to ask if she was okay. Veronica nodded slowly and took a step toward her husband.

Anton struck like a snake grabbing Veronica by the hair and pulling her between Garron and himself. She attempted to fight him, but Anton was taller and he tugged her hair upward, nearly pulling her off of her feet. He rapped his Colt against the side of her head then stuck it in the small of her back. Veronica stopped fighting.

Gracie screamed, "Anton stop, have you gone mad?"

"Shut up bitch, this is all your fault!" Anton snarled and sounded more animal than man. "I've changed my mind. Jacob, Garron, put down your weapons. Hand over the seeds and I will allow you to say goodbye to your wife. Or I will have my men shoot you all and we will collect the seeds from your dead hands, and you will never hold your wife again."

Garron dropped his gun and lifted the small jar above his head. "I'll scatter these in the wind."

"You won't have the chance, I'll cut you down first." Anton nodded toward Jacob, "Now you, put that gun down."

Jacob dropped the gun at his feet.

Anton smiled and said, "You've lost, Shepard. It is over and I win."

An explosion from within the fort lit up the night.

Garron had nearly timed the detonation perfectly. If Anton had not grabbed Veronica, then she, Leah, and Jacob would be safely in the minibus. Garron's mind raced, searching for a solution. He looked to the gun at his feet. Anton had been distracted by the blast, but he quickly turned his attention back on Garron. Garron had not had time to recover his gun.

Garron forced a smile. "You had better send some men to put out that fire. You may be able to save something from the laboratory. Was there anything in there of value?"

Garron saw Anton's anger boil over. He knew that he had pushed the man too far. Garron watched the man's face contort in rage and then he heard the shot.

Veronica gasped and then slumped to the ground. Her eyes never left Garron's gaze.

Initially no one reacted, but Anton slowly raised the gun and pointed it at Garron. There was another shot, and Garron saw Anton's body jerk awkwardly to the left and fall to the ground beside Veronica. Garron rushed to his wife.

Jacob saw Taylor turn toward the walls of the fort. The shot that hit Anton had come from behind them. Two more shots sounded and both Taylor and Whitlock fell dead. Jacob pulled Leah and Phillip toward the minibus. They stumbled into the clearing and found George waiting by the vehicle with a stricken look on his face. Jacob forced Leah and Phillip into the car and asked George to get them to safety. Jacob quickly turned and ran back for his brother. Jacob heard the stiletto of automatic fire coming from the fort. The muzzle flash that he was able to see confused him. Someone was firing from atop the wall down into the fort, not at Garron or himself.

Jacob froze at the sight of Garron holding Veronica in his lap. Garron rocked her back and forth in his arms. Jacob watched Gracie approach Garron slowly and saw his brother push her away. Garron's anguish caused Jacob so much pain that he felt rooted to the spot. Then movement to his right drew Jacob's attention. Anton was running toward the cliff and the footpath that led to Sandy Bay beach below. He ran awkwardly, his right arm flapped at his side. Jacob took a second look at his brother, and then he sprinted after Anton.

***

Garron looked down into Veronica's face willing her to open her eyes. His tears flowed, his head ached, his ears rang. He smoothed his wife's beautiful hair, tucking a wisp behind her ear. He kissed her cheeks and closed eyes. He could not look down at the dark stain spreading across her stomach; he only stared at her beautiful face.

A voice drifted to him on the wind.

"I'm sorry, Garron."

Garron answered, "No, I'm sorry Ronnie, I couldn't protect you, I couldn't save you."

"No, Garron."

He repeated louder so that she could hear over the wind, "I'm sorry, Ronnie."

"Garron, Garron can you hear me?"

"Yes my love, I can hear you."

Garron became aware of someone leaning over him. He looked up from his wife's face to see Gracie standing beside him. Then he remembered pushing her away. Gracie had been the one speaking to him.

She said again, "I'm so sorry, Garron."

Garron screamed, "Leave us alone!"

"Garron, Anton is still alive."

Garron stared at the woman who betrayed him.

"What did you say?"

"He's alive and Jacob went after him."

Garron clenched his jaw, "Where?"

"Toward the ocean, there is a footpath down to the bay. He has a boat."

Garron kissed his wife on her soft lips and laid her gently in the grass.

He asked, "Which way?"

Gracie pointed to the cliffs.

Garron fixed Gracie with a stare.

"You stay with her. Don't you dare leave her alone."

She nodded.

Garron noticed the glimmer of the nickel plated Colt near Veronica's body. He picked it up and ran after his wife's killer.

***

The foot path was difficult to find in the dark, but once Garron found it he moved swiftly with little regard for the 400-foot drop to his left. He thought that he heard voices and slowed to try and judge the distance, but the roar of the wind made it impossible. A rock abutment shot out from the cliff and narrowed the path. Garron had to stick the revolver in his pocket so he could use both hands to navigate the obstacle. On the other side of the rock, the footpath widened again. Garron saw someone on the path ahead of him. He pulled the gun from his pocket. Voices carried on the wind; someone was yelling, but he could not make out what they were saying. He rushed forward and saw as his brother threw himself at Anton. Garron quickened his pace. He watched Jacob and Anton struggling and then they were both gone. They disappeared from the path as if the night had swallowed them. Both men had slipped over the edge and into the dark abyss. Garron slid to the ground where he judged that his brother had gone over the edge and peered down the cliff. Garron screamed his brother's name.

Someone was hanging perilously from an outcrop only eight feet below the path.

Garron felt a moment of relief, but the man that hung by one arm was not his brother. Anton held tightly to the rock and stared up at Garron. Garron searched the cliff face for his brother. The moon provided just enough light to see the crest of the waves below. Jacob was gone.

***

Anton was surprised to see Garron extend an arm over the edge, until he realized that the hand he offered was holding his Colt storekeeper. He saw it shine in the moonlight. Anton's final thought, just before the .45 caliber bullet entered his forehead and ripped through his skull was how much he had loved that gun.

***

Gracie saw Garron reappear from the darkness of the night. She watched as he approached her alone. Garron came back and sat next to his wife once again. He bent over and kissed Veronica once more on the lips and then scooped her up in his arms. Veronica's head and arms hung limply. Gracie tenderly turned the woman's head into Garron's shoulder.

He looked up with hollow eyes and said, "Thank you."

Gracie knelt down to pick up the small clay vessel that Garron had dropped earlier.

He said, "Don't bother; it's empty. I left the seeds to burn in the lab."

Garron turned and carried his wife's body toward George's minibus.

Gracie turned and walked back toward her burning lab.

Garron laid Veronica's body on the seat of the minibus and covered her with a blanket that was crumpled on the floor of the vehicle.

Leah's lip trembled when she asked, "Where's Jacob?"

Garron turned from his wife and looked at Leah with tears in his eyes.

He said, "Jacob's dead."

They held each other and they cried.

Chapter 13

WHEN THE AUTHORITIES arrived, George did most of the talking. He explained that the source of the conflict was a stolen artifact. George used the photographs of the amulet that Phillip found as proof of his story. George told the constables, most of whom were related to George, that Anton had stolen the amulet from Phillip and when the archaeologist confronted the man, Anton went berserk. George's cousins were surprised to see the dead bodies of Anton's small army when they stepped into the fort. George said that the men came ashore illegally and then turned on their benefactor when Phillip explained that the amulet had little monetary worth. George suggested that Anton had promised to pay the men with the profits gained from selling the amulet. George told his cousins that he and his friends were lucky to be alive.

After Garron was promised that Veronica would be cared for respectfully, he showed the police approximately where Anton and Jacob went over the cliff. The next day an extensive search found Anton's body lying on the rocks near the shoreline. Jacob's body was never recovered.

The RAF and the USAF sent personnel to St. Helena from Ascension Island. Questions were asked, conclusions were drawn, and four days later the investigation was closed. Leah and Garron were given transport to London; Veronica's body traveled with them. In London, Leah and Garron hugged goodbye. While Leah was heading home, Garron boarded a plane to Barcelona. Veronica always wanted to be interred in that ancient city facing the Mediterranean Sea.

The service was small and private; only Veronica's closest friends were welcomed. The day was sunny and bright. From the grave site, Garron could see the Mediterranean sparkling. It was a beautiful place to say goodbye.

Epilogue: One Year Later

GARRON WALKED INTO Jason's Spirits on the corner of Fleet and Broadway in Baltimore, just three blocks from his studio. He walked slowly, hunched at the shoulders. Garron was thin and gaunt, but he made that walk several times a week.

The Pakistani man behind the counter greeted Garron, "Good morning Mr. Shepard."

Garron muttered hoarsely, "Hi Henry. Could I have two bottles, please?"

Henry bagged two bottles of Glenmorangie 18-year-old single malt scotch.

"I am happy to see you, but you don't look so good, Mr. Shepard," Henry said with real concern on his face.

Garron slid two hundred dollars to the man and took the bag.

Garron said simply, "Keep the change."

Henry put the money in the register and watched his best customer shrink towards the door. "Thank you, Mr. Shepard."

Garron said, "I'll see you later," and stepped through the door out onto the street.

After the door closed, Henry said, "Not too soon, I hope."

Garron shuffled the three blocks back to his studio. He had been living there exclusively for eight months. It was too painful to return to the house in Locust Point. He unlocked the door and made his way through the dusty gallery. He had not painted since returning to Baltimore, he had not even stepped behind the partition that separated the studio from the gallery. The closed sign still hung in the window, and he had even papered over the windows. Garron slowly climbed the stairs to the second floor and made his way directly to the kitchen where he pulled a dirty glass from the sink. He poured himself a heavy glass of scotch and immediately emptied it. He took the glass and the bottle to the couch, sat, and drank a second glass quickly. When Garron put his feet up on the low coffee table, piles of un-opened mail slid to the floor. He used his heel to push the cascading pile and watched as more envelopes dropped from the table. Under the mail was a highly polished nickel plated Colt. Garron pulled his feet back from the table and stretched to pick up Anton's gun. Garron checked the gun and found one bullet in the chamber; the same bullet he had put there two weeks ago when he wanted all the pain to end. Garron threw the gun to the floor, disgusted with himself for not being able to pull the trigger. He emp-tied the glass once more. Then he slept.

Garron dreamt of Veronica and Jacob. He dreamt of Leah and Gracie. He dreamt of painting and sailing. He dreamt that he was drowning. He dreamt that Malik sat beside him and they discussed losing the women they loved. He dreamt that Malik had given him a picture of his wife, only it wasn't his wife but a statue. Garron dreamt of having a statue made for Veronica.

When Garron woke, night had fallen. He blindly reached for the lamp and knocked a second pile of mail to the floor. The lamp's light caused his head to ache; he immediately turned it off again. He stood shakily and made his way to the bathroom. He urinated and then washed his hands and face. Garron was surprised at the beard he felt when he washed. He wondered when he had last shaved, or for that matter when he had last taken a shower. He shuffled from the bathroom and turned the light back on. He picked his empty glass off of the floor. He scooped up some of the mail and dropped it on the coffee table. On the table he found his bottle of scotch and picked it up to pour himself another glass, but something under the bottle caught his attention. There was a photograph of a monument. The statue portrayed one man standing, holding another man collapsing into his arms. The men were on a boat; a sail billowed behind them. On the sail were three crosses. Garron blinked several times slowly trying to clear the image. He flipped the photo over to find something written in small neat handwriting.

Palos de la Frontera
Andalucia, Spain
M. Qwari

Garron looked around the room expecting to see someone sitting in a dark corner of his apartment. He staggered to the laptop sitting on his small kitchen table. On top of the computer was a plane ticket to Sevilla, Spain. The flight was scheduled for Friday and was leaving from BWI Thurgood Marshall International Airport.

Garron opened the laptop and did a Google search for Palos de la Frontera. He opened the Wikipedia link and scanned the article. Jumping off of the page were words that pained Garron just to see. He saw: Pinta, Niña, Santa María, and the Pinzón brothers. Garron then added the word monument to his search; Google returned several articles. One had photographs of the monuments in Palos. Garron opened the link and studied the images. He saw the same monument on the screen that was on the photograph that he held in his hand. It was described as a monument erected to commemorate Palos' favorite son, Vicente Yañez Pinzón. Vicente stood holding his dying brother Martín Alonso on the deck of a ship. Garron sat back in his chair and studied the front and back of the photograph once again. Then he examined the plane ticket and said aloud, "Subtle."

***

Garron pulled off to the side of the road in Palos when he saw the statue. It seemed to have been dropped in the edge of a field with little thought to its location. Garron stepped from the car and approached the monument.

Malik Qwari was standing under the shade of a tree near the monument. The man met Garron as he approached.

Malik said, "You look better than when I last saw you."

Garron ran a hand over his chin and felt coarse stubble.

"It was a long flight though, and I didn't stop to freshen up."

"Even still, the beard didn't suit you."

Malik extended his hand and the two men shook.

"I don't really remember you being in my studio. I know you were there because of the ticket, but I don't remember."

"That is probably for the best. I was a bit emotional talking about my wife."

Garron hung his head.

Looking at the monument, Malik asked, "So do you think that the sculptor captured the emotion of the two men?"

Garron looked up and examined the faces of the Pinzón brothers. He thought of Jacob, and then Veronica's face flashed in his mind's eye.

"Malik, what are we doing here?"

Malik turned to face Garron.

He asked, "Do you remember much of that night on St. Helena?"

"I remember too much. I've been trying to forget," Garron answered.

"There was a firefight inside the fort. Anton's men were gunned down while you were dispatching Anton himself. It was The Brotherhood."

Garron was stunned. "You were there?" Garron asked.

"No, I was not there. It was a separate chapter of *The Brotherhood of the Three Crosses*, a Spanish chapter. The two chapters knew nothing of the other. When Vicente created the order, he had the foresight to split the knowledge of The Brotherhood between two groups separated by the vast Atlantic."

"And they were the ones on St. Helena?" Garron asked.

"Yes, they knew of St. Helena and the string tree. They had identified the ingredients. Not from a map or list, they were unaware that a list even existed, but from the elixir itself. So they stationed someone on St. Helena to monitor anyone visiting the island. It was our Spanish brethren who took care of Anton's men."

"They had the elixir?"

Malik nodded. "When the Pinta landed back in Spain, the baskets holding the elixir were still aboard. Martín Alonso had the baskets spirited away to the Baetic Mountains before his death. The Spanish chapter has guarded that location with their lives for over 500 years."

Garron shook his head. He said in disgust, "But someone in their organization couldn't help but to identify the ingredients. That sounds too familiar."

"Only they never exploited that knowledge. The Brotherhood in Spain has known the composition of the elixir for 200 years."

Garron was surprised. He had seen the worst in mankind, and because of that his trust in humanity had been spoiled.

Garron asked, "How do you know all of this?"

"I received a call two months ago inviting me to Spain."

"Why did they call you?"

"We share a member." Malik waved to a vehicle parked near Garron's own rental.

The dark sedan's driver stepped from the car. It was Malik's son, Abram. He stepped around the vehicle and opened the sedan's rear door. Abram helped his passenger from the car. Leah stepped from the vehicle wearing a long blue dress and dark sunglasses. Garron could see her smile. Leah then turned back to the car and helped a man with white hair and a cane from the vehicle. She made sure that he had his footing and then Leah ran to Garron and embraced him warmly.

Garron had not seen Leah since Jacob's service nearly a year ago. They had a memorial without the body. He hugged her tightly. Just holding her made Garron begin to tremble and cry.

Leah held on until Garron regained control. Then she backed away and kissed him lightly on the lips.

She said, "I love you."

Garron's voice was tight, but he replied, "I love you, too, Leah."

Leah squeezed her ex-husband's hand.

She said, "I am sorry that I couldn't tell you before now, but it took some time to convince The Brotherhood to bring you in."

Garron said resolutely, "I can't be brought in. I don't want to be a part of any of that. Not now."

The man with the cane had approached slowly. He said, "I was hoping that we could convince you otherwise."

Garron looked at the man with the cane. He wore dark sunglasses and a lightweight suit with an open collar. His hair was full, but was the color of cotton. He stood favoring his right leg, using the cane for support. He looked familiar. The man removed his glasses and smiled at Garron. The white hair confused Garron, but Garron knew that he was staring at his brother's face.

Garron began to cry again and embraced Jacob, nearly knocking him off his feet.

"Easy Gar, I'm still a little shaky," Jacob said through his own tears.

"But how?" Garron muttered.

"The Brotherhood found me clinging to a rock in the surf. I was unconscious and badly broken, but I was breathing. They used the elixir."

Garron said in surprise, "It works."

Jacob nodded. "It helps the body's natural ability to heal and mend. It took a long time, but I am doing okay."

Garron finally released his brother from his embrace, but continued to hold Jacob's hand.

Jacob used the cane to tap his right foot. "My leg was severely crushed, so it's still giving me trouble. But every day I'm a little better."

Garron said, "Are you going to live forever?"

"No, or I don't think that I will."

Garron hugged Jacob to him tightly once again.

Garron said, "I'm really happy to see you." Garron's smile fell. "It's been a dark year. It's been really hard without Ronnie."

Jacob backed away from his brother, but kept one hand on Garron's shoulder.

"I know Gar, I've had someone watching you." Jacob nodded toward Malik.

Garron's eyes widened. "The elixir, would it have …"

Jacob shook his head. "No, it was too late. It would not have brought her back. I am really sorry."

Garron hung his head. "I've been drinking, it's eating me up." Garron envisioned the nickel plated Colt. "I nearly …"

"I know, big brother, that's why The Brotherhood finally agreed to let me bring you here. Although, I wasn't waiting for their approval any longer;

I had already booked a flight. That's when Malik promised to bring you to me."

The two brothers hugged again, crying into each other's shoulder.

Leah said with tears in her eyes, "Okay, you two, I can't take anymore of this, besides we have more people to meet."

Garron and Jacob reluctantly relinquished their embrace. Leah stepped between the two men and guided them toward the sedan. Malik followed. Leah kept the pace slow to accommodate Jacob's injury.

Garron wiped his eyes, "So what's with the hair?"

"It's a side effect of the elixir," Jacob answered.

Garron shrugged. "It's not bad, it makes *me* look younger."

Jacob laughed. "Oh, you're still the older brother."

Leah said, "I like it. He looks more distinguished." She ran a hand through Jacob's hair.

"If by distinguished you mean older, then I agree," Garron quipped.

When they reached the sedan, Garron shook hands with Abram. Abram and Malik hugged warmly.

As Jacob was sliding into the car, Garron asked, "Hey, have you two gotten married?"

Leah was surprised by the question. She shook her head, "Not yet."

Garron smiled. "What have you been waiting for?"

Jacob looked up from the edge of the car's seat and took Leah's hand.

They both answered simultaneously, "We were waiting for you."